THE CRIMSON WRAITH

Legacy of the Hood

J. Griffin Hughes

Copyright © 2020 J. Griffin Hughes

All rights reserved

The characters and events portrayed in this book are fictitious. Any similarity to real persons, living or dead, is coincidental and not intended by the author.

No part of this book may be reproduced, or stored in a retrieval system, or transmitted in any form or by any means, electronic, mechanical, photocopying, recording, or otherwise, without express written permission of the publisher.

ISBN: 9798680660485

Cover design by: Cameron Kramer
Parts 1-4 Covers by: Justin Moore

CONTENTS

Title Page
Copyright
Acknowledgments
Content Warning
PART ONE   1
From "Nights of Justice"   3
Chapter One   5
Chapter Two   32
Chapter Three   66
PART TWO   97
Chapter Four   99
Chapter Five   127
Chapter Six   150
Chapter Seven   171
PART THREE   193
Chapter Eight   195
Chapter Nine   218
Chapter Ten   239
Chapter Eleven   263
Chapter Twelve   276

PART FOUR	301
Chapter Thirteen	303
Chapter Fourteen	324
Chapter Fifteen	334
Chapter Sixteen	353
Chapter Seventeen	379
Be My Hero!	399
About The Author	401
Books By This Author	403

ACKNOWLEDGMENTS

This book has come together thanks to my astute beta readers, Brian, Jackie, and Harriet, whose feedback helped shape the telling of this story; Suzanne, Hemed, Dori, and the others in my local writing community who provided enthusiastic encouragement; the work of Brian Ward and Dr. Andrea Letamendi whose *Arkham Sessions* podcast provided excellent insight into the psychology of masked vigilantes and their adversaries; and my family, who have always believed in and supported my creativity.

Cover art by Cameron Kramer
Parts 1-4 cover art by Justin Moore

CONTENT WARNING

Although this is a story about heroes and villains inspired by comic books, it is not intended for children. Bad things are going to happen, some of the kinds of bad things that happen for real. And they won't all have simple solutions. Good guys won't always be perfectly noble, bad guys won't always be unsympathetic, and the resolution of their conflicts won't always be pretty.

My purpose in this is not to mock heroic ideals—I am no cynic—but to play them out in a world I hope feels true to our own.

And in case this warning somehow misses someone who ought to hear it, I hope the amount my main character curses can alert readers that some R-rated material may be ahead before it takes them by surprise.

PART ONE

J. GRIFFIN HUGHES

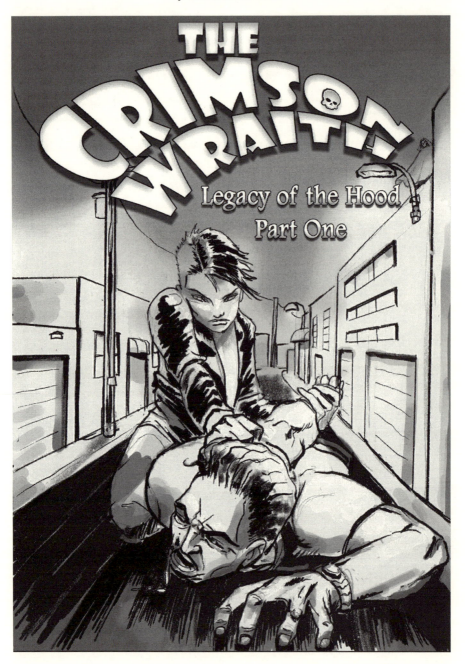

FROM "NIGHTS OF JUSTICE"

by Chief Harlan Goodman (1989)

No delicate blossoms took hold in Titan City. In the year 1609, English explorer Sir Roger Marshal purchased the land from its indigenous inhabitants for a few furs and a lot of lies. He gave his name to Marshal Bay, largest natural harbor in the Eastern Seaboard, and named the two rivers that fed it after his financiers, the Honorable Lord Englehart and coal mining magnate Angus Brennert.

Those who built Titan City's gridline streets and established its factories did so with determination to scramble and scrape without succor. And to those who so gambled their fortunes, the city repaid triple or nothing, launching dynasties and shattering dreams.

Amid the Elysian Hills ringing Titan City to the west, down whose slopes the Englehart carved its path, the most fortunate of Titan citizens built private play palaces. From these stately manors, they gazed down upon Titan City's lights, its smoke, its workhouses, its ships, and its struggles. Their descendants would come to reap the choicest of rewards for the least of labors.

And to commemorate the victories of industry, Titan City erected a statue named "the Spirit of Prosperity" at its easternmost edge above Keaton Park. A one-hundred-foot-tall armor-clad angel, she opened her arms to the Old World of

Europe, inviting any and all to a land rich with opportunities for the taking.

CHAPTER ONE

2019

Rats scurried along the gutters of South Titan's newly renovated warehouse district, seeking the scent of sizzling meats rising into the October night air from street vendors' sausage and pretzel carts. Somewhere, a late-night reveler laughed explosively at a joke whose punchline did not carry quite as well down the echoing alleys. And in darkened doorways of gentrified boutiques, the homeless slept in cardboard shelters they would tear down at dawn's first light.

Gracie stomped down the sidewalk past them. The sounds of her biker boots resounded from the walls around her as she headed from the dance club to the Titan Metro station. She kept her fists shoved into the pockets of her black leather jacket, and glared through her dark hair, cut jagged and boyish. Her face wore that "don't-fuck-with-me" hardness so many Titan citizens kept as standard procedure upon its streets.

She did not feel as angry as she looked. No, the night had not gone quite as planned, but any plan made with her roommate Kristen that involved more than sweatpants and television had slim chance of becoming reality; Gracie knew that. Kristen bailing on coming out to dance at Terpsichoria because her dickhead boyfriend Zack was "in a mood" might be annoying, sure, but not unusual. The only thing that bothered Gracie about that was, if Kristen had been with her, she figured she might have had an easier time dismissing that guy in the too-tight t-shirt who refused to accept her not wanting to dance with him. He was the kind of man who saw a woman alone as having a target on her.

Dancing with guys was not the reason she went to Terpsichoria—not to dance with guys or talk to guys or anything in the guy department, really, and usually it didn't have to do with any person of any gender. Gracie went dancing for the sake of dancing, for the feel of her body in motion—one gesture flowing into another, her limbs growing warmer and warmer in the dark, as her heart rate rose to the rhythm of the music. That was what made everything in life bearable. And it always had. From when she was a little girl fleeing her parents' shouting matches, she'd learned that the only way to calm the grief or rage or desperation she felt was to move her body hard and fast, to sweat, to burn from within until nothing but peaceful silence remained. Without that, Gracie wasn't sure what she'd do.

This night was just a maintenance dance. Kristen had been paying enough of her share of the rent that what Gracie made at Sprang & Sons Used Books & Media kept the lights on for them both. They ate decently, thanks to what Kristen brought home from her waitressing job at Starpoint Diner to supplement a breakfast-cereal-based diet. The two spent more money feeding Kristen's dogs Jerry and Joe than themselves, and that suited them both just fine. All in all, Gracie was pretty pleased with this roommate situation and figured she lucked out when she answered Kristen's ad.

There was also the fact that Brianna, one of Gracie's co-workers at Sprang & Sons, had shown her how to apply for a need-based education grant from the Finn Foundation, which opened the door for Gracie to go back to school. It didn't sound like Gracie would have to repay the money either, so long as she kept her grades up, and now that life flowed a little more smoothly than it had for her as a teenager, making those grades hadn't been that hard for her. Sometimes it was almost fun.

But no matter how good life may have looked, she knew better than to think troubles had ever gone for good. Gracie had to stay vigilant, certain she would never know when the next thing would show up to throw her life into chaos.

That next thing would pull up to her at the stoplight. But for the first time in her life, she did not face it alone. An unseen presence was there as well, watching.

Through the open passenger window of his white Mustang, Tight-T-Shirt-Guy shouted, "Well, look who it is! Miss Too-Good-To-Dance-With-Me." Underneath the car's base, purple neon lights glowed.

Gracie rolled her eyes. Of course, a douchebag like this would have a car like that, looking like it floats down the road on clouds of shitty cologne. She didn't even break her stride. "Fuck off, dude."

But he kept pace with her, rolling into the intersection. "What's the matter? What don't you like about me, huh?"

"I said fuck off."

The engine growled. The car lurched forward. For a second, Gracie thought she might be done with him, but no such luck. He swung sharply in front of her, blocking her path on the crosswalk, and vaulted out of the car. The slam of the driver's side door rang loud as a gunshot in the night air.

Thirty feet above the two, perched atop a building with a faded sign for Chew-Rite Gum painted on its wall, one red-gauntleted hand grasped a fast-repelling winch, while another made sure the grappling iron held securely in place.

Tight-T-Shirt-Guy swaggered toward Gracie. He was drunk —drunk enough to say out loud things he ought to keep quiet if he wanted to stay part of polite society. "I know you're a dyke and all..." In fact, Gracie did date boys now and then but didn't care to correct him. "I don't mind. Hell, I like a challenge. All it takes is one good dick, right?" He gave a lopsided leer. "And it would be my pleasure to be your first."

As he drew closer to her, Gracie kept her feet planted, her eyes on his, watching for the first flicker of intent.

Above them, the red-gauntleted hand reached into a belt pouch and plucked one, two, three smoke pellets before snapping it closed. Its arm reached back, brushing red cloak aside, ready to throw.

Tight-T-Shirt-Guy reached out to touch Gracie's hair That was a mistake. Her small frame played to her advantage in a fight like this. Already, he slightly unbalanced himself to look down at her. His reach over-extended him, and it was all over before it began.

With the fluid ease of someone who had performed this move way too many times, Gracie took hold of his wrist with both hands, jerking forward and down, and pulled him off his feet. She kept her grip firm and side-stepped his stumble, bringing his arm behind him and pushing into his back.

His chest and then chin hit asphalt. The hollow crack of his skull told Gracie he'd been stunned. After that, her grip on his arm and knee in his back were all it took to subdue him. The blood coming out of his face was just a bonus.

The one who watched them from above paused, deciding not to interfere, extremely curious as to what might happen next.

With his words muffled by his face pushing into the ground, Tight T-Shirt Guy shouted, "You little bitch!" He attempted to throw her off, but a further twist of his wrist shot pain along his arm that cautioned him against trying too hard.

Gracie's tone remained steady, simply stating the facts as she said, "If you move, I break your arm."

"I'm gonna break your face!"

Another twist of his wrist made him scream and then shut up. "What you are going to do," said Gracie, "is go home. You are going to sleep this off. If you're lucky, you won't remember being such an asshole tonight. If you're very lucky, you will, and then you won't ever try this shit again. Understood?"

"Fuck you," he muttered into the street. She started turning his elbow slowly, letting him feel the torque working on his joint. "Okay! Okay!"

"Okay, what?"

"Okay, I give! Whatever you want!"

She stayed there, held him, and listened to his breathing, waiting for it to ease, for his acceptance of defeat to sink in. "I'm going to release your arm now, and when I do, you are going to stay right here and count to ten before you get up. Do you understand?"

"Yeah."

"Start counting."

And he did. "One... Two..."

Gracie released him gradually, watching for the slightest sign of movement, easing her weight off his back.

"Three... Four..."

She didn't start running as soon as she stood. Her first steps backward were measured, wary. Her eyes found a shadowy alleyway leading from the street. She could disappear quickly there.

"Five... Six..."

Quietly she withdrew into darkness. "Seven..." From behind a garbage bin, she watched him. "Eight..." His head turned, and, no longer seeing her, Tight-T-Shirt-Guy staggered to his feet.

"Fucking bitch." She heard him spit, saw him look around for her, and, not finding her, he shouted, "Fucking bitch!" He got back into his car. The engine roared, and he shot off down the road in a neon purple haze. Gracie watched him go and then kept watching the point into which he disappeared.

From underneath his hood, the observer watched the same, then turned his attention to the alley where he'd seen Gracie escape. Tapping a control band on his wrist adjusted the light sensitivity on his mask so he could see her even in shadow. A directional microphone allowed him to hear her as well.

Choked back for the duration of the confrontation, terror seized upon her in safety. Her veins ran cold. Her stomach clenched and lurched. Suddenly she was sobbing, and she let herself fall into a crouch, gripping her knees.

"You're okay, goddamn it," she said to herself. "You are fucking okay. Stop it. Just stop it!" But the more she shouted at herself, the more the trembling overtook her.

The unseen figure heard every ragged breath, every shuddering word. He wanted to comfort her but decided it may not be the night for that. He let her take her time and watched as she emerged from the shadows to continue her walk to the Titan Metro station. They would talk. Later.

Elsewhere...

His shift in the kitchen having ended for the night, Lawrence didn't mind following Mr. Burton back to his room to make sure the elderly gentleman and his walker made it all right down the thickly carpeted hallway. They passed by the pair of cockatiels who served as pets for the entire third floor. An orange construction paper notice announced the week's activities for Sunset Gardens residents. And from one door after another, no sound other than the occasional cough arose.

In his slightly quaking voice, still carrying the sounds of a more refined age, Edward said to him, "Lawrence, you do make a lovely chicken pot pie."

"Thank you, Mr. Burton."

"I mean it. That is a real gift you have there."

"I am glad you enjoyed it, Mr. Burton."

"Please, Lawrence, just Edward."

Edward Burton must have cut a fine figure in his day. His strong jaw still jutted proudly from sagging cheeks. He had gentle eyes, a brow that once must have held a commanding arch, and he liked to dress well. Edward was the only man in residence at Sunset Gardens to wear an ascot and jacket to the dining room.

"It's not as if I would eat just any old chicken pot pie, you know," Edward continued. "These days I must be much more careful about how much I consume. And your chicken pot pie, Lawrence, is a treat for which I save myself." He laughed. "It isn't easy. The women on this floor do everything in their power to fatten me up. They barrage me with cookies and muffins and cakes."

"Yes, sir, Mr. Burton. All the women do think highly of you."

"Oh, please. I have no interest in anything any of them are offering me, not from their kitchens nor any other room of theirs—not that I have much time left for romance if I did."

"You don't have to talk like that, Mr. Burton. Who knows how many more years you got ahead of you? Might have a whole lot of life to enjoy."

"Simply being a realist. I've out-witted and out-fought death over and over, but we all end sometime."

"I do suppose that's true, Mr. Burton."

"Call me Edward, Lawrence."

"Yes, Mr. Edward."

"Oh, honestly..."

They came to Edward's little apartment, and Lawrence paused there to let him unlock the door. More like a cave than anything, that's how Lawrence would describe Mr. Burton's apartment. Always a shade covered the window. Table lamps around the sitting room provided tiny pools of illumination. And a cave of wonders it was too, not full of the same sentimental knick-knacks as other residents. Lawrence marveled at the bronze scarab that might have come from a real Egyptian mummy for all he knew. There was some kind of Japanese knife that looked like a miniature samurai sword, an arrow tipped with an ornate silver head, and a strange theater mask with a long, pointed nose.

"You sure have some wild stuff, Mr. Burton," said Lawrence. "Must've lived an interesting life."

"That's a curse, you know." Edward set his walker aside and took hold of the snakewood cane with silver Derby handle that he used in that smaller space. "A Chinese curse. 'May you live in interesting times.' To live in a peaceful time, boring even, that is a blessing." He turned to gaze upon the items displayed on his shelves and, for a moment, appeared to yield to the pull of memory before looking up sharply with a smile. "Don't suppose I could entice you to stay for just a little longer? There's a bit of brandy an old friend brought me."

"Sorry, Mr. Burton. I gotta get going."

"Of course, my boy." He saw Lawrence to the door and locked it behind, not to keep someone out, but to keep someone in.

As he turned back inside, Edward adjusted the grip on his cane, readying it to swing. "It's no use," he said to the intruder he knew was there but could not see. "You haven't got room to stay hidden, although I suspect you know better than to try and hide from me, whoever you are."

No one else would have recognized the signs of the intruder's presence. He had been raised to notice the tiniest of details: a slight shift in the stack of papers on the kitchen counter revealed someone had brushed past them during his absence; some of the photos on the refrigerator door sat ever so slightly askew. The intruder had not been able to resist touching them. Anyone else might have missed these, but not Edward.

"Come out," he said.

No one did.

"Very well. You want to do this? All right. Let's do this." Edward began to stalk his intruder, taking small, shuffling steps. His right leg dragged a little. To keep his cane ready to swing, he braced himself with his left hand against the hall door, the kitchen counter, the back of a chair. "And what must you be calling yourself, my shy friend? A present-day incarnation of the Shadowmaster, are you? The Puzzle Prince? Queen Cleopatra? El Toro Terriblé?"

At a slight hint of motion, he spun around, cane upraised, and nearly toppled over. There in his unlit hallway, just outside his bathroom, stood the intruder, their features indistinguishable in the dark.

"That's it. Come on then. Show me what you came for."

The figure stepped forward into the light, revealing their face to him.

Abashedly, Edward relaxed, seeing no threat. "Oh, I'm sorry. Forgive this old fool a bit of dramatics..." It was then he felt the first bolt of pain strike, running up and down his limbs, gripping his frail and long-suffering heart. His body tightened, and he brought down his cane to steady himself but could not do so before the second bolt struck. His legs crumpled, and he fell.

Edward knew he broke a bone in his fall, but he also knew that he wasn't going to have to worry about walking, not anymore, not ever again. This was the end. His body was too old, too weak, and too worn, and the poison was too strong. He reasoned that he must have received it before he had come back to his apartment, maybe an evil ingredient added to Lawrence's chicken pot pie. But it wasn't enough for his murderer to simply rest in the knowledge of Edward's impending death. No, they wanted to see the life drain from him.

As his vision blurred and darkened, the face that drew close to Edward was not one to which he could attribute any motivation. He had been murdered by somebody who wanted to watch him die, and he did not even know why. Then, he knew nothing at all.

1940

Across the rooftop of the Finn Industries warehouse, the two figures faced each other. Their respective cloaks—one red, the other blue—billowed in a shared breeze. Within the red hood, a white skull glared from empty sockets. The black mask within the blue had no shape too it, just two jaggedly torn holes through which a pair of eyes blazed. This would be their final confrontation, the decisive battle between the Crimson Wraith and the Blue Banshee.

"It's not too late!" the Crimson Wraith called out. "Surrender now and let me take you peacefully to the authorities! You don't have to make this any worse!"

"But it *is* too late, Crimson Wraith," the Blue Banshee replied. "Far too late—not for me but for the children."

The Crimson Wraith could not help but leap from his perch, advancing on his adversary. "What have you done?"

The Blue Banshee matched step for step. "Can you really not hear their cries? I would have at least thought you'd smell the smoke. And what do they say?" He came to a doorway leading down from the rooftop and flung it wide. "Where there's smoke, there's fire!"

Only now could the Crimson Wraith hear small voices crying from below, rising up along with the thick smoke. "You fiend!" he cried, grabbing a pellet from his belt and hurling it as he charged his foe.

The Blue Banshee dodged, and the pellet struck a chimney behind him, exploding with a burst of light and smoke. He had his own weapon to deploy. Pulling the drawstring on the device at the center of his belt, the Blue Banshee shattered the air with a fierce siren's whine. It stunned the Crimson Wraith, made the world seem to spin around his throbbing head, and he was unable to dodge a blow that fell squarely upon his skull-masked cheek. A punch to his abdomen followed, cushioned only slightly by the Crimson Wraith's leather doublet.

"You should know better than to underestimate me!" The Blue Banshee shouted. "Don't you think I learned my lesson underestimating you?" He clasped both fists together and brought them down hard, delivering a hammer blow to the Crimson Wraith's shoulder.

The Crimson Wraith fell to his knees, but that brought him eye level with the Blue Banshee's belt. He snatched the still-screaming device and hurled it away, sending it over the rooftop edge to crash on the street below. Silence followed, but the Blue Banshee did not relent. A knee into the Crimson Wraith's chin sent him sprawling backward.

The Blue Banshee loomed over his downed opponent. "Not bad. Always were so clever, weren't you?"

"You make this sound like a game," the Crimson Wraith groaned. "Only a madman makes a game of death."

"Am I mad? Am I, indeed? And who made me mad?" With that, the Blue Banshee tossed his mask to the ground and showed his face.

His skull concealed the Crimson Wraith's surprise. "Robert Caine?"

"That's right, William Finn." He kicked away the Crimson Wraith's mask to expose the man underneath. "Or should I call you 'brother'?"

The kick that unmasked him made Will spit blood to his side. "You gave up the right to call me that when you murdered our father."

"And yet you insist on calling Josiah Finn *our* father when he ignored me, his own true son, to lavish attention on you, an orphan plucked from the street." Robert stomped his foot down on Will's chest. "An orphan just like the seven boys I've bound up in the building below us. I think they are getting quieter. Perhaps the smoke is taking its toll." He began to laugh. "Finally, vengeance is mine!"

But the sound of that laughter re-awoke within Will the anger that first inspired him to don the mask and cloak, to defend the defenseless, not as any mortal man but as a creature from beyond the grave—the Crimson Wraith! He would not let the Blue Banshee claim these innocent lives.

Will summoned all his rage and, with a cry, drove a sharp punch into the side of Robert's knee. His enemy cried out. Another strike followed, then another and another until bone shattered under flesh. He followed through by grasping the Blue Banshee's boot and giving it a vicious wrench. Robert Caine would never walk unaided again.

Leaving his crippled opponent wailing like his ethereal namesake, the Crimson Wraith charged, unmasked, toward the doorway from the rooftop. Deep within, flames lit up the darkness. There were, in fact, no more cries from the Blue Banshee's captives. They had all lost consciousness, and Will found them slumped in the ropes that held the children bound in a circle, tied with their backs together against a wooden beam.

With a utility blade pulled from his boot, Will began cutting the boys free, when one, the tallest of them though not even ten-years-old, coughed himself back to consciousness and looked up at his rescuer. Terror and ash covered his face.

"Don't be afraid," said Will. He pushed his hood back to let the boy see him fully. The yellow light of flames illuminated his face. "I'm here to rescue you. You are going to be okay. Understand?"

The boy nodded.

"Good." With that, he cut the bonds free. "Can you get to your feet?"

The boy did.

"Now, what's your name?"

Across the room, a piece of ceiling fell into the fires that tore at its base. The boy started, on the verge of panic.

"Stay with me." Will brought his face between the boy's gaze and the inferno spreading around them. "Tell me your name."

"Eddie," the boy croaked.

"All right, Eddie. I'm Will. Can you help me?"

Eddie nodded.

"I need you to help me get the smaller kids to safety. Can you do that?"

"Yes, sir."

The two worked quickly to move the others out of harm's way. Will kept coaching the boy as they did, "Keep your head low. That's it. That's just how to do it." He gave Eddie his cloak to cover his face so he could breathe.

Soon they had all the children down the stairs and safe on the sidewalk. Then Will ran back up to what remained of the roof to rescue Robert and make him stand trial for his multiple crimes, including, most recently, the kidnapping, the arson, and, ultimately, the murder of their father, Josiah Finn. But Robert was nowhere to be found. All that remained were the Blue Banshee's black mask beside the Crimson Wraith's white skull. Will took one in each hand before tucking the Blue Banshee's mask into his belt.

Suddenly the rooftop groaned underneath him. Already its black tar had begun to melt from the heat, and the damage was worsening. He threw a grappling iron around a metal railing and launched himself over the side of the building as the structure crumbled in flames behind him.

Back on the ground, he found the children starting to come around, Eddie standing over them, holding up the littlest, who coughed and coughed in Eddie's arms. "You did an excellent job, Eddie," said Will. The clamor of fire trucks rang in the distance, drawing near.

"You saved us, sir."

"No 'sir.' Just Will. Now I want you to do me one more favor, okay?"

"Yes, Mr. Will. Anything."

"The firefighters are on their way. The police will be here, too. I want you to do whatever they ask and answer any of their questions. But, please, I'd rather you not tell them my name or that you saw my face. Can you do that for me?"

Eddie nodded and handed the red cloak back to Will.

"You're a good boy, Eddie. I'm very proud of you." Will put his gloved hand on the boy's shoulder. "Tonight, you were a hero."

As Will started to turn away, Eddie called out, "Am I ever going to see you again?"

"I promise." Will smiled. "And when you do, I want you to pretend that you've never met me before, okay?"

"Yes, Mr. Will."

"Just Will. But that's between us." He slipped the skull back over his face. "Remember, only very special people get to know the secret of the Crimson Wraith."

When the authorities questioned him, Eddie was true to his word. He told only the details of the night that he was asked to tell and gave no secrets away. The children all returned to their orphanage, and in the weeks that followed, Eddie calmed the fears of his fellows by telling them about the mysterious figure who had saved them, a man who seemed like a nightmare in red but was in fact kind and brave and strong.

It was a real thrill to have the millionaire industrialist William Finn visit their orphanage soon after. He said that he felt just awful that their terrible ordeal had occurred on one of his properties, and he wanted to make an in-person donation. In addition to a sizable check made out to their new orphanage, he brought new shoes for all the children, new clothes, and new books for their education. There was even a bit of chocolate. And when he got to shake hands with the oldest boy and hear him tell of how he had helped the Crimson Wraith to rescue the others, Will smiled at his bravery as if he had not seen it himself first-hand.

"Eddie, I think that shows a lot of character," he said.

"Thank you, Mr. Finn."

"Please, call me Will."

"Yes, sir," Eddie couldn't supress a smile.

"I think you have great things ahead of you, Eddie. I really do. So, I'd like to ask you a question. Would you like to come home with me and live in my house and be my son?"

Tears leaped into Eddie's eyes. "Please." And young Edward Burton threw himself into William Finn's outstretched arms.

2019

In the past three minutes, Howard had shifted two books from the first stack to the third, four books from the second to the first, and five books from the third to the first and second. These stacks represented, as he told Gracie, "Buy Now," "Buy

Next Week," and "Buy Later."

There was no line behind him, which was probably why he chose to do his shopping on Tuesday mornings. It still bothered Gracie, though, something about the way he whimpered and sniffed in agitation, squinting through his thick, black-framed glasses. Why his distress over the perfect purchasing plan got to her, she did not know, but it did.

"Now, if I have early Stephen King tonight," he muttered, "then I'm going to want the P. G. Wodehouse as a palate cleanser tomorrow morning... Or should I shift into Barbara Kingsolver for a little substance?" Howard slid a wisp of his long gray hair behind his right ear.

Probably Gracie could have pushed through a couple of pages of her psychology text before he finished, but how could she concentrate with Howard's whimpering? This would be the perfect time to do some shelving, but she'd already put up all the new arrivals. Gracie chewed her lip and scanned the store for some other task that could take her away from Howard long enough for him to make his decision.

"...But do I want to start with King tonight? I'm having meatloaf for dinner. Does Stephen King go with meatloaf? What if I don't have the meatloaf? If I were to read the Wodehouse instead, then I could maybe get a bit of curry on the way home. Or a pork pie! Oh, yes. Then what would I read in the morning?"

The nice thing was that Howard had to be the most difficult regular customer at Sprang & Sons Used Books & Media. The rest were simple and straightforward, definitely not shitty, and, for the most part, super polite and friendly. It was an older, public-radio-listening crowd, a bit slow and soft spoken maybe, but that worked for Gracie just fine.

It was a good gig all-in-all, probably the best place she'd ever worked. The owner Rich—one of the "& Sons" who had taken over the store from his father—was more laid back than she thought someone could be and still operate a business. He was a sixty-year-old product of the "flower power" generation who spent most of his time at the store just hanging out. Half of the time, he would be playing his guitar in his office. When he was working, he didn't work hard, and he didn't seem to expect his employees to have to either.

All that worked okay for Gracie. It was stable, calm, and peaceful. She liked working with Brianna, and she liked working with the books. They smelled nice.

"Excuse me, miss?" What the hell? Miss?

Gracie looked over to the man who had called out to her. It wasn't Howard but some other guy, a new guy, wandering around the aisles. He had to be in his, what? Late thirties? Kept himself in good shape. Could pass for younger if he dressed differently. Maybe he wasn't a douchebag, but he sure shopped in the douchebag department of this clothing store. His look seemed to be trying a bit too hard to say, "class but still cool," with a houndstooth coat that it really was not cold enough for and a purely ornamental cashmere scarf. There was so damn much product holding his hair in a Ken-doll coif. And—oh God—was that a spray tan?

Anyway, whatever he looked like, he had called Gracie "miss," so he could go right to hell as far as she was concerned.

Then he did it again. "Miss?"

She held up her finger and forced a smile. "Just one second." As much as she wanted away from Howard, the tone of this probable-douchebag's voice had Gracie wanting to make a power play. *That's right. I'm the one behind the counter. I decide who gets my help and when.* Anyway, Howard appeared to have it all sorted.

"Okay! I think that does it." Howard beamed in relief, perfection achieved. "I'm going to start with Dashiel Hammet this evening!"

Gracie looked down at the first stack and sighed. She wished she had caught it earlier. That would have saved them both some time. And she didn't want to say it, but she couldn't help herself. "Howard, you've read that one before."

"What? No, I haven't."

"Yeah, you did." It wasn't that Gracie tried to keep her customers' reading history memorized. Some things just stuck in her head.

"No, see, because when I read something and then return it, I put a little yellow sticker on the inside."

Gracie picked up the copy of *Nightmare Town* before her and opened its front cover to him. She didn't need to look for herself. She just knew it was there, Howard's little yellow sticker. And it was. His eyes squinted behind his glasses in disbelief, and he took the book from her to more closely inspect, as if dubious as to the sticker's origin. "Well, yes, that is one of mine..." The selection process would have to start again.

"It's cool, Howard. You take your time." Gracie came out from around the counter and made her way over to the other customer. Figured she might as well get this over with.

She kept a little of that service industry sing-song tone in her voice as she said, "Yes?"

He shelved the personal motivation book he'd been thumbing through, something called *Unchaining Your Inner Prometheus* that promised it would help make all your dreams come true like a paperback genie in a lamp. Apparently it didn't do its job well enough to stay on the shelf of the person who bought it new. "Oh, yeah. Hi," he said, as casually as if he hadn't summoned her over. "I was wondering, I'm looking around here, and I couldn't see if you had a True Crime section?"

Not what she was expecting, but then she wasn't expecting a guy like this in a store like that at all. Wouldn't he have someone he could pay to shop for him? Or read for him? "Sure. It's right over here."

They passed Howard, still seeking something unattainable in his book selections, and dived back into a dim, isolated corner at the intersection of Horror and History, just five shelves worth of non-fiction about some of the worst humanity had to offer.

"Here you are," said Gracie. "We got your Torso Killer, your

Manson Family murders, Zodiac, Gacy, even a little Bonnie and Clyde."

"Perfect! Thanks!" His face lit up with an eagerness that she found a little troubling. Gracie wasn't going to linger there. Howard's ambivalent company seemed preferable, some humble and honest OCD.

A light must have shone down from the heavens and showed Howard the way. He made his selections but found no exultation in that victory. Doubt clung to him even as he took his bag of books out the front door. "I hope that was right..."

And so, Gracie was left alone with New Guy seeking his jollies in True Crime, at least for the next twenty minutes before Brianna got back from lunch. Whatever he was after, she figured it was bound to be sick, something to startle his fellow partygoers at the monthly mask orgy. Suddenly, her stomach clenched, and she flashed back to the guy who followed her from Club Terpsichoria the other night—his leer, his reach, and then him spitting his anger into the concrete as she pressed the hard places of her body into the soft places of his.

"Oh, miss?"

For the love of God... "Yes?" Gracie didn't stand up, didn't look back.

"Could you... I mean... I can't seem to find..."

She didn't like this. The timing struck her as suspicious, as though he had waited for Howard to leave to get her on her own. And something in the tone of his voice was off, like he cared more about getting her attention than getting any book on any of the shelves. Gracie felt her pulse quicken. Whatever bullshit this was going to be, she had to be ready.

Walking back toward him, Gracie stayed keenly aware of how much space she had on either side. She wanted to keep whatever room she might need to swing or bolt. Two good steps away from him, she stopped. He stood bent over the lower shelf, rifling through the books. If either hand made a move to his pocket, she'd rip it off him.

Gracie's sing-song voice flattened. She couldn't help it.

"What is it?"

"Well, I'm trying to find... I can't seem to locate any, um..."

"What?"

He stopped, turned, and looked up to her, now a tad sheepish. "I was looking for anything you might have about, um, the Crimson Wraith?"

Gracie kept her eyes locked on his. There was something there she didn't like, something insincere, but it didn't read like a threat. Not yet, anyway. She sighed and relaxed slightly. "I think we've got a few of his things in the comics and collectibles..."

"Oh, no!" he straightened up suddenly. "I was looking for maybe a case history? Some of the pieces about his early career are out-of-print now, so I thought you might have a relic or two..." She could see how that might be valuable at the next orgy, something about Titan City's most famous masked weirdo.

The Crimson Wraith had been a big deal when she was a kid. There was a guy who dressed up as the Crimson Wraith to talk to her school about what to do if a stranger tried to lure them into a van. He gave out stickers with his white mask and red hood and deputized them as Junior Wraiths, which didn't mean anything because everyone knew the Crimson Wraith's sidekick was called the Wily Wisp, but you didn't hear people talk about the Wily Wisp as much.

Gracie heard rumors that there was once an actual, real Crimson Wraith stalking the streets of Titan City at night, fighting a war on crime, "defending the defenseless," and supposedly thwarting a series of villains just as cartoonishly costumed as he was. Word was that he had tried to stop some of the Zero Hour bombings twenty years ago. Whatever. If any of it was true, it wasn't like it did Gracie any good.

"I don't know, dude. You're just gonna have to keep looking." She turned back on a bit of her service industry cheeriness. "That's part of the fun anyway, right? The hunt?"

The childlike disappointment on his face did not appear to

agree. "Right… The hunt…" He returned to the shelf, and Gracie turned her back to him, but she didn't get more than one step away. "Oh, here we go!" She turned to see him happily holding a paperback with heavily worn edges. His excitement fell just as quickly as it rose. "Aw, but I've already got this one."

The cover read *Nights of Justice: A Study of Titan City's Crimson Wraith*. "It's one of the better histories anyway." He flipped open the back cover to her to reveal the photograph of an older police officer in uniform with several medals in place. "That's Chief Harlan Goodman. He featured strongly in the Crimson Wraith's career during the sixties, seventies, and eighties, so if anyone knows, he knows."

Gracie nodded. "How nice for him." And she returned to the register.

1973

They followed each other out of the Kronos-Kola bottling plant in a line, their wrists bound and each one chained to the next, like a mother duck leading her little ducklings behind her. First in line came Otto von Kemp, a.k.a. the Buzzard, bald and hook-nosed, his fur-collared coat drenched in explosions of beverage equipment from the factory he had been using to launder money. He sneered at the arresting officers who pushed him forward, "You keep your filthy hands off me! Don't you know who I am? My attorneys will eat you alive, every one of you! You'll see! You'll all see!"

Behind him followed all the crooked cops who had served on his payroll. Most had been around a long time and thought their seniority gave them immunity. They scowled at the junior officers arresting them and especially at Lieutenant Goodman, who stood apart, surveying the scene.

Not one of them surprised Goodman by being there. They were the kind of cops who thought they were above the law because they enforced it, swaggering braggarts to a man.

He rose up the ranks alongside them and knew these faces as the ones who most regularly and gleefully made trouble for him as the first black police officer of Titan City. They tried to make his career a short one. For his entire first year, he didn't have a locker at the station and, when he did, they broke into it, replacing his sidearm with a roughly carved spear, his uniform with a costume cheetah-skin tunic, and his cap with a chicken bone attached to a note that read, "To put in your hair."

Watching them marched away, Goodman grit his teeth to stifle any expression of triumph. He had never given them the satisfaction of seeing him angry, not once in almost twenty years of service, and indulging in an emotional display now would have let them see how much they got to him.

But beside him, Officer Jorge Villagraña, who joined the force only six months prior, marveled openly at the parade. "It's like Christmas!" he said. "Christmas and New Year's and Thanksgiving all rolled into one!"

"Let's not celebrate too hard. Remember, men died for this."

"*Sí,* men like O'Neil. It's all there in the papers we found inside, everything the DA could ask for to stick the Buzzard and the rest of those *pinches pendejos* for racketeering, extortion, narcotics trafficking, arms dealing, and the murder of Officer Adam O'Neil."

"A victory for justice," said Goodman.

"Yes, sir," said Villagraña. "But can I ask one question, though? Who was your anonymous tip? Who was the Santa Claus who wrapped all these Christmas presents for us?"

Goodman looked at Villagraña gravely. "You can ask."

Villagraña saluted. "Yes, sir. Whoever he is, you can thank him for me." He looked once more at his former colleagues being shoved into the paddy wagon. "*Feliz Navidad.*" And he returned to assist the others.

In all his years of service and after, Harlan Goodman never could explain how it was that he knew when he suddenly stood in the presence of his old friend, the Crimson Wraith, but it came with a slight tingling at the back of his neck. He first felt that sensation twenty years prior, when the "Scarlet Stranger" stepped in to save his life during his first year on the force.

Goodman had been walking the beat one night and turned out to be the first responder at the break-in of a savings and loan in Little Italy. Things didn't go well, and he got pinned down behind a parked car, taking crossfire from two assailants. With his face to the ground as bullets whizzed above, young Officer Goodman's gaze traced the patterns of the tire tread in front of him. He wished he told his wife that morning how much he loved the apple crumble she baked the night before.

Then one gun fell silent. And then the other. Goodman kept right where he was, unsure of what the silence meant until he saw the red leather boot of his rescuer touch the ground beside him. He felt that tingle at the back of his neck, and then looked up to gaze for the first time upon the red hood and skull mask that made criminals tremble.

Standing outside the Kronos-Kola bottling plant, watching the Buzzard and his men being hauled off to jail, Lieutenant Goodman felt that tingle again, and knew he was once more in the company of the Crimson Wraith.

"It was all there," Goodman said without turning his head. "All just as you said."

He heard the Crimson Wraith whisper, "Good."

"Not hurt, are you?"

"Not in any way that matters."

Lieutenant Goodman nodded, and then a touch of emotion almost overtook him. "I know that you're not him. You're not the one I first met in that mask. The way you move, that's not something that's in a man who's been fighting thirty years. But that's all right. You're doing right by him, by his memory."

There came no response.

Goodman continued. Somehow, talking like this was easier, not facing his listener, knowing there would be little said in return. "I counted him as a friend, you know. Funny to say that seeing as we never spoke face-to-face except with a mask between us, and then only about Titan City and its criminals. But it's true. This isn't the kind of city that gives a man a lot of reasons for hope. There were times when I was certain I'd come to the end of my rope, but if he could keep fighting, I knew I had to as well.

"And I never believed any of the things they said about him and that boy, not for one second. If he is still around somewhere and if you know him, please tell him that, from me. Tell him I never doubted him."

No answer came, and Goodman knew none would. He was alone again, the silence that followed his words like that following prayer, tight and hopeful. A prayer to the dead.

2019

The whole ride home on the Titan Metro Bus, Gracie periodically looked to her phone where she had the midterm grades opened. Only her math class had posted so far—a 98. She had never gotten a 98 on anything in high school, not even her art class, which had been mostly participation. That was her weak point in that and in every class; Gracie didn't participate. She rarely came to class and rarely did the work. School just never seemed important back then. None of it tied into any kind of future that she could imagine for herself.

All school meant was not being home for part of the day, and so long as she wasn't home, Gracie could be out in the woods behind the teacher's parking lot with the other equally unmotivated kids. They had things to offer her, things she needed—acknowledgment, belonging, laughter, comfort, and safety or at least the feeling of it. Sure, there were times when maybe Biscuit would be off his meds and try doing something that might get him seriously injured—say, attempting to light his farts on fire—but they all at least tried to look out for each other. Three or four voices would quickly talk him down from danger. Somehow, he still managed to rip off his eyebrows in one super-glue-related incident. But those grew back.

Always her teachers or the school counselor *du jour* would say things like, "You're so smart. If only you applied yourself..." Son of a bitch, who'd have thought, years later, she'd find out they happened to be right? She sure as hell didn't. So, every time she looked at that number, that 98, it was like, *Well, what do you know?*

This wrapped Gracie in a glow that made all the grim faces on the Titan Metro appear a little more benevolent— the mother of two surrounded by a sea of stuffed grocery bags while her children fought over an electronic device that *bleeped* and *blorped* in their hands, the businessman of apparently African extraction whose richly accented tones seemed so proper as he tiredly explained some matter over his phone to someone who must have been just not getting it, the early-cut waitress still in her tip apron half asleep with her head resting on a folded-up jacket pressed against the window. In Gracie's mind, in her A+ mood, these people weren't all bad, not even half bad, because they came from a world that was itself not half bad. And she could see that because she herself wasn't half bad at all.

It made Gracie smile at the shopkeeper who sold her a chocolate Cupid bar at the little store beside her bus stop that offered the usual beverages and magazines in addition to dried beans in bulk, canned Middle-Eastern imports, and house-baked pita that was always stale as hell by the time Gracie ever thought to try some. The teenage boys in their puffy jackets telling jokes on the corner didn't seem all that sinister as they laughed with each other and called out to her as she approached, "Hey, beautiful, what's up?" Gracie didn't even feel like flipping the bird as she passed by.

So, as she neared her apartment building, it seemed odd that the two dogs she heard barking in extreme distress sounded just like Kristen's dogs, Jerry and Joe—and it was. She found them in her yard, not on leashes, their attention fixed on the front door, either angry at being outside or at whatever was happening within.

Gracie broke into a run. Jerry and Joe showed some relief to see her as she sprinted past them and flung open the door. They ran inside after her to continue their barking at Zack, Kristen's boyfriend, who they never seemd to like much, but this behavior was new, different.

He slouched on the torn-up couch, watching something with zombies on the television and holding a half-empty bottle of a cheap rum called Medusa's Head. A snake-haired woman snarled from its label.

Zack winced at the dogs' barking, scrunching up a face that showed a growing bruise on his cheek and a cut just above his eyebrow. "The fuck, Gracie? Why'd you have to let those shitheads in?"

"These shitheads live here," she said. "Unlike you. Where's Kristen?"

"Sleeping it off." He nodded toward the bedroom he shared with his girlfriend, rent-free.

Turning to look in that direction, Gracie's gaze passed the kitchen. On the floor, overturned milk bowls and multicolored pieces of children's cereal mixed with broken glass—and blood. Gracie didn't take time to ask why. She bolted to the bedroom.

"Kristen?" There came no response from the darkness inside as Gracie opened the door. She saw the shape of her roommate on top of the tangled sheets of the frameless futon mattress. Crouching by Kristen's bedside, Gracie reached out to touch her roommate's hair and felt something wet, sticky. She turned on the bedside lamp.

The wound on the side of Kristen's head had not been bleeding long, but long enough to cover her face in dark red streams. They ran down cheeks whose topography distorted from still-swelling bruises. Drool bubbled on her torn lips, indicating she still was breathing, even if she did not respond to the light against her eyelids. Gracie didn't need to be the world's greatest detective to figure out Kristen's boyfriend had done this to her.

She wheeled around, propelling herself back toward the living room where Zack now stood with Joe and Jerry barking at his feet. He raised the bottle of Medusa's Head to bring it down on them but never got the chance.

At a full run, Gracie grabbed Zack by the lapels of his shirt, drove him backward, and slammed him up against the wall. Her lips peeled back into a tight sneer, rage beyond speaking. Electric hatred leaped between their eyes.

Zack raised the bottle once more, this time to bring it down on Gracie, but she shifted and flung his body to the side. He crashed to the floor and the weapon fell from his hand, skittering out of reach and spilling its contents.

Jerry and Joe went for his thigh and shoulder respectively, keeping Zack distracted as Gracie leaped onto his chest to drive her first punch into his cheek. Blood flew from his mouth, sending a spatter over his shoulder.

She quickly landed one, two, three more blows to his face before Zack managed to fling her off him and get up onto his feet. Gracie recovered quickly and hurled herself at him once more, but he grabbed hold of an over-full ashtray and threw it at her face.

The explosion of ash stunned her, choked her, and as she tried to cough herself free, Zack delivered two sharp jabs at her head and chest that sent Gracie stumbling backward into the kitchen, where she splashed to the floor with the spilled cereal and milk and glass.

Zack spat some curse Gracie didn't quite hear. Her head was ringing from the impact. Suddenly, she doubled over as Zack kicked her in the gut, once and then again.

She reached out for anything to use in her defense and her fingertips found the neck of a broken beer bottle that must have been responsible for the glass on the floor. When Zack went to kick her again, she drove its jagged edge into his calf, and he howled in pain. Zack pulled back his bleeding leg and fell. His head caught the corner of an empty milk crate they used as a table, and it knocked him out cold.

Jerry and Joe kept yipping at him, still and quiet as he was, and Gracie climbed back to her feet. Her whole body burned. It was always the moment right after a fight that hurt the worst. She shook as she looked down at him. Still, she held the bloodied bottleneck in her hand. He was helpless. She was armed.

How easy would it be to end him? What would it cost her to remove a piece of shit like Zack from the world? And might that cost be worth it? The fight was over, but would anything really be over after? Would he just end up hurting Kristen again? Or someone else? Who could Gracie keep from harm by just taking one simple, decisive action?

She pursed her lips. It would be easy, she told herself, like carving a pumpkin. It only takes one motion, one line, ear to ear across his throat. That's all. She could do it. She could do what needed to be done.

And then, as she focused on Zack's face, Gracie saw tendrils of a strange mist begin to curl around him. The fog that engulfed Zack reached toward her, expanding into the room. Then she heard a voice that seemed to resonate within her bones say, "Don't..."

Gracie looked up. She hadn't noticed the dogs going quiet.

It was as if he had stepped out of the cover of *Nights of Justice*—the Crimson Wraith.

He stood there, surrounded by an otherworldly haze, dressed all in red like something out of a Renaissance Faire with tall cavalier boots and leather gauntlets. A black belt with silver skull-shaped clasp wrapped around his waist over a red doublet with black brocade. And from within the shadow of his red cloak's hood, the white skull gazed at her with no eyes visible in its darkened sockets.

Gracie blinked. "You have got to be fucking kidding me."

CHAPTER TWO

1922

On the exhaust-choked streets of Titan City, shiny new motorcars carried well-to-do businessmen this way and that. They honked arguments at each other, each seemingly in someone else's way, all needing to get where they were going without a second's delay as if their life depended on it. And watching them from his street corner vantage point on a warm July afternoon, young Will Singer held aloft The Titan Gazette and called out the news of the day, trying to make a sale.

The headline read, RAILROAD STRIKE ON SIXTH DAY—a story gone stale, not all that compelling to passers by, no new drama, no twists or surprises. So, Will did what he could to bring it a little pizazz, shouting, "City council in panic! When will it all end? Children going hungry!"

True, he had not read anything in the story about hungry children, but he figured it a safe bet that somewhere some children were hungry. Anyway, *he* was hungry. The stone-stiff crust of bread he took for breakfast from the orphanage had been digested a long time ago. Will hoped to sell enough papers to get something nice to eat soon—a real fresh apple, say—with a little left over he could deposit in the shoebox he hid under his cot.

A voice full of sly self-assurance said to him, "Sounds like sad days, little man. Sad, sad days." The speaker was an older boy, a former newsie with whom Will worked a couple of years back. He had grown taller, taken to combing his blonde hair into thick waves, and his chin had filled out thick like it could take a punch and give the knuckles that did it something to remember him by.

"Hey, Whitey," Will said. "Say, you don't want to buy a paper, do ya?"

"Papers? Nah, kid. Why should I *buy* the papers when I'm gonna be *in* them someday?" He winked.

"Funny, Whitey."

"Not funny at all, little man. Real serious. I'm going somewhere, and fast. See, I know some people, important people. They say they like the looks of me. They say they see potential."

"Yeah?"

"Oh, yeah." He hooked his thumbs into his suspenders and gave them a cocky tug, puffing his chest. "I got potential in spades."

"That's great, Whitey. Good for you."

"Good for me? Hey, maybe good for you. Maybe you got potential too, Will. You ever thought of that?"

"Me? What kind of potential?"

"Well, you got drive, don't ya?"

"Drive?"

"Yeah, drive. You want things. You want to get things."

"Oh, sure. I guess."

"You don't want to be calling out to passing cars all your life. No, not you, Will, you want to be *in* those cars, sitting at the wheel, with a tasty dame at your side. I tell ya, that's the life for a guy with drive. You wear the finest clothes. You sleep in the softest beds. You eat the best food, all brought to you by waiters in fancy white gloves."

"That sure sounds swell." Will's stomach rumbled in agreement. He could all-too-readily imagine silver trays of succulent meats being laid before him.

"Swell and how," said Whitey. "I knew you had some drive in you."

It felt good to hear the older boy's approval, so Will smiled.

Whitey continued, "And that drive means you have it in you to do whatever it takes to get the things you want."

"Whatever it takes?"

"That's right. That's how it is for guys like us, guys with drive. We don't let nothin' stand in our way—not nothin' and not nobody."

"Nothing and nobody? What are you saying, Whitey?"

"I'm just sayin' sometimes drive means you got to get one over on the other guy."

Will frowned. "Who's the other guy?"

"Who's to say? But it don't matter, do it? Whoever that sap may be, what matters is what *you* want. That's your drive. You go for what you want even if you gotta go through your Old Aunt Edna."

"I don't have an Aunt Edna, at least I don't think I do." Only vague memories of Will's mother remained for him. Influenza took her years ago, and Will did not remember her having any sisters. Otherwise, he would have gone to live with them instead of the orphanage—at least he hoped he would.

"I'm not sayin' you got an Aunt Edna. I'm sayin' that, if you did, you wouldn't let that gray-haired biddy get in between you and your drive, would ya?"

"I… I don't know…"

"What? What don't you know? You said you got drive, don't ya?"

"Sure, I do!"

"That's what I thought. So, what about Old Aunt Edna?"

He did not want Whitey to think he was soft, so he came up with the strongest words he could muster. "She can go eat beans!"

Whitey laughed. "Yeah, she can, a whole big bowl of 'em. All right, kid. Maybe you do got what it takes. So, here's the deal. Me and my new friends, tonight we're gonna be meeting over at that movie theater on Wilson Avenue, just off 43rd, you know the one? The Regent?"

"Is that the one that's playing the vampire movie now?"

"Sure is, kid." His grin sent a chill through Will's spine. "*Nosferatu.*"

"Yeah, I know the one."

"Good. You meet us there tonight, ten o'clock sharp, got it?"

"But curfew is eight!"

"You gonna let that get in your way?"

Will had never snuck out of the orphanage at night. Other boys did, he knew that, but never him. Getting caught meant extra chores and no supper, at least the first time. He never saw a second time, but always there was the threat of not being let back inside, left to sleep on the street. Could Will manage it? Did he have the drive? "I'll be there," he said.

"I think you will, kid. I think you will."

As he sat down to supper at the orphanage that night, Will's nerves got between him and his soup. A few sips were all he could get down. The boy on his left took notice. "Not hungry, Will?"

"Not really."

"Then, can I have it?"

"Sure." He slid his bowl over, and the boy began emptying it almost before Will had pulled his fingers away.

By the time for evening prayers, Will had worked out his plan. He lay in bed with his eyes open, listening as one boy after another drifted off to sleep around him. After a while, he felt his eyelids getting heavy. They drooped all on their own, and he shook himself to try to keep alert. He had to show that drive.

Suddenly he realized he had given in to a long blink and fallen asleep. For how long? He did not know, but he knew he needed to get into action!

Will quickly changed into his street clothes under the covers then swung his legs over the edge of the bed, where he had placed his shoes in a spot where they would be easy to slip onto his feet. Then he tucked his laundry sack into bed to make a shape under the covers like his body still lying there. It would not pass close inspection, but it might fool someone just peeking in from the doorway.

There was no chance he could escape out the front. The caretaker's big mutt kept an eye on the door and would bark like the devil at anyone coming in or out, so Will made his way to the washroom. There, he stood up on the lid of a toilet to get to the window beside. Every other time anyone else opened it, that window squealed something fierce, but at dinner, Will had pocketed a pat of butter and he slathered that over its hinges. Then he tugged at the window handle, gently at first. He did not hear the slightest creak. Swinging it all the way open, Will worked his way through and stepped up onto the ledge.

An open window could catch someone's attention. Maybe they would get woken by feeling the draft inside and come to shut it, locking Will out again, so he took a little bit of twine, the same as he used to tie his papers, and wrapped it around the handle to pull it just barely shut. A tiny wad of chewed-up Chew-Rite Gum pressed into the frame would keep the latch from locking on its own.

For just a moment, as Will clung to the side of the building, there on the second story, some fifteen feet above the ground, he wondered what in the world he thought he was doing? And what was he doing it for? Could Whitey provide that dream he had spun, that luxury only drive could win?

He did not know. But he would never know if he did not try, so Will shuffled his way along the window ledge to the corner where the bricks jutted out a little more, and he could get a better hold. He slid one foot down over the edge until it found purchase in the building's uneven face and worked his way down until he was dangling from his fingertips with almost ten feet between him and the ground.

How was he going to get back up here? The thought suddenly struck him, but he knew it was too late. He would have to figure that out later. Will pushed himself away from the building and rolled with the fall when his feet hit the orphanage lawn. It hurt, but he hadn't broken anything, hadn't twisted anything. A bit of dirt on his pants, nothing more. He had done it. He was free. Will could not help but smile as he set out to see what Whitey had in store.

The dark majesty of Titan City by night spread out before him. Pools of light spread across pavement, glistening from streetlights above. Day-familiar alleyways disappeared into impenetrable shadow at every turn. The growl of workday traffic transformed into late-night revelry with the giggles of citizen celebrants. Flappers in their shimmering shift dresses and modern bob hairdos draped from the arms of pin-striped playboys with shiny, slicked-back hair. Voices called out to him, grown-up voices made looser and louder with drink. "Hey, kid? Where you going, kid? Ain't it past your bedtime?" The night showed Will a whole new face of Titan City, and he wasn't sure which of the two was real and which was the mask.

Whitey hissed at him from behind a trashcan in the alley beside the Regent, "You're late!"

Will could not see the older boy very well, nor could he see the other four who surrounded him until he came closer. They were all about the same age as Whitey, none of them over fifteen. These couldn't be the big shots who saw potential in Whitey, who admired his drive. No, they had to be others with that same drive and potential, trying to impress the ones who said they saw it. From the sneers and squints they shot his way, Will wondered if their potential was the potential to knock his teeth out of his skull. It sure looked like it.

"I'm sorry," he whispered.

"This the kid you got?" one of the others asked Whitey.

"Yeah, this is Will." Whitey grabbed hold of the younger boy's shoulder and drew him close. "This here cheese is gonna bring us a big, fat mouse." The way he squeezed Will's shoulder fell somewhere between a show of confidence and a threat. The bit about "mouse" and "cheese" made no sense to him, but the others seemed to understand.

"I don't know, Whitey," said another. "Kid looks like he doesn't have the nerve."

"Then he's got you fooled just like he's gonna fool our mouse! See, Will here promises me..." Whitey looked him hard in the eye, a sharp, predatory glare. "He says he's got drive. And he's gonna show us. He's gonna be a real tasty piece of cheese tonight..." Will knew the next words that were coming so clearly, he could have mouthed them along with Whitey, "...or else."

None of the boys had anything to say to that. They were all looking at Will. His eyes had adjusted well enough for him to make out the mix of hardware store weapons each of them carried—a wrench, a lead pipe, a wooden beam, a hammer, a length of chain. If he did not say the right thing, right then, Will had the strong impression he would not have to worry about how to climb back up to the orphanage window from the ground because he would be six feet below it.

His voice squeaked as he spoke. "Beans to Old Aunt Edna."

The words sank into their ears. Will felt his left leg begin to tremble and fought the urge to wet himself. Then all five boys erupted into laughter.

"Beans!"

"Did you hear that kid?"

"Beans to Old Aunt Edna!"

"That's a good one!"

"What'd I tell you, boys?" said Whitey. "Ain't he the perfect cheese? He's gonna make us real fat cats for sure!"

Then he spelled out for Will their plan and his place in it. The "mouse" would be one of the people coming out of the movie, man or woman, they did not know yet, but Max—he was the spotter—would pick someone with the right look to be their mouse and pass the signal onto Jackie-Boy, who would be the one to point out the mouse to Will. Then Will would come running out of the alley as the "cheese," crying about how his ma had fallen back there away from the crowd, and she was not getting up. He would beg the mouse to come help.

"Then we'll handle the rest," said Whitey, and he gave that Nosferatu grin again. "But you got to be real convincing with your crying. I'm talking the full waterworks, get me?"

Another boy, Harvey, the one who carried the wooden beam, said, "You think we need to help him get those tears, Whitey?" He clapped the beam against his open palm.

"Nah, you don't need no help there, do you, Will?"

Will quickly shook his head.

"Sure, you don't. You're gonna be a real little Shakespeare tonight."

"Shakespeare! That's funny!" The fifth boy, Wheeler laughed. "Will Shakespeare! Get it?"

"That's right," said Whitey. "Will Shakespeare."

Will forced a smile.

All the boys stood in position as The Regent began to release its audience into the street. The well-dressed men and women of Titan City murmured in fear and wonder over the director Murnau's sublime study in shadow and the terrifying portrayal of the fiendish vampire, Count Orlok.

"How did they get him to look like that?"

"Oh, those eyes... those eyes..."

"And when he was creeping up the stairs? I could just perish!"

Who would Max pick to be the night's mouse? One of the silver-haired ladies with pearls around her neck and mink around her shoulders? Or a young couple enjoying their night out, the gentleman throwing his cash this way and that to win his girl's admiration?

When the signal came from Jackie-boy, Will looked to see that it was a broad-shouldered man who had caught his eye. This cheese did not look like a chump, but Will figured what gave Max the idea was the shiny gold watch the man had pulled from the pocket of his long camel coat and the fact that, as he reviewed the time, all the other bodies passed around him. This movie-goer had come to the Regent alone.

"Get to it!" said Whitey, "It's showtime for you, Shakesepeare."

Fear brought real tears real fast to Will's eyes, fear of violence from the others, fear of this man seeing right through him, fear of getting into trouble, maybe losing his place at the orphanage. If he did not show what he was made of and show it soon, Will's world was going to turn several shades of awful and quick.

Wishing he never left his bed that night, he ran forward to tug on the mouse's sleeve. "Hey, mister!"

The mouse looked from his watch at Will, showing his neatly trimmed mustache flecked with gray and his spectacle-framed eyes. His spoke in tones smooth and refined, the sounds of comfort, the sounds of money. "Good Lord, son. What is the matter?"

"Please, mister! It's my mom. She's real sick. Something happened. I don't know. She fell. She's right back here and she fell and…" Will hadn't planned what to say, but the jumble of words just served to make him sound even more distressed. He pulled the mouse's sleeve in the direction of the alley.

"Now, hold on a minute here. Just breathe. You say your mother fell?"

Will nodded. He pulled again, harder, hoping to get the mouse in place before his story fell apart. Questions were not what he wanted.

"This sounds very serious. Tell me, son. How long since she has eaten? Has she had anything to drink?"

"Uh… I don't know… Maybe…"

He leaned down to speak eye-to-eye with Will. "Listen carefully," he said. "Your mother is going to be all right. I'm going to make sure she gets proper medical attention, okay?"

Looking into the man's eyes, Will forgot for a moment that he did not actually have a mother waiting there in the darkness, down in the alley where Whitey and his boys stood with weapons in hand, ready to commit violence. And forgetting that, he felt oddly comforted by what was being told him.

This was a nice man. He would make it all work out all right.

The mouse turned and took one step toward the alley, toward danger and maybe even death. But Will cried out, "Wait!" He had his hand on the man's sleeve still, the soft wool gripped firmly between his fingers.

"Don't worry, son. We'll make sure she gets the care she needs."

"No, you see..." And it all came out of him like a broken floodwall. "I'm sorry, mister. They made me do it. My mother ain't down there. It's a trap!"

From the alley, Harvey shouted, "I knew the kid was yellow!"

"Get the snitch!" Wheeler shrieked.

"Run, mister!" He shoved the man hard away from the alley and felt the man's hand wrap around his wrist to pull him along too. Suddenly, Will was running at his side, feet fumbling against the pavement, struggling to keep up with the rest of him. Whitey, Harvey, and Wheeler exploded from the alleyway. Max and Jackie-boy charged from the opposite sidewalk.

The last scattered movie-goers turned to look at the ruckus and only glimpsed for an instant the back of millionaire industrialist Josiah Finn, who had mourned the death of his wife and daughter for many years, fleeing from the gang. At his side ran the orphan Will Singer, whom he pulled with him into the safety of his limousine, into the comfort of his home, and ultimately into his family.

2019

Jerry and Joe slinked away from Gracie and the Crimson Wraith as the two stood face-to-mask in the strange, deepening fog that had arrived just ahead of the Crimson Wraith's appearance.

"Don't," the Crimson Wraith repeated, keeping his red-gauntleted hand raised to her.

Gracie didn't. She didn't anything—didn't move, didn't blink, for a moment she didn't breathe, and she didn't let go of the broken bottleneck with its viciously sharp edge.

The words came hard through her clenched jaw. "Don't what?"

"You can put that down. You don't have to use it."

"Wait... Are you..." She looked at Zack, that useless, abusive piece of shit, motionless on the ground. "Are you trying to protect him?"

"The fight is over," the Crimson Wraith said. "You can let it be over."

Gracie exploded. "There is a seriously fucked-up girl back there! Her eyes... Her face... I don't know if she's going to be okay!" Tears came now. "And are you really trying to protect the motherfucker who did that to her? Aren't you supposed to be some kind of hero, defending the defenseless or some shit?"

"He can't defend himself, but it's not him I'm trying to protect. It's you."

"Me?" Gracie couldn't help but laugh. "You don't know me. You don't know anything about me."

"I know you've never killed before. Whatever else you've done doesn't change how taking this man's life would affect you."

She raised the jagged glass, pointing it toward the Crimson Wraith's palm. Zack's blood darkened the bottle's emerald sheen. "Maybe I'm okay with that. Maybe it doesn't matter how it affects me. Maybe the only thing that matters is stopping him from ever doing anything like this ever again."

"Maybe," said the Crimson Wraith. "Maybe not. But one thing is certain; if you kill that man, I will have to bring you to justice. And I believe you might to more good for that girl he hurt—and who knows who else—from this side of iron bars than in prison."

The fight began draining from her, taking Gracie once more to that terrible, shuddering, cramping pain that came right after a rage. She watched the glass vibrate in her trembling hand, and although she wanted to scream, the only sound that came from her was a defeated groan. Her arm fell. Her shoulders fell. Her head hung, no longer meeting the Crimson Wraith's expressionless gaze.

"Who are you?" she said. "What do you want?"

"I want you to let me take this man to the police, and I want you to take your friend to the hospital. She needs help. You take her. I will take him."

Gracie nodded. "Okay."

The Crimson Wraith swiftly scooped up Zack's body to throw over his shoulder. "I've contacted an ambulance for you. Make sure you've got her identification. Be ready to stay the night with her." Then he went for the door. Gracie hoped the Crimson Wraith would bang Zack's head against the frame as he went out. He didn't.

With the Crimson Wraith's exit, the fog began clearing. Jerry and Joe started to whimper. The open doorway remained dark, empty. And then she did as the Crimson Wraith had asked her, collecting Kristen's purse, phone, and a change of clothes.

She thought maybe she should call Kristen's parents, but Gracie wasn't sure what their relationship was like. In the months since she met Kristen and moved in, the subject of parents hadn't come up, and they'd made no physical appearance. So, maybe there was a reason not to call them.

The EMTs didn't take long to arrive. When had the Crimson Wraith called them? How long had he watched? Had he seen Zack do this to Kristen without stepping in?

Gracie stood in the hallway as they checked Kristen to see if they could move her and asked questions for which Gracie had no answer. How long had she been unconscious? What had been used to hit her? Were there any drugs or alcohol in her system, what kinds and how much? Gracie knew none of that. After a minute of them attempting to rouse her, Kristen did make a sound. She puked all over her bed before lapsing into weak sobbing. Then the EMTs got her up on the gurney.

Riding with her in the back of the ambulance, Gracie held Kristen's hand. Through some of her sobs, she could make out words like "hurts…" and "sorry…" and "please…" and "baby…" That was what Kristen called Zack. She didn't seem aware of her environment or who was in it.

When they arrived at St. Gabriel's Hospital, Gracie filled out the admitting paperwork again with little insight to offer on things like allergies or existing conditions. She listed herself as "emergency contact," and then she had to sit in the waiting room with assurances that she would get to see Kristen soon and that her wounds were "not that bad." Wherever Kristen's wounds fell on the scale of badness didn't matter to Gracie. Kristen shouldn't have had them at all. What would a doctor say about the wounds she had given Zack?

All around the waiting room, the late-night miserables sat in various states of discomfort. In the corner, a syndicated sitcom played on TV, something that hadn't been on the air in five years called *Easy Does It* about a single dad trying to raise three children while running a pizza shop. There was no way Gracie could stand killing time by watching that or reading any of the magazines arranged in stacks, not that night. Gracie needed to get up and get out. She needed the night air.

Out the front door she went and started walking, past the marble statue of St. Gabriel at the church's fountain, past the nurses smoking around the corner from the ambulance bay, over the footbridge that led to the parking deck, where she stopped halfway and turned to look out over the street below and the city beyond.

The cool night breeze felt good against her face. In the distance, so much of Titan City spread out before her. She saw the flashing red Kronos-Kola sign and the glittering golden spire of the Snyder-Finn Building. And as the light and motion of Titan City swirled underneath her, Gracie thought back on the night, on Zack and Kristen, and on what went down before the Crimson Wraith showed up.

She didn't have to crack open her psychology text to know she had some serious "displacement" going on. The scene in the apartment she'd walked in on came way too close to what she saw growing up, nearly identical to the aftermath of one of her parents' fights, only then Gracie had been too small to do anything but cry and listen to the sound of her father's hands against her mother's face.

Their fights would build up from nothing, the fire sparked by something as inconsequential as Salisbury steak still cold at the center, finding ample fuel in the amount both had to drink in the hours before. After Gracie fled the dinner table, filling her room with music to drown out their noise, she could still hear the terrible words they used against each other. Then wordless screaming. Then blows.

Only one time, when she was just entering her teenage years, did she dare step out to scream, "Stop it! Stop it! Stop it!"

Her father turned his anger on her, hand raised to remind Gracie who put food on their table, but her mother threw herself between them and shoved Gracie back into her room. Gracie could still smell the sickly-sweet gas station wine on her mother's breath as she said, "Just go to sleep, sweetie. Just go the fuck to sleep."

How was it that Gracie managed to find herself once more in a home with these same characters playing out the same drama around her? It must have been like some kind of scent that she had picked up on when she'd first met Kristen, something that made Kristen feel familiar because Gracie grew up with it even though she ran away from it at age fifteen. And now that the source of that familiar feeling had shown itself, what the hell was she going to do about it? Gracie was too tired to begin to figure that out.

1930

Along the dark halls of Finn Manor, whose high ceilings disappeared into gloom, the walls bore portraits of those with whom he shared no blood but who his new father Josiah Finn urged him to call "family." However, for William Singer Finn, every heart that beat within those walls felt like kin to him —the staff of maids and cooks, the butlers, the driver, the groundskeeper. And in each of these, he found, more often than not, a smiling face who delighted in indulging the young master.

The only notable hold-out came from one particular housemaid, Miss Delilah. She always seemed cold and curt toward Will, but he would not avoid her because she also had a son, Robert, who lived on the grounds. He was very near in age to Will himself and knew all the best hiding places and secrets of Finn Manor. Sure, if Will got into trouble, it was only ever at Robert's urging, but the redness across his backside— administered by Miss Glenda, Finn Manor's head of household —could be fully justified by whatever wonder Robert had shown him. These included the body of a fallen deer on the estate grounds out beyond where they were permitted to go, a false-bottomed chest where the *chauffer* stashed a few "bathing beauty" photos, and the hallway panel that opened into a hidden passage leading to his father's study, which he was not allowed to enter without supervision.

In time though, after Will had been brought up-to-speed through the education of private tutors, Josiah enrolled him in the same boarding school that he and his father and his father's father attended, the prestigious Ellsworth Academy. There the children of Titan City's elite prepared to take their places among its upper echelon. The street grime had been well scrubbed from both his fingernails and his manners before he encountered children his age who had been born into wealth. Will received their scrutiny but not their scorn. And he made himself loveable with his easy smile, friendly jokes, and sympathetic ear—the outgoing charm he had practiced while selling street corner newspapers.

Besides, when children tested him with schoolyard challenges to see what he was made of, there was no way they could frighten Will more than the dangers of Titan City's streets. He laughed at any threats they gave, and bravado has a way of winning esteem. However fine the clothes he wore or the social circles into which he received admittance, Will would always know what it meant to be hungry and desperate and alone.

It could be no surprise then that Will found himself less drawn to the company of the other students than to the son of the groundskeeper, a round young man of just a few years younger than him named Chester Chumley, whom the other boys called "Chubby" Chumley so often that Chester had taken to calling himself that name as well.

There was plenty to like in the friendship of Chubby Chumley. He never cheated at cards, never gloated in victory, and never raged in defeat. He knew interesting things about motor car engines, and his collection of adventure magazines could not be beaten. Many a fine Saturday afternoon they lay on opposite workbenches of the Ellsworth garage, poring over copies of *The Argosy, The All-Story*, and *Amazing Stories*, where Will met such heroes as Zorro, the Shadow, and Tarzan. After a weekend spent in this way, Will would return to his studies at Ellsworth with at least a little eyebrow raise for the company he kept. But should any off-color comment on the subject come his way, Will just laughed and shrugged and paid it no mind, so Chubby's common character did not seem to stain him.

Will excelled in the study of chemistry and Latin, and after his classwork, he ran track and performed in student theatrical productions. While the former did much to make Will shine in the eyes of the other Ellsworth boys, with their love for physical competition, the latter brought him to the attention of the young women of the Fletcher School for Girls, who arrived by bus to perform the female roles of Ellsworth's plays.

He received more than one love note from his castmates.

Will even experienced a few furtive kisses in the shadows of the Ellsworth auditorium. And with one girl, Sylvia Madison, who played opposite his leading role of Macbeth as Lady Macbeth, he experienced his first romance. She warmed to his gentle demeanor, and when he felt ready to share them with her, she thrilled at his tales of surviving the streets of Titan City, so when he invited her to the spring formal, Sylvia answered an enthusiastic, "Yes."

The night of the formal, Will and Chubby met on the steps of the Ellsworth Courtyard. The sun had set, and the moon had risen. The still-warm night air carried with it the scent of new-blossomed flowers. Tea lights all around the stonework and shrubbery illuminated eager young men and just-as-eager young women as the Ellsworth boys welcomed their Fletcher counterparts by the fountain, by the rose bushes, by the statue of Major Malcolm Ellsworth, proud founder of the academy.

"Gosh, Will, tonight is gonna be something, isn't it?" said Chubby, wearing a borrowed suit. "Boys and girls, all together and… just… Gosh!"

Will smiled. "Maybe. Could be. You never know."

"My hair is okay, right?" Chubby asked. "I don't want to look like a total bumpkin for Kelly's cousin."

Normally, Chubby did not take part in Ellsworth's social events, but for the spring formal, one boy, Kelly Winchester, had told Chubby that his cousin would be visiting and needed a chaperone. "She's just the girl for you, my boy. Just the girl," Kelly had said. While Will didn't think much of Kelly, a teammate of his from the Ellsworth running squad, it warmed his heart to see Chubby so excited.

Sylvia beamed as she approached Will and Chubby, "Well, aren't you boys a picture?"

"We are?" said Chubby. "Gosh! Just look at you!"

Will smiled. "He's not just whistling Dixie. You are an absolute vision."

And she was. Her blonde hair tumbled in elegant waves

down pale shoulders left bare by her shimmering satin gown. In the moonlight, she sparkled, silvery and luminous.

"Oh, me? Well, it's nothing, really."

Of course, her modesty was false. Will knew that Sylvia knew her own beauty. But she did not make a fuss over it nor permit others to do so, and that was something Will liked about her very much.

Then Kelly called out, "Chubby, my boy! Aren't you looking dashing?" He strode up to the three, surrounded by his coterie, a girl on his arm and several young swains with their respective ladies in tow.

"Gosh, thanks," Chubby replied.

Will went to shake Kelly's hand. "You're a real pal, inviting Chubby here to look after your cousin."

"Thanks, chum," Kelly said. And Will noticed something distracted in Kelly's demeanor that suddenly troubled him. "Now, you'll be an absolute gentleman, won't you, Chubby?"

"Of course! You can count on me! One hundred percent!"

Some of the others had started to gather around them. Later, Will would wonder which of them already knew what Kelly had planned and who had just followed the gravity of a gathering crowd, guided by curiosity.

"Promise me," said Kelly. "I've told her that you will show her a very enjoyable evening."

"And how! A more enjoyable evening couldn't be found!"

"You promise?"

"God's honest truth, I do."

"Very well, my boy," said Kelly, a grin just beginning to overtake him. "Here she is!"

At that, Kelly gave a whistle, and four of his followers who had held themselves back from the growing throng came forward with Kelly's "cousin" trotting between them on a leash. She was a fine specimen, a well-fed Yorkshire sow with a wig affixed to her head and an emerald green gown over her back whose skirt had dragged through the mud.

Kelly crowed, "Like I said, Chubby, my boy! She's just the

girl for you!"

All around them, laughter erupted, the privileged teens delighted by such mockery. It was quite a sight, and only Will, Sylvia, and Chubby himself did not join their laughter.

"Gosh," Chubby murmured.

Will noted a trembling in his friend's lower lip, and then Chubby took off as fast as he could, trying to outpace the onset of tears.

"What now, my boy?" Kelly called out after him. "You don't think you're too good for my cousin, do you? Doesn't that beat all? And he promised to show her a good time!"

Will only barely restrained himself from grabbing Kelly by the scruff of the neck. "That was a rotten trick. What business do you have mocking him like that?"

Kelly remained unmoved. "Surely, Chubby can take a joke, can't he? All in good fun, Will. All in good fun."

"It didn't look like good fun for him," said Will, fist clenched at his side.

Sylvia placed her hand against his arm. "I'm sure Chubby will be just fine," she said. "Let's not let this ruin the evening."

"Ruin?" Kelly crowed. "Why, my dear, this has *made* the evening! It's the absolute tops!"

Will turned and saw the warning in Sylvia's eyes. He held his anger in check and began imagining how he could exact Chubby's revenge. Later, as they danced, he and Sylvia conspired, developing a plan that would reduce Kelly to the same laughingstock he had made of Chubby that night.

"A good fright," said Sylvia, "that would do him. Show him that he's not such a big man after all."

Will agreed. "Let's have him whimpering like a babe."

"But how?"

Then Will remembered the first film his father Josiah had taken him to see, *The Phantom of the Opera* starring Lon Cheney. The scene that scared him most was when the Phantom came striding into the ball dressed as the Masque of the Red Death, from the story by Edgar Allen Poe. "What a fearsome terror he was," said Will. "It had me frightened for weeks after."

"That's it!" said Sylvia, "Let's trick Kelly into thinking he is facing death itself! Then he might reconsider his ways."

So, it was agreed that Will would dress as the frightening figure, wearing as elaborate a costume as they could cobble together from the schools' theater supplies. And when they informed Chubby of their plan, he volunteered his mechanical skills to heighten the illusion's effect. "I'm sure I could find a way to create a fog of some kind."

"Chubby, you're a genius!" Will cried, remembering some of the experiments from his chemistry class. "We could use liquid nitrogen! That would really sell it!"

"Liquid nitrogen? Gosh!"

After a week of planning and preparation, Sylvia convinced a friend of hers to send a private note to Kelly. It swore up and down how highly she thought of the young man and how she would be keen to show him just how highly if he might be able to sneak away from Ellsworth some night to *rendezvous* at a location where they could enjoy a bit of privacy. She suggested as the perfect site a little church that sat just up the road between the two schools. When Kelly sent a note back to indicate his agreement, Will knew they had him.

"What can I say, boys?" Kelly bragged at the dining hall table over dinner that night. "Some of us simply have it, you know?"

Some do have it, thought Will, overhearing. *And, tonight, Kelly Winchester, you are going to get it.*

Several beds in Ellsworth emptied themselves after lights out. Not satisfied to simply announce his romantic conquest to his toadies after the fact, three of them joined Kelly out onto the darkened lawn and down the road toward that little church where Will, Chubby, and Sylvia lay in waiting. The trio heard them all laughing as they approached.

"That's far enough, my boys," said Kelly as they drew up to the churchyard gate. "We must allow the young lady a modicum of privacy, mustn't we?" The others laughed and offered rude words of encouragement as Kelly climbed the fence and began to approach the church steps.

Sylvia's note said to meet her in the grove of trees just beyond the graveyard on the left side of the church. As Kelly rounded the corner, he called out to her in a whisper, "My sweet? Your prince has arrived."

Hiding behind the trunk of a tree, Sylvia called back to him, "Over here! Oh, please, don't keep me waiting a moment longer!"

The young stud checked his breath with the palm of his hand, smoothed back his hair, and then strode toward the sound of her voice, brazen as anything. "Then wait you shall not, my dear. You will find Kelly Winchester a punctual paramour..."

But as Kelly moved into position, Chubby quickly wound the crank on the small gas generator he had set up to power the evening's effects. The sound startled Kelly straight away. Thick waves of fog poured toward him from four different directions, creeping around the headstones around him. The acrid bite of sulfur met his nose as if the gates to Hell had just opened to engulf him. Then a hollow, echoing voice, Chubby's through a series of metal tubes, called his name, "Kelly Winchester..."

With faltering courage, he shouted back, "Very funny, Sylvia! Oh, yes, a real cracker!"

As if in response to Kelly's word choice, thunder crashed from above as Will struck a metal sheet on the church rooftop. Turning toward the sound, Kelly spun around to see a figure standing beside the steeple, silhouetted against the night sky, cloak billowing in the breeze, its face hidden in the shadow of its hood. At this point, Kelly soiled himself.

Then the figure opened its arms toward Kelly as if inviting an embrace. It stepped forward, off the rooftop, yet remained floating in empty space before descending toward him. The pulley system Chubby rigged up slowed Will's flight, giving their victim ample time to take-in the phantom's fearsome visage as he entered the glow of a lamp hung from an opposing tree limb. In its light, the figure's costume burst into a blood-red blaze, within which the bright white death's head grinned.

The sound that came from Kelly shocked his companions at the gate. They turned to find its source and saw their proud leader vaulting over the churchyard fence in full panic. Terror tripped him up, and Kelly caught the hem of his trousers on an iron spike, tearing the fabric and sending him face-first into the dirt below. His toadies ran to him, freed his leg, and helped him to his feet, whereupon he re-commenced his sprint without a word of explanation.

2019

As soon as Gracie walked through the door of Sprang & Sons, Brianna hit her with, "Whoa, are you all right?" Gracie nodded. Brianna squinted at her. "Are you sure?"

"I'm sure."

"Are you sure you're sure?"

"I'm sure I'm sure."

But Brianna's voice rang with a dubious tone when she said, "Okay…"

While everything else in Sprang & Sons seemed old, dried out, and dusty, Brianna brought warmth and life to that almost-dead place. Having her at the shop meant there was always someone taking care of things, more so than the owner himself. Rich possessed a keen eye for good product and had developed a network of loyal customers with whom he could shoot the shit for hours, but he wouldn't notice if some kid left a candy wrapper on the shelf and it sat there for weeks.

That was what Brianna brought. She fretted over the shelves and floors and the strangers who wandered in, everything in the shop really, and Gracie knew she herself was one of those things. Sometimes it was nice. Brianna would bring Gracie sweet tokens she never asked for—scratch-made cookies from home, an extra pair of socks she got from a buy-one-get-one deal, a free movie pass she picked up somewhere. But the thing that happened last night, though, that wasn't something Gracie wanted to invite Brianna to fret over.

What would Gracie have said, anyway? "I came home to find my roommate beaten all to hell, got into a fight with her dirtbag boyfriend, and then received a visit from Titan City's very own costumed vigilante..."

She couldn't even imagine how Brianna would respond to that. How would anyone respond? Sure, she would want to help, but what sort of help could she actually give?

In fact, something in Gracie's gut screamed against the idea of letting Brianna know what had happened, either because she didn't want to admit it was a real thing that really happened or because it mortified her to think of bothering Brianna with it. Could have been either. Could have been both. Regardless, Gracie knew her night's adventure would have to stay secret.

For the most part, the day went by normally, and that gave Gracie some relief. She didn't think she could take any more excitement. The usual customers, some new faces and some old, came in the usual waves and did the usual business.

Gracie knew she shouldn't keep checking her phone but couldn't stop herself. All it showed her was the last line of text she'd sent Kristen before she left the hospital room, "Please call me when you can. Please let me know you are okay." With each hour that passed without reply, Gracie got more and more worried at just how bad her roommate's injuries must be.

As Brianna went to take her lunch, she asked, "Want me to pick you up something from the bodega?" Gracie shook her head. She had no appetite.

Alone in the bookstore finally, Gracie did what she'd wanted to do all morning. She went back to the True Crime section and picked up the copy of *Nights of Justice* that rich douchebag had pointed out to her. Reading it in front of Brianna would have brought questions Gracie didn't want to answer.

She rang herself up for it without using her employee discount. They were supposed to write in a ledger which books they had purchased with their discount, but no discount meant no evidence of sudden interest in the Crimson Wraith. And Gracie would have a safe forty minutes to start reading it before Brianna got back.

The author, former Police Chief Harlan Goodman, wrote it after he retired from his thirty-five-year career in 1989, as he put it, "after having passed the fear of exposing secrets and of any harm that may come to myself or my loved ones as a result." In his introduction, he went on to say:

Rumors and fear have often surrounded the Crimson Wraith and his sidekick the Wily Wisp, and perhaps that is just what he intended by taking up his crusade in so mysterious a manner. He has, at times, been branded both murderer and pervert by those who enjoy the luxury of observing criminal activity from a comfortable distance. How fortunate for them. But for those of us who place our lives on the line for the safety of this city, it remains unspoken wisdom that, without the assistance the Crimson Wraith has provided, these streets would be far less safe...

Goodman went on to describe his first meeting with the vigilante and sidekick, the gunfight from which they saved him:

Perhaps it may paint me a biased narrator that I owe the Crimson Wraith my life. So be it. I believe my personal experience with him gives me greater insight than those who wonder at him from afar...

Then Gracie looked up from the page and realized she had been reading for longer than was safe. She hid the book in her backpack only five minutes before Brianna walked in.

On her bus ride home, the book remained hidden, and her texts to Kristen remained unanswered. She sent another, "Going to apartment to change and clean. Will feed J&J. Coming to hospital after."

The sunset splashed fire across the gleaming glass windows of Titan City's financial district as Gracie's bus drove by. Skyscrapers belched out swarms of professionals in crisp suits to be hassled by the street vendors pushing the evening paper at them. When she reached her stop, Gracie stepped gingerly onto the sidewalk, employing extra caution, as if the concrete itself had betrayed her the night before, giving no warning of what would await her when she got home.

She had her keys at the ready as she walked up to her dark apartment. Weird to come home to it at night without any lights to greet her. From inside, she heard Jerry and Joe start-up their barking as soon as she stepped foot on the walkway. Probably they both had shit the carpet at least once.

Then a woman's voice came from behind. "Excuse me, Miss Chapel?"

A jolt shot up Gracie's spine. She turned to see a woman of about forty-years-old stepping out of a car, her hair scraped back in a tight ponytail, wearing a navy pantsuit.

Gracie answered. "Yeah?"

The woman held up her hands. "Please, don't be afraid. I'm just here to talk. Can we step inside?"

Being told not to be afraid suddenly put Gracie on edge. "Who are you?"

"My name is Esperanza Villagraña, and I work with Titan City Police. I would like to speak to you about last night."

So, maybe the Crimson Wraith had come through, turned over Zack to the proper authorities, and made sure that son of a bitch was going to get what was coming to him.

Esperanza gestured toward the door. "Please, can we step inside?"

Gracie remembered something about how you are safe

from a vampire inside your home unless you invite them, but, still, she nodded. "I have dogs," she said.

Esperanza nodded. "I can hear them, yes."

Jerry and Joe didn't trouble Gracie's visitor, Esperanza just smiled and said to them, "Good doggy. Yes, you're a good doggy." They were letting her pet them before Gracie turned on the lights.

"I need to…" Gracie muttered. "The dogs haven't been out all day."

"You go right ahead," Esperanza said and sat down right where Zack had been the night before. "Please, take your time."

With one eye back to her visitor, Gracie leashed the two dogs and let them out the back. She stayed on the porch step, keeping firm as they tugged at her to be let loose. This wasn't the time for that.

Their business done, Gracie gave the dogs their treats and then sat in the opposite Esperanza. "Okay, what's up?"

"First, I want you to know that you are not required to say anything to me. Do you understand? That is your legal right."

As Esperanza adjusted in her seat, Gracie caught sight of the badge on her hip The bulge in her jacket had to be a sidearm. Shit, had Kristen left any weed lying around? Gracie saw an overturned ashtray. Looked like the dogs had happily gobbled up any unsmoked butts. Good doggies, indeed. "That's cool, yeah."

"Now, I need to ask you a couple of things," Esperanza continued. "First, have you had any contact with your roommate today?"

"No, nothing since I left the hospital this morning."

"Well, she has regained consciousness. And we have spoken with her. Miss Chapel, do you have any legal counsel?"

"You mean an attorney?"

"Yes."

"No. God, no. Why?"

"Well, you see, after her boyfriend was placed in our custody, we went to speak with your roommate about the incident last night and asked if she wanted to press charges. She says that she does not." And her eyes met Gracie's meaningfully. "But he does."

"He does what? Want to press charges? What can he charge her with?"

"Once again, I want to remind you that you are under no obligation to relate to me any details of how you remember last night. But we took his statement, and as he tells it, you assaulted that young man without provocation…"

Gracie shot up from her seat. "Motherfucker!"

"Please, please. Stay calm. There is no need to raise your voice. Sit."

Thinking about Esperanza's gun, Gracie lowered herself back into the recliner. Her knees were starting to feel weak, anyway.

"Now, that is just how he tells it. A judge will have to make his own determination, but the charge in question is particularly serious. It includes an allegation that you attacked him with a bladed weapon?"

"What? No! Well, yeah, but…"

"Please, you do not need to say anything. But the wound on his leg does seem to support his claim. And so, the charge being made against you is that of aggravated assault."

"Aggravated assault? That son-of-a-bitch…"

"Tomorrow, I would like for you to come down to the station of your own volition. Can I trust you to do that?"

The jigsaw pieces started coming together in Gracie's mind. "Am I being arrested?"

"I have handcuffs with me if I need them. But I do not think I need them right now. Do *you* think I need them?"

Gracie shook her head. Her mouth felt dry. "I don't want to go to jail."

"I do not want that for you either." Her voice lowered. Eyebrows raised. "And neither does our mutual friend."

"Friend?"

Esperanza nodded slowly. "In red..."

Holy shit. So, Goodman wasn't the only cop in the TCPD in tight with the Crimson Wraith.

Esperanza continued. "Please, listen. As an officer of the law, I am not in a position to give you legal advice, you understand? But I am not just here as an officer of the law."

From her shirt pocket, Esperanza pulled a business card with a few words scribbled on the back that she handed to Gracie. The front read, *Bradley Hancock Attorney-at-Law*. On the back had been written the words, "I met a man at midnight."

"Even if you already possessed legal counsel of your own," she said, "Mr. Hancock has a special affinity for this sort of case. You will not need to pay him for his services. Simply say the words written there when you call."

"I met a man at midnight?"

"He will understand. And he will help. He is someone with whom we also have a friend in common."

The police, a lawyer, and a costumed vigilante, all working together. Who else was in on this? Gracie couldn't keep herself from saying, "This is fucking nuts."

The statement didn't alter Esperanza's steady tone. "Yes, it may seem that way."

"Look," Gracie felt tears starting to well, and she fucking hated that. She still couldn't believe she was getting charged with a crime, but this woman seemed reasonable. Maybe she would hear Gracie out. "Look... That guy? That creep you say is charging me with assault? Yeah, he is not a good guy. For real. He is a very-not-good-guy." It was a long shot, but if this police chick was getting real with her, then maybe she could get real right back. "He beat the shit out of Kristen. She's not in the hospital right now for falling down some fucking stairs, you know? This apartment doesn't even have stairs!"

"*Cálmate, por favor*." Gracie didn't speak Spanish, but she heard the word "calm" in there, and Esperanza's pleading eyes filled in the gaps. "Our justice system, it isn't perfect. It is a tool, and a tool can be used by good people or bad people. Mr.

Hancock is a good person. Call him. He will help you. And the man you met last night, he is a good person too. He is going to do everything he can to make sure justice gets done. So, please, do not worry. Tomorrow morning, you call Brad and talk with him, and then you come downtown to see me."

Gracie turned over the attorney's business card in her hand. "What about you? Are you a good person too?"

"I try. In my own way. Good night, Miss Chapel." And she left.

Meanwhile...

The elderly residents lounging in front of the doorway of Sunset Gardens, in defiance of autumn chill, looked up and smiled at the gentleman who approached. They didn't know his name nor recognize his face, but he was a handsome young man—young to them at thirty-nine years old—sharply dressed, with briefcase in hand and a proud bearing. He appeared to be doing well in life. That was enough to smile about. Kevin Snyder smiled back, although he did not feel like smiling.

At the front desk, he signed in and let the receptionist know who he was and why he was there. She had been told to expect him and asked if he would wait just one minute. She rang the Sunset Gardens director, a small and effusively polite woman who came out to meet Kevin. As she shook his hand, she said, "Mr. Snyder, it is a pleasure to see you. We didn't expect you would be coming personally to retrieve your godfather's belongings. You must be a very busy man."

"My godfather was very important to me," he said.

"Oh, of course, and very important to us as well." The director continued to hold his hand well past the point of politeness. "Mr. Burton was loved by everyone and will be so deeply missed."

"He was special," said Kevin. "One of a kind."

A tall man, one of the Sunset Gardens staff, approached the two of them, and when the director saw, she drew him in to shake Kevin's hand as well. "Lawrence! This is Lawrence, Mr. Snyder. He works in our kitchen. He was the last one to be with Mr. Burton before his passing."

"How do you do, sir?" said Lawrence.

"The famous Lawrence," said Kevin. "My godfather gave your cooking high praise in his letters."

"He did? Well, damn... I mean. I'm sorry," said Lawrence, apparently feeling he should be more formal in his tone to the CEO of Snyder-Finn, certainly while the boss was there to see.

"It's okay," said Kevin.

The director said, "Mr. Snyder, I am putting Lawrence here at your disposal. If you want help boxing things or carrying them out, Lawrence is your man."

Lawrence said, "Any way I can help, just name it."

"Thank you," said Kevin. "Thank you both. I think I'd just like a little time alone in his space first if you don't mind."

"No, no! Not at all. You take your time. And if you'd like me to send Lawrence over to you, just ring the front desk, and he'll be on his way."

They both walked Kevin to what had been Edward's apartment and unlocked the door for him. The director left then, but Lawrence held back. "Mr. Snyder?" he said, shamefaced. "I just wanted to let you know... See, the night he passed..." He looked back over his shoulder to see that the director had cleared the hallway. "I don't think this is like a liability thing, but I don't think she'd want me saying this. I just got to, though, because I feel so bad."

"Go ahead," said Kevin. "It's all right. I'm not holding you accountable for my godfather's passing."

"Well, that night, he invited me inside with him. And I didn't go because—man, I hope you don't mind me saying this —I think your godfather was kind of... um... sweet on me..."

Kevin nodded, unable to suppress a small smile. "I think you may be right about that."

"Okay! Now, he's a nice man, and I do like our chit-chats and all that. I mean, I did like them. But I didn't think it was a good idea to go inside with him. Didn't want him getting the wrong idea, you know?"

"I'd say that is understandable."

"It's just..." Lawrence chewed his lip. "I keep wondering, maybe if I had been there with him when he had his heart attack... Like, if we could have gotten him help, maybe instead of just finding him there the next morning..."

What if Lawrence had joined Edward Burton that night? What would he have seen? Kevin hoped to soon find out.

"Please, don't trouble yourself over it," said Kevin. "You did the most anyone could have expected of you. And your cooking brought my godfather a whole lot of joy."

Lawrence smiled at that. "Thank you," he said and left Kevin to enter the apartment alone.

With a heavy sigh, Kevin gazed across the little living space, taking in relics from decades of adventure, artifacts of the man who was responsible for passing on the legacy he now carried, which had become his life's mission. *God damn it, Eddie. I wish you would have let us do more for you.*

Then Kevin set his case on the kitchen table and snapped it open to reveal the gadgetry hidden within. It was time to get to work. He started by withdrawing his earpiece from the suitcase and inserting it, giving it time to connect to the Wrist Communicator he revealed by slipping off his jacket and rolling up his left sleeve. Tapping a few commands into its touch screen, he sent a hailing call back to the Crypt. A crackling sound came through his earpiece and then a voice. "Line secure, Specter Prime. Ready to receive."

"Ready to deliver, Crypt. Deploy Haunts." He took a step back from the briefcase, which began emitting a low, soft buzz.

"Deploying Haunts," said the voice. "Fly, my pretties, fly." From inside the briefcase, three tiny red drones rose into the air, came together in a triangular formation, and started toward the opposite wall.

"This is a small space, Crypt," said Kevin. "You sure you got their flight patterns tightened up?"

"That I have, SP. Been running them on unpiloted drills through the manor's passageways."

"And how successful have these drills been?"

"Let's just say that, if they were getting graded, the Haunts wouldn't have to worry about losing their Finn Foundation scholarship."

"Let's hear it for academic excellence. It looks like a little over 700 feet square. About how long will it take to map?"

"Not more than thirty minutes."

"Okay, collecting video next. I'll start with the doorway."

He took a kitchen chair with him and stood on it to reach the ceiling just above the doorway. He directed his attention to a tiny dot that would have looked to anyone else like nothing more than an exposed screw. Drawing a Utility Pick from its sheath in his Wrist Comm, Kevin took hold of what was, in fact, a tiny camera, only about three centimeters long, embedded in the ceiling. Flicking a switch on the Utility Pick set it whirring, unscrewing the camera and withdrawing it from the wall. Setting it down beside his briefcase, he repeated the process with six other cameras hidden at six other points throughout the apartment. Once all were collected, he unclipped the embedding sheath from each one and inserted the first camera into an input slot in the briefcase computer.

"Uploading doorway cam now, Crypt."

"Receiving video data now, Specter Prime," the voice responded. "I just hate we had his security set up like this. These should have been broadcasting directly here. We could have kept it on a constant feed."

"Eddie wanted his privacy," said Kevin. "You know how he was about that. And after the things he went through, I figure he deserved some peace more than we deserved a piece of him."

"I know. And that was all fine before, but these cameras

only record about two hundred hours of footage. What if there's something further back we missed? Some clue?"

Kevin didn't respond.

"Sorry, man," said the voice. "I know. This isn't the time for *what-ifs*."

"It's okay, Crypt. We're all affected by this."

"No kidding. I can't believe Stephen is taking it so well."

"What makes you think he's taking it well?"

"I don't know. I woulda thought he'd take some time off, but he hasn't slowed down at all. If anything, he's working longer days than ever."

"What do you think would happen to someone like Stephen if he didn't have work to occupy him right now?"

"Oh…" said the voice. "Yeah, I can see that."

Kevin uploaded the video from the remaining cameras and then started looking over the apartment with his own eyes. Over the next several days, he would return and return to gather more evidence, checking for fingerprints, shoe impressions, and so on. He knew it would be difficult to find anything that might point toward Edward's killer. The cleaning staff had come after the coroner removed Edward's body. No one had preserved the crime scene because no one knew it was a crime scene.

Edward had a provision in his will stipulating that a sample of his blood should be made available to his next-of-kin, which at the time happened to be Kevin. This provision may have come off as paranoia in others but was pure practicality for a former crime-fighting legend. Toxicology testing at the Crypt found in Edward's blood traces of aconite, also known as monkshood and wolf's bane, the "queen of poisons." But Kevin did not think it best to alert the police. Edward's killer may be easier to find if they did not know they were being hunted.

The voice came through his earpiece again, "Hey, Specter Prime. You've got a friend reaching out on the private line."

"Patch it through, Crypt."

Then another voice, a woman's spoke. "It's done," said Esperanza Villagraña. "Your message is delivered."

"Thank you," said Kevin. "How did she take it?"

"Confused. Angry. Afraid. About what you'd expect."

"Angry? Tell me about that."

"Angry about how things shouldn't be like this. About how it isn't fair. About how he's the one who committed a crime."

"Okay," said Kevin. "Good."

"I have to say, can't see much reason to get too involved there."

"You didn't see what I saw, the way she handled herself with that guy, both of those guys."

"Uh-huh," said Esperanza. "I know that tone. I heard it from Michael when he started talking about a certain someone fifteen years ago. You're not really doing this, are you?"

"I don't know what I'm doing yet," said Kevin.

"But you know what you want to be doing."

"It's early days," he said. "We're just getting to know each other."

"No, you are getting to know her. She doesn't know a thing about you or about what you get up to at night."

"And it wouldn't be safe for her to know that. Not yet."

"Kevin, I just—"

"Codenames," he interrupted her. "Please."

There was a silence of Esperanza collecting her thoughts. "I just hope you are being careful," she said, "Because once someone puts on the hood, it does not come off easily."

Kevin couldn't argue with her there, and he knew better than to try.

CHAPTER THREE

1939

Below them, the Englehart River rushed through the ice clinging to its shores. Falling snowflakes caught streetlights in their crystals, shining in the darkness. And Will pressed his back against the cold metal railing of the 6th Avenue Bridge, his eyes upon the barrel of Robert's gun, which pointed squarely at his chest.

"That's it," a sinister smile tore open Robert's face. "Now, jump."

"Why?" Will asked, feeling foggy and strange. "I don't understand."

"Jump!"

"Just tell me why…"

Days before, Will was called back from London, where he had been handling the European accounts for Finn Industries after his college graduation. Troubles brewing on the continent had put business awry. That man in Germany had everyone very concerned, but he wasn't what brought Will back to Titan City. It was a telegram from Miss Glenda. "Your father has passed away. Please come home."

He boarded a ship the next day. Acquaintances offered condolences that he accepted politely, numbly, dazed by the shock. Then, when his ship reached Marshal Bay, and Will saw the Angel of Prosperity reaching out her arms to greet him, he wept. He was home, but the man who had made it home for him was no more.

Miss Glenda sent a driver to pick him up from the docks, and as the car pulled through the gates, Will saw majestic Finn Manor crouching against the flat, white winter sky. He could not imagine its dark halls without his father's love to illuminate them. The late nights of laughter and music from the society balls, Easter egg hunts on the lawn, and the towering Christmas tree filling the air with sweetness—where would these be without Josiah Finn?

Will met Miss Glenda inside and received the details of how his father had fallen ill. They laid Josiah Finn beside the grave of his wife and daughter in the plot behind Finn Manor, burial site of the Finn family going back for generations. Mourners included all of Titan City's elite, even the mayor and chief of police.

At the reading of the will, the family attorney spelled out how the estate would transfer. "All property, lands, and holdings of this house, Finn Manor, and of Finn Industries, both its local and international assets, are conferred in total upon my one and only heir, William Finn." From scrounging pennies off the streets of the city, he had become a millionaire, but as he listened, Will thought how quickly he would have traded it all to have his father back once more.

His boyhood pal Robert Caine returned for the funeral. Robert had grown muscular and broad-shouldered, becoming a serious and studious man who had also been sent to school and received responsibility within Finn Industries and its Titan City businesses. He ran more and more of the operations as Josiah had moved toward retirement. That night, Robert and Will sat in the parlor over a bottle of Irish whiskey Will had brought from Europe.

"This wasn't easy to come by," Will said as Robert poured a glass of the brown liquor for each of them. "Ireland and Great Britain have been in a trade war for a while. Strange how two nations so close to each other could feel such bitterness."

"Familiarity breeds contempt, Will," said Robert. "You get to see what someone else has. You get reminded of what you do not."

"Maybe," said Will. He raised his glass. "To Josiah Finn. My father. Your benefactor."

"To your father." Robert raised his glass as well.

They spoke a little about their time apart, how neither found a woman to settle down with, and both wondered if they ever would. Suddenly, Will started to feel strange, heavy. It seemed as though the light from the fireplace was dimming, its warmth contracting as shadows stretched all around him.

"Something wrong?" he heard Robert ask. Robert rose to his feet just as Will's legs gave out underneath him.

When Will began to regain awareness, it first came with the smell of leather, then the pressure of his face against a car seat, his body jostled by the rhythmic rumble of the ride, then jerking forward as the vehicle came to a halt. A car door clicked open. Biting winter cold wrapped around him, and Will was dragged out into the night, shoved onto his feet against the bridge's railing.

His eyes took time to focus on Robert, on Robert's gun, and Robert patiently waited to let the moment sink in for him.

"Why?" The question seemed to anger Robert. "Why? You still haven't put the pieces together? All of those fancy schools, and still can you be so stupid?"

Will accepted the challenge. "You want the inheritance for yourself, so much you are willing to kill over it, even your oldest friend."

"You were never my friend!" The words seemed impossible, but Robert shouted with too much conviction for them not to be true. "I have hated you since I saw you, since he brought you to our house, *my* home."

"Then take it," said Will. "Take everything. Take the money. Take the house. Take whatever you want."

"Do you really think this is just about money? So, very stupid, Will. Do you think I would murder you merely for your fortune? That I would have murdered him for his?"

"You… murdered… him?"

"Oh, yes. Arsenic, Will. It works slowly, over time. Requires patience and planning, both of which I possess in abundance. I made sure Josiah had a little bit added to his dinner, night after night, until…"

"But he gave you everything! He sent you to school! He's set you up as a man of business. What more could you want?" And understanding dawned for Will Finn. "You wanted him to be your father."

"No!" The gun shook in Robert's hand. "He *was* my father!"

The snowflakes seemed to swirl at the force of Robert's shout. They settled slowly on his shoulders, on the muzzle of his gun.

"For years, I held that secret! Years! It was my mother's wish. She had been having an affair with him while his wife still lived, and when she died, my mother thought her time had finally come. He would bring their love into the light. But the noble Josiah Finn wouldn't dare disgrace his wife's memory with scandal. What would their fancy friends think? He told my mother that it could never be and pushed her away from him, but not before she allowed herself to get pregnant with his child, with me.

"She went away, bore me in secret, and when she returned, years later, to beg for her job once more, she told Josiah that I was not his, that I was the product of her marriage to some drunkard slinging cod for Infantino. When she passed away, I came to him with the truth. Was I the fool then? Thinking he would acknowledge me? Thinking time might soften the severity of his pride? Thinking I might, in all my laboring over the years, have shown myself worthy of his recognition?"

"I had no idea," said Will.

"Of course, you didn't. And that is why I have to make sure you don't die tonight without understanding how I have suffered."

"I'm sorry," Will said. And he meant it.

"Yes, you are very sorry. You are overcome, in fact. The regret, the grief, knowing just how little you deserve everything that has come to you—it is too much to bear. And that is why tonight, you have decided to take your life, to jump from this bridge." Robert steadied his arm. "You have until I get to one. Ten... Nine..."

What Robert didn't know was that the lifestyle his father —*their* father—had granted Will meant so little to him that he secretly spent years sneaking away from high society and returning to the seedy streets that first had raised him. In dark basements throughout London—in the Camden docks, in a Chinatown grocer, and in several Brixton pubs—Will had found strange and unexpected joy in fighting for sport.

"Eight... Seven... Six..."

A fortnight could not pass without him finding his way there, squared off against another shirtless man in some grimy hole, while the crowd around them shouted for blood and placed their bets. He learned how to take a punch and how to give one, how to stand and how to step. And from that knowledge, Will possessed absolute certainty that he had no chance to disarm Robert. His opponent stood too far away, and he could feel how dulled his senses still were by whatever it was Robert drugged him with. There was no chance at all.

"Five... Four... Three..."

Turning to face the night, Will said a prayer and jumped.

Behind him, he heard Robert give out a long, strange cry. It was a terrible, shrill, keening sound of rage and pain and triumph, the wail of a banshee. Then the Englehart River struck him like a wall of ice, and its depths drew him down into darkness.

2019

There wasn't much sleeping for Gracie that night. She tried, but everything in her head felt jumbled and on fire. Hard to sleep when you have that going on inside.

First thing she did was she cleaned the whole apartment

up and down, left to right, and back to front. Bringing order out of chaos sometimes calmed her. She even cleaned Kristen's room. Her roommate wasn't totally stupid, right? Surely, she had some shred of self-preservation. No way could she stay with Zack after this. So, Gracie folded Kristen's socks in the hope that maybe, just maybe, her roommate wasn't a lost cause. Maybe she would come to her senses, charge Zack with beating her into unconsciousness, and then he would be the one going to jail.

The cleaning did eventually get Gracie to where she could sit still with her laptop. She signed-in to each of her online classes and checked to make sure she was caught up there. Finally, she turned the light off around 1 AM. No luck sleeping then. At 2 AM, she got up to try to walk off her nerves. Jerry and Joe, the little bastards, had been snoring in happy doggy dreamlands, but they took their leashes, shook off sleep, and joined her outside to circle the block a few times. Gracie could easily have kept going, but Jerry and Joe started lagging behind her, so she returned to the apartment for their sakes. Back in bed, she lay in the dark for thirty minutes before giving up again.

Was she really going to jail? That made no sense. None of this made any fucking sense. It wasn't that she needed answers. She didn't even know enough to ask a decent question, so Gracie started searching stories from *The Titan Gazette* that included the term "aggravated assault," hoping that might give a sense of what to expect. The results weren't pretty or reassuring. Was the world so broken that she could be sent away for, what? Maybe two years? More? All because she kicked the ass of a guy who beat up his girlfriend?

Closing her eyes took Gracie immediately back to that night. She could feel the broken glass bottle in her hand, see its edge catch the light as it trembled in her grasp. And then she was looking down on Zack. And then there was a fog. And then there was him, the Crimson Wraith.

She closed her laptop and picked up her copy of *Nights*

of Justice again. Maybe she'd get a better feel for this whole Crimson Wraith business there, even if Goodman was writing about shit from way back. That guy in the mask who she saw, he wasn't like a-hundred-years-old. No way. Not with how he scooped up Zack like that. But, whatever, same mask, same name, and both had friends at TCPD, so maybe there was some connection.

In the 1940s, the activities of the Crimson Wraith and his faithful boy sidekick, the Wily Wisp, were known primarily by those themselves involved with Titan City crime, either in perpetrating or thwarting it. These phantoms haunted wrongdoers and earned the silent respect of those interested in public welfare.

Awareness of their adventures gradually grew, reaching a tipping point coincidental with the heightened paranoia of the 1950s. Enough of the citizenry heard about the Crimson Wraith and Wily Wisp to question the rightness or wrongness of their activities. If the Crimson Wraith worked for the good of all, why do so in secret? This question guided a series of investigations that sought to put an end to his crime-fighting career.

Rather than retiring, however, the Crimson Wraith transformed, both in costume and method. The skull that hid his face moved to his chest, and he wore, instead, a domino mask, as the Wily Wisp had before. This allowed him to smile at onlookers and for them to recognize his humanity. In public appearances with city officials, most frequently Mayor Kelly Winchester, the Crimson Wraith aligned himself with the forces upholding order in Titan City.

There appeared at this time a new class of costumed criminal to challenge them. It was then that such figures arose to prominence as Deadly Nightshade, the Puzzle Prince, Frostbite, Queen Cleopatra, and, most famous of all, the Troubadour. The crimes they committed manifested almost as performance art, including larger-than-life props and elaborate ploys, seeming as much a show for the benefit of onlookers as the actual acquisition of ill-gotten gains...

Goodman's tone, so calm and matter of fact, didn't directly resolve any of Gracie's fears, but it presented the world as understandable, and if it wasn't exactly safe, at least it wasn't total chaos. With that last balm against the worries of her upcoming fate, she found a few hours of sleep until Jerry and Joe had to let her know it was time for them to shit again. She obliged them, and then made the call to Hancock. It was about 11 AM.

He sounded startled by her call. "Hello? Hey? Yeah?"

"Um, is this Bradley Hancock?"

Suddenly his voice became all professional. "It is. Yes, it is. Bradley Hancock, attorney-at-law." He quoted his business card exactly.

"Right. So..." Gracie swallowed. "I was told I should call you..."

"And I'm glad that you did. Tell me, what can I do for you?"

"You see, there was this guy... and I... I met him at midnight..."

Silence. And then, "Say that again?"

Gracie flipped over the business card. "I mean, I met a man at midnight."

"I see. All right. When can you come in?"

"Come in where?"

"My office. If you 'met a man at midnight,' we need to speak in person."

"Right. Yeah, okay. I mean, I guess, like... now?"

"Good. See you soon."

She made it to his office by noon. It sat amid the crush of shops on Dixon Street, above a vintage clothing store called All Today's Yesterdays, between the office of a small architectural firm and a shop that sold artisanal chocolates. Hancock had told her to look for the window with the St. Andrew's flag sticker, a white X on a blue background, and there it was, the only identifier to his otherwise unassuming office. She went to the door that led to the upstairs unit and pressed the buzzer built into the rough brick wall.

"This is Bradley," his voice said from the box.

"Yeah, it's Gracie."

"Come on up."

The buzzer sounded, and the door unlocked. It was surprisingly heavy and hard to open. Right away, she noticed a camera facing her from above. Seemed paranoid. But the walls were painted a soft, warm beige leading up the flight of carpeted stairs that immediately greeted her. And it smelled nice inside, maybe from the chocolatier next door, a hint of vanilla and cocoa. It felt like walking into a cookie.

Upstairs she found a tiny waiting room with the usual table full of magazines in front of deeply cushioned seats that looked decades old. An electronic chime announced her entry. She must have tripped a sensor to set it off. And Hancock came out of the door to his office with hand outstretched, a big smile, and a voice that filled up that tiny space.

"Miss Chapel, welcome! Come on in!" He seemed young, just a few lines of gray creeping into his beard. A green polo shirt clung tightly to his large frame, and there was a warm twinkle in his eye, the kind you see in pictures of Santa Claus.

She took his hand, and he waved her into his office where a half-eaten calzone sat in an open cardboard container on his desk. Gracie noticed, in addition to the shelves of legal tomes and framed law degree on the wall, a memorial statuette of clear crystal that read, *In Recognition of the Survivors of Zero Hour. Titan City, January 1, 2000.*

"So," he said, taking the calzone from his desk and depositing it into a small refrigerator underneath, "you met a man..."

Gracie nodded. "At midnight."

"At midnight. Right. Right... First off, whoever told you to call me, you don't need to tell me, and I don't want you to. That isn't important. What's important is that whatever help I can give, you've got it. So, tell me what's going on."

She did. Hancock sat back and listened as the details from

the other night came haltingly out of her, all the way up to the Crimson Wraith's appearance and the trip to the hospital after, then Villagraña appearing and telling Gracie to turn herself in. She took Hancock's cue of not mentioning it was Villagraña who gave her his card, but she did notice him smile slightly at the mention of her name.

Only when Gracie finished did he ask further details, but nothing about the Crimson Wraith. The night of their fight, had Gracie been intoxicated? Did she think Zack was? Was there any illicit drug use? Had there been any previous altercations between them leading up to this? Had there been any sexual relationship or even flirtation between them? How long had Gracie known Zack and Kristen? Did Gracie have a previous record of an arrest of any kind?

Then he was quiet. He leaned back in his chair and looked at the ceiling. A heavy sigh hissed out of his nostrils. The longer he sat there, the more Gracie felt her stomach start to knot. Hancock's head bobbed like he was counting in his mind. He chewed his lips. Finally, he spoke.

"Well," he said, "in most circumstances, I'd say you'd gotten yourself in a real pickle. This is just the sort of situation where what is lawful..." He pointed with his left hand in one direction, "...and what is right..." then his left hand pointed in the other, "...occasionally miss each other." Both hands crisscrossed in front of him. "Situations like this tend to favor the plaintiff, not the defendant, especially with the evidence of actual physical harm. Normally a judge would look at a young woman your size and think, 'Hey, no way is she a danger to society,' and that would work for us. But if this guy staggers into court with a wound like it sounds you gave him..." Hancock shrugged.

"What the fuck? That's ridiculous."

"Not really. Laws are there to protect people from getting their legs cut up and punish people who do the cutting."

"Well, what the hell else was I supposed to do?"

"Call for help, either a domestic abuse hotline or, if it seems dangerous enough, the police. Have you heard about that thing where women in trouble call the police department and order a 'large pepperoni pizza'? That's the standard sign to get help from law enforcement for a domestic abuse issue. But whatever else you could have done, I don't think trying to handle it on your own was a good idea in this circumstance."

"So, what you're telling me is that because Kristen wouldn't defend herself—because she *couldn't* defend herself—and because I didn't just stand by and do nothing, now I'm screwed?"

"In most circumstances, maybe. But these aren't most circumstances."

She waited for him to say more. He didn't, so she had to prompt him. "What the hell does that mean?"

Hancock shrugged. "Honestly, I have no clue. But someone sent you to me on his behalf, which means he thinks we've got a shot at seeing real justice done. I'll have to make some calls, but I know two things. First, when an officer of the law asks you very nicely to come downtown, you very nicely do so, especially if it's the captain herself."

"The what now?"

"Did she not tell you? Oh, yeah, Captain Esperanza Villagraña of the TCPD, daughter of former Lieutenant Commander Jorge Villagraña."

"She didn't say she was a captain."

"There's a lot she doesn't say."

"Okay, that's one thing. What's the other thing?"

Hancock's face became suddenly serious, and he said, with reverence, "Always trust the Scarlet Stranger. He's human. He can't be everywhere at all times. He can't stop a bullet in midflight or turn time back on itself, but the man who wears that hood cares about this city and everyone in it, even the ones who frankly don't deserve it. And if he cares about you, he's going to do everything he can for you, which is, actually, a lot."

Gracie caught Hancock's eye flickering to the Zero Hour statuette and wondered if that had been the midnight where

Hancock had met the man himself.

1939

Too hot. Way, way, way too hot. Will was smothered, damp, and could not move. Something heavy wrapped around him, but to his surprise, it was no burial shroud. He became aware of a hollow ringing tone that would fade from his attention but never, for the rest of his life, ever fully leave his hearing, and with it, a sensitivity to loud and piercing sounds.

Pushing against his bonds, he twisted and let out a groan. A voice seemed to reach him through a tunnel. "Easy there, Will. Easy now. I've got you. Gosh, you had me worried."

Blankets came away, loosened from his limbs by large, steady hands. Will blinked his eyes and became aware of a dim red light—not the fires of Hell but coals casting their warmth out of the grate of a cast-iron stove. The hands helped him sit up in the small bed he occupied. He tried to speak but only got out a croak.

"Let me get you something to drink," said the figure who loomed in silhouette against the oven's glow like Hephaestus among the fires of Mount Vulcan. He lifted a pot of coffee off the top of the oven, poured from it into a tin cup, and handed the cup to Will. And as he did, the light caught the corner of his face and lit up smiling eyes that Will once knew so well.

His heart leaped. With the coffee having just eased his cracked lips, he shouted, "Chubby!"

"That's right, Will. It's me. Now drink up, all right?"

"But how… How did you…?"

"Oh, you know, same as anything, I guess—the hand of God and a bit of dumb luck. You floated right past my tug, so I did like the Good Book says and became a fisher of men."

"Chubby… you… you saved me."

The boy he had been showed once again in the face of the man who smiled at Will. "Like I said, real dumb luck. What were you doing going for a swim like that anyway? In the middle of the night? In the middle of winter? And not exactly in your swimsuit..."

"It's... I..." Will didn't know where to begin—the news of his father's death? The confession of Robert's guilt? The bridge? The gun? But a coughing spasm overtook him as a bit more of the Englehart worked its way out of Will's lungs.

"Gosh, you really did take a big drink, didn't you? That's okay. You get your rest, Will. In the morning, I'll fix you up a nice breakfast, and you can tell me all about it."

Sleep came dark and heavy for him, dreamless with a pervasive dread down in his bones. But morning brought with it the smell of bacon, and he ate what Chubby fixed them over the little stove of the boathouse he made his home.

"Yeah, it's a good life," said Chubby. "Mostly, I'm pulling garbage scows for the city. But, now and then, one of the big boys needs a tug. That's when they call on Chubby." He beamed.

There were only a few of his personal effects of his there among the rigging. Will's wet clothes hung by the stove to dry. He had a pair of long johns to borrow in the meantime. They draped loosely over Will, who kept the blankets from the cot draped across his shoulders as he sat at Chubby's table.

"Feels like being back in your dad's garage," Will smiled.

"Well, gosh, it was Ellsworth's garage."

Will shook his head. "Your dad took care of it. He made it his."

The damp, salty smell around Will seemed more real than the aromas he had found anywhere else since he arrived in Titan City. It was like those Chinatown basements where he had felt truly himself. Maybe the life Josiah Finn gave him was never meant for Will in the first place, and if so, what would there be to miss? It would be like waking from a dream.

"Don't suppose you have room on that boat for a second mate, do you, Chubby?"

"Not much room. Wait... For you, Will? Of course! But,

why?"

"I don't think..." Will didn't know what he wanted to say, what he wanted at all. "I don't know, Chubby. But I think I won't be going back to Finn Manor any time soon. Probably best I lay low."

"Sure, Will. Sure. Long as you like. Low as you like. You sure you want that, though? I guess you maybe don't want to talk about what happened last night, but, gosh, it sure seems like one heck of a mystery."

And then Will told Chubby everything, the whole story from the telegram about Josiah's passing to that leap from the 6th Avenue Bridge, not one detail left unsaid. "Robert's face, Chubby... That look... I never knew. But I can't say I never saw it. No, thinking back now, I think there were times when it came through, like his true face peeking out from under the disguise he wore. God, how did I not know? How was I so stupid?"

"Stupid, Will? Not you. Not ever. No, if someone lies like that to you, that's on them. Isn't your fault for believing it. You remember that night of the dance when Kelly said he was setting me up with his sister?"

"I do. Never forgotten it. Not for a minute."

"Well, that was a real dirty trick, and you said it. Same thing. It was wrong of him to play that trick but not wrong of me to believe it."

"And then we played a trick of our own."

"Did we ever!"

Chubby leaped up from the table and went over to a trunk that sat in the corner of the room. He opened it, and out of that trunk, he pulled the very same red cloak and white mask from that night.

"I've never forgotten that night, Will. You showed me something. You showed me that friends, real friends, they'll always look out for you. And if you've got a good friend in your corner, then there isn't a thing in the world that can keep you down, not for long." Lovingly, Chubby looked down at the mask and its empty eyes, and an idea stirred in Will.

Rising to join Chubby, he gazed into the face of the skull mask as well. "That was some kind of night."

"Sure was. Gosh, Kelly was sure he'd seen a ghost!"

"A ghost…" Will reached out and took hold of the mask. Age had dulled the brightness of its white down to yellowed ivory. It looked more like true bone than it had over a decade prior. "A ghost, freshly risen from his grave." Will placed the mask over his face. "Like me."

2019

Gracie received a text from Brianna. "Heard you aren't feeling well and taking time off. Good! Could tell you need the rest. No offense. Can't be a superhero all the time."

Rich had been cool about it when Gracie asked if she could get her shifts at the bookstore covered for the week. And her attendance at class was in good enough shape that she could afford to be absent, but she emailed her professors anyway, claiming an unspecified "personal emergency."

That had been Hancock's advice, to be ready to check out of her life for a little bit. She wished he would have specified how little of a bit that was, but he said he just could not be certain yet.

What awaited Gracie at the TCPD station and what would come after were total blanks. Hancock kept assuring her that he would do something, but she didn't know what that was. Apparently, he didn't either—not yet. She was totally in his hands without a clue what that meant. After a while, all the not-knowing just short-circuited her ability to worry. It was too big a space for fear to fill. So, she did as she was asked, moving mechanically without much thought, making the preparations Hancock suggested.

He told her, "Don't leave anything in your apartment that you have any strong feelings about." Mainly what she had feelings about were her jacket, boots, and laptop. She shoved those into a garbage bag along with her copy of *Nights of Justice*.

Then Hancock showed up to drive her downtown, and she met him at the sidewalk, garbage bag in hand. He was smiling. And Gracie couldn't decide if that pissed her off or not. He asked, "You ready?" She lifted her garbage bag in answer.

As Gracie buckled her seatbelt, he started his car back up. Hancock's radio came to life with '80s hair metal howling on the classic rock station. "Okay, here's the plan," he said over sound of white guys singing big feelings. Aggressive guitar and drums provided a soundtrack to his words. "It sounds like you are going to be charged with a crime and arrested. Being arrested is going to basically involve the stuff you've seen in movies—fingerprints, mugshots, that sort of thing."

Great, Gracie thought. She'd get to have her face on that gas station paper with all the new arrests of the week.

"Now, once you are arrested," Hancock continued, "you would normally be held in jail until your trial comes up. And honestly, with the backlog of cases, that can sometimes be months."

Months? Ice hit Gracie in the gut and sank to her toes.

"But!" Hancock held up a finger. "We've got a friend of a friend willing to cover your bond. With that, you can be released under the expectation that you will return to your appointed court date."

The thought of owing some stranger for paying her bail didn't sit well with Gracie. "I do have a little bit of money," she said. "How much would it be?"

"Honestly, it depends on the mood of the magistrate. First time aggravated assault—I'm thinking probably in the four-to-seven-thousand-dollar range."

"Fuck..."

"Well, if you show up for your trial, you can get that money returned to you. But let's say you were hiring a bail bondsman, they usually charge you about fifteen percent of your total bail, and that's their fee."

"So, like, several hundred dollars?" She wondered if she could make that work.

"Exactly. But you don't have to worry about that. We've got this covered."

Nope. She did not like that one bit. That was an unthinkable amount of debt to carry from someone she didn't know. "Okay, so this friend of a friend who's got it covered, did he 'meet a man at midnight' too?"

"He's got his reasons," said Hancock. "You can ask him what they are when you meet him. Right now, all you need to know is that he will make sure you don't have to stay in lock-up overnight and that he's got a place for you to crash until trial if you need one. It is not a good idea to go back to your apartment after this. You shouldn't have contact with your roommate or her boyfriend before you see them in court."

"Right... Right..." Either this was a sweeter deal than Gracie could have ever imagined, or it was a trap. "And what does this guy want in return for bailing me out and housing me?"

Hancock must have caught the suspicion and fear in her tone. He looked over at her. "If it seems like too much, we don't have to do it this way. You aren't required to take the offer. If there's someone else you feel more comfortable crashing with, that's totally fine."

There wasn't. Sweet as Brianna was, Gracie wasn't ready to get close to her like that. "No, I just... I'm not really... This whole being rescued thing... It doesn't feel like me."

"I get that. Okay, well, the guy who's offered to put you up, he runs a business. Maybe he can find some work for you there, you know, give you the chance to feel like you're earning your keep."

Gracie nodded, and the conversation went silent until they came up to the Titan County Justice Center.

Originally built in 1933, the Titan City Justice Center showed the sleek art deco style of that age with a great glass arch intercut by gleaming towers that speared upward into the deepening red of the autumn sunset. In its courtyard, a reflecting pool shaped like the eight-pointed star of a compass rose burned with the brilliance of the blazing sunset above.

That was the pretty front door the public went through. Hancock went around the side, driving down into an underground parking deck where he had to wave his courthouse ID to guards with rifles to be let through.

When they stopped, he handed Gracie a pen and asmall, torn piece of paper with a phone number on it. "Write this on your arm," he said. "Once you finish processing, you'll have emptied out everything in your pockets. After the magistrate sets your bond, call this number and let them know that's done and how much. You'll be out in three-to-four hours, tops."

Gracie nodded. Then she realized something. "I'm... scared," she said, not because she felt like Hancock could do anything about that, more that it surprised her. This wasn't like looking over her shoulder at some guy who seemed to be following her on the sidewalk or casting a wary glance toward a darkened alley. This was way big, bigger than her, big as the whole weight of the Justice Center over Hancock's little car in the underground parking garage.

He nodded. "Feeling scared right now makes sense. Come on."

1939

"Murderer..."

The husky voice did not fully rouse Robert when first it spoke. He merely shifted in his sheets at the sound.

"Murderer..."

The second time drew him forth toward waking, but his eyes were slow to open.

"Murderer..."

And when he was awake enough to realize the voice was

no dream but something there in the dark with him, Robert's eyes shot open wide. He looked up from his bed to see, standing above him, a shape shrouded by gloom with an unmistakably skeletal grin gleaming within its hood.

One gloved hand raised and pointed at him. "Murderer…"

Terror took all words from Robert. Only a strangled shriek escaped his lips. He bolted from bed and ran to the door to find the knob refusing to turn. No matter how he struggled and jerked, it would not budge. "Let me out!" he screamed.

"Murderer…"

The hooded figure drew closer. Robert was sure that he could smell the vile sweetness of decay. But if the knob would not give, he could only use the hidden door that led into the secret passages of Finn Manor.

Into that darkness, he fled, fast as he could, until suddenly he saw before him that ghastly grinning figure he thought he left behind. With a shriek, Robert halted in his tracks and turned to push his way into the first room he could, the one that led into the office of Josiah Finn.

From the top drawer of the heavy wooden desk, he grabbed the revolver Josiah kept there. When he heard the voice call to him once more, "Murderer…" Robert turned and fired, emptying all six shots into the thing that followed him inside. The smoke of those shots drifted into a haze, and yet the ghost remained standing, unaffected, unstruck by a single bullet.

"You cannot kill me again…" the figure said.

"Again?"

"Yes, you killed me, Robert… You killed me and our father…"

"You? And our father? No… Will? Is that you?"

"You killed me…"

As the ghost reached out to take hold of him, Robert fled into the hallway, where the house staff, frightened out of sleep by all the noise, were running to the source of the sound of gunshots. In a tone of deep concern, Miss Glenda said to Robert, "Mister Caine, what on earth is going on?"

But Robert had been reduced to a gibbering mess. "The ghost…" he said. "The ghost…"

"A ghost, Robert? What ghost?"

"There!" He pointed inside the office. Those gathered all looked through the doorway and saw nothing. The ghost had vanished.

"You must have had a bad dream," said Miss Glenda. "This has been such a hard time for all of us, with the recent loss of both the elder and younger Mister Finn."

"No, Will was there! He was right in there, I swear. But he can't be! He can't! I killed him!"

There came a gasp from among the servants, who exchanged horrified expressions with each other. "Robert?" said Miss Glenda. "Did you just say that you killed our Will?"

And then Robert saw behind her, down the hall and through the window, Will's ghost hovering outside, some thirty feet above the ground. Its cloak fluttered around it, dark against the moonlit sky.

Robert shrieked and ran, away from the staff who called out after him as he hurtled down the southern stair to the Finn garage. There he grabbed a ring of keys from its hook and leaped into the first car he could, the Packard. But, when he turned the key, the engine refused to start. Robert stomped on the pedals and tried again. Nothing. And then he caught sight of the red cloak in his rear-view mirror.

Stumbling from the driver's seat, Robert scrambled his way into the Studebaker, the next car beside him. But once again, he turned the key without response. And still Will's ghost drew slowly closer, one gloved hand outstretched as if to drag Robert down into the underworld with it.

"Damn you, Will Singer! You'll never get me!"

Finally, Robert ran to the Lincoln-Zephyr, a car painted the same shade as the ghost's attire. This time the engine did start for him. Robert shot out of the garage and went thundering down the Finn Manor drive, nearly running over a night watchman who had to leap out of the way from his frantic escape. The guard at the front gate, seeing no sign of Robert slowing his approach, rushed to open the way to him.

Too late, a call came to the gatehouse from inside Finn Manor. "Don't let Robert escape!" Miss Glenda shouted. "He's just confessed to Will's murder!"

"I'm sorry, ma'am," the guard replied. "He's already run off."

"Then phone the police!" she said.

As Robert whipped around the curving roads winding down the Elysian Hills at speeds that would have been dangerous even in daylight, he started to think he might be free and began to breathe more easily. Where was he going? He did not know. North perhaps? He might cross the border into Canada, then make his way to Europe. But just as he approached the 6th Avenue bridge, the Zephyr began filling with a smoke that burned his nostrils. It reeked like the pits of Hell.

"No!" Robert shouted. "No, no, no!" He rolled the window down, but still the smoke was too thick, too biting. Between his stinging eyes and the blinding haze, he couldn't see a thing, and so he slammed the breaks and brought the Zephyr to a screeching, spinning halt right on the bridge itself. Spring thaw had cleared the ice and snow, leaving its span a dark, steel web illuminated by streetlamps.

Falling from the driver's seat with burning lungs, Robert spat out as much of the foulness as he could, nearly retching from it. And then a pair of red boots appeared before him. He looked up and saw the ghost's skull staring down.

"This was where you did it... This was where you murdered me..." Two hands reached for him, grabbed Robert by the shoulders, forcing him closer to stare into those empty, dark eyes. "Confess... Confess... Admit your crime, Robert... Turn yourself in... Confess..."

Trapped in that gloved grip, his neck bulged and twitched as horror overtook him. Robert screamed, shrill and sharp, a sound that tore through the air, and, strangely enough, seemed to harm the ghost. It recoiled, releasing Robert and staggering backward, clutching its head as if in pain.

Robert tore himself from the ghost and began running, unaware of where he was going, fleeing frantically toward the dark, when suddenly the air in front of him exploded in a flash of light.

Behind him, the ghost commanded. "You will come with me... You will come to the police... You will tell them how you murdered our father... You will tell them how you murdered me..."

With his back still toward the ghost, Robert shouted, "Damn you, Will Singer! Damn you back to hell!" Then he turned to look over his shoulder. "I'll see you there." Certain now that he could not escape his crimes and preferring to face ultimate judgment right away rather than await its coming in a prison cell, Robert turned and ran toward the bridge's railing.

Behind him, the ghost began to run after him. It leaped to tackle its murderer, but the distance was too great. Robert toppled over the same bridge he forced Will to jump from, into the same frigid darkness rushing to the sea.

2019

Fifteen seconds. Seven cameras with two hundred hours of video on each, but it was fifteen seconds of footage that Kevin focused on. They came from the one camera that had faced the entrance to Edward's apartment. And in that fifteen seconds, the door could be seen to open. Light cut into the darkness of the front hallway, and a figure stood there, silhouetted for just a moment, a rough outline of a person holding the door open with their right hand. Their left hand raised, apparently holding something, and then the footage ended. Then all the footage ended. Every camera in every room cut out at that exact same time.

Kevin did not like that. Not one bit.

"My first thought was EMP pulse," said Danny, who had

been on the headset while Kevin was at Sunset Gardens. They both watched the monitor from inside the Crimson Wraith's Crypt. "But an EMP would be too messy, affecting too many electronic devices within its radius. And in an assisted living facility, that could include things like pacemakers and oxygen machines that would draw a whole lot of attention."

"What does that leave us with instead?" asked Kevin.

"Okay, so you know where Sherlock Holmes says that, like, once you rule out all other options, it has to be whatever you're left with, no matter how crazy that may be?"

"That was his creator Sir Arthur Conan Doyle's justification for believing in ghosts."

"Well, this is crazy, but it's got to be that this person here had something that allowed them to specifically shut off all the cameras we had in that place, just them and nothing else."

"What would that take?"

"First, this person had to know the cameras were there. Then, they had to know what model of cameras they were, that they could be switched off and on remotely. Finally, they had to know the frequency on which to communicate with the cameras."

"That's a lot to know."

"It's *too much* to know. Each cameras is a custom piece, built in-house, running an operating system I designed. It shouldn't be possible."

"But that's what happened."

"If somebody knows all that, then they probably know a whole lot of other things. Maybe things about, you know, the rest of us. And who knows about us except…" Danny didn't like where the sentence was going, and so broke it off.

Kevin finished it for him. "Except us?"

"Yeah."

"Which suggests that someone who we've trusted with our secrets maybe wasn't trustworthy after all."

"Why even do it, though? Why Eddie? He was on his way out as it was. He wasn't doing anything to anyone. Couldn't they just wait it out a few more years and let the man pass on his own?"

"It doesn't seem like there could be a rational motivation, so we have to be looking for an irrational one. And that again points to someone who knows us, someone with a personal vendetta who knew him and knew that Eddie had worn the hood of the Crimson Wraith."

"This is real bad."

"It's not good," said Kevin. "So, let's start identifying suspects. You were able to get into the Sunset Gardens payroll files?"

"Took a bit, but yeah. Here are the print-outs of the personnel." He handed Kevin a folder. "No new hires in the last ninety days. No terminations since Eddie's murder. And not likely they'd be paying anyone under the table because they have to pass quarterly financial inspections to qualify for their state subsidies. For the past five years, they've done so with flying colors."

"So, whoever murdered Eddie had been working there for a while and is working there still."

"You'd think, right, that if you murder someone, the next thing is you get the first train to anywhere else."

"But they didn't. That tells us something else."

"What's that?"

"Running away arouses suspicion, but it's a strong instinct. Whoever did this might have a psychological profile that more readily rejects emotion in favor of strategy."

"Like a psychopath?"

"Potentially. Or there could be something else at stake, something very important to them. Maybe one of the staff has a loved one in danger and acted on orders from a third party holding that loved one hostage."

"Ugly."

"It's just another possibility. They could also be very well supported, working in partnership with someone assisting them in resisting the urge to flee the scene of the crime."

Danny stared long at the silhouette on the screen. "Kevin, man, I am liking this less and less."

"Then let's take care of it, quickly as we can. I'm going to start investigating some of these employees, see whose shape roughly fits that of the person on the screen and start to watch their movements."

"So, you're going out tonight?"

"Yes, I'm afraid I won't be here to welcome our guest."

"Our guest? Right. The new girl." Danny pointed at the screen. "Sure this is a good idea, taking on a fresh face while we got this happening?"

"She needs help," said Kevin. "Besides, as you say, she's a fresh face. Whoever murdered Eddie has access to information about us, old information. Whoever that is, we can at least be sure Gracie Chapel has nothing to do with it."

1939

So many steps of that night Will had been able to foresee and plan—the place in the secret passage where Chubby should also wear a cloak and mask to box Robert in, loading blanks in the pistol his father kept in the office, the time to have Chubby lower a mannequin dressed as himself to sway outside the hallway window, disconnecting the starters in all the cars except the one in whose trunk he would be hiding while Chubby followed Robert into the garage, the smoke machine placed under the Zephyr's seat, and the arsenal of flash pellets in a pouch on his belt.

But he did not know just how sensitive his hearing had been made as a result of his icy plunge in the Englehart, nor how sharply Robert would scream, nor how that pain would disorient him. But what he truly could not anticipate was not a weakness of his but a strength, for Will was not a murderer. It was not in him to seek to resolve a situation with death. He could not yet foresee that, finally trapped on the 6th Avenue

Bridge, Robert would want to end his own life. Because of that, Will was not prepared to close the distance between them, to catch Robert and halt his self-destruction. It was a lesson he would consider how to learn from later, but in the meantime, Will had a life to reclaim.

The story sold nicely on the front page of *The Titan Gazette*, a tale of murder and intrigue, concluding with a madman's suicide and one of his victims reappearing soon after, rescued from drowning by a humble tugboat pilot. The house staff of Finn Manor all welcomed Will eagerly. His miraculous return offered some resolution to so much chaos. And while a bit confused at first, Will's attorneys made all the necessary arrangements to restore his position as living heir to Josiah Finn's financial empire.

It was several days of phone calls, appearances, and interviews before Will had the chance to escape his formal duties and go visit Chubby once more. He looked forward to taking off his coat inside Chubby's boathouse and having a cup of stove-top coffee. He could even change into a pair of borrowed overalls and go out on the tug again, perhaps bring a scow on down the Englehart.

But most importantly, he wanted to offer Chubby a job, to invite him to come work for him up at Finn Manor, tending the garage there. He could not know if it might offend Chubby's pride, but Will wanted to do something. It seemed fitting. After all, how can you repay someone who saves you from the brink of death, then helps restore to you the life you just lost? And working in the Finn Manor garage, maybe Chubby could feel he was earning his keep and permit Will to lavish him with an income and lifestyle far beyond what the tugboat could offer. Will hoped so anyway.

It was about dinner time when Will pulled up to the boathouse. The sun had just sunk down behind Titan City's Elysian Hills, leaving thin smears of blue against the sky and stretching all the shadows below. Will hoped he could convince Chubby to let him take them both out to get something to eat, maybe a couple of steaks and good cold beer. But when Chubby answered the door, Will's jolly mood left him.

"Gosh, Will," Chubby said weakly. "It sure is good to see you."

And as good as it was for Will to see Chubby too, it was not good to see him like that. "Chubby! What in the world?"

Someone—or several someones—had given Chubby a sound beating. His face looked an absolute wreck, a purple mass of lumps that appeared horrific even silhouetted in the doorway by the lamplight behind him. And the way Chubby leaned hard on his left leg looked like his right had been banged up pretty badly too, maybe broken even. He had it wrapped in a homemade splint, a hospital visit being perhaps a bit out of his means.

"Oh, well..." Chubby began, attempting levity. "Soon after the story broke, I guess some guys figured, what with me having fished you out of the river, must have meant you gave me some kind of big reward. And, gosh, when I told them there had not been any kind of money for it, they didn't exactly believe me, not until they took their time to make sure I was telling the truth."

"This is terrible. I'm so sorry. Who did this to you?"

"Bunch of boys who call themselves the Titan Pike Gang. Real rough characters. Not the kind I usually have anything to do with, but I guess that doesn't keep them wanting something to do with me."

Seeing Chubby like this, hearing his story, something stirred in Will, a certainty that he never before knew in life. This Titan Pike Gang made him think of Whitey and his boys, and Will suddenly realized that all those times he sought violence in those dirty London fighting rings, he had in fact been training himself, preparing for the day he could stand up to the violence of others, to protect those who could not protect themselves, as he could not as a boy—to defend the defenseless.

He said, "Coming after you was the Titan Pike Gang's last

mistake. I believe a certain ghost shall rise again, old friend, and he will not rest, not ever, until justice is well and truly served."

2019

Inside the station, Hancock and Villagraña nodded at each other.

"Captain," he said.

"Mr. Hancock," she said.

Gracie saw so much in that gesture, those five syllables, the way he stiffened, and his eyes brightened when he caught sight of her, the pinched but kind smile she gave him. No, they hadn't ever been a thing, but it was clear to Gracie that Hancock had been carrying a torch for Villagraña for a good long while. He looked like a boy gazing upon the high school prom queen, and he was some little band club nobody. It was sweet. And sad.

"Miss Chapel," Captain Villagraña acknowledged Gracie. "Thank you for coming in. Please step this way."

Gracie looked to Hancock, who nodded. "See you on the other side," he said and then exchanged another nod with Villagraña by way of good-bye.

She didn't have to hold a sign up for her mugshots, so that part was different from the movies. And her fingerprints were taken by an electronic scanner instead of stamped with ink. Then, Captain Villagraña brought her to a waiting area with the other women who had just come in. Other criminals, Gracie thought. "Please be seated," Villagraña said. "Your name will be called in a bit." So, Gracie joined the other arrestees slumped in chairs that all had been bolted to the concrete floor.

No eye contact. Gracie knew enough to avoid that, but there were eyes checking her out sideways, sizing her up. She caught brief glances and ignored muttered commentary about her background and supposed sexuality. Not hearing things was important. Just sit and wait and be nothing until she got the bond from the magistrate and could call the number on her arm that promised salvation.

About an hour later, Gracie heard her name called and was directed down a hallway to the magistrate, a woman behind bulletproof glass who seemed a lot like a bank teller. The magistrate reviewed Gracie's charges and then gave her the bail amount. "One charge of Assault with a Deadly Weapon. Bail set at five thousand dollars. Sign here."

The magistrate printed a form with Gracie's charge and bail amount and pushed it through a slot in the glass between them. Gracie signed and returned it. Then the magistrate made a copy that she sent back through to Gracie. "You can go back to your seat now." The magistrate never made eye contact with her once. Maybe that was a rule too.

But now Gracie had that dollar figure, so she went to the phone. There was only one, an old-style model attached to the wall. She saw others go up to make use of it already. It cut any call after a few minutes, so arrestees would keep calling back whoever they were talking to if there wasn't a line. Someone was on the phone when she got back. Gracie didn't want to try to jockey for her turn, so she sat and waited. But then a more aggressive woman came up and took the next call before Gracie could get up. That was fine, Gracie told herself. She wasn't there to have any kind of conflict—any kind of conversation, really—with anyone. She just wanted to pass in and out of this place like a ghost, unremarkable and forgettable.

Finally, Gracie was able to place her call. On the second ring, she had a moment of quiet terror where she wondered if maybe there wasn't anyone waiting for her call at all. Maybe this had just been a lie Hancock told her to keep her calm, help her go quietly. But on the fourth ring, a man answered, his voice smooth, reserved, and cultured.

"Is this Miss Chapel?" it said.

Weird when someone you don't know knows your name.

"Yeah, it's Gracie. I was told to call?"

"By Mr. Hancock, yes. You have been provided with a dollar amount for the bail then?"

"I have. Five thousand."

"Very good, miss. I will commence with your release."

"Okay," she said. After the line clicked, Gracie thought it really, really would have been nice to have gotten a name from the guy.

She went back to her seat, and after about two hours of counting cracks in the walls and pretending not to listen to the prostitutes and drug addicts bicker with each other around her, a guard called her name and sent her toward the door. Just under four hours she'd been there, like Hancock promised, and she was getting to leave out the door she came, with her jacket, wallet, and phone returned. Then they pointed her to an outgoing desk where a well-dressed man in his late seventies stood waiting, his hands clasped behind his back.

"Miss Chapel, I believe?" His hair and mustache, both bright white, shone in contrast to skin too deeply tanned to ever fade. He smiled at her through glasses so thick they made his eyes seem small and far away.

Gracie nodded. "That's me. And you are?"

"My name is Stephen, miss." He bowed slightly.

"Okay, so you're the guy who... um..."

"I am in the employ of 'the guy,' as you put it. And my employer has seen fit to cover your bail and offer you a place to stay until your trial."

"Right," she said. "Okay, let's do this then."

"This way, miss," he said, and led her toward the parking deck.

She definitely di not enjoy this "miss" business. But when she saw the car he was taking her to, she thought she could put up with it a bit longer.

It was a classic, a classic so classic she had no idea how old it must have been, one of those cars that, if you see it on the road, you stop and stare out of respect even if you don't know a thing about cars. At least you know no one made a car like that since Al Capone was "Public Enemy Number One."

Its dark red exterior still shone, crisp as a candy-coated apple laced with chrome. Its hood rose high and proud like the prow of a ship, looking ready to slice through traffic.

"The fuck kind of ride is this?" Gracie couldn't keep herself from asking.

"This," said Stephen, holding the door open, "is a 1939 Lincoln-Zephyr."

PART TWO

CHAPTER FOUR

2019

Not once in her life did Gracie ever have reason to pass under the blue lights of the Arch of Mercy and cross the 6th Avenue Bridge. She'd heard about it, knew it was there, and sometimes even saw it shining out in the distance. It served as the portal between her world—the Titan City of real people, working and struggling and getting messy with life—and the almost fantastical world of Elysian Hills, where those who owned everything in her world—the streets, the buildings, the businesses, the government, and, yes, even the people—lived just above it all, beyond the struggle.

Yet there she was, being chauffeured—*chauffeured,* a word Gracie didn't think she could spell, much less experience—across the 6th Avenue Bridge by the manservant of some unknown savior. Maybe this is a trap, she wondered, but perhaps some cheese might be worth a mouse getting its neck broken just to taste.

Riding in the back of the Zephyr was luxury aplenty itself. It seemed odd to her that something so old didn't show signs of crumbling decay. Its leather seat had to be about the most comfortable thing she ever sat on. And it smelled fantastic. Gracie realized that meant somebody must have cared for it, very much, and worked to put that care into it over the years. She wondered what that must be like.

After crossing the Englehart River, Stephen took them up the winding hillside paths, all thick with trees in the process of giving away their foliage to autumn brown. Surrounded by the trees stood homes, each more beautiful than the one before, then entryways into private communities nestled away in comfortable seclusion. Finally, after quite a bit more climbing, they came to the foreboding gates of private estates, and at one of these, the Zephyr slowed to a stop.

Stephen punched a few buttons on a device clipped to the visor above him, and its iron gate began to slide open. Gracie flashed back to the Justice Center holding cells from which she had just been rescued and wondered about the difference between security for keeping people out versus keeping people in. They passed a gatehouse, where Stephen nodded to the guard stationed there and then continued down the drive.

Seeing the mansion for the first time that way, illuminated by lights from below and silhouetted against the moonlit sky above, with darkness etched all along its length between, Gracie wasn't sure if the gothic monstrosity was bigger than she could see or much smaller than it seemed. Shadows obscured its size. There were, little pokey bits coming out here and there that probably all went by technical architectural terms for which Gracie just didn't have the jargon. This part here looked kind of like it came from a church, and that over there like a castle, the type of tower where rich old English dudes would lock up their wives after they went mad.

"Holy shit," she muttered.

"Indeed," said Stephen.

They drove up to the entryway, where a young man came down the steps to greet them. Not dressed as another servant, he wore a slick, colorful windbreaker and pre-distressed denim jeans, casual but comfy street fashion that had to come from one of the nicer stores. And like his outfit, his hair and beard had a deliberately unkempt style to them. It takes a little work to look like you don't work, which would have made Gracie hate him on sight except for the easy bounce in his stride and the way he smiled at Stephen when he saw him step from the car. He didn't have an asshole's smile.

"Welcome back. Did you get the—?" And then the young man saw Gracie. "I guess you did." For a second, Gracie caught him checking her out, but he didn't say anything about it more than, "Hi." Then he extended his hand to Stephen. "I'll take the Zephyr down to the garage for you."

Stephen said, "Miss Chapel, as you may be staying with us for an extended amount of time, allow me to introduce Mr. Daniel Cole, our house mechanic."

Like a break-dancing robot, the young man pivoted in her direction, swiveling his torso. The hand he had held out to receive the keys instead extended to shake Gracie's. "You can call me Danny," he said.

"Gracie," she said, declining his hand.

"Cool. Yeah," Danny acknowledged the snub and turned back to Stephen. "Keys?" The keys exchanged hands, and Danny nodded goodbye before taking the Zephyr around the building. Then Gracie followed Stephen inside.

The way the air around you sounds tells you when a space is spacious. Gracie didn't need sonar to be able to hear how high the ceilings inside were, nor how solid the walls. Just like its stone exterior, everything inside the mansion seemed built to withstand the passage of decades, if not centuries. The windows sure looked gothic enough for centuries anyway. Not a simple square among them, no, each was dagger-shaped or had batwing-edged curves up to its point, with stained glass to boot.

"I shall show you to the room where you will be staying," said Stephen, guiding her up the carpeted stair. "My employer extends his apologies for being unable to greet you himself, but business has detained him."

"That's cool," said Gracie, continuing to take it all in, the paintings and sculptures and brass candlesticks along the walls tucked away in—what were those things called again? Scones? No, sconces. That was it. *Who the hell lives like this?*

"Understandably," said Stephen, "you may wish to have a little privacy this evening and a chance to rest. Are you perhaps hungry at all?"

Gracie couldn't deny it. "Kind of." She hadn't bothered to eat all day.

"And do you hold to any dietary restrictions of which I should be aware?"

"No, not really."

"Then I will warm up a little something for you."

"That's... Thanks." Gracie didn't know what to expect. It wasn't like Stephen presented her with a room service menu, so she did not know what to expect but figured she would just keep going along with whatever was coming her way.

The bedroom that he said would be hers sat on the second floor, looking out over the front lawn. Its bed bore way more pillows than she could have wanted. A small desk stood by the window.

Stephen opened the closet for her, "You will find a laundry bag here should you wish to have your clothes cleaned. Simply place it outside your door."

That wasn't a service Gracie felt like using. Already there was so much strangeness. Handing over her clothes would be just too much.

"And here are towels, a robe, and sandals should you wish to bathe. The toilet and bath are the third door down your left." From his inside pocket, he pulled a card and placed it on the desk. "The wi-fi password. You will find a wireless charging device for your phone in the top drawer, along with a few standard stationery items. And should you require anything else, simply pick up the phone at the bedside and dial zero. If you wish to make an external call, please dial nine first."

"All right. Cool. Thanks."

"Of course, Miss Chapel."

Yep, still didn't like the sound of that "Miss" business, but Gracie couldn't deny it seemed fitting, considering her circumstances.

Receiving all this guidance, all this direction, she felt childlike and lost. If Stephen had opened the closet door to reveal rows of doll-like Victorian dresses and told her she would be expected to wear a different one for each day of the week, she would not have been surprised. This was all just that weird. And she'd probably do it too, no matter how she hated it because, well, Gracie *had* just gotten her ass pulled out of jail by a stranger, so she did feel a sense of gratitude. But also, there was something about all the opulence around her. Everything from every direction reeked of money, and it made her feel like she wanted to comply. Gracie did not like that.

After stripping off her jacket and boots, Gracie tossed the excessive pillows from the bed and started looking over the last messages she and Kristen had exchanged, the silly back-and-forths they had. There were a variety of memes shared between them—animals looking cute or stupid and probably both, celebrity fails, unintentionally suggestive headlines, and foreign signage poorly translated into English.

As to their actual conversations, Kristen carried most of them. It seemed to require little effort for her to do most of the talking for them both. She had so much to complain about at the restaurant, mostly the customers—requests to order something off-menu they had no reason to expect was ever on the menu, complaints when their food arrived just the way they asked for it but not the way they wanted it, and expectations that she must be an idiot because she earned her money serving them. Most of Gracie's replies were a series of supportive statements. "Ugh, really? Come on! She sounds like the absolute worst."

Sometimes Kristen would have good news, say, announcing that she was bringing home some particularly tasty treat. "Bitch, your girl just got this insanely delicious dark chocolate raspberry cheesecake and two free bottles of rosé! Shit is about to get real!"

That particular night, they watched a nineties movie full of high school drama and afterward took videos of themselves speaking in ridiculous accents that Kristen posted to social media. Remembering good times like that was painful to Gracie, but she couldn't help herself. It was one of those wounds you know you shouldn't poke at, but you do anyway.

A knock on her door interrupted Gracie's rumination. When she opened it, she found Stephen had a rolling cart in the hallway, and its tray held a bowl of rice topped with shredded meat and vegetables in some kind of red sauce, with a scoop of black beans and some fried plantains on the side. It smelled amazing, like peppers and garlic, with just a little bit of sweetness. Gracie's stomach gurgled in anticipation.

"What is that?" she asked.

"Tonight's dinner," answered Stephen. *"Ropa vieja con tostones y frijoles negros."* He wheeled the cart into her room. "I hope that will suffice. When you finish, simply leave the tray outside."

"Like the laundry bag, right," said Gracie. "Do I... Am I supposed to, like, tip you?"

It impressed Gracie that Stephen managed to smile at that in a way that didn't piss her off. "No, Miss. Not at all."

"Thanks," she said.

Stephen started to make his way out of the room, then stopped and said, "It is understandable that you might feel a little overwhelmed to receive this hospitality. You may feel reassured to know that you are not the first in this house to receive unexpected generosity from the hands that now reach out to you. And like you, many of us found ourselves feeling, perhaps, a touch undeserving at that time. However, we found that what we had been given was not a favor we were expected to return, like a book borrowed from the library. Instead, what is asked of us is that we make the best and most noble use of that gift as we can, which in some cases, might be in providing service."

"Service?" Gracie asked. Again, the Victorian dresses came to mind.

"Service," he repeated. "By which we extend what we have received to others who may benefit, such as yourself." And with that, he left.

As Gracie lay down in that foreign and fantastically soft bed, waiting for sleep, she remembered one of the places where she stayed for a few years between running away from her parents' house and finding a room with Kristen, an East Town flophouse down by the docks near the Brennert River. Some rich college kid owned it, bought it with money from his family, she heard. He rented it out cheap, never paid for the upkeep, and had tenants sleep three or four to a room. Mostly they were kids like Gracie herself, fresh off the street or from a shitty home, not able to afford much.

The kid who was their landlord sometimes hung out with them. Although he came from money, he didn't dress or act like it. Partying with him constituted part of their rent. He usually supplied the drugs, since he did a bit of low scale dealing. And there was always one girl or another he was fucking on a regular basis. Her rent was covered in full.

Then one night, a couple of years in, he suddenly took notice of Gracie, said it was a shame they hadn't gotten to know each other better. It wasn't a secret that he was looking for someone new after his latest girl moved out. Gracie left the next day. Better, she figured, to walk than to give him the opportunity to do something she might have to break his jaw over.

When she woke the next morning, after her first night in the mansion, Gracie found a note slipped under her door. "Please notify the kitchen by phone when you are ready to take your breakfast. My employer wishes to join you."

So, when she decided she was ready to eat—couldn't lie around in that strange bed forever—she made the call and told Stephen she was ready to come down. "Very good, Miss Chapel," he said, "I shall lead you to the sunroom where my employer will meet with you." In just a minute, Stephen appeared at her door, then guided her back down the stairs to the rear of the mansion.

Gracie's eyes needed a minute to adjust to the sunroom's glare. Its white marble floor reflected so much light, as if the sun shone from both above and below. Flowers and ferns hung around a small glass table with lace tablecloth, upon which sat serving plates decked with an overwhelming assortment of foods with just two places set to enjoy this veritable breakfast buffet. And at the opposite end of the table, facing her, sat Stephen's employer, who rose to greet her.

"You must be Gracie," he said, smiling.

What Gracie didn't say was, "Of fucking course," because the man standing before her—Stephen's employer, her benefactor—was none other than the douchebag who appeared at Sprang & Sons looking for books about the Crimson Wraith.

1979

Hank Mills didn't mean to kill his wife, and he wanted the Crimson Wraith to know that. Titan City's "Scarlet Stranger" caught up with him about a block from the tenement building Hank ran from, appearing right in front of him after an explosion of blinding light, surrounded by his Infernal Mists, a thick fog that smelled like it came straight from Hell.

But it wasn't like Hank had not expected him. After all, he lived in a building painted with the Crimson Wraith's tag —a white skull in a red circle—among the rest of the graffiti sprayed along its exterior. That meant this was a protected space. There would be no escaping the Crimson Wraith's justice. But still, Hank had run. It wasn't something he thought through—a thoughtless action, just like the kind that killed Carla.

They had fought out on the landing, right in their apartment doorway. He hated it when they did that. Fights were just a thing couples had, Hank knew, but not out there for everyone to hear. And Carla had a lot of fight in her. He liked that when they met. And he liked the way she danced, the way her dress clung to her body when she did, and the way her golden hoop earrings flashed in the darkness. She seemed so exciting, and back then Hank wanted excitement.

So much of his life then was just a grind, always had been. As far as he knew, that was the only kind of life he could have. When he started work at the Infantino Fishery in high school, he knew there wasn't much more he could look forward to in life. It had been the same for his dad, his uncles, and his brothers. You work hard, break your back, take pride in what you do, and someday, maybe you can retire with some grandchildren to bring you a beer as you sit on the couch watching the game on Sunday.

When he graduated high school, Hank started slinging full time for Infantino. He saved his money and moved out of his folk's place, into a house with some other guys who worked at the fishery. They showed Hank how to go out and have a good time, drinking beers at places that catered to the working man and to the women who came from the same Titan City neighborhoods they did, women like Carla.

The boys noticed him noticing her as she was talking loudly with some other girls, and they kept pushing him to walk up and say something. Hank was shy, too shy to speak to her, but he figured he could talk to the bartender and buy a round for her and her friends, which he did. The girls accepted the round, raised their glasses, and smiled at him.

His friends told him that was his "in" and that he should go talk to her. Hank couldn't. But Carla could. She came over after they finished their drinks and said, "What the hell? You some kind of creep or something? Buy a lady a drink, but can't say hello?"

He fell in love with her right away.

Their courtship was brief. She did the talking for both of them, and he did the earning for both of them. Hank worked hard to show Carla a good time. They married a year later and got an apartment together. Children didn't happen, but they had some fun nights out.

In time though, fun fades. Hank wasn't creative. He knew how to work hard and make money. A couple of years in,

Carla got bored and started going out without him, while he worked longer and longer nights, hoping to win back her love by saving up to buy them a house.

This was where they started fighting, and soon she started hitting him. Hank let her because you don't hit a woman, and he was a big guy. He could take a hit, and he did—first from her fists, then her shoe, then a saucepan. But none of these hurt like the night he came home to find her suitcase ready in the doorway. That's when she really let him have it. "Enough of this!" she screamed. "Enough of this and enough of you!"

"The fuck are you going?" he said. Hank couldn't imagine she would actually leave. He had been working so hard to ignore all the signs.

"You don't need to know where I'm going. You don't need to know because we are done. You hear me?"

"Goddamn it, Carla—"

"Don't you 'goddamn it, Carla,' me!"

"You're my wife!"

"And this is our divorce!"

"Where are you going?"

"I ain't sayin'!"

"Where the fuck are you going?"

"I'm going to my new man!"

"Your... what?" Hank knew he was slow, but he just couldn't believe what she said. Hank was a good person. He thought Carla was a good person. Being wild and maybe a little self-centered didn't make her a bad person, did it? And only bad people cheat on their spouses. "Carla you haven't... Have you?"

"Haven't what? Huh? Haven't what, you big dumb ape?"

"Carla, don't say that."

"I'll say what the fuck I want!" she screamed.

"You didn't..."

"Yes, I did! Oh, I sure did!" Her dark eyes blazed, and she was grinning, teeth sharp enough to tear his heart apart. "I found myself a man. I found myself a *real* man."

"Stop it," said Hank.

"Does that hurt? Does that hurt your little baby heart to hear?"

"Goddamn it, Carla! Stop it!"

"A real man who knows what a woman needs. That's what I found. A real man who can treat me like I deserve."

"I never done nothing wrong to you!"

"What have you done right? You want to tell me that?"

"I work!" he shouted. "I work every damn day!"

"Like a mule! Like a brainless ox! You're not a man! You're not a man at all! Just some big dumb animal!"

She never said that to him before. No one ever said that to Hank before. That's something you just don't say. And Hank had never felt like he wanted to put his hands on her before.

"Shut up," he said.

"You don't tell me what to do!"

"I said, shut up!"

"Fuck you!"

"Get out," he said. "Go on then."

"Oh, I am gone," she said. "I am already gone."

"Get out!"

She picked up her suitcase, had one foot out the door. "And I ain't never coming back!"

Then Hank broke, "You get the fuck outta here, you fucking bitch!" And that's when he shoved her.

Stupid. You never hit a woman, never lay a hand on her in anger. But he did. And he really was a big guy, even bigger than he knew. And she was smaller than he thought.

Maybe she never expected him to ever come at her that way, didn't respect him enough to think he had it in him. And if she had, if she thought him capable of violence, maybe she wouldn't have cheated on him, not out of fear, just because it might have made him a little more interesting.

But when the force of his shove hit her, it surprised them both. Carla went flying backward, tumbling down the stair.

Hank watched her fall. Their eyes held each other in mutual amazement, and then she was a bundle of spinning hair and limbs all tangled in her overcoat, until her body reached the landing, head first, with the heavy crack of breaking bone.

"Carla?" He started down after her. "Carla? Oh, shit! Oh, fuck! Carla!"

Heads aren't supposed to twist at that angle. As he reached out to her, Carla's eyes fluttered and then stopped all movement, lids still open. Before his fingertips touched her, Hank saw the blood starting to expand from her opened skull, a dark puddle reflecting the flickering neon lights above and the shimmer of her gold hoop earrings.

From an open doorway, there came a scream. "He killed her! Oh, my God, he killed her!" The neighbors who watched the fight from their doorways had all seen him shove her—witnesses, every one of them.

That's when Hank ran.

And that's why, when the Crimson Wraith caught him at the end of a blind alley, appearing suddenly from an explosion like a demon straight from hell, Hank pleaded with him. "I didn't mean to kill her! Swear to Christ I didn't!"

"I believe you," said the Crimson Wraith. Those red gauntleted hands extended to him, open, unarmed. "You want to make this right?"

Hank nodded.

"Then listen to me. We have just a few minutes before the police arrive."

"No," Hank moaned. "No, no, no..."

The Crimson Wraith gently shushed him. "Listen."

And Hank looked deep into the dark, empty sockets of the skull mask, sharing a gaze with eyes he couldn't see.

"If you want to make this right, I want you to hold onto that. It's a good thing. You can't change anything about what's happened. You can't undo what has been done. But you can do the best you can going forward. Do you understand? You can do that and keep doing it, no matter what. Will you promise me that?"

"Promise you?"

"Yes," said the Crimson Wraith. "Promise me you will live to make things right, whatever it takes."

This wasn't what Hank thought the Crimson Wraith was supposed to do, not to someone like him, someone who killed another. Hank thought he was supposed to get his ass kicked, maybe even killed for having killed Carla, a life for a life. "You want me to promise..." said Hank.

The Crimson Wraith nodded. "That you will live to make things right, whatever it takes."

"I... Okay..."

"I want to hear you say it."

"Say it?"

"Say it."

"I promise," said Hank, "That I will live. That I will make things right, whatever it takes."

2019

"It's you," said Gracie. "*Nights of Justice*. Good book, but you've already got it."

"It is," he said. "And I do. Care to sit down? Help yourself."

She didn't. The coincidence did not sit with her well enough for her to sit just yet. "And so you 'met a man at midnight,' and all that?"

He nodded. "I've met the Crimson Wraith. You can say his name here. It's a safe space."

"Is it? Oh, good." Gracie did not feel safe.

"You seem like you'd like some explanations," he said.

"More than I'd like bacon and eggs right now, yeah."

"Why don't I start by telling you my name? I'm Kevin Snyder." He let silence follow the last syllable with an ease that suggested he was used to allowing new acquaintances a minute after he name-dropped himself.

As far as Titan City went, his name held a lot of weight.

Kevin Snyder succeeded his father as CEO of the Snyder-Finn Corporation, a multi-billion dollar corporate powerhouse formed by the acquisition of Finn Industries by SnyTech Global. It owned the renamed Snyder-Finn Building, which towered over downtown Titan City, the historic Finn Manor, where Gracie had apparently just spent the night, and the humanitarian Finn Foundation, which paid for Gracie to go to school.

She imagined this got Kevin Snyder laid a hell of a lot. Even she couldn't help being a little staggered by the impact of his name, but she pressed on.

"Hi, Kevin," she said.

"Hi, Gracie," he said.

"Kevin, just to help me get the full picture here, in addition to owning about half of Titan City, you are friends with its very own superhero?"

"Is the Crimson Wraith a superhero?" said Kevin.

"Is he what now?"

"Is he a superhero?"

"He dresses up in a mask and fights crime. The guy belongs in a comic book. Most people would call that a superhero."

"But does he have any superpowers?"

"I don't know. I haven't gotten to that part of *Nights of Justice* yet."

Kevin answered his own question, "He has been said to appear and disappear at will, surrounded by his Infernal Mists. He can see in the dark, throw his voice, and seem to be at two places at once, but most of these could be attributed to skill or trickery. We live in the real world. There aren't any superheroes here."

And that was Gracie's limit. "Thank you for *man-splaining* your weirdo pal in a hood, but that doesn't help me feel any better about finding out you are the dude offering me help after randomly showing up in my store just a few days ago. That kind of coincidence comes off creepy as fuck."

"Coincidences happen."

"Do they, Kevin? Do they really?"

"From time to time."

"From time to time? Okay, great. Well, at this particular time, coincidences seem a whole lot like they are fucking with me because right after you turn up at my shop, my little life got way fucking fucked up. And now, here you are again, pulling me out of the mess that just happened to hit right after I just happened to meet you. Do you see what I'm getting at here? Can you understand how it might look pretty damn weird to the casual observer?"

"Are you suggesting I had something to do with the charges that got you arrested?"

Gracie wanted to say "yes," that somehow he engineered the entire thing to make her feel indebted to him, creating a problem from which he could rescue and then force her to wear a closet full of Victorian dresses.

But she couldn't bring herself to say that. It was way too far of a reach. The fact was, Gracie knew Zack had been a piece of shit and wanted to tear him a new one since she first met him. The fight she had that night had been a long time coming.

She took it down a notch. "Let's just say that I would really appreciate hearing what your angle is here. You and the Crimson Wraith, what exactly is your deal?"

Kevin nodded. "My deal. Me and the Crimson Wraith. Sure. Okay, a few years back, I was in kind of a bad spot. It's personal, and you and I don't really know each other, so please excuse me staying private about it for the time being. This wasn't the kind of trouble that ends up in the papers, and it wasn't something I thought I could get help from the police for. I didn't know where else to turn and started to think there wasn't anything that could be done.

"Then, I met him. And he helped me. When you get helped by the Crimson Wraith, he expects you to give that help to someone else. So, now I'm helping you. But if you don't want that help, you don't have to take it. You don't have to stay here. Stephen can drive you back into the city and drop you off wherever you like. You don't owe me the money I paid to bail you out of jail. I think you ought to try to make your court date, but that's your choice. Whatever you do with what's given you is your choice."

Her bullshit detector wasn't registering anything. Everything in Gracie's gut told her Kevin was dealing straight, at least in spirit. There were things he wasn't saying, but he said there were things he wasn't saying, and that was okay. He didn't owe her his life story.

"Cool," she said and sat.

Stephen, who had remained in the room during their exchange, said, "I shall leave you two to your breakfast then."

"Thank you, Stephen," said Kevin.

"Yeah, thanks, Stephen," said Gracie. She started putting food on her plate and then poured herself some coffee. Kevin took a few pieces of bacon from another plate before offering it wordlessly to her. She accepted. The sounds of utensils on plates were the only ones in that little room for a moment. Gracie let Kevin pour her a glass of orange juice and then asked, "So, what's it like being a billionaire?"

"It's nice," he said and handed her the glass.

"Yeah, was thinking it might be."

They started to eat. After a few bites, Kevin asked her, "How was getting arrested?"

"Not good, Kevin. Not good at all. I do not recommend it."

He nodded. "That makes sense."

Gracie ate a bit more and then sighed. "What am I supposed to do here?"

"Well, I can show you around. Feel free to make yourself at home…"

"No, I don't mean, like, here, in this space, in your house, or mansion, whatever. I mean 'here' as in… arrested and released and waiting and…" Gracie groaned in desperation, "Jesus fuck." Oddly, she felt bad cursing like that in front of Kevin. He did seem like he might be a kind of decent guy—maybe a little stiff and weird, too clean-cut, but decent. "I'm sorry."

It did not appear to disturb him. "What do you want to do?" he asked.

"I don't know. Not be waiting for trial?"

"Fair," he said, "Yeah, I can see that."

"But that isn't an option though, is it?" she asked.

"Not really, no."

She sipped at her coffee. "I heard you might have some work for me."

"If you want. I understand sometimes that can be good, having something to occupy you."

"Probably. What kind of work were you thinking?"

"There are some odds and ends that I could find for you to handle at Snyder-Finn—carrying documents around town, maybe picking up coffee, nothing too demanding."

"You mean like a secretary?"

"Not exactly. I've already got those. Besides, I don't know how good you are at taking dictation."

"Can't say as I ever have, Kevin."

"Don't worry about it then. No, what I was thinking of was finding space for you in the courier pool."

She ate a bit more and then said, "That sounds all right. Could maybe fit in a couple days. I'd like to keep working at Sprang & Sons too. And going to class. You know, try to keep life kinda normal. At least until… Do you know how long until I have to go to court?"

"That's a question for your attorney."

"Right. But do you think I'm going to have time to finish the semester? It would be nice to get those credits in before… Am I really going to jail?"

"Jail is where you would wait for your trial, which you don't have to worry about, now that your bond is paid. Prison is where you get sentenced to stay after trial, if you're found guilty."

"Great. Prison, then." And suddenly Gracie thought she might start to cry. She didn't want to. She fought it back. Scrambled eggs started to quake on her fork.

"Oh, Mr. Hancock delivered a bag of your things this morning," said Kevin, either not noticing or not wanting to address the shimmer rising in Gracie's eyes. "Is there anything else you want to get from your apartment? A few extra changes of clothes, perhaps?"

She nodded, set down the fork, and wiped at her eyes with her napkin. "I guess. Can I? He said I should keep my distance from Kristen."

"It's worth asking. And if you need to go into town to buy a few things, Stephen could take you."

"Yeah, if I'm going to come work for you, I don't know that I have, like, business clothes—not for, you know, your kind of business."

"Stephen could probably help you there too, take you shopping."

"I don't know if I could afford those kinds of clothes."

He nodded. "Maybe if you let Stephen know your measurements, he could see if there is something in your size just lying around."

Gracie realized she had absolutely no appetite anymore. She set down her fork. It really was too much, being taken care of this way, all of these needs of hers anticipated by someone else, handled for her before she thought to ask. It felt so strange, so wrong. Would it be better to be sitting in a jail cell? She would be wearing clothes that someone else provided there as well, a striped jumpsuit courtesy of Titan County. She would be eating someone else's food and sleeping in someone else's bed, all way less nice than what Finn Manor offered. But maybe that lack of luxury would make it easier to take.

"Are you finished?" Kevin asked.

Gracie nodded.

"Come on. Let me show you around the manor then. Do you like bowling?"

1984

His public defender didn't do him much good. Still, it helped that Hank had come along peacefully when the arresting officer arrived, "showing sincere remorse and a desire for rehabilitation," as the attorney argued. What didn't get mentioned in the courtroom was the fact that the Crimson Wraith had been on the scene. A detail like that doesn't get said out loud, but the judge and assistant district attorney were aware. Hank ended up receiving five years for one count of manslaughter, the minimum sentence for that felony conviction.

Those who commit violence against women can find themselves targeted while in penitentiary, as Hank found out his third day. He was sitting with his lunch tray when another inmate approached. "Heard you killed your wife," he said.

Hank was a big guy, but this guy was just as big. He stood over Hank with fists clenched at his side, hard and heavy fists that had clearly done some swinging. Looking at those fists, Hank could just imagine their knuckles cracking open his jaw. And imagining that image, he wanted it. He wanted to hurt for what he'd done. So, he nodded and extended his chin, ready for the blow.

But another inmate interrupted. "Easy, Vito," he said, speaking low. "You know who brought this guy in, right? The Scarlet Stranger got 'im..."

Vito looked at the interloper, clearly unhappy with this piece of information. The force he had been preparing to put into his punch huffed out his nostrils like an old train engine letting off steam. His fists unclenched, and he pointed a finger at Hank. "You watch yourself," he said. Then he turned to walk away.

Denied the punishment he craved, Hank leaped up, lunch tray in hand, and slammed it against the back of Vito's head. This dispelled whatever forbearance the Crimson Wraith's touch had given him.

Vito turned with bulging eyes, shocked at such a move. A guy had to be crazy to do a thing like that. And Hank thought,

Yeah, maybe I am crazy. The blow that Vito crashed into the side of his face felt fantastic though, and Hank threw punches back, just to make sure Vito would keep swinging. Guards swept in to pull them apart, bringing the weight of their batons down on both combatants. Afterward, Hank savored every ache that radiated through his body as he spent the next twenty-four hours in "the hole," solitary confinement.

When allowed back into General Population, he found others kept their distance. The fact that the Crimson Wraith had captured him was like a plague. It made him untouchable. Word was that the Crimson Wraith would know if you harmed one of his and would make you sorry for it.

Hank couldn't have that. He craved their violence, and when the craving became too much for him to bear, he picked a fight wherever he could, sometimes with a new inmate who hadn't yet heard of his protected status. That first year, he spent a lot of time in solitary, and with each infraction, his time got longer. Sometimes he got a little stir crazy there, not having anyone else to deliver his punishment for him, and he would punch the walls just to feel the concrete stab into his fist.

It got harder and harder for him to pick the fights he wanted, though. His reputation for being a "batshit motherfucker" started keeping more inmates away than the Crimson Wraith. Finally, there came a day when he couldn't seem to get any response.

Hank went right up to a Puerto Rican gang when they were all sitting together in the yard, and he stepped on the toe of one of the member's shoes. All of them saw it. The inmate stood up fast, moving with those sharp reflexes honed by the prison's atmosphere of always imminent violence, but when he got eye-to-eye with Hank, he stopped and cast a look over to the gang's leader, who shook his head.

The gang member muttered, "*Pendejo loco*," and sat down again.

This confused Hank. He felt the need to point out what he'd

just done. "I stepped on your toe," he said.

"You sure did," said the gang leader. "And he's real sorry about that. His toe shouldn't have been in your way."

"I stepped on your toe," Hank repeated.

"Hey, *gringo*," said the gang's leader. "Listen to me. You ain't getting your fix here. See, if a man is a man, he doesn't go kicking a dog. And that's all you are—one crazy, fucked-up animal. So, go on, dog. Get outta here. We ain't got nothing for you. Not today. Not any day."

Animal. That's what Carla had called him. As sharp as the frustration was that clenched inside of him, Hank felt something else too, hearing those words. He felt shame. He realized this was how they all looked at him, all the other inmates. He had become too low, too pathetic to even bother with. And he thought about his promise to the Crimson Wraith, his promise to make things right, whatever it takes. This was not doing it.

He signed up for a psychological rehabilitation course, three hours a day of sitting with a state-appointed therapist among a group of other inmates convicted of violent offenses. They talked about what their backgrounds were like, their childhoods, their school experiences, their families. Conversations came haltingly, and some days they didn't come at all.

Hank talked about Carla. It surprised him one day when one of the other guys in the group said about her, "You didn't deserve the way she treated you. That wasn't a way for anyone to act, man or woman."

It felt strange to hear another person say Carla might be in the wrong for something. Hank always figured he had to be in the wrong, right? Hadn't he failed to be the man she needed him to be? Wasn't that why she did those things? And how could she be in the wrong when he was the one who killed her? It didn't make sense to him, but Hank listened anyway.

Their therapist tried to show them new ways of expressing their emotions verbally instead of physically. Hank learned how to have a conversation with himself, inside his head, to ask questions about what he would get out of whatever it was he felt like he had to do. Would it get him where he wanted to be? Before, he always thought talking to yourself made you crazy, but apparently, it could be a way to get sane.

He completed six months of that course, then went back in for another, serving as a mentor for the next batch. It didn't seem like doing much at first, just sitting in a circle and talking, but he felt different by the end of it, like his head was clearer, quieter. Maybe he wasn't the same dumb animal he had been when he entered. Maybe this was what the Crimson Wraith wanted for him.

In his last years of incarceration, Hank got a job in the laundry room, and that gave him a little spending money, which allowed him something sweet from the commissary now and then. He never had been a reader before, but there wasn't anything else to do some days, so he read a bit here and there, books like *The Mark of Zorro*, *The Adventures of Robin Hood*, and *The Maltese Falcon*. He didn't think any of that made him any smarter, but it helped to pass the time.

And eventually, his time ended. The guards came to tell him he would be going out into the world once more. His five years had passed. And in all that time, only once did he hear from anybody from the outside. It was a letter from his father during his very first week, saying how ashamed his family was that he had turned into a killer, how he was no longer their son and no longer welcomed there, so don't even bother ever trying to contact them in future.

No one came to meet Hank when the prison gates opened to release him. So, he started walking down the street with only the clothes he came in wearing and the cash that had been in his pocket.

2019

The Finn Manor bowling alley had no ball return because

there were no ball returns in the 1800s when the mansion was built. So, Gracie and Kevin's bowling balls rumbled down the shiny wooden lane that had been refurbished at least a few times in the past century. Then they had to be collected at the end and the pins set back up by hand. No electronic scorekeeping either, Kevin scratched that out onto a paper scorecard for them.

Around the fifth frame, though, Grace had enough. Kevin's ball hit the gutter once again, costing him the spare. As it clacked against the back wall, she said, "Okay, you can stop that now."

"Stop what?" said Kevin.

"You're letting me win."

"What?"

"Your gutter balls, they are going way too straight into the gutter. You're aiming for it."

He walked to the back and began resetting for her the three pins he knocked down. "You know, I could just be not very good."

"Sorry. Try again," she said. "You live in a mansion that has its own bowling alley, and the very first thing you invite me to do is play against you. This is far from your first game."

"Even so. I really could be bad at this."

"Nope," said Gracie. "Ain't buying it."

"How come?"

"The way you move, your stance and whatnot. You know what you're doing, so you can stop doing it."

Rejoining her at the other end of the lane, he said, "Are you sure?"

Gracie readied her ball. "Look, it's fine. I get it. You're trying to be a nice host. Whatever. But I don't need you to fake it for me. If we're going to play, let's play. All right?"

"All right."

As of that frame, Gracie had him beat 63 to 35. Then he played her for real, as she asked. They ended with her scoring 128 and Kevin winning with 131

"Good game," she said. "So what else does this place have?"

What else Finn Manor had included many of the things that seem required for a mansion. It possessed a study where various little curios shared shelf space with old and important-sounding books. Its parlor held its own fireplace and a large antique globe. There was a big open ballroom with a big old piano to host big fancy balls because that's what rich people do. Long hallways opened into several guest bedrooms, and little sitting areas by the stairs provided space to gaze up at the stained glass windows and contemplate just how goddamn rich you are.

Outside, there stood the naked statue of some athletic guy holding a harp. He was maybe supposed to be a Greek hero or something. Fountains that did not flow in the cool of Autumn and rose bushes that would bloom in spring interlaced with stone walkways leading out to a broad lawn ringed with trees climbing into the wooded Titan hillside.

Also, it had a graveyard, well, "family plot" as Kevin called it. Tucked just off to the side off the massive rear lawn, surrounded by trees, there sat a mausoleum with the name "Finn" carved above its door. Around it stood dozens of headstones and a few small pieces of statuary.

"So, this is your family?" said Gracie.

"Not by blood."

"What?"

"These are the Finns. When my father took control of Finn Industries, the manor came with it, and they came with the manor."

"That's... Okay, I'm sorry, but that really is super weird. You know that, right? Like, not just that you have dead people in your backyard but dead people who you have zero connection with."

"My father wanted to tie our name to a name that had been part of Titan City for as long as anyone could remember. That's what he got."

"You're talking about him in past tense. He pass away too?"

"He has, yes."

"I'm sorry, man. Is he here now?"

"No," said Kevin. "He's with my mother down at Poplar Hill."

"Oh." As far as Gracie was concerned, that didn't make things any less weird. If anything, it made them weirder.

Then she noticed one of the graves had fresh earth, extremely fresh. Its headstone read, *Edward Burton Finn (1931-2019)*. "But you're still taking new additions? Finns still get buried here even though you own the place?"

She saw Kevin's face struggle. When he talked about his father's death, Kevin reacted as blandly as if he were talking about the weather. But from how he looked at her when she mentioned Edward Finn, Gracie felt bad for asking.

"I'm sorry," she said. Even though he hadn't said anything, clearly, there was a lot to say. "Fresh dirt and fresh wounds, huh?"

"It's okay. You didn't know." He turned to Edward's grave. "Families are... complex. Eddie and I were close. At least, I wanted us to be. He was a good man. I respected him a lot."

"I'm sorry," she said again.

They made their way back up to the house, and Kevin went into town to be businesslike and do business things that businesspeople do. Gracie just lazed around for a while but sitting still gave her mind time to wander off to her legal situation and all the yawning void of not-knowing that awaited. She wanted distraction. She needed to get back to Terpsichoria soon and dance out these feelings. In the meantime, she thought she'd wander around the halls a bit more. And that's when she smelled something cooking.

Following the scent led her into the kitchen, which sat right between the dining hall and the ballroom. There was space in there to fit a team of cooks, but it only held the guy who took the car keys from Stephen when they arrived.

He stood in front of the stove, working a frying pan over one of the burners and kicking up a whole lot of meaty smoke.

And as he did, he sang, softly and lazily, "Ain't too proud to beg, and you know it…Please don't leave me, girl…"

Gracie knew he didn't hear her approach. Probably she could have stayed there watching him for a while. But before Gracie decided how to announce herself, he slipped a spatula under something on the pan, turning to deposit it on the plate beside him, and caught sight of her in the doorway. He nearly dropped the spatula in surprise.

"Motherf—!" he blurted out but stopped himself and took a moment to regain some composure. "Hi."

"Hi," said Gracie.

"Grace, right?"

"Gracie," she corrected. "I forgot your name. Sorry."

"Danny. Daniel Cole."

"Cool. Hey, Danny. That smells good."

"Fried bologna," he said and started assembling his sandwich.

"Okay, that was not what I was expecting."

"What?"

"Fried bologna. Here. In Finn Manor, of all places."

"Why not?"

"Because this kitchen is attached to a ballroom. I didn't figure bologna to be big on the menu for whatever charity galas get hosted here."

"We're full of surprises. Want one?"

"I'm good," she said.

Danny smirked, "Didn't ask if you were good. I asked if you wanted one."

"Well then, allow me to politely decline your offer to fix me a sandwich."

"What you are declining—*politely*—is my offer to leave out the stuff for you to fix yourself your own sandwich."

"What a gentleman."

He took a big bite of bologna and said through a mouthful of it, "That's me."

Gracie smiled. "So, you live here too?"

"Room and board," said Danny after swallowing. "Part of the package."

"Sweet deal, you and Kevin and Stephen here, little bachelor paradise you got going on." She watched him put away bread and mayonnaise and American cheese, then thought about something. "So let me ask you, both your roommates have told me about how they got help from a certain someone, and now they want to pay that help back."

"Yep."

"And you living here too, I gotta wonder, does that apply to you as well? Did you… meet a man at midnight?"

Danny shut the refrigerator door and turned to look her over, not like he did the night before, not the way a guy checks you out to see if he's interested. This was how a woman looks at a man to see if he's safe to walk home with—a threat assessment.

To Gracie, it felt strange to be on the receiving end of that for a change. She tried to read the result in his eyes but couldn't find it. Seemed like maybe the jury was still out. And as he walked past her, he said nothing, gave no answer to her question, one way or the other. He just chewed his fried bologna and kept going.

There was one place, though, that couldn't help but give answers, all kinds of answers, often the wrong kinds, but it couldn't be faulted for being thin on information. Back in her bedroom, Gracie pulled out her phone and started seeing what she could find out about her benefactor online.

Kevin Snyder made a strong social media presence. His postings were way too polished, clearly something that someone else—or a team of someone-elses—took care of for him. A few of the older pictures seemed fun and personal, swimming with models off the coast of Greece and hanging out with the attractive actors on the set of the remake of *Viva Las Vegas*. There were magazine covers and fashion shoots, ads for public speaking events, and publicity photos from humanitarian work in foreign countries. Occasionally, a supposedly inspirational image would appear. One had a dog in sunglasses looking into the distance from the driver's seat of a classic red convertible. Above him appeared the words, "Your motive will drive you toward your goal." And below, "That's why it's called *motor-vation*." His business wisdom seemed based on puns and misspellings like that.

Nothing about Kevin's online persona looked like he could have any connection with Titan City's masked vigilante. His posts all appeared frivolous, vapid, and self-aggrandizing. It almost surprised her Kevin hadn't posted a selfie with his notorious friend. But then, while many thought of the Crimson Wraith as a hero, he was, after all, a criminal, taking the law into his own hands. Maybe getting chummy with the Crimson Wraith would have looked bad for the CEO of Snyder-Finn, no matter how many points it might earn him at the country club.

CHAPTER FIVE

1984

They didn't want Hank back at the Infantino Fishery. "You gotta understand, we're a family business," the foreman told him. "People around here know each other's wives, each other's kids. They knew Carla."

"I didn't mean to," said Hank. He couldn't say it in full, couldn't say, "kill her," not back out in the world, in the office of Infantino's, in the light of day and all.

"No, of course not. No, no one would think that of you. But it doesn't look good, you know? I'm sorry. That's just the way it is."

"Okay," said Hank.

"I wish there was more I could do, honest." Maybe he honestly did and maybe he honestly didn't. But it wasn't any help to Hank either way.

The shelter where he stayed over on 76th and Bickle Street regularly posted flyers for places willing to hire people with problems in their background, and that's how he ended up washing dishes at Bobby D's Delicatessen. It wasn't much, but it was something. When you're starting from zero, that's what counts, anything that kept him from having to beg for spare change outside the elevated train station. Some guys could pull in a decent amount panhandling, but Hank wanted—he *needed*—something to do with himself, something more than just standing with his hand out or sitting beside a cardboard sign.

Washing dishes kept him busy, kept him fed too. Bobby didn't mind guys having a bit of soup on their break or making themselves a little sandwich. So, that was good. And the work was hard, hard on his body, standing over that steaming dish pit for hours at a time. That was good too—the ache in his bones at the end of the night, the burning in his legs, and that stabbing pain he got from where his old shoes were giving way in the sole. Part of Hank still felt like he deserved to hurt.

Bobby's little sister Iris managed the deli. Hank liked her. She could talk as tough as any of the guys and never let them get away with being sloppy or lazy. And her daughter, Betsy, worked the register after school. Betsy seemed smart. Hank could just tell that from how she talked. She was going places, definitely getting into college. And she smiled and looked Hank in the eye when she said, "Hi," to him. She didn't know he was a killer. To her, he was just a man doing a job. It was like having a secret identity, and that felt nice, being able to pretend he was just like anyone else.

The night that Hank met Jasmine, Betsy celebrated her sixteenth birthday at the deli. She brought around slices of cake from the bakery across the street, a yellow cake with white frosting and strawberries. "Thanks," said Hank, looking up at the piece she handed him on its paper napkin. "I'll get it on my break."

"Hey," she said. "It's my birthday. You can eat it now."

He wasn't going to disappoint her. So, he wiped the suds from his hands and accepted the cake.

Everyone stopped working. For five minutes, the whole kitchen, wherever they were standing, was just having cake. Even though they weren't all sitting at a table together, it kind of felt like they were sharing a meal. And Hank thought maybe he could do this. Maybe his past could disappear like dishwater down the drain. Maybe he could just be a person again.

Walking home that night, Hank pulled his red hooded sweatshirt up over his head to fight a touch of early spring chill. He set his fists in his pockets and hunched his shoulders.

On the streets of Titan City, a person wanting to avoid trouble often has to pretend they don't see certain things and don't hear others. From the doorway of a hardware store where he was bedding down for the night, an older man, his wild gray hair rising straight upward from his forehead and one lens of his glasses cracked, pointed to Hank and cackled in a strange, sing-song voice, "I know the Crimson Wraith's secret! Yes, I do! I know it all!" Hank didn't turn his eyes from the sidewalk ahead of him.

But one block later, the sound of Jasmine's cry came from the alleyway between a Chinese restaurant and a record shop, both closed for the night. There was no way Hank could pretend not to hear her. His rehabilitation training told him to pause, to ask himself what he wanted to accomplish and choose a rational course of action. What would get him to where he wanted to be? Yet, hearing that sound, everything inside of him leaped, and without being able to think, he broke into a run. There was a woman in peril. Hank had a debt to repay.

Hank could make out little more of her than that her skin was dark, her hair was light, and her purple sequined dress glimmered in the alleyway where she had been knocked to the ground. A white man stood over her. He wore a tank top and broad-brimmed hat. His hair came down to his shoulders.

"Fucking scratch me? Man, you got some nerve, you know that? Owe the kind of money you owe, and you fucking scratch me?"

"I don't owe you shit, Matthew. I earn my money."

"On my fucking block, you earn it!" And he kicked her in the stomach.

Hank could feel that kick as if he were the one receiving it. He could not allow this to continue. "Stop!" he bellowed.

Matthew turned in response. "What's this? What'chu looking at, Little Red Riding Hood? Go on, now. Get back home to Grandma's House."

From the ground, the woman called out to Hank. "This

ain't got nothing to do with you! I got this!"

It seemed Matthew didn't appreciate the two of them being in agreement about Hank leaving. "How about you just shut the fuck up—" And then he was screaming as she sank her teeth into his ankle. "Fucking bitch!"

He raised a hand to strike her, but Hank charged him up from behind like an angry rhino, driving an elbow strike into Matthew's ribs that sent him flying.

Spitting Matthew's blood from her lips, the woman made it to her feet, and turned her anger toward Hank. "What did you do that for? I told you, I got this!" He could see now that her hair was a bright golden wig. Its strands tangled across her face.

From the ground, Matthew coughed and groaned. "All right, Little Red. You want the wolf? You got the wolf!" And he shot up to his feet, swinging a knife in an upward arc toward Hank's stomach.

Hank had plenty of blades come at him in prison. He was used to getting out of their way, which was the only reason this one didn't spill his guts all over the concrete, but he didn't manage to miss it entirely.

Stepping back, the woman whipped off one of her high-heeled shoes and threw it with startling accuracy at the hand holding the knife, knocking it free from his grasp. Matthew turned to her in shock, "How in the shit?"

Now disarmed, he had nothing to defend himself against Hank, who delivered a right hook across the jaw, three gut punches, and an uppercut that threw him back into a pile of overstuffed garbage bags from the Chinese restaurant.

Although the fight was done, the woman was not done with Hank. "What part of 'I got this' did you not understand?"

"You needed help," said Hank.

"You think I need you to tell me what I need?"

"He hurt you," said Hank.

"Man, I been hurt way worse by way better than this punk. Look at you, starting to bleed all over yourself."

"I didn't want to let him hurt you."

"Well, give this man a medal! You think, just because you got a red hood over your head, that make you the Crimson Wraith or something?"

"No." That thought hadn't occurred to Hank. The suggestion shocked him. No way could Hank see himself in the role of the man who handed him to the police.

"You sure acting like it. And you gonna be a for-real ghost you don't get that knife wound looked at."

"It's not that bad," Hank said, then saw just how much blood was making its way down his pants.

Maybe the knife cut a little deeper than he thought. It hadn't felt deep, but it hadn't felt like much of anything at all, not with the adrenaline coursing through him. Running in and fighting for someone else was a whole different thing than picking fights in prison to punish himself. It had a rush to it, something that propelled him forward effortlessly.

Hank said, "It does look bad."

"Yeah, I told you it did," she said. The woman looked out toward the street, appearing to be figuring something out in her mind. "All right, look, my place ain't far from here. It's a damn sight closer than St. Gabriel's anyway. I ain't no doctor, but I got a needle and thread, and I seen every episode of *M*A*S*H* on the TV. And maybe you did help me out with Matthew, just a little."

She looked down at Matthew's unconscious body, *lo mein* noodles strewn across his chest. "Sucker punch me with them weak-ass baby-boy fists!" Hank couldn't blame her for kicking Matthew where he lay, returning the kick he'd given her. "One for the road," she said and led Hank to the sidewalk.

"My name's Hank," he said, as they stepped out under the streetlights.

"You can call me Jasmine," she said. So, he did.

2019

Since Gracie never got her name on the lease, she didn't have to worry about being on-the-hook for paying next month's rent, so at least there was that.

"Unfortunately," Hancock told Gracie over the phone, "it would have simplified things for your case if it actually had been. We could have argued the fight was a matter of you defending your home, which includes the property and persons therein. Not being on the lease himself, Zack wouldn't have a leg to stand on—which isn't a reference to you... with his leg... and the bottle... Well, you know what I mean."

Not having her name on the lease also meant that Gracie didn't have the right to just walk back into the apartment and get things that she left there. That's where having a lawyer is helpful. They know how to ask for things and who to ask for them. Hancock got permission from the court for Gracie to return, so long as she did so in the company of a sheriff's deputy, who would make sure no further violence occurred between her and Zack.

"And you can be sure that he'll be there," said Hancock. "Right now, the territory in dispute isn't so much the apartment or the things you left. It's your roommate. He's not going to want you saying anything that will make her rethink pressing charges against him. And, as much as you may want to, I'm going to strongly suggest you don't say anything to her while you are there, not one word."

That pissed Gracie off. "Why the hell not?"

"You're the defendant. Things are stacked against you. You're the one whose behavior is being watched. You know how when they read your Miranda rights, it goes, 'Anything you say can *and will* be used against you'? That still applies. So, in order to give them less to use, you want to say and do as little of anything as possible. It gives us our best shot at presenting you to the judge as *not* being a danger to public safety. We want him to see that you regularly follow the rules of society and that one night of violence was not indicative of your nature."

Gracie wanted to punch something. Like she was a danger to the safety of anyone who didn't deserve it? But she knew that was just the kind of impulse she needed to practice keeping in check.

She got cleared to go back to the apartment that Saturday morning. Danny brought up a white utility van from the Finn Manor garage to meet Gracie and Stephen at the mansion's front steps. "You sure you guys don't want another pair of hands?" he asked, giving the keys to Stephen.

"Nah," said Gracie. "Isn't like I left a washing machine there. Just need a ride, and Jeeves here has that covered."

Stephen bowed slightly. He wore his casual weekend attire, a cardigan, khakis, and a pair of loafers. It made him look kind of like a Latino Mr. Rogers.

Danny said, "You sure? I'd be more than happy to lend a hand."

"Look," said Gracie, "I know that I am just a weak and feeble woman, but, trust me, I will, in fact, be able to pick up a couple boxes and a bag of clothes all by my wee little self."

Danny looked to the side, biting back something else it seemed he wanted to say but was choosing not to. "All right then. You two have fun."

As the van rumbled down the roads of the West Titan hillsides, Stephen asked, "Are you looking forward to seeing your roommate again?"

Gracie shrugged.

"What sort of person is she, exactly?" he asked.

"I don't know. The fucked-up kind? She's fun. Her taste in men is trash. But she was easy to live with, and we always got along—when her boyfriend wasn't there, anyway."

"Oh?"

Sitting up in the front seat of the van with Stephen took the whole butler thing down a notch, and Gracie liked that. It made her feel more comfortable, not just comfortable with him but comfortable in general, which was a damn relief to find after the past week. It made her feel like sharing. "Yeah, I mean, I kept my distance from them when they were together, but when Zack is over, it isn't like there is anyone else in the room for her. You could be choking to death on a peanut and she wouldn't notice."

"I see," said Stephen. "She gave him the full focus of her attention then?"

"You betcha. And she does everything for him too. I mean, like, *everything*. She fixes his dinner, opens bottles for him before he even asks. Oh, and laundry. Every week she does his laundry, folds his underwear and all." Gracie sighed, "I guess some women are just like that with a guy."

Stephen smirked, "Well, I perform a similar function for Mr. Snyder, although I receive compensation for my service. But in my romantic relationships, I have shown affection similarly. I enjoy taking care of those I value. And doing so provides a kind of compensation itself."

"Yeah, I don't know about all that, but just since I've been here, I've seen you treated way better than Zack does Kristen. Nothing she ever does for him is right. Always, he finds something to complain about."

"Then what do you imagine she receives from their relationship, if I may ask?"

"Well, he does bring the weed. And maybe the sex is good. It's loud at least."

"Oh, my..." said Stephen, shaking his head.

A police vehicle sat on the street in front of her former apartment—not subtle at all. Gracie noticed neighbors looking their way as they passed by windows. None of the faces there wore disinterested expressions. It wasn't a neighborhood with neutral feelings about a police presence.

The deputy met them on the sidewalk, led Gracie and Stephen to the apartment door, and knocked for them. Jerry and Joe started barking. Kristen answered, her face still bruised and bandaged from the beating, and Zack, the asshole who gave it to her, stood behind her, leaning on a crutch.

Things went quietly, all under the deputy's gaze, which mostly looked bored. Probably that was a good thing. When someone wears a gun on their hip, you want them as disinterested as possible in whatever you might be doing.

Gracie boxed-up and bagged-up her towels, sheets, clothing, toiletries, books, and a few pieces from the kitchen. Yes, it may have just been a plastic cereal bowl, but it was *her* plastic cereal bowl, damn it.

The dogs stayed right at Gracie's feet the whole time. Hancock had warned her to try to avoid interacting with them just as much as with Kristen. They weren't her dogs. But it broke her heart to have those two looking up at her, wanting her attention, and not be able to acknowledge their existence. She forced herself to ignore them just like Kristen and Zack ignored her. Every time she passed through the living room, their eyes remained focused on the sci-fi drama on the TV screen, taking no apparent enjoyment from it, Zack's bandaged leg sitting propped-up on the milk crate coffee table that had knocked him unconscious, ending their fight.

When, at last, her things were gathered in the van, Gracie said to the deputy, "Okay, that's it." The deputy nodded and waited for Gracie to walk out the door.

She made one look back. She couldn't help herself. And Kristen noticed the gesture. She looked up from the television, up at Gracie, and there was nothing in her eyes. It was almost like looking at the picture of a face and not a real face at all. No trace showed of their late nights giggling, drunk and stupid together, no evidence of the hung-over mornings when Kristen might fix them pancakes and scrambled eggs, giving Gracie's a whole lot of extra hot sauce, just the way she liked. They may as well have been strangers. And before Gracie looked away, she saw Zack take hold of Kristen's hand, interlocking his fingers with hers.

Heading back, as soon as the apartment disappeared behind them, Gracie erupted into tears. Stephen handed her a tissue.

Once they came to the Finn Manor front gate, he paused at the guard station to pick up the latest deliveries. They included two items that he handed to Gracie, the first one large, light, and soft, wrapped in plastic. "This should contain a suit appropriate to your role as courier for Snyder-Finn." Then he handed her the second. "And a letter has arrived for you, apparently not by post. This must have been dropped off by hand."

"A what now?"

"A letter. It appears to come from our mutual friend."

The cream-colored envelope was soft to the touch, an old-fashioned paper, maybe hand-made even, something you could draw a pirate's treasure map on. It bore a seal of red wax stamped with the image of a skull. The letter inside said only, "Tonight. Midnight. Finn Mausoleum. We should talk."

1984

Every time Hank stepped over something—or *someone*—strewn across the hallway of Jasmine's building, the wound in his abdomen burned. Stairs were murder. He leaned on her up the three flights. And when Jasmine opened the door to her apartment, it was like breaking apart a dull, gray stone to discover a geode blazing with vibrant crystals within.

Color hung from every wall in the form of long scarves and feather boas of pink, purple, turquoise, and gold, framing the posters and cut-out magazine pages of sex symbols like John Travolta, Madonna, Prince, Freddie Mercury, and Grace Jones. Dresses hung from a rack in the corner like a flock of exotic birds perched tightly together, their plumage almost too bright to look at. Pairs of her shoes, high-heeled and strappy, stood underneath. Jasmine's cosmetics covered the tiny folding card table pressed up against her one window.

She helped Hank to her couch, across from a television on which stood three polystyrene foam heads—one with a black wig, another silver, and a third empty. Seeing that she didn't have a second room to her apartment any more than she had a closet, Hank figured the couch must double as Jasmine's bed. There wasn't a kitchen either, just a hot plate sitting on top of a small refrigerator barely big enough to contain a gallon of milk.

The only inner door cracked open toward a bathroom. More of Jasmine's costume pieces and cosmetics could be seen within. Once she had placed him on her couch, she stepped into the bathroom to change out of her street clothes. A few minutes later, she emerged wearing a nylon cap over her head, wig in hand, which she added to the other two on the television. She had removed her dress as well and instead wore a loose, flower-printed kimono, torn at the shoulder and frayed at the edges, with a thin white camisole visible underneath. Hank could see her form was less curvy than it had appeared before, with more masculine angles to it. Wig removed and her make-up wiped away, her transformation was dramatic.

"You're a man," said Hank.

"Listen," said Jasmine. "I do not need you bleeding on my couch, trying to tell me what I am. I will put your big beefy ass through this window, are we clear?"

"We're clear," said Hank. He hadn't meant to offend. Hank never met a trans woman before. He didn't know the difference between a trans woman and a gay man, but he associated the two. Some prison inmates had sex with guys willingly, and they were usually easy to get along with. Maybe Jasmine would be too.

"Good," she said and collected her medical supplies. These included a needle and thread in addition to a roll of toilet paper, some duct tape, a towel, and a bottle of Medusa's Head rum. "Want a drink before that wound of yours gets a taste?"

Hank shook his head.

"Suit yourself," she said and took a swig before kneeling at his side. "Lift up your shirt." What he showed her made her whistle. "If you aren't the luckiest motherfucker…"

She was right. It didn't look good. Jasmine slipped on a pair of latex gloves and got to work, first toweling away the blood that began to cake on the hairs of Hank's stomach.

As she did, he looked around the room and noticed on the wall opposite the image of a black woman wearing a crown and holding a scepter, like a princess. Catching up on five years of missed pop culture was taking Hank some time, but he recognized most of the media figures on Jasmine's walls except for her.

"Who's that?" he asked.

Jasmine threw a glance over her shoulder. "Oh, her? That's Miss America, Vanessa Williams."

"Miss America is black?"

The question looked like it hurt Jasmine because she had to close her eyes and let it roll through her. "Lord Jesus, give me strength. Yes, Vanessa Williams is black, and, yes, she is Miss America. And it don't mean shit they took her crown away from her for those sexy pictures she took. That is her body, and it ain't nobody else's damn business. Vanessa Williams is *still* Miss America no matter what they say."

"Oh," said Hank, "I didn't know."

"What? How did you not know? You been living under a rock."

"Prison."

"No shit? I done some time too. You know…" She gestured around the room as if it would offer better explanation than any she could give. "For reasons…"

"You're a prostitute," said Hank.

"Boy, you ain't got one single drop of tact, have you? We don't say 'prostitute,' we say, 'lady of the night.'"

"Lady of the night," Hank repeated. Again his mind chewed over understanding Jasmine as a lady.

"That's right. And what about you? Seem like maybe you got in a fight or something. Was that what happened? Got you an assault charge?"

It would be the first time Hank managed to say it out loud

to anyone since the Crimson Wraith. "I didn't mean to kill my wife."

That made Jasmine stop again. She looked at him hard. "You didn't?"

Hank shook his head.

"You sure about that?"

He nodded.

"For real?"

"For real."

"I guess that's a real shame then. This gonna hurt." And then she poured the rum on Hank's wound.

And it did, better than any of the fights he ever got in. Pain flashed like a wall of white in his brain. He felt it shoot down his thighs and electrify his heart. Hank wasn't sure what kind of sound came out of him, but he knew it wasn't quiet.

When the wave had passed through him, Jasmine asked, "You done?"

"Yeah."

"Well, this is the part where I stitch you back together."

Every time the needle entered Hank, it was terrible, a tiny bit of awfulness that happened over and over again, a pinch on a pinch on a pinch, each one overlaying the other, the cumulative effect bringing heat to his cheeks. And it made Hank want to speak.

"I told him I didn't mean to kill her," he said.

"Who did you tell, honey?"

"The Crimson Wraith."

"Did you?"

"I did. He caught me. I told him I didn't mean it."

"Well, then, it's a good thing you told him."

"And you know what he told me?"

"What's that?"

"He said... He made me promise... that I would live... And I would make things better... Whatever it takes."

Jasmine started tying off the stitches. "That why you did what you did tonight? Why you ran like some fool superhero down a dark alley to save a woman you didn't even know from *what* you didn't even know?"

"Yes."

Jasmine folded the toilet paper several times before taping it over the stitched-up wound. "Well, even if yours truly don't need no rescuing like that, I guess someone ought to be doing it, now the Crimson Wraith himself gone missing and all."

"What?"

"Yeah, that's how it is. No one seen him in about a year now. Places he used to protect, it's open season there again. Gangs arming up and assholes like Matthew trying to stake their claim on this block or that."

"That fucking sucks."

"It does," said Jasmine. "The streets are dangerous out there. Could use someone like the Crimson Wraith evening the odds."

"You think so?"

"Of course, I do. He did more for us than cops ever did, and that's for damn sure. They never get the really scary motherfuckers, just harass people on some minor shit, thinking we easy pickings."

"Minor shit like..." Hank halted himself, "...ladies of the night?"

"Ain't like we hurting nobody."

"Guess not," said Hank. "I wonder if I could do it."

"Do what? You wanna try hooking? No offense, sweetie, but I don't know if they make dresses in your size."

"No, not that. I mean... I wonder if I could, you know, make streets safer... Like the Crimson Wraith did."

"Whoa... Just, whoa... Are you serious? You want to be the Crimson Wraith? You mean, for real?"

"Well, maybe... yeah."

"Huh, well, ain't that something? The Crimson Wraith right here in my home, bleeding on my couch and shit."

"I'm not bleeding anymore."

"No, you're not. And who do you have to thank for that?"

"You. Thank you, Jasmine."

"You're welcome." She got up, started putting away her medical supplies, then she stopped and turned to look at Hank. "You ain't bullshitting are you? About doing this Crimson Wraith thing? I mean, you want to do it for real? Like, *for real* for real?"

"I do," said Hank, and the more he thought about it, the more he liked it. He considered the strategies from his rehabilitation group. Becoming the Crimson Wraith—doing a job it seemed no one else could do or wanted to—seemed like the best way to fulfill his promise to make things right, whatever it takes.

"Well, then..." Jasmine opened a footlocker and started rifling through it. "Boy like you who goes off running into knives ought to have himself some help."

She pulled out a purple domino mask, something she apparently found useful in her work. Then she slipped it on and stood up straight with hands on her hips and her chest puffed out. Jasmine's kimono draped from her shoulders like the cape of a hero from the cover of a comic book. It made her look just like the Wily Wisp, crime-fighting sidekick of the Crimson Wraith.

"And, honey," she said. "Help is right here."

2019

As she waited for her appointment with the Crimson Wraith that evening, Gracie picked up *Nights of Justice* once more:

> *No clear consensus can be determined for the starting point of the Crimson Wraith's career. It was not as though he announced his arrival to all major media outlets.*
>
> *The first police report that mentions his name does so in the year 1942, as part of a statement taken by a wit-*

ness to attempted robbery. The witness, one Agnes Addison, describes a kind of "phantom" in red who emerged from a cloud of smoke to thwart two young men fleeing a jewelry store. She described the figure as "terrifying." Agnes lost consciousness from shock and woke an uncertain amount of time later in the arms of a TCPD officer who had responded to the jewelry store alarm. He found the miscreants bound head-to-foot and Miss Addison resting on the sidewalk with her handbag placed under her head as a pillow...

When Gracie came downstairs, she heard Kevin laughing, his voice just sharper than the muffled laugh track accompanying him. It came from the study, which she would pass on her way out the back, and she thought about maybe just going out the front and circling around before deciding that might be going to an unnecessary length. Gracie hadn't told anyone else about the invitation she received. Although it seemed like everyone at Finn Manor knew the Crimson Wraith personally, the letter came just for her, and it came sealed, so Gracie felt maybe she should keep quiet about it, even if they met in Kevin's backyard.

The door to the study stood open, and as she approached the sounds of paired laughter, she found Kevin sitting with his feet up, a bag of microwave popcorn in his lap, wearing a pair of pajamas she guessed cost more than her entire wardrobe. And on a side table that probably usually held buckets of ice for chilling champagne, Kevin had placed a tablet on which a television show was playing.

It wasn't one she'd ever watched, but Brianna talked about it at work. The show was called *Nice One, Donna*, about a single mother working as a nurse and recovering from alcoholism, going to meetings and all that, but apparently in a funny way. And there Kevin was, laughing along with it while eating his popcorn. Weird to be reminded that this mansion, as old and fancy as it was, was also just some dude's house.

He noticed her and paused the show. "Not too loud, am I?"

As if he had been watching TV next door to her bedroom instead of down a staircase and two hallways away.

"No, you're fine. Good show?"

"It's won awards."

"I heard."

"You want a late-night snack or something? Stephen's gone to sleep at this point, but you know…" He shook his popcorn at her.

"That's okay. Just felt like stretching my legs."

"Sure. Of course. I get that."

How did this guy seem so normal? Rich people weren't supposed to be normal. Here he was, as mundane as anything, not a hint of twisted debauchery to him. Surely, there at least had to be something creepy in the basement, right?

But what was really weird to Gracie was how she noticed the space on the couch beside Kevin, and, for just an instant, she got an image of herself sitting there with him, sharing that popcorn, watching a sitcom where everyday folks work their gosh-darned best to live a good life and take care of each other, one day at a time. It wasn't a romantic image, no cute cuddling of this forty-something bachelor or any of that, just being there and being herself with someone who felt okay being himself and everything being just fine.

That image had never been her life. It was more foreign than the butler providing in-home room service or going for a ride in an antique luxury car. Being here in this space that felt so far away from the struggles of the city, the struggle of just being, to have this peaceful space where the terror of what fresh hell was coming next didn't hang in the air like evil potpourri, where there wasn't that constant threat of shouting and fighting and things being thrown, where she didn't need to have one eye looking over her shoulder to see who was going to try to screw her over next but in fact had total fucking strangers going out of their way to be helpful, and not because they were getting paid—it was Bizarro World, everything upside down and backward from her own. Or was hers the Bizarro World? Was this actually how things were supposed to be?

She left Kevin. The sounds of the show and his laughter returned as she made her way out the back door. The flashlight on her phone helped her find her way down the steps, down the garden path, back towards the family plot.

Graves in the backyard. Right. *This* was the Bizarro World.

She approached the Finn Mausoleum. No red-cloaked form stood among the headstones, so she called out softly. "Hey! Crimson Wraith guy? You here? It's midnight. I know that's kind of your thing…"

Then she saw the first wisps of fog start to curl past her ankles. Gracie stopped and stood there as it began to cover the graves around her, thickening and rising up to her knees.

She knew he was behind her, but she did not turn around before she heard the softly echoing voice say to her, "Please, turn off your light."

"What? Feeling shy? Afraid I'll post pics of us online?"

"Please," he repeated.

"Fine." Gracie switched the light off of her phone and pocketed it. "I'm going to turn around now, ok?"

"You may."

And there he was, a spectral shape shrouded in darkness, his cloak appearing blood red where moonlight struck it through the trees, just a bit of the whiteness of his skull visible within the shadows of his hood. Even though she'd seen him before, even though she knew to expect him, Gracie felt an instinctive fear clutch at her as she stared into the hollow blackness of the empty eye sockets gazing back at her.

Then he said, "You saw your former roommate today."

"Yeah, I did. And her boyfriend. And everything is pretty fucked. So, I guess I'm going to prison, and he is going to keep on making a punching bag out of her whenever he feels like it."

"That may not have to be your fate. Or hers."

"Really? 'Cuz I'm not seeing any way around it."

"A judge might consider either dropping your charges or reducing your sentence if certain factors are in place."

"You mean like if Zack says, 'Hey, sorry, judge. I'm really the bad guy here'? Yeah, I don't see that happening."

"People have a change of heart sometimes."

"Not that I've seen," said Gracie. "In my experience, an asshole is an asshole is an asshole, pretty much forever."

"There's a lot you haven't seen."

"Hey, I've seen a fuckton more than you would have any idea about—way more than I wanted to, way more than anyone should have to. Don't go telling me what I have and haven't seen, okay?"

He took a step toward her, floating in the rising mist. "What a terrible thing that is."

"What?"

"To see so much that nothing can surprise you, to know the score before the game is even played, with no doubt of its turn-out at all. That is a terrible, terrible thing, and I am sorry that it has happened to you so young."

Gracie swallowed. "Well, maybe a few things have surprised me, just recently. You, for instance. And your friends." She gestured to the mansion.

The Crimson Wraith nodded. "They have surprised me too."

"Okay, then. So, let's say you want to surprise me a little more, huh? Say there is a chance things can work out differently, like, a really, really small one. And I'm not saying there is that chance, but, you know, for argument's sake, if there were that chance, then what would that look like?"

"First," he said, "it would involve me asking your permission to help you and to do so in the best ways that I know."

"What does that mean?"

"It means I would ask you to trust me."

"Do I have a choice?"

"You do. I will not take any further action unless you want. You can leave things up to Bradley and the courts. And he is good at what he does. He's honest, and the District Attorney respects him. That counts for something."

"All right, say he pulls off a miracle for me. That's great, but Kristen..."

"We cannot make her leave her boyfriend."

"Why the fuck not?"

"Because she is choosing to be with him. And she will continue to be with him or with someone like him until she makes a different choice. Sometimes people are drawn to what's destructive to them. They hurt themselves with another person's hands. But those hands don't have to be his, and the choice to harm her is one that he could be persuaded to reconsider."

"Persuaded?"

Instead of answering what kind of persuasion he had in mind, the Crimson Wraith said only, "Will you let me help you?"

For someone who talked her down from carving into Zack just recently, the Crimson Wraith sounded an awful lot to Gracie like he wanted to have Kristen's boyfriend "sleeping with the fishes," the way mobsters said in movies. She had no idea what exactly he was planning, and she realized he wasn't inclined to tell her unless she came on board.

Well, she thought, what did she have to lose?

"Okay," said Gracie, "Let's do this."

Afterward...

As Kevin entered the Crypt, Danny was removing the costume he wore during the meeting with Gracie, returning it to its place among the high-tech battle suits of the Crimson Wraith. "Well, that's that," he said. "Looks like we're doing this."

"It looks like it."

"She say anything when she passed you on her way upstairs?"

"Just 'goodnight.'"

"Not a lot to read from that."

"No, but there was a difference in her tone and movements. She has seemed scattered and desperate since she arrived. Now, there is something different. There's hope."

"Well, then," said Danny, "My hope is she turns out to be worth it."

"You don't seem too big a fan of hers."

"Kevin, man, she's a hard case, walking around here like she invented trouble. I mean, yeah, she's in a tough spot, but can she ease off the attitude?"

"She's lived a different life than either of us. It's made her a different kind of person."

Danny said, "If that kind of person wants our help, she could make helping her a little easier. We do have other things going on right now."

"That we do. You said you noticed something in the scans of Edward's apartment?"

"Sure did. Take a look at this." Danny sat down in front of the Crypt's computer array and began typing. A still image appeared from the recording of the security cameras in Edward's apartment, facing into the kitchen space. On the screen beside it, another shot of Edward's kitchen appeared, scanned by the Haunts that Kevin had brought in with him.

"What are we looking at?" Kevin asked.

"The refrigerator. Took a lot of flipping back and forth between all the angles to notice the difference."

Danny began zooming in both images on the refrigerator door. Just as another man of his age might have photographs of his children, grandchildren, and great-grandchildren held to his refrigerator by magnets, Edward Burton Finn—former Crimson Wraith, former Wily Wisp—kept images of his extended crime-fighting family.

In one, as a young man, he stood among those beside William Finn and his wife on the day of their wedding. Decades later, a middle-aged Edward sat shirtless beside a similarly younger Stephen in a canoe, both smiling up at whoever was taking their picture on the shore.

A laminated newspaper-clipping, yellowed with age, marked the death of Officer Adam O'Neil of the TCPD with a photograph of the deceased. Yet that photograph bore a suspicious resemblance to an older man in another, his appearance obscured by a beard and dark glasses, standing beside Edward and Stephen and a dark-haired young man in cap and gown for his college graduation.

That same college graduate leaned against a motorcycle in another photo, arms folded grimly in a blue-jean jacket appropriate for the 1980s, his hair grown out into a shaggy mullet. In yet another, he sat with Edward and Stephen at a small restaurant eating sandwiches piled high with sliced meats. Finally, he appeared on a magazine cover that read, "The 90s are NOW! Finn Industries CEO Michael Conroy envisions 'limitless horizon'!" His photograph there showed the mullet trimmed. He wore a blazer and tie but still the blue jeans.

What appeared to be the most recent photo on the refrigerator showed an unsmiling blonde man in his twenties wearing a trench coat and red, circular sunglasses, standing in the Finn Manor garden. Beside him, beaming for all she was worth, stood none other than a teenaged Esperanza Villagraña in a black rock band t-shirt, cut at the waist to show her midriff, her hair pixie short. She was giving the camera a peace sign.

Looking from one screen to the next, Kevin said, "In the second image, the photos have shifted slightly."

"Bingo. Had to be our killer, right? You said it's probably someone who knows us, someone with a personal vendetta. He must have recognized some of these faces. Hell, maybe he recognized all of them." Danny kept flipping between the two images, the before and after. "I thought I could put together a program to measure which ones moved and how much. Maybe that could help us determine what the killer touched, and that might be a clue about who they are."

Kevin pointed. "It's that one."

"That one?" Danny looked harder at the image Kevin indicated, the photo of Edward, Stephen, and the young Michael Conroy sitting down to lunch together. "You sure?"

"The photos around it moved more, but that's because they were obscuring it. In the second image, it can be seen more clearly."

"So the killer wanted to get a better look at this one, the photo with all of them together. Why?

"Edward, Stephen, and Michael all appear in other photos as well. But this photo has one face that does not show up anywhere else. Look here." In the background of the photograph, in the deli's kitchen, one cook stood out, the only one looking right at the camera.

"Is that... Hank?" asked Danny.

"That's Hank," said Kevin.

CHAPTER SIX

1986

Sunday nights, the sign above the Golden Sphinx stayed dark. The strands of lights winding up the potted palm trees out front did too. Desperate and lonely men of Titan City would have to look elsewhere for titillation. The bar was closed.

But between their protective iron bars, light shone through the red lace curtains covering the windows. And inside, past the foyer fountain that continued to burble whether or not anyone was there to see it, past the chairs set upside-down on the unoccupied tables, past the silent DJ booth, and past the empty stage with its brass poles from which no dancer dangled or spun, a door led to the dressing room. And from that door came screams and the sound of fists on flesh. Then a voice, a woman's voice dripping with venom, saying, "I just don't understand it, Tamara. I really don't. It is incomprehensible to me. Do you know what that word means, Tamara?"

Another woman's voice whimpered. "Please. I'm sorry. Please."

"Beyond understanding. That's what it means. Your behavior, Tamara, why, it is beyond understanding."

She paced back and forth as she spoke, wearing a backless silk gown that clung to her sinuous shape. Her hair in braids, each tipped with gold, brushed her shoulders. The band across her head bore the image of a cobra.

"Didn't I take good care of you?" she continued. "Didn't I

give you everything you need?"

"Yes, Miss Cleopatra," gasped the girl held down to the tabletop by four large men, all wearing matching suits of shimmering gold fabric.

"Queen!" Her nails slashed suddenly across the girl's cheek, drawing blood. "I am *Queen* Cleopatra, you little bitch! I wear the same crown as my mother before me! I rule the same kingdom! And you will address me as fitting!" Then, as if only just noticing the wound she'd inflicted, Queen Cleopatra pouted, "Now, just look what you made me do. You've made me go and ruin the merchandise. No way now to earn the money you owe."

"I will!" Tamara cried. "I'll pay you back! I'll do anything! I promise! Anything you say!"

But Queen Cleopatra had her back to the girl now. Her attention focused instead on a large basket, whose lid she opened. Then she reached inside with a long, hooked instrument.

"I'm afraid it isn't up to me anymore, Tamara. Now, we submit to the will of the gods of the Nile."

From the basket, she drew forth a cobra, its body draping from the end of the hook. The cobra arched up its head to fan its crown.

"And the gods," said Queen Cleopatra, "have a way of showing us their will."

Thrashing for all her worth, Tamara fought to free herself from the grip of the four men who exchanged uncomfortable looks among themselves as Queen Cleopatra and her cobra approached.

"Easy now," she cooed. "You don't want to upset my little pet, do you? He might render his judgment too quickly if you do. I think you ought to stay nice and still and let him think about whether you deserve to keep breathing..."

Suddenly, darkness fell, swallowing them all. Queen Cleopatra's men muttered in confusion, and she shouted, "Someone go see what happened!"

Then the emergency lights switched on, giving the room a reddish glow. And standing there, where he had not been before, was a huge man wearing a red hooded sweatshirt and a black ski mask with skull painted on it in white—the Crimson Wraith!

"Boo," he said, then swung at the nearest of Queen Cleopatra's men. That one punch sent his target spinning back into a make-up mirror, shattering it, as the other three men released Tamara to reach for the guns they kept in their jackets.

Suddenly free, Tamara tumbled over the side of the table, away from Queen Cleopatra and her cobra, almost running into the Wily Wisp, who stood in the dressing room doorway in her purple domino mask and golden wig, along with sequined crop-top, purple hot pants, and go-go boots.

"Sorry we didn't get here sooner," said the Wily Wisp. "You run on home now, honey, and thanks for the tip." Tamara needed no further encouragement.

Then the Wily Wisp whistled, warning the Crimson Wraith, before pulling a flash bomb from her purse and throwing it on the ground, temporarily blinding all but the two of them.

"My eyes!" Queen Cleopatra shrieked, lifting her free hand to cover her face and nearly dropping the hook that held the cobra.

The Wily Wisp leaped forward, giving generous room to the writhing viper. "A snake? Really? You brought a snake? Bitch, this is not *Wild Kingdom!*" Grabbing the basket and its lid, she captured the animal, who was much happier back inside.

But Queen Cleopatra kept hold of the metal hook and slashed at the Wily Wisp's face, a slash she danced backward to avoid. Then came another and another. Each one the Wily Wisp dodged.

The flash bomb forced one of Queen Cleopatra's men to drop his pistol. The other two, the Crimson Wraith grabbed by the wrists to jerk their arms down. They doubled over in front of him, dropping their guns. Then he cracked their heads together, and both crumpled to the floor.

The one remaining opponent began hammering punches into the Crimson Wraith's side. He responded by wheeling around with a backhand strike that sent the man spinning. Then he took the off-balanced attacker by the back of the head and drove him, face-first, down, into, and through the table where Tamara had been held, knocking him unconscious.

As she continued to evade Queen Cleopatra, the Wily Wisp grabbed one of the dancer's feather boas and entangled the hook on its next swing. She then ripped it out of her opponent's hands and cast it aside. The villainess screamed in rage, but before she could react further, the Wily Wisp wrapped the boa around Queen Cleopatra, pinning her arms to her sides.

"Release me!" she screamed. "Release me this instant!"

The Crimson Wraith stepped forward. "No," was all he said and took hold of her arms in his massive hands to keep her from wriggling free. "Cuffs," he said to the Wily Wisp.

"The man wants cuffs. He gets cuffs." The Wily Wisp pulled a pair of handcuffs from her purse to bind Queen Cleopatra's arms behind her back, then did the same for her men.

"You'll pay for this," Queen Cleopatra spat. "I swear that you will pay for this. Only a fool crosses a queen, Mister High-And-Mighty Crimson Wraith!"

"We'll have the authorities here for you soon," the Crimson Wraith said. "Animal protection too."

"That's right," said the Wily Wisp, standing up from latching the last of the handcuffs. "You're done, girl. No more Queendom for you."

A cold chuckle came from the back of Queen Cleopatra's throat. "You think this is over? No, not by a longshot. You think you can just do away with me, with Queen Cleopatra, just like that? Who do you think you are?"

"Actually," said a man's voice, "I was wondering that too."

The Crimson Wraith, the Wily Wisp, and Queen Cleopatra all turned to look at the stranger who had joined them. He wore a black jumpsuit and domino mask, his hair a dark and shaggy mullet. On his chest, he bore the letter "Z."

"Did I miss the party?" he asked.

The Wily Wisp reached into her handbag for another flash bomb, but the Crimson Wraith raised his hand. "If he wanted to fight, he would have."

"You got it. I am definitely not looking for a fight, not with you anyway. I *was* looking to fight her." He pointed to Queen Cleopatra. "But you two managed to beat me to the punch, several punches in fact."

"Who are you?" said the Crimson Wraith.

Queen Cleopatra scoffed. "You're all in the same superhero game and you don't know each other's names? He's the Zephyr."

The man with the "Z" on his chest bowed.

In response, the Crimson Wraith introduced first himself, then his partner.

"Funny enough," said the Zephyr, "I have heard of you both."

The Wily Wisp said, "Can't say the same of you. New in town?"

"Oh, no. I've been in Titan City a long time, long enough to have heard that the Crimson Wraith had disappeared and that now he's back. I'd been hoping to get to meet you, since we do play the same game, as her majesty put it. Thanks for bringing us together, Queenie."

She rolled her eyes. "I'd rather clutch the viper to my breast than to hear you continue prattling on."

The Wily Wisp said, "We could arrange that, you know. Got that snake right in its basket. All we got to do is open it."

"No," said the Crimson Wraith. "We don't kill."

"Well, shit," said the Wily Wisp. "She don't have to know that."

"Yes, she does," said the Crimson Wraith. "She tried to do wrong. Now she needs to learn how to do right."

The Zephyr said, "Has to live if she's going to see justice, huh?"

And the Crimson Wraith nodded.

"I respect that," said the Zephyr. "Besides, Queenie, you've been too bad a girl to have it all end too quickly. I followed a nice long trail of money laundering, drug trafficking, and bribing of public officials to find you here. There's a whole lot of evidence that is going to have you behind bars a whole long time."

"We got her on all that too," said the Wily Wisp, "Plus her doing some real bad things to some real good girls—some who ain't walking no more, some who ain't breathing."

"That's terrible," said the Zephyr, sounding sincere.

They left Queen Cleopatra and her men bound to the poles on the stage of the Golden Sphinx, then went outside to watch the arrival of the TCPD from a rooftop farther away. Among the officers on the scene came Captain Harlan Goodman himself. Immediately upon exiting his vehicle, Goodman looked up to scan the surrounding buildings. When he saw the skull watching the street below, he nodded and then turned to speak to the others around him.

"You have Goodman's respect," said the Zephyr. "He has been a friend of the Crimson Wraith a long time."

"I never met him," said the Crimson Wraith.

"But I have," said the Zephyr, "back when I went under another name." He removed his mask. "My name is Michael Conroy, and before I was the Zephyr, I fought alongside the Crimson Wraith as the Wily Wisp."

Jasmine removed her mask, "Get outta town. For real? The original Wisp?"

"Original? No, just the most recent. Before you anyway."

"I'm Jasmine," she extended her hand.

"Nice to meet you," he said. "Pretty good moves down there."

"Pretty good?"

"I didn't mean any offense. I don't think I caught the whole show."

"Well, honey, I give one hell of a show."

"I bet," he turned to the Crimson Wraith. "And you, what made you put on the mask?"

Hank slipped it off. "I met the Crimson Wraith once. He was good to me. Then I heard he was gone, and I thought somebody needs to do this."

Michael nodded. "He was good to me too. And, your right, somebody does."

2019

Looking down from the Snyder-Finn Building gave an almost god-like perspective on Titan City. That vantage point encompassed so much, the entire sweep from the Spirit of Prosperity up to the Elysian Hills, with the Englehart and Brennert rivers surrounding. The motion of all the individual lives below seemed coordinated into a single flow, like the murmuration of birds. And to behold it by night, with the streets' grid lines transformed into valleys of light, throbbing with headlights and LED billboards and traffic signals—all reflected against the sheen of glass windows, framed by the darkness of asphalt and concrete—imparted a wondrously strange and eldritch beauty to the sight.

But, dangling from his ankles, Zack was in no position to appreciate the view.

"I want you to know that you are suspended securely."

Zack heard the Crimson Wraith's voice in his ear, just over the roar of high-altitude winds around him. Rope tied his wrists behind him and connected to his ankles. It extended up to an empty flagpole, which held him away from the wall of the building, then back down to the balcony where the Crimson Wraith gripped it tightly with both hands.

"Let me go," Zack moaned, still groggy from the blast of the Crimson Wraith's knock-out gas. "For fuck's sake, man, just let me go…"

"I'm not going to let you go, and that's why you are not going to fall, not unless you make me."

"The fuck, man? What do you want? Fucking shit, what do you want?"

"Don't act surprised. You haven't exactly been a model citizen, have you, Zack? You like to throw your weight around. You like to throw your fists around. When people don't give you what you want, you take it. Isn't that right?"

"No, man. Not me. I swear."

A tremor seized Zack's whole body, head to toe, the invisible force of an electrical shock, making him flail and jerk in a way that did not seem at all safe, given his position. In his ear, the Crimson Wraith's voice roared, "Do not lie to me, Zack!"

The shocks shuddered their way out of him. Zack whimpered, "I'm sorry. God damn it, I'm sorry. I'm sorry, man. I swear."

"What you're feeling now is not remorse. It is fear. You're afraid, aren't you, Zack? Somewhere along the line, you learned that fear is powerful, didn't you? Someone taught you that lesson long ago, and you took it to heart."

"What are you talking about?"

"The fact that I do not believe you are sorry," the Crimson Wraith said. "But I am. I'm sorry for whatever happened to you, whatever made you become this."

"Made me become what?"

Three inches. A drop of three inches was all it took to start Zack screaming again, three inches closer to the ground.

The Crimson Wraith continued, speaking calmly over the screams. "You are cruel, Zack. You are cruel and brutal. And this is why you are here right now. You are here because you have shown that this is the only form of communication you respect. I would rather it wasn't this way. I would rather not talk to you this way. But if you won't listen to anything else, you need to listen to this."

Zack shrieked, "What do you want from me?"

"I want you to give me a promise. And I want you to keep

that promise. You are going to keep it because you know now that I am watching you. I will always be watching you. And I can always bring you right back here."

"I promise! Anything! I promise!"

"Kristen. Your relationship with her is over. You will leave her and never have anything to do with her ever again. Do not see her. Do not speak to her. Do not message her. If she is ever again hurt in life, it will not be by your hand. Promise me that."

"Yes! I promise!"

"Say that it is over between you."

"It is over, man! Me and her are done!"

"Good. And then you will contact the District Attorney. You will inform her that you wish to change your statement regarding your fight with Gracie Chapel. You will let the DA know that you were the first to pick up a weapon. You were the one to escalate the confrontation, and she only took up her own in response."

"Fine! I'll do that!"

"You'll do what, Zack? I want you to say the words. Tell me."

"I'll say that I did it! I'm the one! I was the first to grab a bottle!"

"And is that the truth?"

"It is! It's the truth! I had a weapon first!"

"Then the truth," said the Crimson Wraith, "will set you free." Slowly he drew back the rope to bring Zack up and over the ledge, safely on something solid once more. "Now sleep. And remember." The Crimson Wraith held his gauntlet over Zack's face. A cloud of sweetly smelling mist poured from his hand, and the world around Zack faded to nothing once more.

"That should do it, Gracie," said the Crimson Wraith.

Miles away, his spoken words appeared on the screen of the phone in her hand, the phone which also received images captured by the camera in the Crimson Wraith's mask, allowing her to see everything he saw, displayed for her in shades of night-vision green as she read the transcription that appeared below.

Gracie watched the whole rooftop conversation between the Crimson Wraith and Zack with a drink in hand, sitting in a corner by herself at Terpsichoria, her face lit up by the screen. Of course, there were plenty of others equally transfixed by their phones around her, so Gracie didn't seem out of place. A few fellow patrons came up trying to start a conversation. Nothing out of the ordinary—people typically go to clubs to socialize, to meet and be met, and some were even acquaintances she'd seen there before. Gracie brushed them all off, placing her phone face down as they approached to hide the screen.

When Zack had been sent off to dreamland and the video feed shut off, the status message from Crypt read, *Subject being returned to his vehicle*, and Gracie clamped her hand over her mouth to keep from crying out in exultation. She wanted to laugh. She wanted to scream. She wanted to dance. Fortunately, there was a dance floor nearby.

Every mix the DJ spun seemed perfect, all the other dancers on the floor, fun and full of life. It had been too many nights since Gracie came to the club, too much terror and uncertainty shackling her feet. Now, though, she danced with a fierce joy that she had not felt pour through her body in years, maybe ever.

Earlier That Day...

No routes of the Titan Metro Line made their way into the Elysian Hills beyond the Englehart River, but Gracie didn't want Stephen to give her a ride directly to Sprang & Sons. That would bring more questions from Brianna than she wanted to answer. Instead, she asked him to bring her to the 6th Avenue station in something less anachronistic than the Zephyr. Fortunately, not everything in Kevin's garage made such a bold statement. It felt much more comfortable to her to step out of the gunmetal grey 2007 Mercedes-Benz—still eye-catching, sure, but maybe that wouldn't call the attention of quite as many panhandlers on the sidewalk.

Most of the ads posted inside the station had a Halloween theme to them. One claimed Chew-Rite gum as the secret to a vampire keeping his fangs sparkly. Another announced the arrival of cinnamon-maple-bacon-flavored Kronos-Kola —a truly horrifying concept. A third advertised the pumpkin maze in Keaton Park, promising age-appropriate spooky times for young and old alike.

Then Gracie caught sight of a poster that would not have merited her attention before, *The Crimson Wraith's Guide to Safe Trick-or-Treating*. A cartoon of the Crimson Wraith held out its cloak, upon which appeared a list of things like, "If you wear a mask like the Crimson Wraith, take extra care to look both ways when crossing the street..."

Did the Crimson Wraith get a cut of whoever got paid to print public service announcements with his likeness? Or did he get like a tax write-off? Did whoever made these even consult him? Not like he had an agent for them to contact and negotiate rights or anything—or did he? And probably it was in the best interest of anyone in Titan City who wanted to use the Crimson Wraith's likeness that they do so respectfully. Gracie figured if anyone had ever tried to make a Crimson Wraith porn parody that they'd find themselves getting a none-too-happy meeting from "a man at midnight."

But these were the realities of living in a city with its own masked vigilante who had, somewhere in his eighty years, earned the tacit approval of official law enforcement. And when you're a kid growing up with this sort of thing, it gets to be so bland and commonplace that you can make fun of it as a teen for being just so hokey, never once having any sense of the reality underneath. It was like having George Washington's face on the one-dollar bill—the least valuable paper currency, easiest to loan and most disappointing to find as the only bill in your wallet—and to forget that, not only was this face the face of an actual person and the first President of the United States, but that he was a soldier. In the line of duty, he killed people, running them through with his saber or opening up their skulls with his musket. He faced death, dodged it, and visited it upon others only to one day have school kids laugh about how, with his puffy wig, you can turn his head into a mushroom if you fold a dollar bill just right.

As she settled into her seat on the train, Gracie pulled out her phone. A text message from a blocked number had given her the link to download and install an app with the name "Tombstone." Its icon appeared to be a game, a red deck of standard playing cards with the image of a white skull on the back. When she opened the app, a simple menu offered access to a video feed, which currently had the status "Inactive" and a chat window with "Crypt" that read, *Specter Prime in preparation. Will notify when in motion.* That message remained unchanged. No updates Gracie had missed. She would go on about her day and try not to look at her phone every five minutes.

The Crimson Wraith told her to expect this, that she would receive notifications as he began his attempt to persuade Zack. He said he might need her help, guidance for how to proceed, depending on how things went, so she would be able to communicate with the Crimson Wraith this way, and it would allow her to see everything he did to Zack.

But since she couldn't just sit there on the train, waiting for her phone to buzz, Gracie pulled open *Nights of Justice* once more:

> *As more stories of the Crimson Wraith began to surface, reporters of The Titan Gazette employed a variety of alliterative names for him, including the Red Rogue and the Fiendish Fantom. The name Crimson Wraith did not appear until 1944 in connection with a story regarding the theft of a cache of weapons stolen from the U.S. Military, recovered*

in Titan City's Little Tokyo area. A photograph accompanied this story. Although his form appeared grainy and indistinct, being photographed at a distance and in the dark, the pale image of his skull mask could be seen clearly, turned in the direction of the camera. This image captivated the public imagination, and so the name attributed to him in that story, the Crimson Wraith, was the name by which the public would know him...

Returning to Sprang & Sons felt strange. Her last day had seemed just like another usual shift in her on-going routine, but that routine had been shot to hell. A lot had happened for Gracie lately.

Brianna met her with wide, worried eyes at the door. "You should go talk to Rich," she said. Gracie poked her head into Richard Sprang's grubby little office, its walls a mottled mass of faded newsprint cartoons and rock show fliers. A stack of disordered boxes with old receipts stood in one corner. It always looked to Gracie like he had made a nest of old paper for himself, the way a hamster might. And she could tell by his distracted response that her talking to Rich was Brianna's idea. It had nothing to do with him.

"Oh, you're back?" he said, slightly startled by her.

"I'm back, yeah," said Gracie.

"Good. Good. You feeling better?"

"Yep," Gracie realized she could answer that vague question honestly. "Feeling much better."

"Glad to hear that." Then he turned back to the vintage guitars magazine in his hand and the article he had been reading before.

"What did he say?" Brianna asked Gracie when she came back.

"Nothing really. Glad to see me back."

"Guess he doesn't know then. I wasn't going to tell him. You don't have to worry about that. But you might want to think about getting ahead of the story."

She blinked. "You think I ought to what now?"

"Oh, Gracie," Brianna sighed. "I saw, okay?"

"Saw what?" Gracie knew the answer but couldn't help but ask.

"The arrest. Your mugshot. I get an alert on my feed for local news that shows me pretty much all the arrests. Normally don't pay it any attention but... Well, damn, honey. Are you okay? I've been worried like crazy about you. What's been going on? Were you in jail? Did you just get out? I'm... I'm asking too many questions. I'm sorry."

"No, no. It's fine. Really." Gracie felt bad that Brianna felt bad, that she'd let her work friend worry. But what the hell should she say to her now? "Things lately, they've been kind of... complex."

"Oh, I get it! Something like this isn't always something you want to talk to people about. Talking can make it too real maybe. You may not even want to hear yourself say the words." She put a hand on Gracie's arm. "But you know you can talk to me about anything, right? I mean it, anything."

It was sweet. Gracie knew Brianna would have said something like that, given her the sympathetic arm touch. Maybe telling her about it wouldn't have been so bad, if things had gone differently. Probably Brianna would have called her from outside if Gracie had wound up spending time in jail as she awaited her trial. After her release, would Brianna have let Gracie sleep on her couch?

"Thank you, really," said Gracie. "It's okay now. Or it's going to be okay. You don't have to worry." It felt strange to say but stranger to feel. Things were getting handled, and by a superhero, no less.

"You sure? No shame in asking for help, you know."

"Right, of course." Gracie wasn't sure she believed in that. Asking for help wasn't ever anything she'd known was an option. If you ask someone for help, you're showing them they have something you need, something they can hold over you. But this time, help had been offered to her, and she kept looking for an angle without finding it. So, she accepted help. It felt weird but it also felt nice. "I've got help. Good help. Like, legal help. And stuff."

"Oh?" said Brianna. "Well, okay then. Good. I'm glad to hear it." She didn't ask further. Maybe it was clear that if Gracie wanted to give more details she would have. "You just don't forget, if there is anything else you need..."

"I'll let you know. I promise. And thank you."

Then there was work to be done, and Gracie appreciated having something to keep her occupied, but before the day was out, she felt her phone buzz. Sure enough, it was Tombstone. She opened up the app to see a message from Crypt, *Subject has left the house. Following.*

She now found access to a live video feed and a stream of stills taken every fifteen seconds from the feed previously. Scrolling through these, she saw Zack leave the apartment, walk to his car, and enter. The live feed showed Zack's car in motion on the road, the camera following him from some distance above.

Seeing this video, being part of spying on Zack, it was the definition of creepy, and, on some level, Gracie wondered if she should have moral qualms about this, but the fact was that she didn't. Knowing this was Zack being spied on, all Gracie felt was excitement. He was a bad guy. He did bad things. And now, they were going to stop him, even if it meant being creepy about it. Was this how it felt to be CIA?

A question appeared on her screen. "Do you know where he may be going?"

Gracie typed her reply. "He drives for one of those rideshare things. Headed uptown to find commuters."

"Good. Can use that. Beginning process of accessing his mobile device."

Accessing his mobile device? Definitely CIA shit.

After closing Sprang & Sons, Gracie headed over to Titan Community Polytechnic campus, grabbing some falafel from a street vendor on the way. Today was supposed to be about revisiting her routine, and that meant going to class. By the time she arrived, Tombstone had begun displaying the screen of Zack's mobile phone, showing the rides he had taken that night, his location on a map, and even what music he had playing in his car—lots of easy listening for his customers, something she'd heard Zack complain about in the past.

Gracie typed in the chat window, "Class about to start. Have to keep my phone away for the next 3 hours."

Crypt responded, "Message when free. Will set up contact point."

Probably the funniest thing about all of this was that Gracie had been working toward a degree in criminal justice, not like she planned on being a cop, but maybe someone who worked in a crime lab or handled legal documentation. Brianna had pointed her in that direction, saying she had a cousin who worked at a domestic violence shelter filing court orders on victims' behalf and that there were a whole lot of jobs in the legal system that didn't require a law degree or going to the police academy. Gracie hadn't ever thought of having a career before, just making money and paying rent, but Brianna painted a picture for her of a way more stable life than she ever imagined for herself, something with benefits and vacation time and raises. It all sounded good. Gracie wasn't sure that career path would still be open for her with an arrest on her record, but she didn't want to screw up her GPA.

As hard as it was, while knowing the Crimson Wraith was stalking Zack, Gracie paid the best attention she could to the video the instructor showed about the history of Japanese-American internment camps during the Second World War. Then she answered the comprehension questions with her discussion group. That night, she spoke more and raised her hand more often just because doing something, even speaking in front of the rest of the class, made the time go by much more easily. It got her instructor's attention too, and after class, she stopped Gracie to say how good it was to hear so much from her.

As soon as she made it out of the classroom, Gracie had her phone open once again. She messaged one word, "Ready."

A new ride showed up on Zack's screen. Crypt said, That is Specter Prime. He will collect subject at that address.

Suddenly, Gracie realized that Crypt was not the Crimson Wraith himself and wondered how the vigilante managed to have a secretary. But that was something for another time. Instead, she messaged back, "Ok. Headed to club."

Going to Terpsichoria was part of the plan as well. The Crimson Wraith said she should be out and be seen, so she brought a change of clothes that were a little more attention-getting to switch to in the college bathroom—a crop top and black leggings, still with her same leather jacket and boots, black lipstick, some sparkly eye make-up, and a pair of hoop earrings. Her reflection almost made her laugh, and when another student commented, "Girl, you fierce," on her way out the door, Gracie couldn't help but smile.

This was not what she expected of someone who had nearly gotten sexually assaulted the last time she went to the club. But then, she'd been arrested since. For beating the shit out of a guy. Left him with stitches. Nearly killed him. Why, some might even accuse her of being a danger to society. And she almost hoped that Tight T-Shirt Guy would show up and try some shit. If only she had taken a picture of Zack lying at her feet so she could say, "Here's what happened to the last guy…"

The Crimson Wraith made contact while she was changing, and when she checked her phone on the Metro ride to Terpsichoria, she found the video from above Zack's car no longer broadcasting. Instead, there was a new feed showing the car's interior, aimed at the dashboard. It showed neither Zack nor the Crimson Wraith, who must have been wearing some kind of "plain clothes" disguise to be picked up by Zack. The image on her screen shifted slightly from moment to moment, suggesting the camera being used was attached to someone, maybe hidden in a tie pin, like in old spy movies. And at the bottom of the screen appeared a transcribed conversation, with no speaker attributed. Just a stream of small talk:

My wife, she took the car. Took everything.
That's awful. Just awful.
Not married are you?
Me? Oh, no. Oh, hell, no.
Never do it. Just a trap.
Yeah, man, I hear you. Got this girl now. She thinks I'm a fucking god.
Don't do it. Don't marry her. You'll regret it.
No, I'd never marry her. See, I got her wrapped around my finger. She pays for everything. Does whatever I say. Got a real sweet deal.
You got to be kidding me. Doesn't she make you buy flowers and all?
What? No way. That's some loser bullshit right there. Oh sorry. Didn't mean to curse.
No, go ahead. You are right. That's what it is.
That's what it is. It's all bullshit.
So you don't buy flowers. You don't get her gifts. She pays for everything? And does whatever you say? Like she's at your command?
You got it. I'm not saying she's my slave. [laughs] Okay, maybe I am.
Got to tell me your secret. How do you do it?
How do I what?
How do you make her do everything for you?
She knows who's in charge.
Yeah?
Oh, yeah.
Never questions your authority?
Not if she knows what's good for her.
And if she doesn't?
[laughs] Then I have to remind her, don't I?

The Metro car suddenly sang with the sound of a ring on Gracie's right hand striking the metal handrail that she punched in a flash of anger. Eyes turned toward her. A few passengers shifted away. It seemed to Gracie like pocketing her phone for the time being would be a good idea.

She was waiting in line at Terpsichoria when she felt the phone buzz in her jacket. A notification on the screen read, *Subject acquired.* Luckily, the weekday crowd didn't keep her in line for long. Gracie got checked-in and went right to the bar. There she ordered a whisky sour and took it to a dark corner where she could look at her phone without others seeing her screen.

Tombstone wasn't offering any video feeds, just a status update, "Subject acquired. Specter Prime and subject in motion." Subject acquired? How?

Going back through the screenshots of the previous video feed, she found the action they depicted was blurry, difficult to make out. Then as Gracie kept rewinding, she realized some kind of fog had filled Zack's car, obscuring the screen. She watched it clear away, disappearing up the sleeve of the jacket worn by the person who also wore the camera, the Crimson Wraith. His hand covered Zack's face, and a startled expression peaked through the fingers.

Still Gracie scrolled backwards, seeing the hand release Zack, his expression return to ignorance, and finally there appeared at the bottom of the screen the last two lines of transcribed conversation:

> *You sure this is your stop, man?*
> *No. It's yours.*

Holy shit. Holy fucking shit. It was happening. It was actually happening. Gracie downed her drink way too fast and then went back for another.

Somewhere, out there in that dark and writhing monster of

a city, hidden away in a corner of concrete and shadow, Zack was completely at the Crimson Wraith's mercy. A pair of red gauntleted hands were dragging his sorry ass around, and Gracie knew just where they were headed next because the vigilante had consulted her on it.

She'd asked, "So, what, are you going to kidnap him to some 'undisclosed location' where no one can hear him scream and beat the shit out of him for a few hours? Like, tie him to a chair and cut off his ear or something?"

"You've been watching too many movies." The Crimson Wraith's mask and augmented voice kept her from being able to tell if he was amused or not.

"Well, what the hell else is going to do anything? Give him a pair of 'concrete shoes' and toss him into Marshal Bay?"

"No killing."

"No killing?"

"No."

"Not even a little killing?"

"The dead can't face justice," he said. "They don't get to learn from their wrongs nor suffer for them."

"But if you aren't going to kick his ass, then how else are you going to stop him? Hell, how will you stop him even if you *do* kick his ass? Obviously, this son-of-a-bitch can just brush off an ass-kicking and go right on being a son-of-a-bitch."

"We can show him that his actions matter. We can show him that he is not above receiving their consequences. We can let him know that someone is watching him and holding him accountable."

"Few broken ribs could go a long way toward accountability."

"If it has to be that way, then that's how it will be, but what if Zack shows up in court with brand new injuries as well as a change in his story. How will that look to a judge?"

"Probably like someone forced him to change his story."

"Exactly, and that makes your case look worse, not better. What we want is for Zack to tell the District Attorney he now remembers the night differently, without any apparent coercion."

"How are you going to make Zack say that without kicking the shit out of him? You just gonna ask him nicely to stop being an abusive fuckwad and think about other people?"

"I intend to take a more psychological approach."

"Lay him down on a couch and make him talk about his feelings?"

"Not quite. Tell me, how do you think Zack feels about being in the dark? Or restrained? Or maybe high places?"

And that's what they had settled on, dangling Zack from a very high place, the highest place in Titan City in fact. "Give him a sense of perspective," Gracie had said with a grin.

And that was just what the Crimson Wraith did.

CHAPTER SEVEN

1986

The Titan Metro ride up to the 6th Avenue station wasn't exactly comfortable for either Hank or Jasmine. Typically, she didn't like going out during the day. It never felt safe for her to dress the way she felt most herself when the sun was out, so she threw on something a boy had left at her apartment one time, left her wig and make-up at home, and told Hank to call her "Jay" while they were in public. He said he would try to remember. Nothing changed the way she moved or walked though. It was clear that more than one young man saw her and wanted to call her something very not-nice, but one look at Hank at her side kept their tongues still. His size intimidated plenty even when he didn't have on the Crimson Wraith's hood and mask.

And they had to go during the day since nights were when the two patrolled the streets. Usually, Hank finished closing Bobby D's around 10:30 PM, and that gave him and Jasmine just enough time to suit up and start stalking criminals by midnight. This day, Hank had a half-shift scheduled, allowing him to accept Michael's invitation for lunch before he had to go back and work the dinner shift.

Hank wasn't comfortable, though, because he wasn't someone who got invited to lunch, not up on the West end of 6th Avenue, definitely not over by Englehart. He was an East Town guy. On top of that, this invitation from Michael seemed to be about Hank being the Crimson Wraith, and he was afraid. He didn't want to hear someone say he shouldn't be doing that, thinking they knew better than him. But Michael had known the Crimson Wraith who sent him to prison, and he had been a good guy, so Hank would hear what Michael had to say.

They walked out of the 6th Avenue Titan Metro station to find Michael standing in front of a beautiful classic car in polished bloody burgundy with gleaming chrome accents. "Oh, shit," said Jasmine. "What kind of car is that?"

Michael grinned. "It's um… It's a 1939 Lincoln-Zephyr."

"Zephyr? You mean like…"

"Yeah, exactly like that."

Jasmine lowered her voice. "You named yourself after a car?"

"Hey, it's a really nice car."

Hank asked, "Where are we going?"

Michael pointed up to the Elysian Hills, and Hank nodded. No, he did not think he was going to like this at all.

As they rode on over the 6th Avenue Bridge, crossing the Englehart River, Jasmine could not get enough of the car. "It *looks* like money. It *feels* like money," she said as she ran her fingers over the seats. "Honey, it even *smells* like money."

"Right?" said Michael. "That's why I tried to steal it."

Hank said, "You stole this car?"

"Tried to," said Michael. "Only tried to. I was seventeen and thought I knew everything. Ran with a group of guys who operated from Dini Street to Robinson."

"That's East Town," said Hank.

"Sure is."

"See," said Jasmine, "I knew there was something I liked about you."

"Aw, thanks," said Michael.

Hank said, "You were in a gang?"

"Had to be. Never knew my parents. Couple of aunties raised me. And you want to make it out there, you don't do it alone, right? We called ourselves the Red Birds. Dunno why, really. Maybe the Crimson Wraith made the color red sound cool and dangerous. We didn't get into heavy stuff. Most hardcore was some B&E, but typically we kept to pickpocketing and a bit of car theft. So, when I saw this beauty..." Michael patted the steering wheel. "Oh, man, it was everything I could have wanted and more than I could have imagined. I thought to myself that if I could jack a car like this, then my whole future would be made for me. And I guess it was. But let's just say, you steal the Crimson Wraith's car, you don't get very far."

Hank said, "The Crimson Wraith left this car parked in East Town? Between Dini and Robinson?"

"No, see, I'd gone wandering uptown. Suppose that's what you get for leaving your turf. Found this beauty sitting up on the corner of Warner and 3rd. Although, to be specific, it didn't belong to the Crimson Wraith I knew, the one who trained me, the one I was the Wily Wisp for. It belonged, and it still belongs, to the Crimson Wraith who trained him, and he's the one you're going to meet. He'd been in town handling things at Finn Industries..."

Jasmine stopped him. "Hold the damn phone. Finn Industries?"

Michael laughed. "Yeah, Finn Industries. Wow, you guys are gonna be getting a big history lesson today."

Hank wasn't interested in history.

"You know what's cool?" said Michael. "I've spent years with all these secrets, keeping them very carefully, for my safety and everyone else's. But here I meet you two, and even though I don't know you at all, not as people, I do know that we're doing the same work. So, it feels okay just being open with you, like we're long-lost cousins catching up on family stuff you didn't even know was there to catch up on."

"Guess you don't have to worry about us blabbing to the cops or anything," said Hank.

"Right?" Michael laughed.

Hank wasn't sure how he felt about that either.

When the gates of Finn Manor opened for them, Jasmine

whistled. "Like something out of a fairy tale," she said.

"I know just what you mean," said Michael. "Felt the same way when I first saw it." He parked in front of the manor's main entryway and opened the doors for them. "Gentlemen," he said, with a slight bow.

"Lady," said Jasmine.

"Right, sorry." Michael turned his attention to the interior and called out, "Grandpas! I'm home! And we've got company!"

They appeared down the hall, Stephen wearing the apron he had been cooking in and Edward walking with the silver-Derby-handled snakewood cane he would be holding at the time of his death, but carrying it more lightly in his fifties than he would in later years.

"Honestly, Michael," said Edward. "Must you keep on with the 'grandpa' business? And in front of guests?"

A bright grin cut across Stephen's face, "Forgive the *niño*, Eddie. He is quite excited, yes?"

"Darn right!" said Michael, "Now, Grandpa Eddie, Grandpa Stephen, these are Hank and... I'm sorry."

"Jasmine," she said.

"Jasmine, right. Hank and Jasmine are the Crimson Wraith and Wily Wisp I was telling you about. Hank, Jasmine, these are Eddie and Stephen."

They each shook hands, and as soon as Hank's hand clasped Edward's, he knew. It came from the way a handshake tells you about the person attached to the palm you are pressing. That told Hank this man was a fighter, at least he had been. Still the echoes of that strength and poise, of that readiness, remained. And he knew that Edward saw it in him too. Of course, he would. Edward gave a slight nod of acknowledgment, saying, "It's good to meet you."

Then Stephen said, "Why don't we all step into the parlor?" He gestured toward a doorway to their left, where fine leather sofas awaited them. Stephen opened an antique globe to reveal a drinks set hidden inside. "It is past noon, so might I offer anyone some refreshment?"

Hank shook his head, but Jasmine said, "Oh, you know I'm not gonna say no to that."

"What may I serve you?" said Stephen.

"Well, I don't exactly know what you folks drink up in these parts. Usually, I'm a Medusa's Head girl myself. I ain't fancy."

"Rum then?" said Stephen. "Very well. Ice?"

"Maybe just a little."

Stephen poured her something the same dark, rich tone of the leather and wood grain all around them. "See how this treats you."

Jasmine took a sip. "Oh, this treats me good. This treats me real good."

"Excellent." Stephen then poured for Edward and himself.

"Now," said Michael, looking to Edward, "how about you tell our guests a story, Grandpa?"

Edward sighed with gentle irritation undercut by a tiny current of amusement, but he turned toward Hank and Jasmine nonetheless. His fingers gripped his cane firmly as if bracing for the impact of history, and he began.

"In the year 1940," he said. "I was kidnapped along with several other orphan boys by a villain who called himself the Blue Banshee. We were rescued by the first Crimson Wraith, William Finn, who later adopted me as his son. In 1948, after much training, I began to fight alongside him in a guise of my own creation, the Wily Wisp."

Jasmine broke in. "You were the one who came up with the Wily Wisp?"

"I am. I was the first Wisp, and I joined my father in our secret mission until he passed on the mantle of the Crimson Wraith to me in 1954. I carried that name until my own retirement in 1971. Soon after, I found the man I would train to take it from me."

"That was Adam O'Neil," said Michael. "He was my Crimson Wraith. He was the Crimson Wraith who you met, Hank."

"What happened to him?" Hank asked.

Stephen said, "Sadly, Adam is no longer with us. He has passed away."

Anger flashed in Hank, "You mean someone killed him?"

"No, nothing like that," said Edward. "It was an accident, a terrible fall from a great height one night during an evening's patrol."

"Wait," said Jasmine. "That's it? He fell?"

"That's it," said Michael. "I was there. I was with him. One minute, he's right there on the rooftop with me and then next…"

Stephen explained, "Before he began as the Crimson Wraith, Adam received a severe head injury. It affected his hearing and sometimes gave him dizzy spells."

"My father suffered a similar injury," said Edward. "But it seems Adam's injury affected him more gravely. Those of us around him saw his dizzy spells worsening as the years passed, but Adam pushed on. He was a very driven man."

"I can't believe he just fell," said Jasmine, shaking her head.

"Why is that so shocking?" asked Edward.

"Well, because… I mean… He was the Crimson Wraith. Titan City's own number-one badass superhero supreme."

"We are not super," said Edward. "If we try, if we fight and if we fight in the right manner, we may be able to become heroes. But we are, each of us, only men, nothing more."

Eight years before, another fall, another accident, had changed Hank's life. And the man who caught him, the man who redeemed him, had died just that way too—a fall, an accident.

Hearing this, Hank felt something strange that he wouldn't ever be able to put into words. It was the recognition of a shared experience with someone else, that gut-level connection of being able to understand something very important to them because you've got something just like it very important to you, realizing that means they may understand you right back, in a way few people can.

"I'm sorry," he said to Michael.

But he didn't just mean it about the Crimson Wraith dying. It was about Carla too. And the fact was, for all the years since it happened, Hank had only ever said he didn't mean to kill her. He never said he was sorry. That was the very first time. It felt clean.

"Thanks," Michael said. "It's been almost two years now and it's still... It's hard." Then he shook it off, "But now, you're here! You're both here! And the Crimson Wraith fights again."

"Thank you," said Hank.

"And now," said Stephen, "it is time for the Crimson Wraith to eat again. Eddie, Michael, will you show our guests to the dining hall?"

It was a room and a table far beyond what the five of them required, able to seat five times as many, so they gathered all at one end of it with Edward at the head, a space for Stephen at his right and Michael sitting to the right of that. Hank sat to Edward's left and Jasmine to the left of him.

Along either side of the table hung two massive paintings, each dedicated to the history of Titan City. One offered a peaceful view of the Titan hillsides lush with greenery as they had not been in at least a century, the other showed a whaling ship depositing its bloody bounty on the Titan docks. Along the ship's side could be read the name *Perseverance*. In the wall behind Edward sat a huge fireplace, now dark and empty, and on the mantle above it, the marble bust of a somber, bearded man.

Hank must have been staring because Edward asked, "Curious about our silent dining companion?"

"Who is he?"

"That, technically speaking, is my Great-Great-Grandfather Archibald Finn, a man two whom I have no relation."

Jasmine asked, "You ain't got no relation to your great-great-granddaddy?"

"Blood relation, no. As I said, I am an orphan and the adopted son of another orphan, who was himself adopted by Josiah Finn, son of Cornelius Finn, son of Archibald Finn, whose image you see there. That ship," he pointed behind Hank, "the Perseverance was his, and it made his fortune so that he was able to purchase the land," he pointed at the painting across from Hank, "on which this home now stands."

"An orphan," said Hank. "And the son of an orphan."

"That's right," said Edward. "So, you can imagine I don't put much stock in bloodlines the way that some descendants of the old Titan families do. In my family, we pass along things more precious than blood. We pass along a code, a calling, a mission—things that seem now to have passed on to you." He looked meaningfully to Hank.

But before Hank could say anything, Stephen wheeled in a tray with their lunch. "I took the liberty," he said, "of being somewhat playful with the menu, taking my inspiration from a summer picnic." Upon the center of the table, he began placing dishes heaped with pieces of fried chicken, deviled eggs, corn on the cob, potato salad, and some sort of broccoli salad. "I thought we might eat it family style."

Edward nodded. "A wonderful job, Stephen. Thank you."

"You're welcome, Eddie." He squeezed Edward's shoulder affectionately as he went to take his seat, to which Jasmine gave a little smile. She tried to catch Hank's attention, but the gesture passed his notice.

"Thank you," Hank said to Stephen.

Jasmine said, "Yes, thank you. This really looks like something else. You got boxes for us to take home leftovers?"

Stephen smiled, "I would be quite flattered if you did."

For whatever differences there may have been in the lifestyles of the five of them, they found plenty of common ground in their love for the city in which they lived and protected. Each had similarities in their origins, never expecting to find themselves part of the Crimson Wraith's legacy.

Edward had many tales of past adventures to offer, occasionally prompted by Stephen and occasionally corrected by Michael. Jasmine had a whole slew of questions about the reality behind the mythology of the Crimson Wraith. After all, when she and Hank were growing up in the sixties, the Crimson Wraith and Wily Wisp appeared on lunch boxes, in the toy aisle, and on television.

What she didn't ask about was why the Crimson Wraith disappeared suddenly. She knew there was a book that made some kind of scandalous claims about the Crimson Wraith, and suddenly you didn't see his face everywhere anymore. But Jasmine was entering her teen years then and was kind of over the Crimson Wraith, so she never caught exactly what the fuss was about. Years later, rumors started going around that the Crimson Wraith had returned, not making the smiling public appearances he used to, but working the shadows, fighting street crime instead of costume villains. She realized now those had to be two different Crimson Wraiths, the first one Edward, the second one this Adam person he had talked about.

But Edward did not want to do all the talking. He found plenty of occasions to turn the conversation to Hank and Jasmine and their adventures behind the mask. While Hank's laconic replies did little to further the exchange, Jasmine knew how to spin a yarn, and she kept their hosts entertained.

Michael eventually asked, "So, how long were you working up Queen Cleopatra's chain of command before you got to her headquarters? And on a night you knew she would be there?"

Jasmine looked at Hank. "When was it I told you Mandy came asking about us? That was the Tuesday before, right?"

"Six days?" said Michael. "You got to her in six days?"

"Yeah, I guess that's about what it was."

"Wow! I spent six weeks tracking drug shipments back to that club!"

"Well, we knew we had to act right away when poor Tamara went missing. That girl did not have long to wait."

"But still, that's some impressive detective work there."

"Detective work?" said Jasmine, "Hell, I don't know anything about all that. We just talked to people. And, people, they wanted to talk. They was scared of Queen Cleopatra.

Everyone wanted her gone, just gone."

Michael frowned. "Guess I didn't find people quite as chatty."

"No offense or nothing, 'cuz I know you from the street like us and all, but it's been a little while since you been walking East Town, know what I mean?"

"Yeah, suppose you're right," said Michael. "Something to be said for being street level."

"You know," said Edward, "her mother was an adversary of mine. She went by the name Queen Cleopatra as well. Although it was a different time, a little more innocent perhaps. She also ran girls, but although they flaunted their sexuality, they did so as part of social protests, covering their naked bodies in wet paint and then assaulting city officials who opposed equal rights for women. I remember we had our final showdown in a disco. She surrendered to me after I defeated her in a dance competition. I must admit that I cheated—I made *her* my dance partner."

"Swept her right off her feet, did you, Grandpa?" said Michael.

Stephen smirked. "You rascal."

"Ain't that a bitch," said Jasmine, and she smacked Hank's shoulder. "Now why the hell can't we be Crimson Wraith and Wily Wisp for a dance competition instead of somebody coming at me with a damn live cobra?"

Then Edward said, "Henry, I wish to come to my point in having Michael bring you here. The work you are doing, you are doing in my name, and as such, it represents a lineage of secret protectors who have fought for Titan City and its citizens going back generations."

Hank tensed. Any time someone used his unabbreviated name, it troubled him. That was the name on his drivers license and birth certificate, the one the judge used for him and the one by which he was incarcerated. It wasn't a name that friends or people who wanted to be friends would use.

"That being the case," Edward continued, "I feel as though I have a right to a certain amount of interest in your campaign against crime and its success. Therefore, I would like to ask what we can do for you?"

Hank wasn't expecting that. "What?"

"To support you, both of you. How can we help?"

A glance at Jasmine showed surprise and apparent excitement, but Hank wasn't sure what to do with that. "I think we're okay. Thanks."

"Now, young man, I don't want you to simply be polite. My offer is sincere. Whatever way we can make it easier for you to do what you do, it would be my pleasure."

"Okay. Yeah, I think we're all right."

Michael said, "He's serious, Hank. Money, legal assistance, doctor bills—whatever we can give you, we'd be more than happy."

"Thanks," said Hank. "I just can't think of anything."

Jasmine elbowed him, but he couldn't figure out what she was trying to say.

Here Stephen added, "Well, should something come to mind, you will let us know, I hope? I'll make sure to get you a card with the private number here—the *very* private number."

The rest of the meal continued pleasantly, although the drive back to the 6th Avenue Metro station was a quiet one. When Michael dropped them off, he said, "See you around, maybe? Figure we might end up crossing paths again somewhere."

"Maybe," said Hank.

Michael extended a card with a phone number—no name, no title, just the number. On the back had been written the words, *Where we met*. "That's the 'very private' line. Whoever answers will ask where we met, and you'll say…"

Hank blanked, but Jasmine answered for him, "The Golden Sphinx. I'll hold onto that, thank you. And you *will* be hearing from me. A girl's got rent to pay."

Michael nodded. "Absolutely. The offer still stands. Whatever you need."

As soon as he drove away, the Zephyr once more zooming up into the hillside paths with the other Zephyr at the wheel, Jasmine turned to Hank and smacked him on the shoulder. "What the hell, Hank? Ain't you got no sense at all?"

"Don't hit me," he said.

"They were offering us money—*money*, fool! I don't even know how much, but you saw how those boys live up there? Family going back as old as the goddamn city itself, and saying they want to give you whatever you want—*whatever you want*. Did you get dropped on your damn head?"

But there was too much sadness in the eyes Hank turned toward her for Jasmine to continue her tirade. "They can't give me what I want," he said.

And since there was no other argument to be made, Jasmine just clenched her fists and shouted at the sky in frustration.

"I'm sorry," he said for the second time that day.

Jasmine held up her finger, recovering from the frustration. "No, no, you know what? It's okay. You and your sorry self can have it your way. This girl," she held up the business card. "This girl is getting paid. And next time you need stitches, you better believe I am pulling out this card and reaching out to touch somebody instead of getting my fingers all up in your bloody insides."

"Okay."

"Okay," she said. And then, "You really don't want anything? Not one thing money can buy?"

"This isn't a job," said Hank. "I've got a job. It pays me money. I've got a roof and food and I can usually buy new shoes when I wear the old ones out. But doing what we do at night, that's something else. It's about making things right. Trying to. Because… Because I made a promise."

It didn't look like Hank was going to cry when he said that, and that felt wrong to Jasmine. So, she teared up for him. "You are an idiot. You know that?" And she kissed him on the cheek. "A big, dumb, beautiful idiot."

2019

It was well after midnight—well after the time you "meet a man" who goes by the name of Crimson Wraith—when Gracie got back to the 6th Avenue Metro station. Her body felt warm and worn from the dancing. A few new friend requests buzzed on her phone, people who benefitted from her celebratory mood by receiving her number. The catcalls she'd gotten on her way from Terpsichoria just rolled off her, every single one, because she just watched the biggest asshole she knew beg for his life from the top of the Snyder-Finn building. If that happened to him, it could just as easily happen to anyone else who messed with her, and they didn't even know.

When Stephen held open the door of the Mercedes to her, she bowed to him. "Home, Jeeves."

"Very good, Miss Chapel," he replied with a sporting smirk. "Your day concluded in a pleasing manner, I take it?"

"You could say that, my guy. You definitely could."

They made their way back to Finn Manor, where everyone appeared to be asleep, and soon Gracie was too. The next morning, she woke late, and when she checked her phone, she saw a message on Tombstone. *Last night a success. Should meet one more time. Like before. Same time. Same place.*

That sounded just fine to Gracie. She wasn't sure how things would proceed from here, but then, this was her first experience having a masked vigilante save the day for her, so maybe he had some insight on that. She was curious when she would hear something from Hancock about Zack and was glad to have a half-day at Sprang & Sons to pass the time. When she got back to Finn Manor that night, she found Kevin and Danny in the parlor, side-by-side on a couch facing a flat-screen TV that she had never seen before. Seemed like it must slide in and out of the cabinet below it. Why had Kevin been watching his show on a tablet when he had that available? They had video game controllers in hand and appeared to be playing some kind of cartoon race where Danny had the advantage.

"See? I told you!" he shouted, "Captain Monkey ain't shit on the water level."

Kevin pouted, "But I love Captain Monkey. I grew up with Captain Monkey."

"Well, the past is past, and that's why I beat your ass."

Then Kevin noticed Gracie watching them. "You see what I have to put up with? Want to take the next round? Save me from my misery?"

She held up a hand, "Gonna pass tonight, boys. Got a bit of homework."

"Understood," said Kevin, "There's some dinner leftover on the kitchen counter. Stephen made teriyaki chicken with snow peas."

"It's real good," said Danny.

"Thanks," said Gracie. She felt herself smiling at the two of them, experiencing a warmth that surprised her.

Sometimes there was a glimmer of this feeling back at the flophouse, times when she really did like all her roommates and didn't have the sense that anyone had plans to screw her over, at least not for the night. It never lasted. But these guys, Kevin and Danny and Stephen, kept not taking advantage of her, and Gracie did not know what to do with that. Was this how family was supposed to feel?

They weren't wrong about dinner. It was delicious. Gracie put in some work for her college classes and then scrolled mindlessly through the Internet, killing time until midnight. At 11:50 PM, she figured she had waited long enough.

On her way out, she passed Kevin again, not in the parlor this time but the study, his face toward a laptop screen that, no doubt, displayed all sorts of financial figures in charts and graphs, translated into foreign currencies, the sort of money stuff Gracie felt sure she'd never understand and never need to. He didn't look up when she passed, and she didn't want to bother him. Instead, she went out back, out into the night, out into the garden, and down the pathway to the Finn mausoleum.

When she had roamed around the headstones for a few minutes without an ominous fog surrounding her, Gracie sat on a stone bench and opened her phone to see if Tombstone had another message for her. It didn't.

For a moment, she wondered if the Crimson Wraith would stand her up. Really, that wouldn't be a bad thing, would it? He was a busy guy, she figured. He did a nice thing for her, several nice things, but she didn't expect to get any kind of special consideration. Anyway, she had been hoping for the chance to just say "thanks" to his face—or his mask—and then she'd be on about her life. Have to see what kind of deal Hancock could get. Then find a new place to stay. Hopefully, that wouldn't take long.

And then Gracie noticed the fog curling around her ankles. "Really?" she said. "Do we still need the theatrics?"

He answered in his ethereal, echoing voice, "The Infernal Mist can be a gentler way to announce my arrival than just stepping from the shadows. I didn't want to startle you since you beat me here."

"Infernal Mist?"

"That's what some have called it."

"Yeah, well," she said, grinning, not knowing why seeing his mask made her feel as happy as it did. "You are late. I am on time. So, you got a lot to answer for there, mister."

"My apologies," he said.

A strange joy bubbled inside her to have this superhero seemingly under her thumb for a moment. "Yeah, well, don't let it happen again, or else."

"Of course," he said. "I think last night went well. Zack moved out of Kristen's apartment today."

"Get the fuck out."

"Yes, that's exactly what he did. And he placed a call to the District Attorney asking to meet as soon as possible, so it looks like that conversation is going to happen."

"Really?"

"Really."

"Holy shit."

The Crimson Wraith nodded. "I am hopeful you will hear good news from Bradley soon."

"Holy shit," Gracie said again. "So, I guess that's that, huh?"

"Well, a few things still have to unfold, but it does appear like we are getting the outcome we were after." It felt nice to hear him say "we."

"Thank you," she said. "I mean it. At first, I thought you were an asshole but... I was wrong. You really are a good guy. And having that, being on the receiving end of that... It's... It's nice. It's really... It's really nice."

"You're welcome."

Gracie brushed a lock of hair behind her ear and dug her hands into her jacket pocket. "Um, well, I guess... I'll be seeing you around... Or maybe I won't see you... Maybe it would be better if I don't... I mean, not that I don't want to see you, just that seeing you probably would mean shit got fucked up again and... Yeah... Wouldn't mind doing without that..."

"I understand," he said.

The Crimson Wraith stayed standing there, and Gracie realized it was probably up to her to head back inside, to leave him there to fade away back into the dark, back into the mausoleum, since he was a ghost and all, and that was where dead things made their home. "Guess you can't make a mysterious exit if I'm here looking right at you."

"It does make that more challenging."

"You'd have to, like, point behind me and say, 'Hey, what's that?' And I'd turn and see nothing. Then, when I looked back, you would be gone."

His mask hid any expression, but his shoulders showed a chuckle. "Something like that."

"Yeah... Okay... So, I'm gonna turn around now... And I'm gonna head back in and go inside, get back on with my life and stuff."

The Crimson Wraith nodded.

"Cool... Cool..."

Gracie didn't want to turn around. She didn't know why, but something inside her screamed not to let him disappear, not to let him leave her.

She said, "Not like my life is going to be, like, normal, when I get back to it. Because how do you go back to normal after this?"

"Many feel it demands a shift in perspective."

"'A shift in perspective...' Yeah, I guess you could say that." Then a thought struck her. "How do I pay you back?"

"You don't."

"That's not... That doesn't feel right."

"Why?"

"Because all this, you and Kevin and Stephen and Bradley, this is not... It's not nothing. It's money. It's time. Those are valuable things. What do I do with that?"

"You could do whatever you like with it."

Gracie chewed her bottom lip. "But I can't just do nothing. I'm not like that. I'm not that kind of person."

She remembered then what Stephen had said on the night she arrived at Finn Manor, about the grace of receiving unexpected, unasked-for generosity, of the call to service that he had felt in response, the same as Kevin and Danny apparently felt as well. She looked up at The Crimson Wraith.

"And you aren't that kind of person either. Or you weren't. Because no way are you like a hundred years-old. So, there was some other Crimson Wraith and he helped you and now... and now you're him."

"You think so?"

"Stephen said to me that after The Crimson Wraith helped him, he felt like it was his duty to help other people in the same way."

"And he helps a lot."

"Right. But, you—whoever you are—you got helped and... Now you're the one wearing the mask. The Crimson Wraith.

The Scarlet Stranger. Defending the defenseless."

"I am."

"You are. And, wow, that's... That's a lot..." Still, she didn't move, didn't leave. Something was happening, a thought forming in her mind.

The Crimson Wraith said, "There's a question you haven't asked me, yet."

"What?"

"It's a detail that may have escaped your consideration, but it's important. You may think you have all the information, but if you don't ask the right questions then you can't get the right answers."

"What makes you think I'm going to ask you this one particular question?"

"Because you are putting things together, and you are smart. If you don't come up with the question now, I'm sure that you will later, when you've had time to think more, but I'd rather you go ahead and ask now, before we part ways."

"Okay, so how about a hint? What's this question I'm supposed to ask?"

"The question is why didn't I stop Zack from hurting your roommate myself before you ever got there. Why did I arrive only after you took your revenge on him and beat him to unconsciousness?"

"And not before?"

"And not before," he said. "Think about it."

"Okay, this is real rude because you just said I should ask you a question and then you don't want to answer the question I was supposed to ask you."

"I said you had to ask. I did not say *who* you had to ask. Try asking yourself."

"Why?"

"Because I've just told you there is a clue to find. And now you know that, I want to see if you can find it."

"Right. Okay. Sure, why not?" Gracie thought about that night. "You stepped in when you did because you had to have seen the fight. But it wasn't like someone had called the cops on us or anything. People don't dial 911 in that neighborhood. So, you had to be watching. Maybe you were on some kind of patrol? That would make sense. Our neighborhood wasn't all that great. You saw the disturbance and swept in."

"And then what happened?"

"You told me to stop. I mean, really, you kind of just asked me. Like, you reasoned with me, the way you are supposed to with someone about to jump off a ledge. You didn't attack me, didn't put me in a chokehold or whatever. It was like you knew..." She paused. "You knew I was in the right."

"Go on," he said.

"And if you just showed up when you heard fighting, you wouldn't know that. You'd have to have been watching right from when the fight started."

"Just about."

"So, you could have heard the sounds of Jerry and Joe being all pissed-off in the front yard and then showed up right when I did, but I don't know if the odds are too good there. Kind of a small window of time, not all that likely."

"What would have been a more likely way for me to arrive when you did?"

"Well, if you were following me." This was where Gracie missed not being able to see The Crimson Wraith's eyes. "Wait, were you following me? What the hell?"

"Look at your phone," he said.

"Why?"

"Just look at it."

"Promise you'll still be standing there when I look up? Because it would be a real dick move if you weren't."

"I promise. Please."

Looking down, Gracie saw a notification from Tombstone. There was a new file available to view, a video. Its timestamp did not mean anything to Gracie until she opened the file and saw herself in the middle of the street, facing off against the Tight T-shirt Guy, who followed her from Terpsichoria.

"This was a usual night for me," said The Crimson Wraith coming closer to watch alongside her. "That warehouse district can often see altercations like this, so I tend to keep an eye on it. The roar of this man's engine caught my attention, and when I heard what he said to you, I drew closer, thinking that he may need a forceful hand to keep him from harming you. And he did, but not mine." He pointed to her screen. "This was very nicely done."

"Thanks," she said, feeling very confused and a little uncomfortable but also a little proud. It isn't every day you realize a superhero was stalking you nor hear him praise your fighting technique.

"After that, I wanted to see more of you, to find what else you might be capable of. That's why I appeared when I did, that night at the apartment. That's the answer to the question you didn't ask. And that answer should also tell you something else."

"You watched me fighting Zack, and you didn't step in earlier... because you knew I could take care of myself, just like with the guy who came at me after the club. You knew I didn't need the help."

"And you didn't. Not until the end. Not until you came close to taking it too far. That's where I wanted to step in."

"Thank you," said Gracie. Now that she seemed to be coming to the other side of her legal fears, imagining what might have happened if the Crimson Wraith hadn't stopped her was terrifying.

"You're welcome," he said. "I didn't want to see you making that mistake. I don't want to see anyone hurting their chances in life like that."

"But if you saw me fight off that guy," said Gracie, "And you didn't think I needed protecting, then there's another question to ask."

"And what was that?"

"Why did you want to see more of me?"

The Crimson Wraith nodded. Again, he pointed to the

video. "This woman right here, she is a fighter. But what I saw at the apartment was that, when you fight to defend herself, you are merely capable. When you fight for someone else, that is where your passion comes out, so much passion that it might be dangerous, nearly too much for you to handle. But if you wanted to learn to control it, if you wanted to train to use that passion to fight for the well-being of others, then I think you could do a whole lot of good."

"You mean like, defend the defenseless?"

"Just like that."

"Holy shit."

"I think there could be a place for you with me, Gracie, fighting at my side, and I would consider it an honor to train you to do this, to do what I do, if that is something you think you might like. I understand you might want some time to..."

But Gracie didn't need any time, "I'm in."

"Are you sure?"

"I'm in. I've never been more sure about anything ever."

"Really?"

"Really! Teach me! Be my sensei! Please! Please. If this is an option for me, if this is something I can do with my life..."

"Why?"

"You know why. You probably had this exact same conversation, didn't you? Like, with The Crimson Wraith before you?"

"Yes, I did. Exactly like this. Almost. And that's why you need to say your part of it."

"Okay." She thought for a minute. "I want to do this. I want to fight like you because there are people out there who can't fight for themselves, for whatever reason, and because they need someone in their corner to do the fighting for them. I know this because now you've fought for me and, I got to tell you, it... it makes me want to be a better person. So, maybe if other people can receive this and I can be a part of that, then maybe they will also want to be better people. And maybe if everyone wants to be better, then maybe eventually the whole world just sucks that little bit less, and—God, damn it—that would be great."

He didn't say anything in response right away, so she added. "Please."

Then The Crimson Wraith reached up into his hood, detached his mask and slipped it off, showing her the face of Kevin Snyder, the man who had taken her into his home, who invited her to have microwaved popcorn and play video games with him, and who she first met when he showed up at her work asking for a book about—who else?—The Crimson Wraith.

"That was perfect," he said, smiling.

Gracie shook her head. "Son-of-a-bitch," she said, smiling back.

PART THREE

J. GRIFFIN HUGHES

CHAPTER EIGHT

1948

When boys at school challenged each other with, "My dad could beat up your dad," Eddie knew he had a one-up over all of them, but it wasn't anything he could say out loud. No one else could know that his father, William Finn, was none other than the Crimson Wraith, a secret known only to himself, their mechanic Chubby Chumley, and their housekeeper Miss Glenda.

His dad was an actual superhero. And other boys could read their comic books of *Captain Marvel*, *Dick Tracy*, or *Blackhawk*. None of those were real, not like the Crimson Wraith. He was real. He saved Eddie from the Blue Banshee and tucked Eddie into bed each night before going out to fight crime.

"Who are you fighting tonight, Father?" Eddie often asked.

Usually, Will would not say much. Sometimes he would just be going out to make sure Titan City was safe, keeping watch over the streets to thwart the regular kinds of criminals—robbers and burglars and thugs. But now and then, Will might share a special, strange, and scary story about someone like the Shadowmaster, overlord of the Little Tokyo underworld, or Mr. Echo, who liked to make a game of his crimes by announcing them ahead of time over the radio in vague and coded messages.

Sometimes his father would allow Eddie to join him in the Crypt, the secret underground lair of the Crimson Wraith. It reminded Eddie of the sort of cave where pirates might hide their treasure, and when he told his father that, William smiled and said, "That is actually very close to why your great-great-grandfather built it."

At an ornate wooden desk sat a heavy leather-bound ledger, where his father kept written accounts of all his adventures. The costume of the Crimson Wraith stood in one corner, and the shelves beside it held his various tools and weapons, all crafted by Chubby at the workbench that sat nearby. There was even a small laboratory, just off the main room, for performing chemical analysis on evidence from crime scenes and a darkroom for developing photographs.

When Eddie would emerge from the Crypt with his father, Miss Glenda would tut and say something like, "Now, Mister Finn, surely Master Eddie is too young to know about such things."

But his father would brush her concerns aside. "A son should know his father's business. It may just be his someday."

And that idea, that hint of a future where Eddie too would go out in the dark to defend the defenseless, made his little heart soar. Whenever his imagination took flight, it conjured up images of himself at his father's side. He drew pictures in crayon of the two of them together, his father in his skull mask and red cloak, himself in more conventional comic book hero attire, a yellow tunic and tights with a purple cloak and a domino mask over his eyes, the kind of mask worn by the Lone Ranger or Zorro.

"I'm the Wily Wisp," he told his father.

"The Wily Wisp?"

"Yeah, like in this." Eddie pulled out a picture book of ghost stories and folklore. "It's about a man. When he died, he was too wicked to go to Heaven but too nice to go to Hell. His name was Will."

"Just like me."

"Just like you!"

"And what happened to him?"

"Well, he got trapped in between. And he became a ghost

who walks the world with a lantern to light his way. If you are good, his lantern will lead you from the dark and into safety."

"And if you are not good?"

Eddie shook his little head with that gravity that children sometimes have when declaring just how the world is and must always be.

"I see. And as the Wisp, you'd be like this too? Good to the good and bad to the bad?"

"I would! And while you move through the shadows, I would wave around a light to distract the bad guys until you got up close to sock 'em!"

His father smiled, "Very smart. That sounds like a very good plan indeed."

Sometimes Eddie drew the Crimson Wraith and the Wily Wisp fighting real criminals like the Shadowmaster, and he would ask his father for details about them so that he could get their looks just right. Sometimes they would be saving another little boy like he had been saved from the Blue Banshee.

When Eddie asked how soon he could go out fighting crime, his father would turn the conversation to training. Every day, they spent some period of time in exercise—running the grounds, swimming laps, or lifting weights. They would practice each of the several hand-to-hand fighting styles his father had mastered, often throwing each other laughing to the mats laid out on the floor of the Finn Manor gymnasium. Eddie knew he needed to be strong to fight crime.

"But your greatest strength," his father asked over and over again, "is what?"

"My mind," answered Eddie.

"Correct."

And so, to train his mind, Eddie read. He liked adventure stories best and pored through tales like *Robin Hood* and *Ivanhoe* to learn what it meant to be a hero and practice virtuous ideals. From the cases of Sherlock Holmes and the novels of Agatha Christie—whose newest mystery he always got on the day of its release—Eddie began to learn deductive reasoning, how to observe and theorize.

And those fictional detectives showed him there was no limit to all the other things he needed to know—chemistry, physics, geography, zoology, botany, languages, and foreign cultures. Sometimes after their work-outs, Eddie recovered by spending hours in the library, working his way through the encyclopedia. At times it seemed too much for any one person to know, and Eddie despaired over ever being allowed to don his own mask and hood to fight crime alongside his father.

However, when it came time for him to enter Ellsworth Academy, Eddie found himself well-prepared to undertake the scholastic challenges there. But what surprised him was how much he enjoyed being away from home, on his own instead of at his father's side. It felt exciting to be living, night and day, in the company of his peers, now grown up to something just beyond schoolyard games, playing instead at beginning to be men, independent and capable and daring.

On the school wrestling team, Eddie found his physical prowess prized and admired, but although he enjoyed winning medals for his school at competitions, what Eddie loved most about the wrestling team was all the locker room laughter before and after.

He discovered, as well, an interest in poetry, something that had no relation to the crime-fighting future for which he longed. He took note when his English instructor commented that poetry has a way of expressing those quiet longings a man keeps secret, sometimes even from himself. That resonated with Eddie. After all, the son of the Crimson Wraith had many secrets to keep.

He felt things stir within him as he read the works of John Donne, Lord Byron, and Percy Shelly, but when he discovered Walt Whitman, it was as if Eddie read his own heart poured out on the page. So many times after that, as he stepped toward the wrestling mat, he would hear in his head the words, "I sing the body electric…" and feel that electricity shiver through his limbs. Smiling as he would take or be taken by his opponent in a lock, Whitman's words continued:

The armies of those I love engirth me and I engirth them,
They will not let me off till I go with them, respond to them,
And discorrupt them, and charge them full with the charge
of the soul.

That was what he imagined him and his opponent doing to each other on the mat, charging each other fully with the charge of the soul. There was a joy to it, the same joy he imagined himself having as the crime-fighting Wily Wisp, grinning at every villainous mug whose swings he would dance around until finally landing his own.

Then came Eddie's high school graduation. At age sixteen, he had finished his education, and there was to be a big to-do for all the recent graduates of both Ellsworth Academy and the Fletcher School for Girls. It was held off-campus at the Dionysian, only the swankiest hotel in Titan City, the very one where movie stars and foreign dignitaries stayed when they came to visit. All of the young elite would be there, each celebrating not only freedom from the drudgery of academia but, in most cases, coming into their own private wealth now they were of age.

This was the case for Eddie as well. He would now have access to Finn Industry stock and the bank accounts where his dividends had been accumulating for the past eight years. None of these really mattered to him, though. The only inheritance Eddie cared about was the mask and hood that still eluded him.

For some, their families dictated that they would not come into their wealth until the day of their marriage. This particularly held true among the Fletcher girls, and the anticipation of potential engagements seemed to add extra intensity to that dance. How soon would there be wedding bells ringing and for whom? That question appeared again and again in the eyes of boys looking at girls and girls looking at boys.

What a great relief Eddie felt that his own inheritance held no such requirements. None of the girls said very much to interest him, and he couldn't imagine himself willing to be ensnared by one in matrimonial bonds. Marriage did not fit into Eddie's fantasies of his future.

So, he sat out one song after another that night, declining more than a few invitations from young women who pointed out the available spaces on their dance cards. But it was an enjoyable evening apart from that. His friends all looked so fine in their suits, each one of them a young Cary Grant or Gregory Peck, and he had many a good laugh with them between their dances.

Sometime after midnight, when their party began to calm somewhat and maybe half of the young men and women had departed for home or to some cozy corner for canoodling, Eddie noticed the glasses of the comrades at his table to be in need of refilling and all the bottles around them emptied. It seemed the wait staff had fallen off their game somehow. So, Eddie assured those around him, "Never fear, chaps. I shall remedy this grave circumstance forthwith," and he rose to find the hotel kitchen to procure another bottle or six and keep the party going.

The door through which he had previously noticed the staff emerge and disappear led to an unadorned hallway. Eddie wandered down that hall, passing a cart of cleaning supplies and towels and another of linens, until he came to a swinging door with a sign above that read, *Kitchen*. As he pushed it open, he called out quite cordially, "Excuse me, but our table has run a bit dry..."

And then he saw three of the waiters, all wearing dime store costume party goat masks and carrying in their hands —not bottles, not spatulas, and not even cooking knives—but guns. They held these pointed toward some of Eddie's classmates who stood in a small cluster. Each of the young men had been bound with butcher's twine and wore a pillowcase over his head.

The waiters all looked to Eddie, then to each other, and then back at Eddie, turning their guns his way. Eddie put up his hands. One of them waved him closer. Another lowered his gun to pick up the roll of butcher's twine. And Eddie stepped forward, consenting quietly to be bound, fighting with all his might against the grin that wanted to cover his face as he once more heard Whitman's words in his mind.

None of the goat waiters spoke until they had Eddie gagged, hooded, and bound. And when they did start speaking, it did not seem like they would ever stop. He had no sense of which voice belonged to whom, but since they all wore the same mask, it didn't really matter.

The first voice had a high-pitched whine, childlike almost. "I told you we oughta block the door."

The second voice gruff and like he was speaking out of the side of his mouth. "And raise suspicions? Don't be ridiculous."

The third voice came pinched and nasal. "Yeah, besides, now we got another millionaire brat to ransom off to his rich folks. We're gonna be *rolling* in it!"

"Well, I don't like it," said the first. "What if this fancypants here told his friends he'd be right back?"

"Good thing no one cares what you like," said the second. "I'm the brains around here, so you do what I tell you."

"You think you're the only one with brains around here?"

"If you got a problem with how I'm running this job, you see the door right there," said the second, "Only you won't be going through it on your feet."

The third voice chimed in. "Yeah, take one step, and you'll be leaving a few quarts lighter."

"All right! All right!" the first voice protested. "You don't have to get so rough! I was just saying—"

The third voice cut him off, "How about you stop saying?"

The second voice asked. "You got the ransom note?"

"Sure do," the third voice answered and he read aloud. "If ever you want to see your sons alive, bring a hundred thousand for each to Pier 38 at midnight tomorrow night. No funny business. Signed, the Three Billy Goats Gang."

"That'll put the fear into 'em," chirped the first voice, who Eddie figured had to be the Baby Goat.

"Darn right," said the nasal third voice, apparently the Middle Goat.

"You brats better hope your folks pay up," the Biggest Goat growled to the kidnappees, "Or you might find yourselves at the bottom of the Robinson Street Bridge." Then he laughed. "And don't you know there's trolls down there?"

There came the sound of wheels. Eddie remembered seeing a couple of laundry carts that seemed out of place in the kitchen. It must have been them.

The Baby Goat said, "Time for you filthy rich kids to come clean," and he snickered. Then Eddie heard one muffled grunt after another until he felt himself being shoved into the laundry cart on top of a pile of other boys.

He felt his feet, which had stuck out of the laundry cart, being shoved back in and heard the Middle Goat say, "Better keep yourself tucked in if you know what's good for ya." There were blankets thrown over them all and they were pushed out of the kitchen, down a hallway.

After a minute, he heard the Biggest Goat whisper, "Masks off boys. Looks like we've got company. Not one peep out of any of you rich brats or we toss the whole lot of you in the Brennert like a sack of kittens."

"Aw, that's sad," said the Baby Goat. "Little baby kittens being tossed in the river."

The Middle Goat snapped, "Someone should have tossed you in the river."

"Why I oughta..."

The Biggest Goat cut them off. "Can it, you two." Then he suddenly spoke with an affectation of deference and refinement to someone else who they must have approached in the hallway. "Good evening to you, sir. And a pleasant one it is, I hope?"

There came a reply from one of the stuffy voices like the *maitre d'* types who brought Eddie's father the restaurant's finest bottle for their meal. "What on earth are you doing with that cart here? The laundry is that way!"

"Oh, begging your pardon. I do apologize for having gotten ourselves lost. We're new, you see."

"That's no excuse! Turn that thing around this instant."

"It would be my greatest joy. Only there is just one problem."

"And what is that?"

A thud. A grunt. The sound of a body falling to the floor.

The Biggest Goat said, "I don't quite care for your tone of voice."

"Enjoy your nap, you sap," said the Middle Goat.

The Baby Goat chuckled. "A sap nap! Because you sapped him!"

"Come on. Let's get going," said the Biggest Goat, "He should wake up just in time to bring our ransom note to the police. Then everyone will know the Three Billy Goats Gang ain't nothin' to laugh at."

2019

Should Gracie have known it was Kevin's face under the mask of the Crimson Wraith? She didn't, but, when she saw it, she was not at all surprised. "That day at Sprang & Sons, you were there checking up on me."

"Yes, I was," said Kevin.

He led her around the back of the Finn Mausoleum, where two angelic heralds in brass stood on stone pedestals, their trumpets pointed heavenward.

"And you weren't looking for a book on the Crimson Wraith for yourself. That was for me. You wanted to point me toward it and see how I reacted."

"I did." Kevin took hold of one of the angels and turned it

slowly to face its partner. The statuette moved with surprising ease.

"But how did you know we had that book in stock?"

"You didn't. That's one of my copies. Brought it there right in my coat pocket. You can keep it though."

"Good because I haven't nearly finished it."

"There's a lot you should know about in there."

When he released it, the angel began slowly turning back toward its original position. As it did, a stone section of the mausoleum wall opened inward.

Still smiling, Gracie looked from the secret door to Kevin and back. "Son-of-a-bitch," she said again.

He led her inside and pushed the stone panel into place once more. For a moment, darkness enveloped them. Then small electric lights set into the walls gradually illuminated the stone with their amber glow. In front of Gracie, instead of the sarcophagus one might expect, she saw the gated entrance of a lift system. Kevin opened the gate and beckoned her with a gesture. When they were both on board, he tapped its one control button. The small platform began lowering.

Unable to keep from grinning, Gracie said. "So, there's a secret passage leading from here up into the manor house?"

"There is," said Kevin.

"And that's how you got from your office back here, popping up out of the mausoleum?"

He nodded. "There are a few hidden passages in Finn Manor. When Archibald Finn created his family's fortune with his fleet of merchant ships, he added to his whaling wealth with just a tiny bit of smuggling."

"Oh, Archie," said Gracie. "Such a bad, bad boy."

Kevin continued, "He built his home around a network of secret doorways and tunnels, all leading to an underground lair that he used to keep his illicit dealings safe. Others of the Finn family used them for similar purposes afterward."

"And now you use those passageways as the Crimson Wraith."

"I do."

"So, after I saw you in your office, you pressed a secret button behind a picture frame and slid down a pole, jumped into your costume, and met me back here?"

"Something like that."

"You were late tonight though. Did something hold you up? Seemed like you got here from the mansion a lot faster for our first mausoleum chat."

Danny called up to them from the landing below. "That's because it wasn't him in the suit. It was me." He smiled up at their lift as it lowered toward him.

Gracie's grin widened. "Son-of-a-bitch!"

Danny smiled too. "Sure, is a lot to take in, huh?"

"A hell of a lot."

"Yeah, well, the tour is just getting started." He followed as they continued along the underground passage.

Kevin explained, "During my encounter with Zack, you saw that the Crimson Wraith's mask has cameras that allowed you to see what I saw when I wore it. The mask also has a microphone with speech-recognition technology that allowed you to read what was said. And you have heard how the embedded speakers alter my voice to give it the Crimson Wraith's ghostly echo."

"Yeah?"

"Well, I don't have to be actually wearing the suit at the time for all that to function. So, when you first met with the Crimson Wraith at the mausoleum, I was still in the mansion, seeing you through that camera, reading your words on a screen and speaking into a microphone that projected my voice to you from the suit Danny wore."

"All while you stayed comfy on the couch where I saw you minutes before?"

"You got it."

"Nice set-up," said Gracie. "Very slick."

"Thank you," said Danny. "I'm proud of that one."

"*You're* proud of that one?" said Grace.

"As my mechanic, Danny does more than just keep the cars running. Really, he was responsible for bringing all the Crimson Wraith technology into the twenty-first century."

"Very nice," she said to Danny. "So, exactly, how long have you been on with the Scarlet Stranger here?"

"Just over ten years."

"What? You can't be much older than me! You had to be just a kid when you started."

"Smartest kid in his grade," said Kevin. "Probably the smartest kid in Titan City, smart enough to catch the Crimson Wraith."

"You what?" said Gracie.

Danny said, "My folks needed help, and I didn't figure anyone but the Crimson Wraith could give it to them."

"I tend to notice when someone comes looking for me," said Kevin. "In Danny's case, it seemed like the right thing to let myself be found. And he's been a huge help to me ever since."

They arrived at a heavy metal door with no apparent handle. Kevin approached the security panel to its right, removed his glove and placed his right hand on the screen as he leaned into the retinal scanner and spoke words in Latin, "*In Pace Requiescat.*"

Gracie recognized the phrase. She heard it while at Sprang & Sons. Howard, their regular customer with the sticker system for the books he read, had told her about it as he, without her asking, explained in elaborate detail *The Cask of Amontillado* by Edgar Allen Poe.

"At the end," said Howard, "when Montresor has finally walled-up Fortunado, he walks away to leave him there forever and ends by saying that Fortunado has not been disturbed for half a century. *In Pace Requiescat!* That means 'Rest in Peace...'"

Rest in Peace. Perfect for a man who calls himself a ghost.

Kevin turned to her and said. "Welcome to the Crypt." The door slid open to reveal the secret lair of the Crimson Wraith.

It was stone on all sides, the floor, the walls, the columns leading up to the curved ceiling above, a place where maybe prohibition-era wine casks had once hidden, leaving a vague sweetness to the cool air within. There was a medieval feel to it, except that electric lights now softly illuminated the stone where once candles or oil lamps must have burned.

Beside a skull-shaped archway that loomed over the stairs leading to the mansion above, a series of screens showed feeds from the various security cameras around Finn Manor. Below them, a multi-monitor computer array appeared to be running some program that looked like it might be recording several simultaneous audio inputs whose lines rippled across their screens.

Against one wall, an empty display case—which looked like it might have stored the Crimson Wraith's costume when he wasn't wearing it—stood amid an arsenal of smoke pellets, flash bombs, grappling irons, various pieces of surveillance equipment, a nest of flying drones that she would learn were called Haunts, and gas canisters that must have contained the ingredients of his Infernal Mist. There were worktables with tools nearby, ready to craft, maintain, and repair the equipment that aided his mission.

And in the center of it all, beaming at them, stood Stephen. "So glad you were able to join us Miss Chapel."

She grinned. "So, what you said before about being helped by the Crimson Wraith before and now providing service?"

"It is mostly in the kitchen, yes."

"Don't let him fool you," said Kevin. "Without Stephen, there probably wouldn't be a Crimson Wraith today."

Gracie asked, "Because, what, the Crimson Wraith can't cook for himself?"

Stephen shook his head solemnly. "It is not his greatest gift."

Once she had taken in all of it, the great shadowy sweep of the Crypt of the Crimson Wraith, Gracie turned to look at the three men standing there—Stephen with his wry little smirk,

Danny with his eyebrows raised, and Kevin.

Now she knew what it was in his eyes that she couldn't quite place at their first meeting. It was this. There were depths and doorways within them, some open, some closed, letting you see just enough to know you weren't quite seeing everything—if you were the sort of person who bothered to look, which Gracie was. Life had taught her that she needed to look and keep looking to find out any threat to her safety and survival.

But even at their first meeting, while she sensed the secrets unsaid, she never felt any malice in him. That kind of threat, a person carries in how they hold their spine—the readiness of a predator gazing upon prey, preparing to strike. No, there was an ease in Kevin as he watched, as he waited, as he let her come to him. He made sure this was something that she wanted. And it was.

Seeing the looks those three gave her, Gracie felt something warm bubbling up inside. After all her twenty-three years of feeling that she didn't belong anywhere, maybe she had found where she was really meant to be.

In the video of her fight with Tight T-Shirt Guy, Kevin showed her what he saw in her. In how he dealt with Zack, he showed her what he thought she could do with it, and that was something that felt so right. As someone who had survived for so long on not caring and not hoping, Gracie surprised herself with how strongly she felt the mission of the Crimson Wraith calling to her and how badly she wanted to answer it.

"All right," she said, "Where do we begin?"

1948

If Captain Hargreaves showed any sign of distress before the wealthy parents gathered in the TCPD conference room, it would have been understandable. He downed two fistfuls of antacid before their arrival, and still his ulcer flared in aggravation. For the beads of sweat on his brow, all he could do was dab at them with his handkerchief and mutter about what an unseasonably warm springtime they were having.

The families of the kidnapped boys from Ellsworth Academy all received officers at the doors of their respective estates immediately after the Hotel Dionysian notified police of the kidnapping. The last to arrive at the station, bachelor playboy William Finn, did so by 7 AM. Even though they had all been roused from their beds in the wee hours of the morning, they each had taken time to don their pearls and furs and the things that one does not leave their front door without. And so they surrounded Captain Hargreaves wearing a display of just how much influence each one held over Titan City and his own career.

"What I want to know," one of the fathers bellowed, "is what exactly is the Titan City Police force—which *my* tax dollars pay for—doing to ensure the safe return of my son!"

"All that we can," said Captain Hargreaves. "We have our best people on this. I personally promise you."

One of the mothers sobbed, "If even one hair on the head of my little Geoffrey is harmed, you can be sure that you will be out of a job! And that is my own personal promise to you!"

Through all the noise, William Finn wore a silent, concerned frown. While the otherwise rich and powerful faced the reality of their own powerlessness in this scenario, he had already begun to take action.

It was in cases like this that Chubby Chumley, William's oldest friend and dearest confidante, proved invaluable for more than just his mechanical skill and warm heart. His rustic demeanor and familiarity with the rough-and-tumble parts of town gave him an ability to discover things the wealth of the mighty would bar them from, things the police would struggle to uncover. He slipped easily into the places where the hint of high society or law enforcement would cause all of those inside to close off like a bed of frightened sea anemones.

At that very moment, Chubby was out there, among the

docks where his face was known. He would be starting up casual conversations with those who had been sweating away at their labors before the dawn, moving later into bars where purchasing a friendly beer could open doors. When it seemed appropriate to share his troubles, he would comment on how he was worried about his cousin who had gotten in a pinch with some guys he owed money to, say they called themselves something like "the Goat Gang," and then see if this sparked any recognition.

The meeting at the Titan City Police Station concluded with Captain Hargreaves asking all the parents to begin gathering the funds that the kidnappers requested "just in case." Once dismissed, Will went immediately to the City Planning Office to begin to look at properties around Pier 38, saying that he was considering making a purchase for a new Finn Industries facility. This allowed him to establish a list of locations that might be currently unowned, making them potential sites for the Three Billy Goats Gang to be using for their hide-out. He returned to Finn Manor with several possibilities and welcomed Chubby soon after.

"Gosh, it nearly took all day," said Chubby, "but I think I found something. Turns out there was a thug named Howard, Sam Howard, who got put away last year. He had been causing trouble with his two younger brothers and a childhood friend of theirs as the Barnyard Boys. It sounded like they might be connected, don't you think? Barnyard Boys? Billy Goats?"

Will nodded. "Howard... Howard..." He pulled out the documents he had copied from the planning office. "Here. This shop near Pier 38, Howard Brothers Fine Cigars, now closed for business. This could very well be the place. Gas up the van, my dearest friend. Tonight, the Crimson Wraith rises."

Like all the other concerned parents, Will delivered the cash requested by the kidnappers to the Titan City Police Department. Then he returned home to don his armored tunic, cavalier boots, leather gauntlets, scarlet cloak, and skull mask, readying his belt with an array of smoke pellets and flash grenades, along with grappling hook and rope, and set off into the night crouched in the shadowy rear of a plain white van, which might be used by any sort of common workman, while Chubby took the wheel.

"I sure do hope our Eddie isn't too frightened," said Chubby as they wound their way down through the Elysian Hills toward the city lights.

William said, "He may be frightened, but he is an incredibly capable young man. If they knew what was good for them, the Three Billy Goats Gang would do well to be frightened of *him*."

"And how!"

But Will couldn't help but worry for his son. No matter how many hours of training they put in over the years, there was a big difference between fighting in the gym versus fighting in the real world. And being outnumbered three-to-one made for dangerous odds. He did not want to trouble Chubby, though, so he kept his concern quiet and focused on readying himself for whatever would be needed of him.

They crossed through the city over toward East Town and all the piers and warehouses clustered there along the Brennert River, coming at last to the street where Howard Brothers Fine Cigars lay.

"Slow down a bit," said Will. "Let's just drive past and take a look."

Chubby did, and as they approached the building, passing the other shops before it, he commented, "Looks like one of the streetlights out front is struggling."

Will noticed the lamp flashing off and on, lit for a longer time, then shorter, and then another long and short again. "Morse Code!"

"Gosh! What's it say?"

"C... M... C... C... M... C... Oh, well done, Eddie! Well done!"

"What's that?"

"CMC. *The Count of Monte Cristo*, a novel about a hero wrongfully imprisoned. It's Eddie! He's letting us know he's okay!"

Sure enough, when the Crimson Wraith alighted on the rooftop of Howard Brothers Fine Cigars, he found his son there at the fuse box, sending out the code by flipping the switches.

At his father's arrival, Eddie stood and smiled, "Took you long enough."

The Crimson Wraith opened his arms. "Come here," he said.

Eddie ran over to embrace him. "You weren't worried were you?"

"I was. But don't tell Chubby. Have you already dispatched your captors then?"

"Oh, no. Didn't want to take your fun away, Father. I'm just keeping an eye on them." Eddie pointed to a skylight where the Three Billy Goats Gang, without their masks, could be seen arguing over cards. "Feel like dropping in?"

"Absolutely, but I won't be doing so alone." From within his cloak, the Crimson Wraith pulled forth a package and handed it to Eddie. "A graduation gift. I had meant to let you find it on your bed when you returned home from last night's party, but perhaps this is an even more appropriate circumstance."

"What is it?" said Eddie.

"Open it."

He did.

Children create a world of imagination with crayons, not knowing the difference between what is real and what is not. They grow older and come to distinguish between fact and fantasy, never expecting the line between one and the other to blur, much less be torn away.

And yet, there in his hands, Eddie held what he had first brought into existence on the page, a crime-fighting suit of his very own, tunic, tights, gloves, boots, cloak, and mask, all in purple and gold.

"Chubby made it," said the Crimson Wraith. "And now, I think the world should get to meet my son as the man I raised."

Meanwhile...

"Hey, you're cheating!" whined the Middle Goat.

"And don't you know," said the Biggest Goat, "that cheaters never prosper?"

The Baby Goat chuckled as he wrapped his hands around the peanuts at the center of the table and slid them toward the stack in front of him. "What can I say, fellas? Lady Luck must be in love with me. It's 'cause of my winning personality."

"You show me what you got up your sleeves!" said the Middle Goat.

"I ain't got nothin'! I swear!" said the Baby Goat.

"Oh, you'll swear all right," the Biggest Goat growled. "Get 'im!" The two other goats rose from their chairs to come at the Baby Goat from either side.

"Hey, wait a minute, fellas! It's just a friendly game! No reason to get sore about it!"

"We'll show you sore," said the Middle Goat, taking hold of one arm as the Biggest Goat grabbed the other. Both forced his sleeves upward and showers of playing cards poured from his jacket, a whole deck of them, spilling to the ground and scattering at the Baby Goat's feet.

The Baby Goat looked first to the Middle and then the Biggest, his expression a painful attempt at a smile. "You know, I think I've had enough of playing cards tonight. Anybody for a game of Parcheesi?"

Both the Biggest and Middle Goats raised their fists in preparation to pummel the Baby Goat when the skylight shattered above them. Not one, but two masked vigilantes dropped to the floor, cloaks whirling around them.

Terrified, all Three Billy Goats shouted in unison, "The Crimson Wraith!"

Then the Baby Goat added, "But who's the kid?"

"You can call me," said Eddie, "The Wily Wisp," and he

punctuated his greeting with a roundhouse kick.

<u>2019</u>

Danny called up images of multiple Crimson Wraiths on the computer screen, seven in total, several Wily Wisps as well, and another masked vigilante in a black jumpsuit who looked like neither. Changes in the quality of the photographs showed a progression through time going back before digital photography, then before color. And although each one of the seven Crimson Wraiths were recognizable as themselves, there were differences in the costumes of each.

"I have been the Crimson Wraith since 2005," said Kevin, "trained by Michael Conroy, the same man who trained the Crimson Wraith before me." He pointed to a Crimson Wraith who did not wear a cloak but a red trench coat with an attached hood. Instead of a skull, his white mask was blank, smooth and featureless. The rest of his clothes appeared military-inspired, with combat boots and straps across his chest and thighs holding multiple pouches. "This is Christopher O'Neil, the Crimson Wraith from 1997 to 2001."

"2001? So was he the Crimson Wraith who tried to stop the Zero Hour bombing?"

"Yes, that was him."

"Holy shit."

"You may recognize the Wily Wisp who fought alongside him." Kevin pointed to a young woman who looked more ready for a rave than crime-fighting. Blonde hair spilled from her purple hooded halter top, which bore a yellow "W," and she wore a purple domino mask. Baggy yellow pants clung to her hips.

"Nope," said Gracie. "Don't recognize her at all. Why would I?"

"Because she is now captain of the TCPD."

"Get the fuck out."

"It's true," said Kevin. "Before she wore a badge, Esperanza Villagraña wore a mask."

"Unbe-fucking-lievable." But looking more closely, Gracie could see it was true. That was definitely the woman who appeared at her apartment after her fight with Zack, at least twenty years younger.

"Before Christopher and Esperanza, our mentor, Michael Conroy, wore the hood." Kevin pointed to a Crimson Wraith whose costume seemed similar to his own, but while the leather gauntlets and cavalier boots retained the same red color, his tunic and leggings were black, his cloak black with red lining. "From 1989 to 1994 he was the Crimson Wraith." Then he indicated the man in a black jumpsuit, with a "Z" on its chest. "From 1981 to 1988, he was the Zephyr."

"The Zephyr?"

"Yes."

"You mean like the car?"

"Michael really liked that car," Kevin said with a smile. "Before becoming the Zephyr, he had served as the Wily Wisp under Christopher's father, Adam O'Neil. Adam died in an accident, and Michael didn't feel like he could take on the role of the Crimson Wraith right away. The one who did was a man named Hank Mills."

The figure Kevin pointed to did not look to Gracie so much like a superhero as a boxer in training, wearing a red-hooded sweatshirt and pants. And, over his face, he wore a black ski mask with white skull crudely painted on it.

"Well, that's different," said Gracie.

"Hank picked up the fight without being asked, without being trained. But he had the spirit of the mission, he and his Wily Wisp, Jasmine." Kevin pointed to a black woman whose sequined costume glittered over wiry muscles.

"Okay, she looks fabulous."

Stephen said, "She was quite exceptional."

Kevin continued. "They fought crime in the 1980s, picking up from O'Neil and Conroy in the 1970s."

Adam O'Neil's Crimson Wraith costume looked the most similar to Kevin's. Gracie recognized the jumpsuit that Michael Conroy wore as the Wily Wisp being very close to his as the Zephyr, except in yellow instead of black, a "W" on his chest instead of "Z," and a hooded purple cloak over his shoulders.

"They picked up the fight from Edward Finn, who served as the Crimson Wraith of the 1960s." Kevin pointed toward a faded photograph whose colors seemed off somehow, strangely bright. And he did not cover his face with a full skull mask, only a red domino mask over his eyes, showing off his strong chin and dazzling grin inside the hood of his red cloak. Edward's jumpsuit appeared to be spandex, more like something an old-fashioned circus performer might wear, with a skull image across his barrel chest.

Beside him, an equally muscular and strong-chinned Wily Wisp stood in a matching stance, arms akimbo, wearing a purple silk cloak and yellow tights with the letter "W" on his chest.

"That is Tommy James," said Kevin. "Tommy was Edward's Wily Wisp."

"Wait," said Gracie. "Edward Finn. He's the one who just passed away, right? That grave, up..." It felt weird to point toward the ceiling to indicate someone buried in the ground. "Up there? In the Finn family plot? Wait, Finn... So, his family owned this house? And he made this his base of operations as the Crimson Wraith, and then all of you who came after him..."

Danny nodded. "She's getting it."

"Edward Finn was adopted by William Finn, the very first Crimson Wraith. And when Edward turned sixteen, he started fighting alongside his father as the first Wily Wisp."

The final photograph Kevin pointed to was in black and white, but the look of the two heroes completely recognizable as being of the same lineage as all those before. Here, however, the Wily Wisp looked so much smaller in stature than the Crimson Wraith.

"He was so young."

Kevin said, "They took that photo right here, in the Crypt, after Edward's high school graduation."

"Holy shit," said Gracie. "This is like... It's so much... There's so many of them."

"Eighty years," said Kevin. "Eighty years of fighting. Eighty years of investigating mysteries, dealing with things the police couldn't or wouldn't, going to any length to protect Titan City."

Stephen intoned, "Defending the defenseless."

"That," said Kevin, "is what you will be joining, the legacy you are going to take part in. All these people, and now you."

"Holy shit," said Gracie.

Danny said, "It's a big deal. A real big deal."

"I do have one question," said Gracie.

"What's that?" Kevin asked.

"The capes, I mean, it doesn't look like they are, like, part of the required uniform, right?"

There came no immediate response from the three men.

"Right?"

CHAPTER NINE

1954

Young Officer Goodman remained calm, his posture poised, in the face of the committee and its wrath. Their demands for answers about his association with the Crimson Wraith rolled off him, leaving no change in his expression even as they filled the walls of the Titan Capitol Building with thunder. But the questions were not ultimately for Officer Goodman himself, as William Finn recognized.

Sitting in the stands among the many others in attendance, he subtly whispered to his son, "This is all a show. A lot of noise for the sake of noise. Political posturing and saber-rattling."

Eddie smiled and whispered back, "You mean, a tale told by an idiot? Full of sound and fury? Signifying nothing?"

"As Shakespeare would put it, yes. But I'm afraid it may signify a little more than nothing. These are fearful times. Amid prosperity and comfort, there always lies the fear of what may not be seen and what the unseen might mean."

For fifteen years, Will had pursued his mission to defend the defenseless and bring justice to the criminal elements of Titan City, fifteen years of cracked ribs and bloodied knuckles, barely dodged bullets and blades, as well as those that had not been dodged, just survived and stitched-up after. There had been near-drownings, a few gassings, multiple escapes from burning buildings, some close calls with electrocution, several moving cars and trains leaped-on and leaped-off, innumerable bombs defused, and, on one occasion, an alligator wrestled into submission. After all that, this newly-formed Committee on Community Accountability, the CCA, sought to accomplish what so many villains had failed to do—end the Crimson Wraith.

For many years, Will had operated in total secrecy, completely unknown to the public Then witnesses began quietly sharing stories of his heroism until the night of that fateful photograph. That night in Titan City's Little Tokyo, Will finally defeated the Shadowmaster and prevented him from constructing a nuclear weapon that could have killed thousands if not millions. As he fled the fires that consumed the Shadowmaster's lair, among the police and firefighters who arrived on the scene was one lucky reporter for *The Titan Gazette* who snapped a photograph of the Crimson Wraith that showed his skull mask grinning from within the hood of his cloak. Suddenly the public knew of him. They knew his face and gave him a name.

But the more the Crimson Wraith became known, the more questions arose about him. Yes, he seemed to assist the police in thwarting criminal activity, but how could the citizenry put their faith in an unknown individual? If he did not answer to any democratically elected authority, how could they be assured he shared the principles of the majority? He did identify himself by the color red. Did he possess a covert Communist agenda? And who was this young man who appeared at the vigilante's side? Where were his parents? Was his safety being looked after? Would other youths follow his example?

These questions found their way into the pages of *The Titan Gazette* in a series of articles penned by Senator Frederick Estes, stoking fears of unknown threats and leading, in time, to three assertions: the Crimson Wraith must be found, he must be unmasked, and he must be made to answer for himself. It was the only way to ensure public safety. Soon other politicians joined, as did some religious figures and leaders of volunteer civic organizations. Eventually, they gained enough traction to form the CCA and summon citizens in a series of public hearings in an attempt to uncover the allies of the Crimson Wraith.

"Officer Goodman, what we are trying to establish here are simply the facts." Senator Estes adjusted his glasses and lifted one of the documents in front of him. "Now, right here, on this report, you have confessed to having witnessed the two vigilantes in question, and yet you failed to arrest either. Why exactly is that, Officer Goodman? Have you not sworn an oath to Titan City to uphold the law and protect public safety? Would that not dictate the arresting of said individuals who have engaged in such criminal acts?"

In a level tone, Officer Goodman replied, "If you read carefully, you will see that I did not witness any crime committed by those two. I could not. I was keeping cover from behind a parked car while those who had committed the robbery shot at me. And after the shooting stopped, I encountered men who, yes, were dressed in costumes similar to the descriptions used for these masked vigilantes, but fancy dress is hardly a reason to arrest anyone. You wouldn't have me going around at Christmas to every man dressed as Santa Claus and arrest him for breaking and entering, would you?"

Will and Eddie laughed, but they were about the only ones. The rest of the gallery erupted with outraged voices decrying the arrogance of the officer and his flippant response.

Senator Estes banged his gavel to bring the room to order once more. "Officer Goodman, you will address this body with the respect it deserves, is that understood?"

Eddie scoffed, "How much respect does he think the CCA deserves? This whole thing is just a bunch of bunk! I can't believe they are putting you on the stand."

"Yes," said Will, "How ironic that in attempting to identify his associates, they have unknowingly invited the Crimson Wraith himself."

Unsurprisingly, those called to stand before the CCA tended to hail from the fringes of Titan society, disenfranchised minorities who benefited less from its law and therefore might be inclined toward taking it into their own hands. These included ethnic minorities like Officer Goodman, artists and intellectuals who seemed sympathetic to a counter-cultural agenda, and labor union organizers already suspected of shady activities.

And so, to have William Finn called up by the CCA raised eyebrows. He was one of Titan City's elite, cream of the crop. How could someone like him have anything to do with the Crimson Wraith?

"Mr. Finn," Estes began, "I would first like to thank you for joining us today. It is not often we get to have one of your rank and status here before us, an Ellsworth graduate, no less."

"Ellsworth forever," said Will, smiling. "I'm just hoping I don't miss my reservation at the squash courts this afternoon."

"Oh, sure, sure, I am certain we can have you out in time." Estes kept his tone condescending. The thread of contempt weaving through it suggested he assumed Will to be at best, a rich idiot, and that was just fine by him.

"Excellent. Well, then, what would you like to know?"

Estes began, "Mr. Finn, as I recall, you were not born William Finn, were you? The Finn family, isn't really your family, is it?"

"I was born a Singer, but for the life of me, I cannot sing. Listen." And he warbled out a cracked and strained musical scale that produced chuckles around him.

"So, I see," said Estes.

"You mean, 'so you hear,' I think?"

"Correct, Mr. Finn. So, I hear. And I wonder, was this not difficult for you growing up, knowing that you did not actually belong to the wealth that surrounded you?"

"Well, you know, it was a lot. I will always feel a great debt of gratitude to my father, Josiah Finn, for adopting me into a life I could never have imagined."

"But did it not give you the sense there was something

different between you and the other young men you grew up with? Was there not a tension created from your undeserved good fortune?"

"You know, I suppose there was, at that," said Will. "In fact, I think those were very close to the words used by the man who murdered my father when he attempted to murder me, before his own death by suicide. It was all so terrible..."

Estes seemed abashed by Will's response. "Er, yes... Of course. And you do have this committee's deepest sympathy."

The details of this particular episode of Finn family history were public knowledge, and reminding Estes of them seemed to cool some of his fervor. After all, he would not want to appear heartless in front of potential voters. But although the senator may have been momentarily stunned, he was only just beginning.

Estes went on to ask about Will's business activities and his connections with foreign financial institutions, probing for possibilities of influence there. He asked as well why Will had never chosen to marry, even though he started a family for himself by adopting his son Eddie.

Will answered all these questions in a casual manner, one calculated to appear uncalculated. He presented himself as simply a man married to his work. This much was true, although his true vocation was not the management of Finn Industries but the crime-fighting career of the Crimson Wraith. But if it appeared to others that he worked with more intense focus than was common for those of his standing, the fact that he had not been born into wealth, that he had lived in an orphanage and worked the streets as a paperboy, might explain his motivation.

Afterward, it occurred to Will that he should have known the CCA would not have challenged someone of Will's influence without something substantial, something that, if it were waved in front of his face in a public forum, would fill him with so much shame that he must feel compelled to confess any and every secret he might hide.

Reading from his documents, Senator Estes said, "Mr. Finn, is it correct that you have registered in your name with the license plate number BV1-122?"

"Maybe. It could be possible. I do own more than one car, I'm afraid."

"I believe it is a Buick Skylark, the 1952 model?"

"Oh, yes! Wonderful car. Are you thinking of getting one?"

"I'm sure a man of your standing has no knowledge of a particular social establishment that goes by the name of the Innocents Club?"

"The Innocents Club? What a strange name."

"Strange indeed. It is apparently a cocktail bar that caters exclusively to men, and strange activities have been said to occur inside, immoral activities. The owners and operators of this establishment have recently been arrested for failure to keep their business license up to date, and the District Attorney's office has found them quite agreeable to chat with. They have much information to share."

"That sounds like a win for the DA then, but I don't quite see what that has to do with me."

"Would you be surprised to know that your vehicle, a Buick Skylark with the license plate BV1-122 was seen parked outside the Innocents Club on multiple occasions?"

A general murmuring arose. Such was the power of the leading question over the direct accusation. The suggestion that William Finn, a bachelor still at the age of forty-one, may have frequented such an establishment left plenty of space for lurid imagination to fill.

Although Will did his best to pretend to be confused by all of the CCA's previous questions, for once he did not have to pretend. "It would surprise me. It would surprise me very much," he said.

Eddie was the one who drove the Skylark, and he felt his face burning with shame as he watched his father being questioned for what he had done.

"Mr. Finn, you haven't reported the vehicle stolen. Do you

plan to tell me that it has gone out of your possession at any time in recent months."

"No, I don't plan that at all."

"Then are you ready to share with this committee your reason for frequenting such an establishment on several dates over the past sixth months at very late hours of the night?"

"I… I don't…"

"Or are you ready to provide other information to this body?"

"Such as?"

"The one question we most want to know. Are you now, or have you ever been, associated in any way with the criminal vigilante who operates under the name the Crimson Wraith?"

2019

The morning after the secrets of the Crimson Wraith were revealed to her, Gracie woke up at 6:47 AM, way earlier than she needed, way earlier than she had been told to wake up. The four of them left the Crypt via the staircase up into the hidden hallways of Finn Manor, exiting through the secret door located in the great unlit fireplace of the dining room, over whose mantle the bust of Archibald Finn kept watch. Kevin left the Crimson Wraith's costume below, and wore, instead, a grey cashmere robe with matching pajama pants and slippers.

But before they retired to their respective rooms, Gracie asked, "So, what happens now? I mean tomorrow? Is it up at the crack of dawn for raw eggs, jogging, and push-ups?"

"More like the crack of noon," said Danny.

Kevin said, "Our mission requires us to be ready at the times when crime are most likely to occur. The peak hour for criminal activity, particularly violent crime, is 9 PM, although juvenile crimes tend to occur in the hours immediately after school lets out. Therefore, at the crack of dawn, you should be getting your best sleep, comfortable in the knowledge that most of Titan City is relatively safe. On a quiet night, I might leave off patrolling around 3 AM and find myself in bed by 4. That means I wake up somewhere between 10 AM and 12 PM most days."

Gracie said, "So, basically, you're like a college student? Or maybe a club kid?"

Stephen smiled, "The comparison has been made before."

"It isn't far off from getting used to being a third shift worker, although the night watchman at a corporate front desk can sometimes find it hard to keep his eyes open as the dark hours roll quietly on. The Crimson Wraith gets to experience a bit more excitement than that. The more action you see, the easier those late hours become."

"Are there no early morning board meetings at Snyder-Finn?"

Kevin smirked, "They happen when they have to. Power naps are handy in those cases. But it does help the public perceive me as a self-indulgent playboy when I appear groggy and bleary-eyed for any work that needs me before noon."

Even having been told the value of sleeping in, Gracie felt like a kid on Christmas—not like her own childhood, but a kid who grew up with parents who didn't spend Christmas Eve drunkenly screaming and crying and throwing things at each other. She was too excited to go to sleep easily, and as soon as light entered her bedroom window, she was immediately fully awake. This was a day to look forward to, a day unlike any other. Gracie was going to be a superhero—an actual, mask-wearing, crime-fighting, secret-identity-having, straight-from-the-comic-books superhero.

At first, she thought she might be able to get back to sleep if she did some reading, and now that she had accepted the Crimson Wraith's invitation to be his protégé, *Nights of Justice* took on a much deeper meaning:

> *One of the first theories to arise about the identity of the Crimson Wraith was that he was part of the Titan City*

underworld, not its adversary, seeing as how he operated outside the law, using tactics of fear and violence. The strongest theory was that he worked either as an enforcer for one of Titan City's crime syndicates or a mercenary for hire. When he undid one criminal enterprise, it might have been at the behest of another, if not to advance his own personal underworld influence. Even his thwarting of petty crimes could be seen as claiming territory, asserting that no criminal activity might occur on his "turf" without permission.

Titan City was, after all, no Wild West town of the century prior, no lawless backwater where the only authority came from the barrel of a gun. What then would inspire an individual to take law into their own hands? What, indeed? The motivation of the Crimson Wraith remains a mystery to this day. Those of us who received the kindness of the Crimson Wraith knew his mission to be altruistic, whatever its root, but fear sells more newspapers than kindness...

When the sun rose above the tree line, Gracie decided she wasn't getting back to sleep and may as well grab some breakfast, so she padded downstairs in her sleep shorts and an oversized t-shirt for a punk band called the Fiery Furies.

On her way to the kitchen, she paused at the entryway to the dining room. The secret door to the Crypt was just a few steps away. She hadn't dreamed it all last night, had she? Would it still be there in the light of day? Was it real? Was it really real, for real? Do such things exist and as a part of *her* life?

Her feet carried her into the dining room, a place where she had never eaten since arriving nor seen any of the others do so. It had a strange too-clean quality, not lived in, like some kind of museum reproduction of a dining room. The woodgrain of the floor shimmered where sunlight from the hallway struck. Its own lights, the twin crystal chandeliers above the table, were on a dimmer switch. Gracie brought them up half way, illuminating the room's two massive paintings and the bust of Archibald Finn. *You don't belong here,* his face seemed to say to her, although she knew he said that to everyone.

"Fuck you, old man," she said out loud to him.

As if to spite the Finn family patriarch, Gracie stepped toward him, toward the fireplace underneath. She had seen where Kevin reached under and behind the mantle to tap the switch that closed the secret door behind them when they left. She wondered if she could find it herself. It turned out, she could. With a sound of stone grating against stone, the back wall of the fireplace opened to her, revealing the stairs down to the Crypt. Gracie entered and started downward.

Tiny LEDs at the base of the stairs illuminated just a few steps ahead of her and faded out after she passed. They must have been motion-sensitive. The stairway spiraled down until she came to the security door, very much like the one she had entered from the other side with Kevin and Danny the night before. It had a palm scanner and a microphone to receive the password. Gracie knew it wouldn't work, that the door would not respond to her, but she wanted to do it anyway, to feel what it felt like to go through those motions, doing them for the first time with no one watching, the first of who-knows-how-many times to come.

She placed her palm against the glass of the scanner. It lit up in response to her touch. Then she leaned in to speak the password, knowing nothing would happen. *"In Pace Requiescat."*

But something did happen. And she nearly peed herself.

Danny's voice came to her through the speaker. "You want coffee?"

Gracie blurted out, "Jesus fuck!"

"Whoa, now. Not in any Bible I heard of. That the Scorsese film?"

"You scared the piss out of me!" *Nearly literally*, she thought.

"Well, you woke me up, so that's on you. I get notified if someone activates the Crypt's motion sensors after lockdown."

She thought about the self-lighting stairs. Either those or the palm scanner must have sent him a notification. "Oh, yeah, that makes sense."

"So, anyway, I'm awake now," he said. "You want coffee?"

1954

All throughout the Titan City Capitol chambers, onlookers edged forward in their seats, eager for William Finn's response. News reporters held pencils at the ready while casting glances back toward the exit to see just how quickly they could make their way out the door to phone their editors with what would surely be tomorrow morning's headline. Even if Will had no confession regarding the Crimson Wraith, having proof of his frequenting a bar that catered to the secret homosexuals of Titan City would provide them a glorious scandal.

That was the real purpose of the CCA after all, at least in the minds immune to its paranoid fervor. A body like that did not truly exist for public safety but political power. It created an imaginary war in which its members stood on the side of the righteous. Being able to out a pillar of the community as living in shameful deviancy—as it seemed the CCA was trying to do with Will—would stoke fears of what else may go on unseen in Titan City, so its citizens would cling to those who painted themselves as virtuous protectors.

Will looked out from the stand toward his son, and Eddie saw the confusion in his father's expression. Could Will see the agony he was feeling? He thought he had been careful when he visited the Innocents Club. He always made sure to have a solid alibi. He never imagined he might have been endangering his father like this.

"On what dates," said Will, "did you say that my Skylark was parked at that establishment?"

"I have them all written down right here. Would you care to look at them? Perhaps they will bring up some... potent memories?"

A bailiff handed Will one of Senator Estes's documents, and as he looked over them, he asked, "And what is the location of this Innocence Club?"

"It doesn't seem like I need to tell you, but I will play along. You will find it on Reinhardt Street."

"Reinhardt?"

"Yes, Mr. Finn. Reinhardt Street. Does that jog some memories for you?"

"It certainly does. I have a business on Reinhardt street."

"You do?"

"Yes, that's the sales office for one of my textile export firms, up on the fourth floor of the Wertham Building."

"The Wertham Building?" An aide came and whispered into Senator Estes's ear. The fervor had vanished from his voice when he spoke. "I am told that the Wertham Building stands just around the corner from the structure that held the Innocents Club."

Will beamed. "Ah, well, there you have it. I must confess to spending more late workdays at the office than I really ought. But I'm sorry I cannot claim to have a more interesting nightlife than that."

There were some chuckles from the viewers, but most came tinged with disappointment. The CCA released Will and thanked him for his cooperation. Eddie rose to join his father and the two left swiftly. When they appeared to be alone, Will said softly, "You've been working very hard on those textile accounts lately, haven't you, son?"

"I have," said Eddie. "I really have."

"Good," said Will. "You've never given me reason to doubt you."

Anguish writhed inside of Eddie. At the young age of twenty-two, he was already a man of secrets. But, after all, he had been raised by a man of secrets, the very biggest secret, that of being the mysterious masked vigilante the Crimson Wraith. Next to that, was it so important a secret that Eddie had found special hidden places in Titan City, places like the Innocents Club, where he could experience love and comfort, even passion, that he had never been able to before?

With a casual air, not looking to his son as they continued their way out of the building, Will said, "You know, when I was a young man in London, fighting in those dark and hidden places, exchanging my blood for money that I did not care about, I saw a lot of things."

"I bet you did," said Eddie. "What kind of things?"

"Oh, all kinds of things. It's a big world, Eddie, bigger than most people want to think about, way bigger than they want to look at. And just because they don't want to look at it, does not mean that it is bad. Sometimes there are good people in those spaces where others don't want to look."

Eddie turned toward his father. What was Will implying? Did he already know the things Eddie had only learned about himself in recent years? And if he knew, was he not angry? Was he not ashamed of what his son was?

Then a voice interrupted them. "Mr. Finn?"

Both Eddie and Will turned to look and saw a thick-set man in glasses. "Can I help you?" said Will.

"Well, sir, I do not know. I have been reaching out to everyone who has stood up on that stand. You see, I have information that I need to get into the proper hands, and I do not know if those hands are your hands or if you know whose hands those might be."

"I've got to admit, you have me there. I am not sure I would know myself if my hands are the hands you are looking for."

Eddie said, "Or if your hands know those hands even."

"They may not," said the man. "But if you are someone who cares about the welfare of this city, then you would want to see my information get into the proper hands as well."

"Well, I'm game. How would I know if my hands are the right hands?"

"It would be because your hands know how to get in touch with the hands of the personage about whom you have just been questioned."

"So, we should be all hand-in-hand, as it were?" He turned to Eddie. "Quite the handy story here, don't you think?"

Affecting his usual role of the bored little rich kid, Eddie said, "Maybe we should scram before the men in the white coats come."

"You may think I'm crazy, and if you do, then you are not the one I need to find. Good day." The man began to walk away.

Will called out to him. "And what exactly are you going to tell the one you are looking for if you find him?"

But the man kept walking.

Will turned to Eddie. "What do your instincts tell you, son?"

"That he has something pretty darned serious to share with a certain you-know-who."

"Agreed, and it seems like something that someone should hear. I want you to get a window seat at the diner across the street. If that man leaves, follow him, and when he gets to wherever he is headed, send me a message on your Radio Wrist Communicator, and I'll meet you there."

"Where will you be?"

"I'm heading back home to get the two of us a change of clothes," he said with a wink. "If we have a date with destiny tonight, it is important that we be properly dressed."

For an hour, Eddie sat and drank his coffee at the Starpoint Diner. He picked at a slice of pie while keeping one eye on the humorous cartoons of a magazine, the other trained on the door across the street. The sun began to set, stretching the shadows of Titan City's skyscrapers across the streets below.

Finally, he noticed the man who approached them make his way down the steps. Eddie tossed a few coins on the counter before heading out to the street to tail him. As he did, he whispered into his Radio Wrist Communicator, "Specter Second to Crypt. Specter Second to Crypt. Subject in motion. Am following. Do you copy?"

Will's voice came in reply, "Copy that, Specter Second. Proceed as directed. In motion to *rendez-vous*."

The man walked several city blocks, changing direction enough times that Eddie realized he must be expecting to be followed. It required Eddie to stay close, which meant he had to be extra careful. For just this reason, he wore a reversible jacket and a crushable fedora and kept a pair of costume glasses in his pocket. These allowed him to make quick costume changes while in motion, first removing his hat and changing the color of his jacket, then slipping on the glasses and throwing his jacket over one arm, all so that if the man looked back he wouldn't recognize the same shape behind him for too long.

When the man reached an office building and went inside, Eddie radioed the address to Will. Entering the lobby just behind the man, just after elevator doors closed, Eddie watched as the lights above indicated the elevator traveling to the seventh floor and stopping there.

In minutes, Chubby pulled up in one of their plain white vans that he parked in a nearby alleyway. Eddie knew his father would be hidden within. Night had fallen, and in that deep darkness, Eddie became the Wily Wisp, joining Will already costumed as the Crimson Wraith.

The two began to make their way up the side of the building by leaping to the fire escape from the top of Chubby's van and then creeping up the steps to the seventh floor. Inside, they found it dark and quiet, most of the offices having been closed for the day. But down that hallway, the light could be seen still burning inside an office. The name on its glass-paneled door read *Maxwell W. Gaines Accounting*.

"All right," said Will. "Let's see what business Mr. Maxwell W. Gaines has with the Crimson Wraith."

"Are we just going to go up there and knock?" Eddie asked.

"Of course," said Will. "We don't want to be rude."

But suddenly a very rude sound came from within the office—gunshots, five of them, with accompanying flashes of light. Will and Eddie broke into a run. Then came another sound, that of shattering glass. "Someone's headed out the window!" shouted Will, assuming that was the sound of an assailant's escape. And so, he and Eddie were taken completely by surprise as two men exploded through the doorway, guns still in their hands and fear on their faces.

One held a manilla folder clutched to his chest. The other had an arrow embedded in the flesh of his shoulder. It pierced his coat, which darkened with the blood expanding from his wound. And behind the two could be seen the body of the man who had approached Will and Eddie earlier, Maxwell W. Gaines, shot dead at his desk. The broken window behind him framed the night sky and neighboring office rooftop. Eddie thought he saw a figure there, a form draped in silver, but in an instant, it was gone.

The startled gunmen collided into Will and Eddie, and all tumbled to the ground in a scramble of cloaks and limbs. One of the gunmen, the one who had run into Eddie, wailed, "And the Crimson Wraith too?"

As the gunman tried to get back to his feet, Eddie grappled with his opponent. "Not so fast," he said. "Don't you know it's rude to leave in the middle of a dance?"

The gunman brought up his pistol to fire on Eddie, a deadly shot at such close range, but Eddie grabbed the shaft of the arrow from the gunman's shoulder and wrenched it from his flesh, causing him to scream in pain and drop the weapon.

Beside him, Eddie heard the other gunman's pistol fire and turned to see Will recoil, clutching his abdomen. "No!" he screamed and released a flash bomb aimed right at the pistol. The explosion of sound and light caused the gunman to release his weapon, and he and the other ran down the hall as Eddie knelt at his father's side.

"Talk to me. Where did he get you?"

"I'm fine!" Eddie could hear Will's teeth were clenched behind his mask. "Don't let them get away!"

Eddie did as commanded and began chasing the gunmen, who had disappeared into the stairwell. Hearing the sound of their footsteps above him, Eddie followed upward, onto the rooftop. Both of the men were running toward the edge and appeared ready to jump, not onto a neighboring roof but out onto the street below, out to their deaths. Eddie grabbed two pellets of choking gas from their pouch, but before he could hurl them, first one arrow and then another came flying over his shoulder, embedding themselves in one gunman's calf and the other's posterior. Both went down.

Eddie could not help but turn to see who had fired those two shots. Behind him stood a woman dressed head to toe in silver, wearing a domino mask. Her shimmering blonde hair appeared to glow in the moonlight.

"Who are you?" he asked.

"A friend," she said.

"And what can I call you, friend?"

"For now, call me Lady Luna." Then she pointed to the fallen gunmen. "Stop them!"

Spinning around, Eddie saw the two had their hands at their mouth. He ran to see what it was that caught Lady Luna's eye, but already they had both begun convulsing as a vile-smelling foam bubbled from their lips.

"What on Earth?" said Eddie.

"Cyanide pills," said Will, having silently joined them on the rooftop. One gauntleted hand clutched at the bullet wound in his side. "It takes dedication to a cause to take your secrets to the grave. These men were more than merely hired muscle."

He turned to Lady Luna, "And you seem to be more than merely a woman, no doubt with secrets of your own behind that mask."

"Oh, Will," she said, smiling as she removed her mask. "Why should I keep any secrets from you?"

And Lady Luna revealed herself to be William Finn's girlfriend from his Ellsworth days, the girl who had been there at the Crimson Wraith's very first appearance in the little church graveyard where he terrified Kelly Winchester—none other than Sylvia Madison.

_2019_

Danny didn't look half-bad in his thin white tank-top and plaid pajama pants, and Gracie noticed the muscles in his arm when he reached to take the maple syrup from the refrigerator for their toaster waffles. It surprised her. Apparently, he didn't spend all his time behind a keyboard. The French press coffee finished steeping. She pushed the plunger down and poured cups for them both.

"We'll do palm scans and voice ID for you later today," Danny said. He sat down at the kitchen table and started scraping butter over his waffle. "Then you'll be all set to creep around the Crypt whenever you feel like."

"I wasn't creeping…" Gracie said as she poured sugar into her coffee. "I was invited, given the grand tour and everything."

"Yeah, well, there's a few more details we should probably go over for your tour. I've got projects on the workbenches I don't want anybody putting hands-on until they are ready. And you don't need to be tapping buttons and flipping switches just for funsies. That is some delicate equipment down there."

"Geez. Sure, fine. I won't touch your stuff."

Danny took a big bite of his waffle and looked at Gracie hard, in a way she did not like at all.

"What?"

He shook his head, looked back to his plate, and carved off another bite.

"What?" Now Gracie was getting angry.

"You know this isn't a game, right? This is for real. Maybe you saw some stuff on Saturday morning cartoons that you think told you everything this life is like—*Biff! Pow! Pop!*—and all that. But whatever you think you know, trust me—*trust me*

—there is a whole other side to this that you do not."

"Wow," said Gracie. "I don't know what your problem is, but Kevin seems to think I'm up for this, and last I checked, he was your boss and all, the actual Crimson Wraith. So, why don't you dial it down a notch, ok?"

"See?" said Danny, "*This* is the problem. You think you know what's going on. Day one—hell, day zero—and you want to 'tell it like it is' before you even know a thing."

Gracie was losing her appetite. "Look, Kevin is the one who reached out *to me*. He saw something in me, and he thought I have what it takes. If you doubt that, how about you take it up with him? I don't really give a shit. You don't think I know what's up with the Crimson Wraith? How about *you* don't know what's up with *me*?"

After sucking a bit of waffle from his teeth, Danny said, "You were born in Greenhill, east of Titan, over the Brennert River, on a day six months after your parents Stanley and Desiree Grace got married. He worked off-and-on in construction, probably some under the table because the tax record is spotty. She worked part-time at a few different jobs—gas station attendant, truck stop waitress, pet groomer. Records show cops came to your house to break up domestic disturbances on three separate occasions before that time, which means they probably missed a whole lot more.

"The family qualified for food stamps, and they kept on receiving them at the three-person household rate until your eighteenth birthday, when they stopped being able to claim you, although their utility consumption went down about the time you were fifteen, so you must have bounced before. In middle school, you played softball for two years. That ended after a fight during a game got you kicked off the team. In high school, you repeatedly received disciplinary action for tardiness. Your attendance record shows you only went to class less than forty percent of the time. You got yourself expelled after throwing an Erlenmeyer flask at your chemistry teacher's head—"

Gracie interrupted him. "He was looking down girls' shirts. And fuck you."

"After that, the trail goes dark until you show up a few years later in Titan City, waiting tables at a chicken shack called Smiley's. Got yourself fired from there after five months. Dumped a guy's beer over his head. A few more jobs go like that, with W-2s sent to an address in East Town even though your name never appears on a rental agreement. That used bookstore is the only place you've worked more than a year altogether, on the record anyway."

This time she said it louder. "Fuck. You."

Danny stopped speaking but kept his eyes locked on hers.

Gracie could feel her heartbeat in her chest. Her waffle sat untouched, her coffee cooling. In her mind, she could see herself pouring it over his lap just like she poured that beer over the guy at Smiley's after he grabbed her ass.

Then Danny said, "That's my job, you see? It is my job to know things and to use that knowledge to keep us safe—to keep *him* safe—so he can do the things he needs to do—for us, for everybody, even for you."

"And is it your job to be a dick?" she said, standing, "because you're doing that just great." She left the table with her food still on it and not in his face.

Feeling rage roll through her, Gracie went back up to her room not knowing what the hell she was going to do with herself. She wanted to hit something, but the wallpaper was too nice and the pillows were too soft. One punch at her mattress told her that wasn't going to work either, so she put on her clothes, headed outside, and started walking, not having any idea where she was headed. Her boots brought her to the outer wall of the front lawn, which she kicked. Then she stomped along the perimeter.

The walk didn't give quite the exertion she craved, but she had calmed down some when she rounded the manor building and made her way into the rear lawn. There she saw a figure standing in the Finn family plot, and the sight took her out of herself, distracting from her rage. It was Stephen.

He stood over the grave of Edward Finn, the second Crimson Wraith, the first Wily Wisp, adopted son of an adopted son. And as Gracie watched, Stephen wiped at his face. She felt suddenly torn, wanting to go to him and comfort the old man if she could, but she also felt like she didn't want to disturb him. This seemed like a private moment. With a softer step, Gracie headed inside.

Back in her room, she fell asleep again on top of her covers, still wearing her clothes, minus her boots, which stood by the door. She stayed there until about 12:30 PM, when a knock roused her from a dream of punching out Tight T-Shirt Guy but seeing it all in night-vision green. Gracie rolled out of bed and opened the door to Kevin, who stood smiling in a dark blue jogging suit.

"All right, he said, "Let's get started."

CHAPTER TEN

1954

Seeing Sylvia on the rooftop the night before, masked in her Lady Luna garb, Eddie felt less unease than he did opening the door of Finn Manor to her in her civilian clothes the day after. Maybe it was the smile she wore, the one that said, I'm in on the secret. I'm part of the club. Eddie didn't remember seeing her invitation.

"Good afternoon, Edward," she said. "May I come in?"

She wore red, perhaps a sign of solidarity with his father's crime-fighting alter ego, a jacket and dress with a wide-brimmed hat to match, offset by white gloves and a string of pearls. Her hair fell in the elegant waves of Veronica Lake. Now, in the light of day, Eddie could distinguish rivers of gray running through its gold.

"Of course, Miss Madison. My father is currently resting in the sunroom."

"Has he seen a doctor yet?"

"Sort of. Our mechanic Chubby has gotten pretty handy with a pair of tweezers, needle and thread, and a roll of gauze. I'm told you know Chubby as well."

"That I do. Such a dear friend. It warms my heart knowing the two of them found each other again after school. I only wish I had joined them sooner. So strange to think that Will and I took similar paths while apart and that now, so many years later, we both engage in the same... Shall we call it a hobby?"

Eddie made himself smile. "Call it what you wish."

Yes, he definitely hated her right then. A hobby? This was his mission. It was the mission that brought William Finn into Eddie's life. It was the mission that gave his life meaning. Was it nothing more to her than an amusing diversion?

They entered the sunroom to find Chubby sitting at Will's side, saying, "Gosh, Will. I just can't see you going out again like this, not for some time."

"I know, old friend," said Will. "But there is something in this that others would kill and die for." He held the file they retrieved from the gunmen.

"Perhaps I can help?" said Sylvia.

The two looked to her like puppies at the sound of their mistress's voice. Chubby leaped to embrace her. "It really is you! Gosh, and just as beautiful as ever! Haven't changed even one bit, honest!"

"I can't say the same for you. Not so chubby anymore, Mr. Chumley."

Chubby ran a hand down his svelte frame, across the now-firm abdomen where once his belly had been. "Oh, this? Well, I have to stay in shape for my better half."

"Better half?" said Sylvia. "Did I hear correctly, Will? Did our Chubby go and find himself a wife?"

A voice that bore traces of a Cockney accent caused Sylvia to turn. "He sure did, miss." And the rosy-cheeked Mrs. Chumley joined them. She wore her maid's uniform. The cart she pushed into the room carried a sandwich tray and a big bowl of salad. "Lunch is served!" she announced.

Will gestured to her, "Sylvia Madison, might I introduce my head of household, Mrs. Candace Chumley."

Mrs. Chumley extended a hand. "Pleasure to meet you, Miss Madison."

"And a pleasure to meet you, Mrs. Chumley."

"Oh, please, call me 'Candy.' Everyone does."

Chubby wrapped his wife in an affectionate squeeze. "And everyone knows how much Chubby loves Candy."

She giggled in response. "Oh, stop it, you!"

"But I can't help myself! Not without you to help me."

Eddie looked away. The two of them were utterly unbearable when they got like this.

"Not in front of the company!" Candy said to Chubby. Then she turned to Sylvia. "I guess you know what he's like, don't you?"

"Maybe," said Sylvia. "But maybe not so well as you."

"Why, he is incorri-*gibble*." She mispronounced the word, giving it a hard "G." "Simply incorri-*gibble*."

"So, I see. And how ever do you manage to keep him in line?"

"Salad, miss." Candy smiled and picked up the bowl from the tray to illustrate.

Chubby nodded with a sigh. "Lots and lots of salad."

"It's good for you, my love," said Candy, handing him the bowl.

"You're good for me." He said, taking the bowl from her in exchange for a kiss.

And this, Eddie realized, was why Sylvia's appearance at the doorstep of Finn Manor disturbed him. She was beautiful. She certainly held Will in high regard. No doubt his father would feel a sentimental attachment to their youth together. And now, it seemed, they both shared secret crime-fighting identities.

If Sylvia had any designs on attaching herself to Will, Eddie suspected the odds to be very much in her favor, far more than the women he saw his father escorted by to movie premiers and charity balls. No matter how nice the families they came from, Eddie saw all of his father's dates as accessories only, brought out in public for the sake of appearances. The same held for any girl that he himself ever went out with. These posed no true danger to the sanctity of their household, and Candy Chumley showed just how dire a danger a woman could be.

Sure, thanks to her insistence on his salad eating, Chubby

had transformed into a far more physically fit figure, but at what cost? She had ensnared his mind, enslaved him. Where once Chubby had been teaching Eddie the ins-and-outs of this-or-that mechanical device, always available for any escapade, and full of jokes you don't tell in mixed company, suddenly his comings-and-goings all submitted to her authority.

She interrupted their afternoons together by declaring it was time for Chubby to join her in their constitutional walk around the grounds. He was never allowed to drink beer with Will and Eddie anymore. There was no card playing. And if they had any radio in the mansion turned up louder than a whisper, she claimed it gave her "such a headache." Jazz she could not tolerate at any volume at all.

Thanks to Candy's efforts, Chubby had all the fun taken out of him. Eddie shuddered to think what marriage might do to his father.

Candy said to Sylvia. "I have heard ever so much about you from our boys."

"Have you indeed?"

"Oh, yes! All about your adventures at Ellsworth and Fletcher."

"And none of our more recent adventures?" Sylvia looked to Will with a questioning gaze.

"Do you mean about these boys going off as the Crimson Wraith and Wily Wisp?" Candy asked, just as casually as anything.

Will smiled. "Candy is aware of all of our adventures, Sylvia. Why, she is a vital part of the operation. You see, Chubby keeps all of our equipment going, and Candy is the one who keeps Chubby going."

Candy swiped a hand playfully at Will, "You'd be lucky to have a lady of your own do the same for you someday, you know. And young Master Eddie."

"Oh, Eddie does just fine, Candy," said Will. "I wouldn't worry about him."

He never heard his father say anything like that before.

Will complimented Eddie regularly, always had, praising his determination, skill, and ingenuity even before Eddie turned these traits toward crime-fighting. But to be praised in this way, just after his father must have surely guessed correctly that Eddie had been visiting the Innocents Club, struck Eddie with a strange, hopeful longing.

Did his father know, truly know, what he had been doing? And did he not consider his son a deviant for it? Eddie so desperately wanted to know, but the risk of being wrong terrified him too much.

Sylvia asked, "And what has been keeping you going, Will, in the absence of a wife of your own?"

"Oh, for the sport of it!" said Will. "Quite the game, don't you think, dressing up in shocking costumes and having such adventures?"

"Do you think I could have performed with you so many times on the Ellsworth stage and not know when you are acting? I know you well enough to know you don't really take this so lightly."

Chubby whistled. "Gosh. Couldn't ever get anything past her, could you, Will?"

"No, I don't suppose I ever could. You knew it was me under that skull right away, didn't you?"

"Of course," said Sylvia. "Can't say the costume has changed too much since the night we scared Kelly Winchester. I knew it was you the first time I read about the Crimson Wraith in the papers. The stories have traveled beyond Titan City, you know. At first, I was frightened for you, worrying about the risks you must be taking, wondering if the tragedy of your father's passing had not driven you mad. But then, the more I read, the more I imagined what it was like for you, and the more I envied you.

"That was during my first marriage, and I suppose it coincided with things beginning to deteriorate there. The longhorn rancher who seemed so romantic when I was younger eventually made it clear he wanted nothing more from me than a pretty face to show his friends and a babysitter for the children of his first wife. His lifestyle had luxury enough that I thought I could be happy doing both. I was wrong. So, I started to wonder if I could find what I was missing by going out into the night in a mask. And I did."

"A mask and a bow and arrow, right?" said Chubby. "You were such a good shot back in school. Why, you could have gone to the Olympics with that arm!"

"Maybe I should have," she said. "But there have been many roads not taken over the years. Who knows what things might have turned out differently?"

Will met her eye, and Eddie saw the spark between them. Both their cheeks reddened slightly, and as their faces warmed, Eddie felt something inside his chest burn. *Don't you dare take my father from me.*

Sylvia turned away, breaking their gaze. "I already had a taste for the crime-fighting life when I met husband number two, the film producer. As wedding bells approached for us, I thought to myself, I can put this aside. Let the police do their job. But soon after the honeymoon, I once again discovered that, with this man too, my role as wife was expected to be ornamental. I could not avoid taking up the mask and bow. By the time that marriage failed, Lady Luna had developed quite the career. And I had reached an age where marriage did not seem quite so likely anymore, so I told my family I would be going on a tour of Europe and embracing my role as the 'gay divorcee.'"

"Just like Ginger Rogers!" chirped Candy.

"Just like Ginger Rogers," said Sylvia, "Except instead of dancing with Fred Astaire, I sought denizens of the criminal underworld all across the continent."

Will said, "Some charming dance partners, no doubt."

"Oh, very charming. And then, about five years ago, someone new arrived on the scene, someone who made all the other criminals quake in fear. One by one, I found the underworld powers falling under his control. The lesser gangs were brought together under a single command. The proud old families who resisted this interloper did not last long. But I did not hear a name for this figure until I was in France, where they knew him as L'Ombre Grande."

"The Great Shadow?" said Eddie. "Father, you don't think that could be..."

"Shadowmaster!" said Will, "But I saw him die. I saw it with my own eyes ten years ago."

"Well," said Sylvia, "whoever this Great Shadow is, I discovered he had stolen from various sources materials that he shipped here, to Titan City, under various business names, but all using the same accounting firm for the shipping costs."

"Maxwell W. Gaines."

"Exactly. That was what brought me to his office last night. I watched through the window from the building opposite. When those two men appeared, I knew they were trouble and fired my arrows at them, but I fired too late."

Eddie said, "Maxwell must have put the details together, come to figure out all these different companies were one and the same."

Sylvia nodded. "The materials being shipped could be pieced together to produce one thing and one thing only."

"And what is that?" said Will.

"A nuclear bomb."

Will said, "Exactly what Shadowmaster was attempting years before."

Candy exclaimed, "Oh, my stars!"

"Gosh!" Chubby gasped. "A nuclear bomb? Here? In Titan City? But where could they be hiding it?"

Will held up the file he had been examining before. "This must be the bomb's location." He pointed to the heading of the very first document inside. It read, *Income Tax documentation for Mikado Imports: 2nd Quarter, 1954.*

Sylvia nodded. "Mikado Imports. That must be the place."

Turning to Eddie, William said, "It seems Mr. Maxwell W. Gaines did have something very dire indeed to share with the

Crimson Wraith. And now it is up to the Crimson Wraith to stop this new Shadowmaster, whoever he might be."

"But how?" said Eddie. "I don't think you're going out there tonight with that bullet wound you took last night."

"Gosh, no, Will," said Chubby. "You're just not fighting fit!"

"I didn't say *I* was going to stop him. I said the Crimson Wraith must." He pointed to Eddie. "And tonight, my son, the Crimson Wraith will be you."

<u>2019</u>

The wheels of the treadmills sang under their feet as Kevin and Gracie brought their speed up to a full run. Wires from the electrodes they wore bounced with each step, determined to stay well-stuck to their skin as the two began to glisten with sweat.

"As to your earlier question," Kevin laughed, "No, the capes are not *de rigeuer*—"

"They're not what?" said Gracie.

"Not required. You don't have to wear one when you join me in the field."

He seemed not-at-all bothered to carry on a casual conversation while engaged in an endurance run, and Gracie felt fine to let him go on. Working out wasn't really Gracie's thing. It felt strange to run this way, without something to run from or run to. She didn't have a hard time keeping up, but this wasn't as fun as a night of dancing, that was sure.

"The first Crimson Wraith, William Finn, chose his costume for visual effect. It was all about scaring his opponent, so the cloak was supposed to be kind of a Grim Reaper shroud. Those who followed him mostly kept it as a nod to him and his legacy. They were building on his renown, and so they had to look at least a little like him.

"Of course then you get into the eighties, and Hank didn't wear a cape at all, just a red-hooded sweatshirt. Michael took it back to a cape in the nineties. But Christopher—who came after Michael and before me—he opted for just a long, hooded trench coat. So, you've got some variety.

"But it isn't just for looks. There are certain things you can do with a cloak or cape in a fight. In the Renaissance period, sword fighters would wrap their capes around their off-hand as a kind of ad-hoc armor. Didn't do much if someone was swinging a claymore at you, but against a rapier or something lighter like that, a thickly wrapped cape would be surprisingly useful. Also, the cape might become a kind of weapon itself. A fighter could whip off a cape and hurl it at their opponent's face, temporarily blinding them, thereby setting up a *coup de grâce*."

"Uh-huh," said Gracie. After so much silence and secrecy, it seemed like words were just tumbling from Kevin.

"Now, there are potential drawbacks, of course. A cape can get caught in something. A long cape might trip you up, and footwork is critical. As cool as it may seem to have a cape brushing the floor at your feet, that is asking for trouble. If you'll notice, my cape doesn't go any farther than mid-calf, which is itself risky. Anything below mid-thigh is dangerous. But also, it breaks away, so if I were to get tangled up in something the cape comes off right at the shoulder. And if it does, that's where the technology comes in. Wouldn't want to leave my cape lying around to be analyzed by someone, so Danny set it up so a chemical compound is released that starts quickly eating away at the fabric. Very clever."

At the mention of Danny's name, Gracie got a burst of anger that fueled her steps. She picked up her pace. Kevin's lecture on the tactical aspects of cape-wear faded for her, just more background noise. It wasn't like he was going to give her a quiz on this, right?

She kept her eyes locked ahead, out the floor-to-ceiling glass window looking over the northern lawn and the small pear trees there. The pitch of the treadmill's whine sharpened as her feet attacked the exercise machine with increasing fury.

"Gracie?" Kevin called to her. When she didn't respond, he brought his treadmill to a halt. "Gracie!"

She smacked her treadmill's controls, letting it slow to a stop. Her breathing continued to labor. "What?" she panted.

He looked her over. Concern furrowed his brow. Gracie could tell he was trying to read her with his eye, the same way she read others, and if felt uncomfortable to receive.

"Talk to me," he said. "What just happened there?"

"I just… It's…" *Snitches get stitches*, the saying goes. As much as Danny had pissed her off, Gracie wasn't going to shit talk him, not to the guy who had been Danny's boss for a decade now. But what to say instead? "Nothing," she said. "Sorry, I kind of…"

"You went off somewhere," said Kevin. "Somewhere not good. Your body was here, doing what it was doing. Meanwhile, your mind…" He tapped the side of his head and then made a swirly gesture of his fingers zooming into the beyond.

"Yeah," said Gracie.

"And probably that happens a lot."

She shrugged.

He started removing the electrodes from his chest. "Let's take a break. Hydrate. Stretch. All that stuff. Sound good?"

"Sure," said Gracie. And as she started removing her own electrodes, she felt her fingers tremble slightly.

Maybe this whole Crimson Wraith thing wasn't something she was suited for. Maybe Kevin didn't really understand just how messed-up Gracie was, all the things about her past that Danny had listed off at the kitchen table, the bumpy road she'd taken to get there. Maybe living in a shitty little apartment with shitty little people who act shitty toward each other—like Zack and Kristen, like her mom and dad—was the best she could do in this life. And maybe Kevin would soon realize what a huge mistake he'd made with her.

1954

Although he grew up seeing his father wear the costume nearly every night, Eddie realized that not once had he ever imagined donning the hood of the Crimson Wraith himself. In private moments, he might touch the cloak's hem or run his fingers over its fabric. But it just never occurred to him to find what it felt like to place it upon his own shoulders.

In some ways, yes, it was simply part of his father's uniform, the thing he wore as he went about his work, one night after the other, as much as a police officer's cap or doctor's white coat. On a deeper level, however, a level that Eddie experienced more as emotion than comprehension, the cloak seemed like a religious icon to him. It provided physical connection with a spiritual reality, and that reality was the Crimson Wraith itself.

He knew the Crimson Wraith to be his father's creation, an alter ego he portrayed. But before Eddie had met William Finn, he met the Crimson Wraith, an unearthly phantom emerging from darkness and flame to save his life. After that, it would always seem as though the hood had a reality beyond the man who wore it, as though it was not that his father *was* the Crimson Wraith but that his father simply *dressed as* the Crimson Wraith.

Since his high school graduation, Eddie had spent the past six years receiving greater and greater responsibility within Finn Industries, preparing him to ease his father's workload in another decade or so, maybe even allow Will to move into retirement. But, in regards to their mission, Eddie never imagined wearing any costume other than the purple and gold of the Wily Wisp.

The mask felt the strangest to wear. Eddie had not seen it when he first met his father. The Blue Banshee had unmasked him in their rooftop brawl. And so, Will's own face had been the face emerging from the Crimson Wraith's hood, a real and human face, kind-eyed and strong. He would always see his father that way, and whenever they went out upon their mission, he was always more conscious of the face beneath the grim countenance that so terrified the Titan City criminals.

"I must say," said Sylvia, in her own costume as Lady Luna, "it fits you well." Together, they crouched side-by-side on a rooftop, gazing through their binoculars at the Mikado Imports building opposite them, there on the Brennert River docks. "No one would know you aren't him."

"His current costume isn't quite my size," said Eddie. "This is Father's first, the one he wore when he started fighting crime."

"That wouldn't be his first then," she smiled. "I had the pleasure of dressing him in that when we were back in school."

"Yes, I suppose you did." Edward did not see why she felt the need to keep reminding him of her history with his father.

"You know, he was always the best of men," she said, "even at that age. And in all the years since, I've never met another like him. To be honest, back then I thought there would be more of a future for us after graduation. But there was a distance in him that I never could cross. I did not understand it at the time. Oh, he always gave a warm and glowing presence to all around, sure. He was a great teller of jokes and had a way of greeting acquaintances that made them feel like bosom pals. But none of these ever got close to him. That was an exclusive club. Only Chubby and I were members. Only we were intimate enough with your father to recognize he kept a part of himself held back, hidden from view.

"I thought it had to do with his childhood, you know, before old Josiah Finn adopted him. I knew that made him different from the rest of us in ways I could never truly understand. Now, though, knowing the man he became, I have to imagine there was something else to it, as though the Crimson Wraith were already within him, gaining strength until the right time came for him to emerge."

She looked to Eddie, eyebrows raised, as if seeking confirmation for her theory of his father's psychological development, but the whys and hows of his father becoming the Crimson Wraith had never been questions for him. Whatever the reason, his father simply was the Crimson Wraith. It was a fact of existence, like the fact that fire was hot and water wet.

He nodded to her in a noncommittal way, acknowledging he had heard the words she spoke. And he was suddenly very glad to have the skull mask concealing the expression of contempt that he didn't imagine he could have hid too well in his Wily Wisp domino.

Sylvia lifted her binoculars and once more turned her attention to the docks. "Looks like we may have something." A van approached the Mikado Imports warehouse. "They are driving with their headlights off."

"That's suspicious," said Eddie

"Not to mention dangerous," said Sylvia.

The van parked and two armed men exited the vehicle, going around to the rear where three more men pushed a fourth out onto the pavement. Their captive had difficulty keeping his feet since his arms were bound behind his back. Although he wore a blindfold, Eddie recognized him. After all, he had been at the Titan Capitol Building just the day before.

"Senator Estes! He's been kidnapped! But why?"

"Whatever the reason," said Sylvia, "his life is in the gravest danger. We had better approach carefully."

Sylvia and Eddie slid down from the rooftop on a rope attached to one of her grappling arrows. Then they made their way carefully toward the Mikado Imports warehouse, creeping around stacked crates and barrels to find the most indirect route to the rear, until they spied a side entrance where one of the gunmen stood at guard, leaning against the wall and smoking a cigarette.

"I'm going to have to get close before I can try to knock him out," whispered Eddie.

"Perhaps a distraction would help you," said Sylvia. She fired an arrow in a high arc down the alleyway, above the gunman's line of sight, knocking an empty Kronos-Kola bottle to the ground, where it shattered.

The gunman aimed his weapon in the direction of the sound. "Someone down there?" he called out, never seeing Eddie until the Crimson Wraith's cloak wrapped around his face, blinding him and forcing him to inhale the sweet knockout gas from a pellet Eddie released. Before the gunman could fire off a round, he fell unconscious at Eddie's feet. After binding his wrists and ankles and placing him behind a group of trash cans, Sylvia fired another of her grappling arrows to the warehouse rooftop, and the two climbed up to a skylight where they could survey the interior.

The warehouse floor had been broken into aisle after aisle of shelves, each one at least ten feet high, stacked with a variety of goods to tempt tourists and adorn the restaurants of Titan City's Little Tokyo—so many golden Buddhas, scrolls of watercolor paintings and calligraphy, tea sets and gongs and chopsticks. Along those aisles and around the walkway that encircled them halfway up the warehouse's height stalked more gunmen than had arrived in the darkened van. And at the center of the room, covered in a canvas sheet, something large and round sat on a table, connected by wires to machines whose light steadily blinked beside it.

Eddie whispered, "I believe we've found the Shadowmaster's nuclear bomb."

"You think it's armed?" asked Sylvia.

"I don't know, but I think we need to get the senator out of here so we can deal with it."

"They must be keeping him there." She pointed to an enclosure at the top of the steps to the second-story walkway. The blinds were drawn over its windows, but a light shone inside.

"That looks like the place. We had better thin out this crowd along the way."

"Agreed. I count four on the ground, six on the walkway. Do you want to go high or low?"

"You can work the ground," said Sylvia, readying her bow. "I can take out most of the upper level right from here."

She had skill; Eddie had to give her that. As he dropped to the ground and began making his way from one gunman to the next, pouncing upon them from the shadows to silently disarm and disable them, carving a path of unconscious bodies slumped in the dark, he would turn occasionally to follow Sylvia's progress. It appeared she had a set of blunted arrows crafted just for the purpose of dealing a knock-out blow from a distance. And in addition to being non-lethal, her shots sent the gunmen into unconsciousness quickly and quietly. Perhaps she was doing more than just amusing herself with crime-fighting adventuring after all. What would his father think of seeing her in action like this? Would the ringing of gunmen's skulls sound to him like wedding bells?

Eddie reached the steps to the office and climbed them cautiously, then listened at the door. From the sounds within, there seemed maybe three other men inside with the senator, no doubt all armed, in a confined space with plenty of lighting. Just like entering the warehouse, a distraction would be useful on this occasion. He looked back to Sylvia and found her shimmying down a rope to join him on the warehouse floor.

Once she landed and readied her bow, he indicated with a gesture that she should fire her arrow at the window opposite the office door. She nodded. He readied a trio of explosive pellets, one flash and two smoke. Sylvia fired her arrow, and the glass window shattered.

Shouts erupted within, and Eddie flung open the door, catching just a glimpse of the positions of those within—two gunmen sitting, one standing, and Estes bound to a chair, still blindfolded. Then Eddie hurled his pellets to the ground, shutting his eyes from the flash.

As smoke started to fill the room, he began his attack, delivering his first blows to the nearest gunman with his eyes still closed, then driving his opponent's skull into his knee. He saw the smoke-dimmed outlines of the other two swing their guns wildly in confusion. Ducking low under their gun arms, he swung up sharply with an uppercut to one and flung his cloak in a disorienting whirl at the other before finishing him with a roundhouse kick. As the smoke began to clear, both lay unconscious on the floor.

Bound in his seat, Senator Estes blubbered in panic. "Is that the police? Help! Please, help! Please!"

The irony amused Eddie, to have Estes saved by the very vigilante he sought to destroy. He pulled the senator's blindfold loose to let him look into the dark, empty sockets of his skull-masked rescuer.

"You!" said Estes.

"Me," said Eddie, reveling in the expression of wonder gaping up at him

"But-but-but... You can't..."

"I understand this may be something of a shock, senator. But although you may not be my biggest fan, that does not change my mission."

"I, uh... Well, I..."

"Perhaps we can discuss that later. First, let me get you to safety."

"Yes! Please! Oh, thank you!"

Eddie quickly untied Senator Estes, smiling to himself at what his father would say about this. Maybe the CCA would reconsider its stance on the Crimson Wraith's mission after this night. What an amusing turn that would be.

"There you are, Senator. Now, let me make a quick check on your friends." Looking out the door, Eddie did a survey of the warehouse. The guards that he and Sylvia had taken out of play remained so. "All clear. Right this way, sir."

He started down the stairs, but as he did, he saw Sylvia at the bottom step. She had an arrow ready, aimed right at him.

A single word flashed in Eddie's mind: *Betrayal*!

2019

Gracie had a tough time warming up to beating on the heavy punching bag that hung from the room of Finn Manor that Kevin called "the dojo." She wasn't angry at the bag. It wasn't hurting anybody.

Kevin held it in place for her, watching Gracie's face, watching her swings. "Okay, stop," he said after a minute.

She dropped her hands. They hung at her side in their padded gloves. Her head followed. This was not working out.

"What are you thinking about?" he asked.

"I don't know," she said.

"No, come on. Really basic here. What are you thinking about? No wrong answers."

"I guess," said Gracie, "I'm thinking about the bag. And about hitting it."

"What else?"

"Um, I guess what it feels like, kind of, in my knuckles and in my elbow. And, I don't know, the sort of gym smell in the room, that chemical, plasticky smell."

Kevin smirked. "Yeah, that happens. Either it smells like cleaning chemicals or it smells like old sweat. You try to go for one more than the other. What else?"

Gracie shrugged.

"Okay, listen, you don't have to tell me. That's fine. But what you're thinking about right now, it isn't the same as what you were thinking about one the treadmill, was it?"

She frowned and considered what he was saying.

"Or if it is the same thing, then maybe you aren't thinking about it in the same way. And how that shows is, before, whatever you were thinking of made you angry, and that anger energized you. I don't see that energy right now though. So, if you are thinking about the same thing, then maybe you are feeling less angry about it and more sad."

That did seem to be close to what was going on. On the treadmill, she was pissed off at Danny for making her feel like she might not belong there. Here in front of the punching bag,

Gracie was afraid that he was right.

She shook her head. "I'm sorry. I'll try to focus up here. Let me try again."

Kevin said, "We can do that, but only if you want to."

"I do. I want this. Really. I want to be good at this, to be able to help you. I want to be part of team Crimson Wraith."

"Good. That's what I want too."

"You are giving me your time," she continued. "And I appreciate that. Already you've given me so much." For fuck's sake, was she going to start crying now? Gracie gritted her teeth so the sob caught in her throat instead of making it into her eyes. "Who the hell else has an actual, for-real superhero offering to teach them like this?"

Kevin nodded. "So, once again," he said, "I don't really think of myself as a *super*-hero…"

"Whatever, man."

"But more importantly, it sounds like you're putting some big pressure on yourself. And that makes sense because… well, all of this—the legacy, the mission…"

The jack-ass trying to bring you down over breakfast, Gracie thought.

"It's a lot," he continued. "It was a lot for me too. Probably, it was for most of those before us, maybe every one of them after William Finn, everyone who got to hear about the Crimson Wraith before putting on the hood. If you didn't find that intimidating, there must be something really wrong with you. Or you might just be an asshole."

That made her smile, but then she thought about Danny again, what he said. "Yeah," she murmured, "an asshole."

Suddenly, she got it. She got where he was coming from. Danny thought *she* was the one who was being the asshole, not caring enough about this thing they'd all devoted themselves to, not taking it seriously.

Kevin went on. "Secondly, I'm not going to teach you how to fight, not exactly. It's more that I'm going to teach you how to be a fighter. You already know how to fight. I saw that. You have the speed and strength. You know how to take a hit and keep going. You show awareness of your opponent and your environment. I can help you develop your technique, but it's everything else around the fight itself, that is where I really want to help you."

"What do you mean?"

"The fights I saw you in, you were reacting to an imminent threat, first against yourself and then against someone you cared about. When that threat hit, your body responded. You felt fear and you felt anger. Those drove you to act. They fueled you, just like whatever you were thinking about on the treadmill before. Having that kind of fuel can give you a lot of power, sure, but it comes at a cost.

"If all you have in that moment is fear and anger and instinct, it ends up being really difficult to think strategically, to think long term and remember what you really care about, what you value. You can go too far when you really ought to hold back. Or you can fall short when you really ought to keep going.

"You don't want to rely on finding your fuel for the fight only in what is right before your eyes. Sometimes the reason to fight isn't standing in front of you. Sometimes it shouldn't be something you are afraid of but something you hope for.

"What I want to do is help you find peace in the fight. Does that make sense? I want you to be able to engage an opponent with less fear and less anger, to fight with a clearer head by helping you to be more comfortable with the fight itself. That way you can bring the fight when *you* choose, not when it chooses you. And you can let it go just as easily because you will be in it with a clear head, never losing focus on what matters most.

"Everything we are going to do in this dojo is about finding that comfort, that peace, that focus by making the fight feel familiar, something you can just slip into and out of at will. Sure, you may, some new tactic that you hadn't considered before, but the point isn't about giving you something that you don't have. I can't do that, and you don't need it. You already have everything you need. What I want is for you to let me help you find what to do with what you have because I think what you can do is a hell of a lot. Understand?"

Yeah, there were definitely tears on Gracie's face—not sobs and not sadness but tears all the same. It felt strange to be looking Kevin in the eyes and just let the water slowly slip from hers. It felt strange to have someone, not exactly praise her, but to show her respect and to feel like, hell, maybe she even deserved it.

Gracie wiped at her cheeks with the length of her forearm not covered by a boxing glove. "I think I understand. I'm sorry."

"It's all right. You don't have to be sorry. This is new."

"Yeah," she said. "Real new."

"Well, it's new for me too. I haven't trained anyone like this before. All I know is how Michael taught me, so let's both hope I don't suck at it."

Gracie laughed. "You're doing okay so far, I think."

"Nice. That's good to know. All right then." Once more, he stepped back and braced the heavy bag. "How about you take a minute and close your eyes?"

She did.

"Now breathe, nice and slow. And think about what you were thinking about on the treadmill. Whatever you were angry about then and whatever you are feeling about it now doesn't matter. Choose to think about it. Choose to hold it in your mind. And let it just be there."

The images that Danny had resurrected for her returned to Gracie's mind. *Waffles. White tank-top. Leering eyes. Home. Gas station wine.*

"Okay, now open your eyes and focus on the bag." She did. "There you go. Just focus on it. See it right where it is. Breathe. And now, find your stance. Lift your gloves. Breathe. Focus. Ready the punch. Breathe. Breathe."

In and out. In and out. And on that breath rode so many

memories for Gracie, so many things she really didn't ever want to think about but, fuck it, there they were anyway. And there was Kevin, there in the room with her, this room, this dojo, in this house where he had welcomed her because of something he saw in her, something that she didn't have to pretend to have because she already had it, something she didn't have to pretend to be because she already was it. She already belonged there.

"Now, whenever you are ready, give me one punch—one firm, focused punch, hard or light as you want. Whatever you feel like throwing, you go on right ahead and throw."

And she did.

1954

Suddenly, it occurred to Eddie that it should have made him more suspicious how Lady Luna just happened to appear on that rooftop as they were following a mysterious lead. Perhaps that was the unease he had felt around her, something his father might have had a harder time seeing due to their childhood connection. Her story about following the trail of "L'Ombre Grande" through Europe—had she made the whole thing up? And why?

Then Sylvia shouted, "Look out!" and let her arrow fly. Eddie sidestepped its shaft only to then realize it never would have struck him. Sylvia intentionally overshot him, aiming at a target above and behind Edward—Senator Estes!

But as Eddie turned and saw the senator wailing in pain from an arrow whose shaft drove halfway through his forearm, he also saw the Japanese *tanto* dagger, slipping loosely from the fingers of Estes' hand.

Eddie had thought he was rescuing Estes. And in so doing, he left himself completely vulnerable. If not for Sylvia, he might be dead. Why exactly had the senator tried to stab him in the back? That would have to be worked out once Eddie made sure he was incapacitated.

After the whole CCA campaign, it felt immensely satisfying to Eddie to drive his fist into Estes' face. He knew he struck the senator hard, but still, Eddie was surprised to see Estes' nose fly right off, a shocking sight but not so shocking as to keep Eddie from following with two more swift jab and a punch to the gut that sent Estes stumbling backward and onto the walkway landing. And as he fell, his hair came loose, revealing itself to be a wig, concealing another head of hair underneath.

"You're falling apart, Senator," said Eddie. "Or should I address you as Monsieur L'Ombre Grande—The Shadowmaster!"

Senator Estes laughed, no longer as Senator Estes. Even in pain on the floor, the Shadowmaster's voice carried heavy, somber tones, although no trace of the Japanese accent Eddie expected. "I almost had you, Crimson Wraith. You were fully at my mercy, and you never even knew. If you had been alone tonight, this would have been your end, and I would have my revenge."

How many childhood fantasies of Eddie's included just this very moment? Here he was, the actual Shadowmaster, fallen at his feet. And yet he did not imagine the Shadowmaster to be so young, nor so handsome. The rest of his disguise was falling away. He could not be much older than Eddie himself, and it seemed to him there was a dignity in the angle of his cheekbone, a sensuous fullness of his lip that caught Eddie's breath.

"That was a close one!" said Sylvia, now at Eddie's side.

"Too close," said Eddie. "So, Shadowmaster, the rumors of your death have been greatly exaggerated, have they?"

"No, you fool," said the Shadowmaster. "It was my father who you defeated. He was the *Kagesama*—the Shadowmaster—before me. I am Kagesama Sato Katsumi, son of Kagesama Sato Takahiro. He was the man you killed while my mother and I suffered in one of my own nation's internment camps for its citizens of Japanese descent. She died there. Lost without the man she loved, stripped of her freedom here in the so-called 'Land of the Free,' she took to her bed and never rose again, refusing the food I held to her lips, fading into nothing before my eyes."

"And you thought that detonating a nuclear bomb here in Titan City would avenge the deaths of your parents?" asked Eddie.

"I was treated as an enemy of America when I was just a child. So, I decided, if that is how I am treated, then that is what I will be, one capable of limitless destruction. But that was to be my revenge against them. Against you, Crimson Wraith, my vengeance is something more personal. For taking the life of my father, for breaking my mother's heart, I have made you experience just how it feels to be hated and feared by those who do not know you. The campaign of Senator Estes and his Committee on Community Accountability has made you a monster in the eyes of the city you claim to protect."

How could Eddie remain unmoved by the pain he saw in those beautiful eyes? "I am sorry for the loss of your mother, Sato Katsumi. And for whatever treatment you received as a boy. But your father threatened the lives of millions. He had to be stopped."

"Spare me your show of sympathy, Crimson Wraith. Do not dishonor my defeat with such pretense."

Eddie felt pained to think of how this man must see him—or rather, to see his father, the Crimson Wraith—as a heartless monster executing his will upon the world without compassion for others. But there appeared to be no convincing him. "Where is the real senator Estes? What have you done with him?"

"A few years ago," said the Shadowmaster, "the senator took a trip to Europe. My agents made certain he never returned. I believe he may still float somewhere in the Paris sewers."

Sylvia asked "What should we do with this Shadowmaster, Crimson Wraith? This is your city after all. Shall we radio back to the Crypt?"

He considered their position. His father was not there to tell him what path to take, but maybe he didn't need him to be. The next right thing to do appeared perfectly clear. "Titan City will not trust the Crimson Wraith right now, not operating as we have, so rather than avoid the authorities, I believe it is time to reach out to them." While Sylvia kept the Shadowmaster guarded, he stepped into the warehouse office, picked up the phone, and dialed the Titan City Police Department. "I'd like to speak to Officer Goodman."

CHAPTER ELEVEN

2019

Alone in the Crypt together, things were all business between Gracie and Danny. Kevin had sent her down to get her voice and palm scanned for security, apparently unaware the two had any tension between them.

Danny said nothing about the morning. Mostly he kept his eyes on the monitor as he pulled up the security software. Gracie sat in a chair the "L" of his work desk with a microphone and what appeared to be a portable palm scanner on the desk in front of her. She spoke the password into the microphone a few times, got her palms scanned, and then Danny said, "Okay, you're all good."

Silence followed. It seemed like he expected her just to leave as he opened up new windows on the screen in front and began typing.

Gracie said, "So that's it?"

"That's it."

"Cool." She looked around the Crypt, at the isolated pools of light illuminating the Crimson Wraith costume, weapons, and equipment. "Did you want to give me that more detailed tour you were talking about?"

"Not right now," he said. "Gotta index the data from your work-outs this morning."

"Oh, ok." But Gracie didn't get up just yet. "What does that do?"

His fingers hovered over the keys for a moment. "It gives

me info on what to expect when you're out in the field, what a naturally elevated heart-rate looks like, oxygen consumption, all that kind of thing. And that info gives me something to get an additional warning if something is seriously wrong, like you're drowning or you've been electrocuted. All that fun stuff."

"Fun stuff..." said Gracie.

"Fun stuff," Danny repeated.

"Okay," still she didn't get up. "I saw Stephen this morning, outside, over Edward's grave."

"Yeah, he's there at least once a day."

"The two of them were close?"

"They were lovers. At least they were for about thirty years or so. Then Edward left."

"He left?"

"Yep," Danny turned to Gracie. "See, most of the guys who have been the Crimson Wraith, they don't retire. It's more like they get retired, you feel me? Some bad shit happens, and if they live past that bad shit, well, their fighting days are over.

"Now, Edward, you could say he was one of the lucky ones. Some bad shit happened. His retirement was one he got to walk away from. And then he got to see one Crimson Wraith after the other *not* get the opportunity to live out their retirement like he did. And after Zero Hour..." Danny gave one of those meaningful looks that are supposed to say everything that needs to be said, but Gracie had no idea what that actually might be.

"What happened on Zero Hour?"

"The way Kevin tells it, it was bad," said Danny. "The wrong call was made. Because of that wrong call, Titan City lost two bridges and about two thousand lives."

"Yeah," said Gracie. "I mean I was like three-years-old, but I know about it, what people say anyway. What I mean is, what happened with the Crimson Wraith on Zero Hour. He tried to save everybody, right?"

"Well, some people got real upset that the Crimson Wraith

only stopped the one bomb at the Titan City Justice Center. Those whose loved ones died on the bridges wanted to know why he hadn't been there for them too. Then someone put on the Internet the threats Mr. Echo had given about where the bombs were going to go, and it became real easy to say the Crimson Wraith should have known there would be three bombs and not just one."

"Okay, so he fucked up," said Gracie. "People fuck up sometimes."

"People do," said Danny. "But people don't like it when their heroes do. We had some harsh Crimson Wraith hate going on there for a bit. Crimson Wraith number six, Christopher O'Neil, he retired over that one, Esperanza too. She went into legitimate law enforcement, while he got himself checked-in to one of those places with the finger-painting and the real soft walls, know what I mean?"

"What, like a fucking asylum?"

"Please. This ain't the nineteenth century. It's a psychiatric hospital."

"Holy shit."

"Yeah, well, turns out he had some other stuff going on, more than just the PTSD of a crime-fighting career, but he's gotten good treatment. We see him on holidays sometimes."

"That's... I didn't..." Gracie shook her head. "I didn't know."

"You're not supposed to know. Folks ain't supposed to think the Crimson Wraith is human, much less a human who needs professional psychiatric help. Anyway, the whole Zero Hour thing and the public hate for the Crimson Wraith apparently brought up bad memories for Edward about his time under the hood, so he bounced. Said his good-byes and went to live by himself in an old folks home. Stephen begged him to stay, but Edward had his mind made up. He went, and Stephen stuck it out here, stayed on the mission."

"They broke up over that?"

"Not exactly. Stephen was always over there a few times a month, so, I mean, they still had something good going on I guess. It was cute, two old dudes holding hands on the couch and watching black and white movies."

Gracie said, "God, if I live to be that age, I would want someone holding my hand on a couch like that."

"They were cute," said Danny. "By the time I signed on, Edward was already on his own out there. They asked me to set up some security to help keep an eye on him, so I got to go over there and meet the guy a few times. Real character. Like, classy. Sharp too."

Both were quiet for a moment, and in the silence and shadows of the Crypt, Gracie's mind swirled with all the names of all the people through all the years of the masked vigilante's career—seven Crimson Wraiths, five Wily Wisps, and how many others like Danny and Stephen who supported those crime fighters along the way? How many had dedicated their lives to this mission? And how many had lost their lives in its service?

After a while, she said, "I can see why I rubbed you the wrong way at first. I was definitely only thinking about me and about everything I had going on, getting arrested and shit. To be honest, I looked at you guys up here in what seemed like the lap of luxury, thinking you didn't have a care in the world. I had no fucking clue."

"Well," said Danny, "I guess it ain't really fair to expect you to care about something you don't know anything about."

"But, now, I do know about this and I do care, you know, about being part of what the Crimson Wraith does. I want to learn. I want to be good at it. And maybe I could be. Maybe this is, like, what I'm supposed to be doing with my life. And maybe that's why I haven't been all that good at anything else."

Danny shrugged. "Maybe. I don't know. Honestly, I haven't seen anyone else try since I came on board. But Kevin believes in you. And it looks like you got Stephen's stamp of approval too. I'm sorry I was hard on you. I guess... Well, it's been pretty rough around here lately, what with Edward getting murdered and what a rough time we've had trying to find who killed him..."

"Wait," said Gracie. "Edward was murdered?"

1955

Senator Kelly Winchester's face brightened at the sight of his old school-mate William Finn, arm-in-arm with new wife Sylvia Madison, now Sylvia Finn. He pushed through the other party-goers celebrating his recent election there at his family's estate to shake Will's hand.

"Willie, my boy! I say, the ghosts of our past do have a way of coming back to haunt us don't they? I'm simply chuffed you found your way to my little bash. And here with your blushing bride as well? Sylvia, you finally caught this rambling bachelor, did you? What a coup! Bully for you. Always did make quite a team, the pair of you. But I hope it isn't your fault that Willie here has to walk with a cane, is it? Too much honeymoon gymnastics, eh?" Winchester brayed with laughter in praise of what he considered to be wit.

The bullet wound of the year before had fractured Will's ribcage, the aftereffects of which still caused a struggle for him, including a shortening of breath and a persistent ache. He never returned to his previous athletic capacity. Will walked with that cane for the rest of his life, a snakewood-shafted cane with silver-plated Derby handle.

But he and Sylvia laughed along with Winchester as best they could for so pompous and self-serving a sense of humor as his. She said, "Oh, now, Kelly. What a thought! No, my loving husband here got distracted during a game of polo and lost his seating. Fell right off his horse."

"I swear," Will chimed in, "it was the absolutely most beautiful blue bunting imaginable. *Cyanocompsa parellina.* You know the bird?"

"I do not believe we've been acquainted," said Winchester.

And Will and Sylvia laughed as if he were the cleverest of men.

An assistant of Winchester's approached them, escorting a woman with pen and notepad at the ready, "Senator, this young lady here is a reporter with *The Titan City Gazette*, and she would like a statement from you about replacing Senator Estes."

"Damn shame," said Winchester. "Damn shame, truly, to lose such a fine citizen and patriot like that to a heart attack."

When Officer Goodman arrived at Mikado Imports to apprehend Shadowmaster Sato Takeshi and his accomplices, he decided that disposing of a nuclear explosive device was a step beyond the capacity of the TCPD and called federal agents for assistance. The Bureau of National Safety ordered that the entire affair, including the murder of Senator Estes while abroad, to be kept secret, not wanting the public to lose faith in its government by making them aware of the threat of a nuclear bomb on American soil.

"And he was doing such good work closing in on that dastardly Crimson Wraith." Winchester turned to Will, "Although surely he made a few missteps along the way, thinking you might have had something to do with all that business, my boy, dragging you in front of the CCA. But we cannot fault him for his efforts, can we?"

Will raised his hand. "It made for a humorous story when I arrived at the club later."

"Surely it did!" said Winchester. "Will, give us a few, would you? And please, you mustn't leave before we've had a chance to speak about that matter I wrote you regarding." He gave Sylvia a condescending pout. "Just between us, dear. Boy's talk. You understand."

"Don't I ever," she said with a playful eye roll. "Fear not. I won't let him slip away without having your little meeting."

"There's a good girl," said Winchester, who placed an arm around the reporter's waist before walking away from them.

Without altering her facial expression, Sylvia whispered, "That fat-head can't really suspect the truth about you, can he?"

"Without a doubt," said Will, "Kelly Winchester is a stupendous ass. But other than you, Chubby, and myself, he is the only other person to have seen the Crimson Wraith in his first incarnation back at Ellsworth."

"I suppose he must have eventually come to figure you had a part in that trick of ours as well, since it was *your* girlfriend who lured him into that graveyard."

"Were you my girlfriend?" said Will with a smile.

"Then and always," said Sylvia, and she kissed Will's cheek.

Before this party, Winchester had sent Will a letter that read:

Dear William Finn,

I hear congratulations are in order, old boy! Wedded at last! And to Sylvia Madison no less. Well done! Why, I think a man might lose his reason for such a woman. He might even follow her right past the gates of HELL on a moonlit NIGHT if he was not careful.

Hope you will join me as I celebrate my victory in the senatorial race to replace poor Fred Estes. Who would have thought I had a GHOST of a chance? So I plan to make it a real RED letter day. Music and dancing and enough champagne to split your SKULL.

There is something too I wish to speak with you about. Something personal. I hope you won't think me exaggerating that it could be a matter of GRAVE importance, and it could be to your great advantage to hear what I have to say.

Quite a lark to hear about your testimony before the CCA last year. Who would have thought you had anything to do with that dreadful character? Why, a connection like that could really ruin a man in Titan City.

There could be little doubt what Winchester was suggesting. Will and Sylvia knew they would have to attend to find out what exactly he had planned. And as the hour neared midnight and the celebrants began to thin at the Winchester home, Will sought out their host and followed him to a private office.

"Can I offer you a cigar, William?" said Winchester. He reached into his desk drawer, and Will noticed his wrist make a subtle twist as he tapped something just underneath the desktop ledge. He surmised a button had just been pressed to activate a recording device that would document their conversation.

"None for me, thank you," said Will. "Had to give up cigars after my injury. The lungs don't work quite as they used to. In fact…" He moved to open a window. "Hope you don't mind me introducing a little draft. The air was a bit thick down there."

"Not at all. I'd like you to breathe easily of course," said Winchester. "And you know what allows a man to breathe the most easily William?"

"What is that, Kelly?"

"The truth."

"Well, I suppose it does."

"The truth, William. The whole truth and nothing but the truth."

Will chuckled. "So help you, God?"

"I think you'll find that I'm not the one in need of help."

"I should say not, here at the beginning of what is no doubt a bright political career. Seems like you are doing quite well for yourself."

"I am. The Winchester family has always done well in Titan City. We've always had an advantage in the world. Call it our keen intellect. Call it our savvy and determination. But the fact is we have always known a little more than the other guy, and knowing things gives a person power."

"It does indeed," said William. "Why, if I hadn't known what a blue bunting looked like, I might have missed that wonderful sight, even if it cost me my riding legs."

"And had I not experienced a childhood encounter with

the Crimson Wraith, I might have missed his true identity."

"Is that so?"

"That is so."

"Would you like to share that with him then?" asked Will. And he pointed past Winchester, who turned to see, there in his office, standing behind him for who knows how long, the masked figure of the Crimson Wraith, cloak billowing in the breeze from the still-open window, the sulfurous fog of his Infernal Mist swirling around his boots.

Winchester's face turned the same shade of white as the skull before him, and he staggered backward in surprise, stammering. "He! But you!" He pointed to Will. "And you!" He pointed at the Crimson Wraith. "You and you!" His finger waved back and forth between them. "I was so sure!"

The Crimson Wraith cut through Winchester's babble with his ethereal, echoing voice. "Please forgive me for entering uninvited, Senator. But I wished to convey my congratulations in person."

His scheme frustrated, the flabbergasted Winchester turned his anger on the figure who frightened him so much, so many years ago. "You've got a lot of nerve showing up here!" he said. "You'll find Kelly Winchester isn't scared of you, Scarlet Stranger! Not anymore! I don't know what you're playing at, but one word and I'll have you arrested faster than you can say Jack Robinson!"

The Crimson Wraith held up a hand. "That is what I wished to speak with you about, since you have taken over for Estes. You see, the late senator made me aware of something. I do not want my work to frighten the good citizens of Titan City, only the bad. Those who follow the law and work for their fellow men should have nothing to fear from me, and I wondered if you could help me make that known."

"Is that a fact now? Help you? Will, are you hearing this?"

"I am, Kelly. Every word."

Winchester asked, "And what do you propose, Mr. Crimson Wraith?"

"After your swearing-in, I would like you to hold a press conference, saying that your career will usher in a new age of civility and decency. And when you do, I will join you there to present myself to Titan City."

"Will you indeed? Dressed like this? Appearing from the gloom like some fearful phantom?"

"No, not quite." And the Crimson Wraith reached within his hood to unlatch the skull that he wore over his own features, to show the face underneath. Although he still wore a red domino mask over his eyes to conceal his identity, it was clear the Crimson Wraith was no ghost, but a man, flesh and blood. And he smiled, reaching out with his gauntleted hand to shake the senator's. "Let us make a bright new tomorrow together."

So ended any suspicion in the mind of Senator Kelly Winchester that the Crimson Wraith might be William Finn, and so began Edward's career as the Crimson Wraith. As the senator shook his hand, Edward looked past him to see his father beaming, showing so much pride in his son and successor.

2019

Danny nodded. "Yeah, Edward was murdered."

"You guys were talking like he was real old, so I just thought, you know, 'natural causes.'"

"He was eighty-seven, but someone felt like going ahead and murdering him anyway instead of waiting for his time to come."

"What the fuck? Who would do that?"

"We don't know yet. Kevin thinks it was someone working on the retirement home staff based on ease of entry. We've been watching the likely suspects for weeks now with cameras and audio, even gone through their goddamn trash, everything just shy of sneaking into their homes to look around.

Kevin doesn't like to commit breaking-and-entering without a good idea that it's gonna turn up something, kind of like the cops needing probable cause if they don't have a warrant. Nothing has turned up yet, but we got a lead, and soon as it's visiting day..."

"Visiting day?"

Danny nodded. He turned back to the computer and started opening up a file. "Crimson Wraith number four. Henry Mills. Goes by 'Hank.'" A faded image appeared on his screen of a thick-jawed man in red-hooded sweatshirt and a spattering of what looked to be dried blood on his face. He stared into the camera with a heavy, haggard gaze. Lines and numbers behind his head indicated his height. A placard before him displayed his name, the date of 03-01-1988, and a number that was apparently his arrest record. It was Hank's mugshot. "He's in prison."

"Wait, so one Crimson Wraith ended up in a mental hospital and another got arrested?"

"Yep," said Danny. "Killed someone. That was how he retired from being the Crimson Wraith. Convicted of murder. Got a life sentence."

"Who did he murder?"

"A bad guy," said Danny. "Someone who deserved it." Then he pulled up the image of Edward's refrigerator from the Haunts. "Whoever murdered Edward, they saw all these photos on his refrigerator and moved them away to get a better look at this one." He pointed to the photo of Edward, Stephen, and Michael at Bobby D's Delicatessen, the one that showed Hank in the kitchen in the background. "Kevin pointed out it's the only one with Hank in it, and all the other guys appear in other photos on the fridge. He figures Edward's murderer knew Hank back in the day, so maybe he can help identify them from the retirement home staff."

"Right. So, visiting day, huh?"

"Yup, visiting day." Danny turned to Gracie. "So, hearing all this, seeing how the mission of the Crimson Wraith can land you in prison, an institution, or the grave, are you sure you still want a part of it?"

Gracie looked at the screen, to Hank's mugshot. Just from his expression, the way he was looking into the camera, without knowing any details of what got him there, Gracie immediately felt in her gut like she could relate. His face looked like how she felt after the fight with Zack, the night she came real close to thinking she wanted to kill someone too—a bad guy, someone who deserved it.

"You know," she said, "all that stuff you were listing out over breakfast, all the messed-up stuff in my background? Yeah, see, that's my 'normal.' Years of being on the street or just barely off it, sometimes not knowing when I'm going to eat next, never knowing who is going to come at me with some shit, feeling like I'm living right there on the very edge of surviving..." She shrugged. "I'm used to it.

"Everything you have here, peace and quiet and people giving a damn about each other, not living with the threat of immediate danger—*this* is the stuff that feels really weird to me. Before coming here, I probably walked out the door a million times thinking, 'Someone may want to fuck me up today.' That was just how I thought the world was. Since I was fifteen, I never thought I'd live to see thirty. I just couldn't imagine. And, you know, maybe I still might not.

"I'm not trying to say I'm a badass, like, 'Danger is my middle name' or some shit. What I'm saying is—fucked up as it may seem—thinking that everything could go real bad real fast—that's nothing new to me. You showing me the risks that come with the Crimson Wraith is actually a huge relief because then I know. There's no guessing. I'd rather be out there doing something where somebody really does want to kill me —somebody with a gun in my fucking face—instead of just going crazy thinking about where is it coming from and why am I not seeing it? Better to have a threat be 'here-and-now' and not wondering 'where-or-when.'

"And along the way, if I get to be useful?" She laughed. "Holy shit, man. Useful? That's something I don't think anyone ever called me, not for any use I wanted to be used for anyway. But being able to help people, to prove that maybe I'm not..." She shook her head. "Yeah, I want this. I want all of it. If it can be mine, I'll take it, wherever it takes me."

Then Gracie looked at Danny. She couldn't figure out what the look on his face meant. And he kept looking, just taking her in. It was weird. But she'd said all she wanted, so she let him look.

"All right," he said. "Then you'll have me backing you up all the way."

CHAPTER TWELVE

1966

The sun shone brightly on the steps of the Titan Capitol Building, and three men who stood at the podium, surrounded by members of the press, the TCPD, government officials, and members of the general citizenry who had taken the morning off to witness the ascension of one of the most beloved public figures of their lifetime, Kelly Winchester, as he swore his oath of office as mayor of Titan City. Cheers followed, and Mayor Winchester approached the microphone.

"Eleven years ago, I first began my career of humbly serving the proud and hard-working people of Titan City. And on the night of my election, I met a man at midnight, a man who some thought was a villain, but I knew to be a hero. And this man said the most amazing thing to me. He said, 'Kelly Winchester, *you* are the real hero. You are *my* hero. And you have given me a reason to change my ways.' That was the night the Crimson Wraith took off the skull that hid his face and stepped into the light to join us in making Titan City the greatest city the world has ever known! And here he is today! Him *and* the Wily Wisp!"

The other two men turned and waved to the audience, the smiles under their hoods as broad as their spandex-covered chests. And on those chests, one red and one yellow, the Crimson Wraith bore the image of a white skull while the Wily Wisp wore a purple letter "W."

Stepping to the podium, the Crimson Wraith spoke into the microphone. "Mayor Winchester, it has been an honor to fight alongside you for over a decade now, showing the good people of Titan City that right is right and wrong is—" Suddenly a terrible shriek of feedback cut through his words. "I'm sorry. It seems we are having some technical—"

Again, a blast erupted from the speakers, but this time it did not stop. The piercing electronic scream persisted, becoming louder and louder, rippling through the air and forcing all gathered there to their knees, the Crimson Wraith and the Wily Wisp as well.

And through the writhing crowd strode a group of men in masks with exaggerated, clownish features in the style of the Italian *Commedia dell'Arte*. Each one had a pair of earmuffs to protect them from the sound, and all wore the armor of Roman centurions except for one, their leader, in toga and golden laurels. The nose of his Capitano mask stretched long above his mustachioed grin, the costume of none other than Titan City's famous felonious thespian—the Troubador.

As his centurions began disarming police officers lost to sonic suffering, the Troubador lifted a series of cue cards above his head. *FRIENDS*, read the first, which he tossed aside. *ROMANS*, read the second, then, *COUNTRYMEN*. And finally, *LEND ME YOUR WALLETS*.

Once the police presence had been relieved of their pistols, the centurions began bagging up the billfolds and purses of all in attendance. Meanwhile, the Troubadour made his way up the steps until he stood above the pain-wracked forms of the Crimson Wraith, the Wily Wisp, and Mayor Winchester. From within his toga, he pulled another sign and held it before the Crimson Wraith's face. *HAVE YOU MISSED ME, MY NEMESIS?*

Suddenly, the Crimson Wraith stopped rolling on the ground and smiled up at the Shakespearean scoundrel. Confusion appeared under the Troubadour's mask. Then the Crimson Wraith tapped his ear, directing his opponent's gaze. He had inserted ear plugs from his belt without being noticed.

Suddenly, the Crimson Wraith kicked upward, right into the Troubadour's mid-section. And since the Wily Wisp had crept around to kneel behind him, the Troubadour toppled backward and began tumbling down the Capitol Building steps. His toga unwound and his earmuffs fell from him as he rolled, revealing the Renaissance blouse and breeches that were the Troubadour's typical attire, and exposing his ears to the same sound that had immobilized the entire crowd.

The Troubadour waved his arms wildly toward the two of his henchmen who had hijacked the sound system. "Turn it off!" he screamed, although he could not be heard. "Turn it off, you fools! A plague on both your houses!" They saw his flailing and ended the feedback attack.

The Crimson Wraith and Wily Wisp bounded down the steps to follow him, but the Troubadour leaped onto one of three horse-drawn chariots where all the collected wallets and purses had been placed in two heavy sacks.

"A fine performance indeed, Crimson Wraith," said the Troubadour, bowing, "But forgive me if I do not stay for the curtain call," and he grabbed hold of the reins, urging the chariot's horse onward at a gallop.

"Hurry, Wily Wisp!" said the Crimson Wraith. "We can't let the Troubadour get away!" He pointed to the two remaining chariots, waiting, presumably, for the Troubadour's henchmen to make their escape as well.

As he took the reigns, the Wily Wisp said, "It's a good thing there was a showing of *Ben-Hur* last week at Titan University!"

"That it is, dearest friend," said the Crimson Wraith. "A good education is never not rewarded."

Their horses reared and whinnied, and then they were off, chasing after the Troubadour. And without the weight of the ill-gotten wealth the criminal carried, the Crimson Wraith and Wily Wisp gained swiftly on him, going south down First Avenue before turning east on Dozier.

Traffic screeched to a halt and cars swerved suddenly to avoid their chase. All three charioteers veered sharply to keep from running over an elderly woman making her way across one street with a paper sack full of groceries, then a small child whose red rubber ball bounced into their path. As he sped past a sausage and pretzel stand, the Troubadour grabbed one with mustard and onions right out of the vendor's hand.

"My sausage!" he gasped.

But the Crimson Wraith clapped a dollar bill in the vendor's empty palm as he passed. "Keep the change, citizen!"

Finally, it seemed the Crimson Wraith and Wily Wisp were closing in, when the Troubadour, looking back to them, shouted. "I'll end with a jade's trick!" And he pulled a pair of rubber snakes from inside his doublet. "Best beware my sting!" He cast them back into the path of the other two horses, who reared so violently that they overturned their chariots and sent the Crimson Wraith and Wily Wisp sprawling to the pavement.

"Your steeds are infirm of purpose!" laughed the Troubadour, as he sped away, down the Titan City streets.

The Wily Wisp punched his palm in frustration. "We've lost him!"

"It seems we have," said the Crimson Wraith, "But maybe not for good. Look, when he threw those two rubber snakes, he must have pulled this piece of paper out of his pocket as well." Stopping, the Crimson Wraith picked up from the ground something pink with a torn edge.

"It looks like part of a business card!" said the Wily Wisp, and he read the letters printed there, "But the words are torn in half! All it says is *Nap— No—*. We've got a puzzle with pieces missing!"

"Quick, dearest friend, to the Crypt! Let's see what our new supercomputer can do to fill in those blanks."

Back in the secret lair of the Crimson Wraith, where the great skull archway overlooked the stairs to Finn Manor above, Edward Finn and his companion Tommy James set to work on the clue that the Troubadour had left behind. As they did, they were greeted by Edward's housekeeper Mrs. Chumley.

"Seems like you two had quite the exciting morning, didn't you? Figured you might have worked up an appetite and all, so I made sure to fix you some sandwiches and lemonade."

"Peanut butter and jelly? Oh, boy!" Tommy exclaimed. "And with the crusts cut off!"

"Just the way you like it, dearie."

Although just out of his teen years, there still remained something boyish about Tommy. "Thanks, Mrs. C!"

Edward smiled. "You always take such good care of us, Mrs. Chumley."

He saw then the pinch between her brows, a momentary flinch of something troubling her, but with the Troubadour on the move, he did not stop to ask.

Candace Chumley had stayed on after Chubby passed away from a heart attack in 1963. He was only fifty years old. They never had any children together. Finn Manor was their home and the Finns their family. So, Candace kept on serving, and although she remained dutifully cheerful, Edward could see the weight of mourning never left her. She seemed to weaken more and more from the strain of it.

He lost his father that same year to pneumonia. William had not lived in Finn Manor for some time, preferring instead to travel at Sylvia's side, seeing the world beyond Titan City for the first time since donning the hood, confident Edward had both Finn Industries and the mission of the Crimson Wraith in-hand. When William fell ill, they were in a Swiss chalet on a skiing holiday. Edward had been in the middle of apprehending Deadly Nightshade and so only arrived to see his father on his very last day.

On his deathbed, William Finn said to his son, his sidekick, and his successor, "Be happy. Please, for me. Always the mission has meant so much to you, but I want you to remember to smile. Remember to love." Those were his final words, "Remember to love."

The Crypt's supercomputer compared the letters on the

business card with entries all through the Titan City phonebook, analyzing thousands of entries in a matter of minutes before finally giving out the only entry from that directory that it could be. Tommy took the card it printed with the answer and read it aloud. "Napier's Noses? I've never heard of it."

Edward said, "A costume shop, dearest friend, one that specializes in false noses for every occasion."

"The kind of money he made off with today could buy a whole lot of noses for a whole lot of occasions."

"Or one very big nose."

"But why?"

"Think, Tommy. What did he say to us at the end of our chase?"

"He said that he would end with a 'jade's trick' then said to beware his sting, and he called our horses 'infirm of purpose.'"

"Exactly. Do you recognize those words?"

"They sound like Shakespeare, but I don't know from what plays. Anyway, the Troubadour is always talking like that."

"You had better sign up for more theatre next semester to brush up your Shakespeare."

"I will! But what were the plays?"

"In *Much Ado About Nothing*, Beatrice accuses Benedick of ending a battle of wits with a 'jade's trick.' In the *Taming of the Shrew*, Katherina says to her suitor Petruchio, 'If I be waspish, best beware my sting.' And when MacBeth reconsiders his plan to kill King Duncan, his wife calls him 'infirm of purpose.'"

"Wow," said Tommy. "You really remember all that?"

"A good education..." said Edward.

"I know," said Tommy. "Is never not rewarded. But what does all that mean?"

"Beatrice, Katherina, and Lady MacBeth are some of the greatest women in Shakespeare. Now, who is the greatest woman in Titan City?"

"You've got me there. I mean, Mrs. Chumley is pretty great, sure..."

"Not great in terms of character but great in terms of size."

"The Spirit of Prosperity!"

"Exactly! And a false nose for a woman of that size would be a very expensive nose indeed…"

<u>2019</u>

Morning frost clung to the edges of the star-shaped reflecting pool of the Titan City Justice Center courtyard, holding in place fallen leaves stuck halfway-in, halfway-out of the water. Gracie bundled up in the black overcoat Stephen provided her, wearing the suit purchased for her courier job with Snyder-Finn.

Inside, she joined the line of those waiting to pass through the security inspection. Well-dressed attorneys with their briefcases stood out among them, since, for the majority of those assembled, wearing their cleanest jeans was the most appropriate court attire they could muster. Several young men looked uncomfortable in shirts buttoned way higher on their neck than they were accustomed. One gray-haired mother batted away her adult son's hand when he reached to loosen the top of his collar.

Court was a thing you didn't go to if you didn't have to. And those who had to were those who couldn't afford not to, blue-collar folks who had to call out of work that day and probably didn't have paid-time-off to rely upon. These were Gracie's people. Any one of the bickering couples, each whispering blame at each other for whatever had gotten one of them in this situation, could have been her parents. And it felt strange to look down at what she was wearing and see that she appeared to have been transported out of that world.

Hancock waited for her inside. He had already been far more attentive than an overworked public defender could have offered. She knew too that she had peace of mind walking through those shiny glass doors that even the best-paid attorney could not give. She had the Crimson Wraith, not only as her hero, but also as her mentor.

As she came slowly closer to the metal detectors, Gracie heard a laugh from the other side of the security checkpoint and noticed Captain Villagraña speaking with a couple of officers in a raised security booth. She couldn't help but stare, trying to reconcile the image in front of her with that of the girl she saw photographed as the Wily Wisp over twenty years ago.

Then, Captain Villagraña noticed Gracie's gaze and acknowledged her with a nod. When Gracie exited security, Captain Villagraña strode her way. "So today is the big day?" she asked.

"It sure is," said Gracie. She heard the nervous excitement in her own voice when and thought she sounded just the tiniest bit like how Hancock did when he addressed her. Could he also know the Captain's secret superhero past?

"And how are you feeling?"

Gracie nodded. "Good. Good. A whole lot better than I did when you showed up at my door."

"I have to imagine you must. You've found some very good help since then."

"Yeah, no kidding. It's been..." Gracie's eyes shot around to those in their immediate vicinity. How much could she say? "Kevin took me for the tour... of Finn Manor... like, the *whole* tour..."

"Did he indeed? And did you like what you saw?"

"I do. I really do. I like it a lot."

Captain Villagraña nodded. "I am glad. You know, at some point when your situation with your ex-roommate is settled, you should come over to the house for dinner."

"Wow, really?"

"Really. I am afraid to say that I am not much of a cook, but my wife is a goddess in the kitchen."

"Oh, you have a wife?"

"I do. And I am very lucky that I do. But I guess it is only by luck that any of us get the good people in our lives who make a difference."

"You can say that again. Thank you, you know, for everything."

Captain Villagraña smiled. "*De nada*, Miss Chapel. It is good to see justice served." She went on to other business, and Gracie continued into the halls of the Justice Center.

It held multiple courtrooms and government offices, places to pay fines and fees, places to get copies of official documentation, and, somewhere hidden underneath, the holding cells where Gracie had been earlier that month. Her courtroom had a little waiting space in front of it, and she saw Bradley Hancock waiting for her there. He was texting on his phone and looked up at her approach. "Good morning," he said with a smile. "You ready for this?"

"I am. I've got to be, right?"

"If not, you've got a few minutes to get there. Judge Ghosh has another case finishing up right now. Make yourself comfortable."

"Okay, cool." Gracie sat and pulled out *Nights of Justice*. The book cover caught Hancock's attention.

"Some good reading in there," he said with a wink.

"Oh, you know. Just kinda felt a sudden interest in local legends."

"You don't say?"

"Weird, right?"

"Very." Hancock looked back to his phone. "That one doesn't say anything about the Dingo, does it? Does it get to Zero Hour?"

"The Dingo? No, it only goes as far as the late eighties."

"Right, right…"

Gracie hadn't heard anyone mention the Dingo yet. Another one of the Crimson Wraith's rogue's gallery? What did he have to do with Zero Hour? But just like how Hancock hadn't wanted to know the details of her meeting the Crimson Wraith and never said anything about who it was that paid her bond or gave her a place to stay after, she suspected those were things he wouldn't want to talk about, certainly not in the Titan City Justice Center.

So, she returned once more to Chief Goodman's recounting of a history that was now hers:

> *In his third decade of crime-fighting, the Crimson Wraith altered his mask, moving the skull from his face to the chest of his costume, which gave him an opportunity to smile and be seen smiling.*
>
> *It was a time for smiling. The Baby Boom generation were coming of age, knowing only post-war prosperity and an optimism that would ultimately reject military conscription, racial segregation, and sexual inequality. But the decade that ended in violent clashes for all those causes began with smiles, and the Crimson Wraith smiled along with them.*
>
> *He came to us in the brightness of day, there for all to see, shaking hands with city officials and working in direct and open contact with Titan City Police officers, like myself, appearing in the homes of so many Titan Citizens on their brand new color televisions—such an innocent time, and it is the great pity of innocence that its clutches cannot be escaped but with dreadful disillusionment. Would it were not so.*
>
> *Much has been conjectured about the book that ended the public career of the Crimson Wraith, forcing him to hide his face once more and move his activities back into the shadows...*

A voice whispered her name, "Gracie! Gracie!"

She looked up to see Brianna walking her way. Gracie smiled and rose to accept a hug from her. Brianna gave great hugs. Gracie let herself get smothered just a moment. With her face still in Brianna's shoulder, she said, "Hey, thanks for coming."

"I wouldn't miss it!"

Gracie pointed to Hancock, "Here is my attorney."

"So you're the help our Gracie found!"

"Yes, ma'am," said Hancock, shaking Brianna's hand.

They all sat together, and Brianna brought Gracie up-to-speed on what she missed since her last shift at Sprang & Sons. "You know that shop Tales Resold over on Tate Street? They shut down, and Rich snapped up almost their entire stock. We're sorting through it now, so you've got that to look forward to. But he set it all out for customers to pick anything they want from the pile in the meantime, and you know who got into it?"

Gracie rolled her eyes, "Oh, Howard..."

"Exactly! He got damn near lost in that pile! Spent hours there."

"Rich should put him on payroll."

"I know, right?"

Then Gracie got that feeling of someone watching her, and she looked up to see Zack walking their way. Immediately, his gaze dropped to the floor. An older man, who could have been Zack in maybe twenty-five years, walked at his side—Zack's father, probably. They both wore nice shirts and ties. Zack's appeared newly purchased, while his father's carried the ghosts of old stains.

The woman walking with the two men wore a suit with a much higher price tag than her companions could hope to afford. Gracie guessed who she was before Hancock leaned over to say, "That's District Attorney Nicole Kim. She thought his case was bullshit from the start. Him saying he wants to drop the charges was a huge relief. That's what got us this court date so quickly. She was glad to be done with him."

"I know the feeling," said Gracie.

Then she saw Zack's father notice her and turn to mutter something angry in Zack's ear. But Zack just shook his head in response. He didn't look up, didn't risk eye contact with her. Gracie could read the fear clinging to him the way ice grips a tree branch after a winter storm, making it stiff and fragile.

His night with the Crimson Wraith still haunted him. What must he have thought, she wondered, if Zack noticed that red hood and white skull staring back at him from the cover of *Nights of Justice* in her hand? It made her smile.

<u>1966</u>

The Crimson Wraith Roadster, a cherry red convertible Pontiac Tempest with gleaming chrome skull on its hood, roared down from the Elysian Hill, across the Englehart River, and into Titan City. At a stoplight in Downtown Titan, the Crimson Wraith's old friend, Detective Harlan Goodman, pulled up beside them in his police vehicle. "Sorry to miss the excitement this morning," he called out from his window. "I take it you are on the Troubadour's trail right now. Care for a police escort?"

"That would be ideal, Detective Goodman. We know just where he is headed, and we haven't a moment to lose!"

"Right away, Crimson Wraith!" And Detective Goodman started up his siren.

With Goodman's cruiser at their side, the Crimson Wraith Roadster sped through every stoplight, picking up three more police vehicles on its journey toward Keaton Park. When they arrived at the feet of the Spirit of Prosperity, they found the Troubadour's gang standing guard at the entrance at the statue's pedestal, armed with Tommy guns.

One of the Keaton Park staff came up to them crying, "Thank goodness you are here. The Troubadour and his men have taken over the Spirit of Prosperity, and they are going to stick that thing on her face!"

Looking up to where the staffperson pointed, the Crimson Wraith, Wily Wisp, and Detective Goodman saw a pulley system lifting the largest nose they had ever seen toward the statue's face. The Wily Wisp whistled, "Check out that honker, would ya?"

Detective Goodman shook his head, "It would appear he does not take symbols of civic pride seriously."

"And he would make a mockery of it for all," said the Crimson Wraith. "Detective, you keep his henchmen distracted but maintain your distance. Keep them talking and do not fire. We don't want anyone getting hurt. Wily Wisp, you and I will make our way around back."

"But how will we make it up the statue?" asked the Wily Wisp.

The Crimson Wraith answered, "Carefully, dearest friend. Very carefully. And with the help of the Crimson Wraith Grappling Cannons."

They pulled two weapons from the back of the Roadster that looked like military bazookas, painted red and armed with grappling irons at one end. Each placed a cannon on their shoulder, aimed for the top of the Spirit of Prosperity', and fired. Their grappling irons flew high, carrying lengths of rope behind them, and took hold in the angel's wings.

Both men began to climb. When they reached the top, they found the Troubadour waiting for him with two more of his henchmen, all standing on the slim walkway along the Spirit of Prosperity's arms, from which visitors would take in the view of Marshal Bay.

"Twice in one day, Crimson Wraith?" said the Troubadour. "My, my... People will say we're in love!"

The Crimson Wraith shouted back, "No one could love a criminal like you until you cease your wicked ways and become a productive member of society!"

"Oh, but I do produce! I produce the most important thing there is, that which makes life worth living! I produce art!"

"You sure have funny taste in it then," said the Wily Wisp.

"No true genius is understood in his time."

"And your time is up!" said the Crimson Wraith, launching into battle with the first henchman as the Wily Wisp took on the other. Blows were exchanged before the masked vigilantes wrapped their opponents in their cloaks and swung them crashing into each other. The two henchmen slumped to the floor, unconscious.

They then turned their attention to the Troubadour and saw that he had unsheathed a fencing sword. "Careful!" the Crimson Wraith called to his sidekick. "Leave him to me!"

"Such a gallant gesture!" said the Troubadour, "No wonder the ladies are all so fond. But now I must bid you goodnight, sweet prince! And flights of angels send thee to thy rest!"

The Troubadour charged, but the Crimson Wraith sidestepped his blade, giving his cloak a flourish that disoriented his opponent so that the Troubadour lost his bearings and toppled over the side of the railing. On the ground below, the Troubadour's blade shattered from the impact upon the stone, but the Troubadour's body did not follow. He grabbed hold of the edge of the walkway as he fell and managed to hold himself there by his fingertips.

"Steady me, Wily Wisp!" The Crimson Wraith extended one arm to his sidekick, who took hold of it and locked his arm around the opposite guardrail. The Crimson Wraith reached out to the Troubadour. "This need not be your final act! Let me help you."

His eyes bulging with fear behind his long-nosed Capitano mask, the Troubadour looked down at his feet dangling in empty space. "The better part of valor," he said, "is discretion."

Taking the Crimson Wraith by the hand, the Troubadour allowed himself to be pulled back up onto the walkway, to be handcuffed, to be turned over to Detective Goodman, and then, along with his henchmen, to be taken to jail.

"Good work, Crimson Wraith," said Detective Goodman. "Yet again, you've successfully thwarted that performance art prankster. The Spirit of Prosperity can show her true face with pride, and once the giant nose gets returned to Napier's, the citizens who were robbed this morning can be repaid."

"If only the Troubadour understood," said the Crimson

Wraith, "that the Titan Endowment for the Arts will gladly support the work of those whose creativity uplifts the people of this great city, he wouldn't have to go to illegal lengths to acquire his funding."

"He'll have plenty of time to think about that behind bars," said the Wily Wisp.

"Yes, he will, dearest friend. Yes, he will."

2019

Judge Ghosh tugged at his beard thoughtfully as he looked down from his bench at Zack. "What I am curious about," he said, "was exactly why you decided to ask the District Attorney to drop the charges against Miss Chapel—in your own words please."

Zack looked at the DA who nodded at him, encouraging him to speak. It became clear he had been coached on just what to say as soon as he opened his mouth. "Your Honor, um... the night of the... *altercation*..." Never could that word sound natural coming from him. "...there was a lot of emotions and... you see, afterward, things kind of calmed and because of that... I experienced a change in... *perspection*... I mean, *perception*. And that led me to, kind of, see that maybe I had... *misremembered* the events and... everything."

"Yes, I see," said Judge Ghosh. "This happens."

Here District Attorney Kim spoke for him. "Your honor," she said, "considering this change in testimony, the State would like to move that the charges of Aggravated Assault be reduced to Simple Assault. Speaking with Miss Chapel's counsel, we have agreed to ask for a suspended sentence."

"I see. The Plaintiff may be seated." He turned to Gracie's table, where she sat beside Hancock. "Miss Chapel, would you please share with me why there will not be a repeat of this incident?"

Gracie stood to answer and realized she had the power

of extreme understatement on her side. "Well, your honor, I think that a whole lot has changed since, um, the night in question—for me and for how I understand... a lot of stuff. So, because of that, I don't think I would take the same kind of actions as I did if I were to see what I saw that night. Not again."

"Interesting. And why is that?"

She thought back to a few nights before in the dojo, when Kevin had gone through some hand-to-hand combat drills with her, specifically around disarming an opponent with a bladed weapon. When they started out, Gracie got to be the opponent, pointing a rubber dagger at him, just as she had done with the broken beer bottle that night. He let her attack him three different times and disarmed her three different ways. Then he went through each again at half speed, letting her take in each technique before Kevin took the rubber blade and had her practice disarming him.

Afterward, as they both sat with their water bottles and towels, rehydrating and dabbing off sweat, Gracie brought up the murder investigation. "Hey, so, about Edward Finn..."

"Yes?"

"Danny was telling me a little more about all that. I just knew he had died recently. But I didn't know he was murdered."

"He was."

"So, like, can I help?"

"This is a murder investigation. I'm looking for someone who has the capacity to take a human life in a cold and calculated manner. That's actually a lot more rare than movies make you think. It isn't easy. And a person who can do that is extremely dangerous."

But Gracie would not back down. "You took me out of a bad situation. You brought me here. You're bringing me into the mission of the Crimson Wraith. And I know I'm new, but I don't want to just be sitting on my ass while you figure out who did it and go take care of him. I want to help."

The frown he turned her way was not one she had seen

before. It was sad. It was scared. "I'm going to be honest with you, Gracie. This situation worries me, more than just the fact that it's murder. There are details about it I don't like. They point to whoever this was knowing things about the Crimson Wraith, things going back years. I don't know how much they know about us, and not-knowing puts us at an extreme disadvantage.

"Common crime follows common patterns. Even if you don't walk in knowing the particulars of a case, there are predictable aspects that you come to learn. And you learn ways to protect yourself while working for the best possible outcome. But this isn't like that. This is a unique situation. I don't know what to expect."

"Cool. You sound like you really should have someone watching your back then." She put her arm over his muscular shoulders. "You had my back, Kev. Now, how about you let me get yours?"

It didn't lift the weight of fear and sadness she saw in him, her saying that. But he did look to her and give the tiniest smile and nod.

"You don't think I know what I'm getting myself into," she said.

"You don't," said Kevin.

"No, I don't. But neither did you when you reached out to me."

His smile broadened. "No, I didn't."

And so, in the courtroom on the day of her trial, Gracie looked to judge Ghosh, and said, "Well, Your Honor, I used to think I didn't have anyone I could turn to when things got bad. I didn't trust anyone to care or to do anything that meant anything when I needed it. I figured that left it all up to me, that I had to be judge, jury, and executioner—or whatever. But I know now that I was wrong. I'm not as on my own as I thought. What's that old saying? No man is an island? And because I understand that better now, I can be better for everyone around me and for myself. That means if something like that were to happen again, I could maybe reach out to the right people to handle things in the right way instead of trying to handle it all myself, possibly in the wrong way."

Judge Ghosh nodded. "I'm glad to hear that. I believe I can suspend your sentence for ninety days. If you can complete those ninety days without arrest, then these charges will be dropped. Do you understand?"

"Yes, your honor."

"Good, you may be seated." He turned to Zack. "And as for you, young man, I am very, very concerned that this altercation happened at all, regardless of the details involved. You should understand that I would not like to see you in my courtroom or any other courtroom ever again, particularly if it involves any form of violence against a woman. Is that understood?"

"Yes, your honor."

And that was that. With the clack of his gavel to punctuate the judge's ruling, court adjourned. Gracie thanked Hancock. Brianna ran up to squeeze the fuck out of her in congratulations. And Zack and his dad made it out of the courtroom, fast as they could.

How quickly, Gracie wondered, would Zack find himself on a ferry, headed south, far, far away from Titan City and the Crimson Wraith? Did he have cousins to go stay with? Maybe he would try to start over in some tiny little town where he could come off as hot shit, the big-city boy with big-city swagger. Maybe he would drop into a bar some night and start making friends by spouting off a lot of tough talk. There are always toadies out there, eager to agree with someone who thinks they are king of the world. And sure, there would be other women who liked the look of him, anyone of them potentially his next meal ticket, if she had the right kind of vulnerabilities to his mix of arrogance and aggression.

But maybe something different might happen. Maybe he might think twice before playing the same game with someone else. A memory might flash for him—the sight of Titan

City spinning below him as he dangled from the top of Snyder-Finn, the feel of the winds surrounding him, and the sound of the Crimson Wraith's voice in his ear. And, thinking twice, there might be a chance that Zack would make a different choice next time. Gracie could hope.

1966

The Troubadour had his rights read to him, his hands cuffed, and his mask removed. Thus ended the crime spree of the Crimson Wraith's most remarkable adversary of that age, and thus began the incarceration of Esteban Valentino, a twenty-five-year-old of Cuban ancestry, graduate with honors from the Titan University theater program, convicted on multiple counts of armed robbery, vandalism, and disturbing the peace.

The police vehicles drove away, leaving the Crimson Wraith and Wily Wisp to give autographs to the Keaton Park crowd who returned to watch the spectacle once the Tommy guns were taken away.

Eager hands shoved into the vigilantes' faces an assortment of scrapbooks, comics, and other collectibles to receive their signatures. The duo laughed good-naturedly with the crowd. And then the Wily Wisp leaned into the Crimson Wraith's hood and whispered, "Can we get out of here? That fight has me so worked up, and I am *dying* to get you home…"

It was impossible for the Crimson Wraith not to smile at such eagerness, but he made sure no child left without their cereal-box cut-out mask signed before the two waved their good-byes and made off in the Crimson Wraith Roadster to return to Finn Manor.

They did not talk during the drive. The Wily Wisp just kept smiling at his older lover with restrained desire glimmering in his eyes, occasionally tapping the top of Edward's thigh in anticipation. As they made their way across the 6th Avenue bridge, Tommy sang softly along with a song on the radio, the Buggies' latest single *Love Whispers*. "Oh no, no one else can know, but it's true I love you so. Whoah-oh-oh, love whispers…"

Never before in his life had Edward thought happiness like this could be possible—to be himself, all of who he was, with another person, to love and be loved, fully and completely.

He grew up in a house of so many secrets, the ones his father gave him to keep from the world and the ones about himself he had to keep from his father. And yet here was Tommy James with whom he could share everything. With him, there were no secrets and never had to be.

They met at the Innocents Club a few years back. It had reopened under new management after the CCA raids, but still served the same community. One night, Edward saw Tommy fending off the advances of a man there who, seeing Tommy was young and new, had been too forward in his approach. Edward was alone that night, watching from the bar, and like all those assembled that evening, his eyes turned to take in Tommy as he crossed the threshold, looking like some fantasy cut from the pages of a magazine in his tight blue jeans and high school letterman's jacket, too beautiful to be real.

But Edward had just returned from Switzerland following his father's passing, and William's words haunted him. "Be happy… Remember to love…" It was almost comical how impossible Edward thought his father's final wishes for him were, and he smiled ruefully into his bourbon on the rocks.

So, when Tommy came to the bar and sat near him, Edward did not attempt to flatter and seduce the young man. He had just come that night to drink in a place where he felt like himself, and perhaps because of that quiet sadness, Tommy had been the one to turn to him. "Can you believe some people?" he jerked a thumb at the man he had just brushed off.

"I really can't," said Edward. "I find people in general pretty unbelievable."

"You said it," said Tommy. "More unbelievable than anyone

could ever believe." That was how their conversation began. And as the night went on, the conversation went on.

Edward learned that Tommy had just started as a freshman at Titan University, having come from out west, leaving behind the family farm. He was an athlete, his high school class president, and although he'd had girlfriends before, he knew that his inclinations did not fall in that direction exclusively. As he said it to Edward, "Sometimes you just want something... more... You know?"

Yes, Edward did know, and from the way Tommy's eyes sparkled when he said "more," there was no way that he could keep from falling in love with this boy thirteen years his junior. That night, they danced, and they shared a kiss. Edward did not press for more, and his restraint seemed to surprise and delight Tommy.

When they did share a bed, it felt different from other times Edward had been with a lover. It felt romantic. They had spent time getting to know each other. And Tommy didn't have another life there in Titan City to keep secrets from, not like the men whose wives and children could never know their shame. Whatever other life Tommy had was miles away. It made Edward feel free with him, made it seem like there was a new world of possibilities opening.

And then one night, months later, he felt the need to disclose his final secret. He brought Tommy into the Crypt and said, "There is a place here for you, if you want it, a place in my home, a place by my side."

Tommy began training to join Edward as the Wily Wisp. On weekends and when his classes allowed, he would stay at Finn Manor, and although Edward always had Mrs. Chumley prepare a guest room for his young friend, they spent the night together in his master bed.

With Tommy's entry into Finn Manor came a whole new life. Edward had never thrown a party before, not a personal one, detached from his business as head of Finn Industries, certainly not for the other regulars of the Innocents Club. But

Tommy was a young man who wanted to have parties, and Edward wanted to make Tommy happy. So, he arranged evenings where Mrs. Chumley would be told to leave them and their guests undisturbed after preparing the ballroom, the indoor pool, and a few guest bedrooms, with several bottles of champagne ready to enjoy.

They had one such party planned that very night, and having finally apprehended the Troubadour, after several clashes with him in the past, gave them something extra to celebrate. Edward and Tommy rose from the depths of the Crypt having slipped out of their crime-fighting costumes. Both wore terry cloth robes and both their faces were flushed and bore the sheen of amorous exertions that could not be postponed until reaching the bedroom. Love's call had been answered right there, in the Crypt, in the back seat of the Crimson Wraith Roadster.

They found the house above in excellent condition for their guests, champagne already on ice. The sandwiches were cut and stacked attractively on trays, along with fruit and cheeses and bread baked fresh that morning. They also found Mrs. Chumley standing in the foyer, wearing her overcoat and hat, two suitcases at her side.

"Hey, Mrs. C!" called Tommy. "The house looks great."

"Yes, thank you, Mrs. Chumley, once again you've taken such good care of us. And are you going somewhere overnight? I don't remember you mentioning taking a vacation, but you absolutely deserve it. When will we see you back?"

Her hands remained clasped in front of her. "You won't."

"Pardon?" said Edward.

"Mr. Finn, I will not be returning to your service. I hereby tender my resignation."

"Oh, no!" said Tommy, "Say it ain't so, Mrs. C."

"I'm very sorry to hear that," said Edward, now realizing this must have been the reason for the tightness in her brow earlier.

The truth was Edward never liked Candy Chumley. Her fluttering about and fixing and fussing irritated him. Sometimes he wondered if it might be because he never had a mother, and that seemed a role that Candy pushed herself into for everyone around her. Edward imagined her feelings toward him might be similarly strained. They were never really friends, just attached to two men who were themselves friends. So, Edward was not sad to see her go, but the manner of her going struck him as quietly hostile. "And where, might I ask, will you be going?"

"I'm moving in with my cousin who lives over by the Great Lakes. The train leaves tonight."

Tommy walked toward her, arms open for an embrace, "We are going to miss you so much."

But Mrs. Chumley recoiled, arms raised to keep him back as an expression of unrestrained revulsion erupted from her. "Don't you touch me!"

"Mrs. C?" Tommy held in place, hurt, confused.

"I've had to endure a whole lot since you moved in here, young man, but I will not permit you to defile me with your touch!"

The outburst shocked and angered Edward. "Candace…" he said, his tone urging caution.

She shouted, "That's 'Mrs. Chumley' to the likes of you! I am a good woman, the loving wife of Chester Chumley, and proud servant of your father, William Finn, who was a proper gentleman and would be disgusted—*disgusted!*—if he could see what you have done to his name! This was one of the *good* houses, one of the best, before you came here," she aimed a finger at Tommy, whose mouth hung agape. Tears rose in his eyes. "You with your parties and your perverts, all those dirty, filthy men, giggling and prancing like who-knows-what, an offense to God and Heaven and all!"

Edward shouted, "That's enough!" Hearing her say those things about him was terrible, but to say them to Tommy he could not bear. "Go," he said. "If you want to go, then just go. And don't ever come back."

Mrs. Chumley picked up her suitcases. "You could never pay me enough to."

2019

She returned to her quiet apartment after another long day at Sunset Gardens and slipped off her shoes at the door before returning her coat to its hook. "Honey, I'm home," she said softly. Her cat came out to meet her, a fluffy little monster, responding less to her voice than the opening of the door.

"Have you been a good boy, Bobby?" she asked and held out her prosthetic left hand to sniff as she crouched down to greet him. He answered by pushing his face into the plastic fingers. "I bet you have."

Dinner, she warmed up in the microwave, leftovers from the delivery she ordered last night, washed down with a can of Diet Kronos-Kola. Once emptied, it joined dozens of its brethren in her recycling. She watched one hour of sexy weeknight crime drama and then another before turning off the lights and undressing for her shower. As she slipped into her fluffy blue bathrobe, she felt the weight of the burner phone in its pocket and gripped it hard.

After pulling the bathroom door closed behind her, she made sure the window shades were drawn, and then started the water running. The sound would have helped to muffle speech, but she knew their adversary was too clever to trust that. Even with those precautions, she would only text. Never did she say a word about their activities out loud.

Using only the fingers of her right hand, she typed out, "BB status update. No sign of CW. Confirm DO." Then she waited. He was never long in responding.

"Confirmed BB. He will find you. Be patient."

Be patient? She had been patient for years! "Being patient. Countermeasures in place. Site B at the ready."

"Very good BB. We give our all for LOVE."

"We give our all for LOVE. Over."

Seeing the old man's face had been so satisfying, watching the life drain from him. He thought he knew so much, thought his decades of dressing up and going on his little adventures had prepared him for everything. But he was wrong. She showed him that. And she had made sure that before he died, the last thing he knew was just how wrong he was.

But Edward Burton had not been alone. There were others in the Crimson Wraith lineage, including whoever it was who wore the mask now, the one in the asylum, and the one in prison—*her* Crimson Wraith, Hank Mills, the one who had taken everything from her. Because of Hank, she lost her family, her arm, and any chance she ever had to live a normal life. It was all his fault. Her family had trusted him, and it destroyed them.

She looked back to the screen of the burner phone. *We give our all for LOVE.*

It was coming. He would get his due. All of them would.

PART FOUR

J. GRIFFIN HUGHES

CHAPTER THIRTEEN

1969

Tommy waited until Shirley said she was done eating to rise from his chair, pull a small box from his pocket, and present it to her, on his knees. She squealed in delight and threw her arms around him, shedding and then wiping away tears. Then, after they cleared the dinner table of his small apartment and washed and put the dishes away, they retired to bed calmly and quietly.

Shirley did not feel like making love after. This was not a surprise. She did not seem to have strong desires of her own. There was a shyness to her, a modesty even in their bedroom. Tommy found it endearing and hoped that following her lead might help to free him from the desires he once had. They shamed him now.

After the lights were out, Shirley asked, "Is it really okay that we don't?"

"What? Of course," Tommy said and kissed her forehead. He fell asleep peacefully enough, but as it so often had this last year, a nightmare awaited him.

These nightmares came as fractured impressions of his time captured by Dr. Oblivion and the psychedelic tortures he endured there. The bespectacled face of Dr. Oblivion would float into view, his hair a wild upward surge from his high forehead, saying in his strange, sing-song voice. "We have great work to accomplish, you and I. Oh, yes. What we do together may someday save the world." Sometimes just his voice came to Tommy, employing some form of hypnotic technique. "I will be counting down now from five... Five... Very relaxed... Four... Extremely relaxed... Three... Your limbs feel soft as sand..." This voice could enter any dream, coming to him from nothing, riding on a breeze or vibrating in his skull. "Picture yourself now floating down a lazy, lazy river..."

Sometimes Tommy would feel the tightness of the bonds that held him to the chair in Dr. Oblivion's hidden lair, sometimes the constriction of his arms wrapped against his chest in the straight jacket he had been forced to wear, and sometimes he would feel himself choking on the cloyingly sweet gas the villain forced him to inhale through a mask that covered Tommy's nose and mouth. He never knew what chemical combination those gases contained, but as the days wore on in those dimly lit and heavily walled rooms, the recipe of mind-melting pharmaceuticals seemed to change. Dr. Oblivion would say, "Today, I've prepared something quite special for you..." Or, "Now, I think I've really got it this time..."

Once the gas had softened the walls of his consciousness, Dr. Oblivion would place a pair of headphones over his ears and begin projecting images on the wall opposite. The combination of sight and sound never quite connected. There might be the clucking of a packed chicken coop over old sports footage. John Phillips Sousa's *The Thunderer* played over children on a jungle gym intercut with hogs being slaughtered. A baby's laugh rang out while vermin ate away at a fox's corpse on a forest floor. And President Nixon delivered his first address to the nation on the Vietnam war as a pair of snakes writhed in their slow-motion act of mating.

Amid all these images—sometimes in the middle of something he had seen before – would erupt a white skull against a field of red, and with it, the sound of sirens blaring. The same sirens exploded across his brain if ever Tommy dared to close his eyes to what was being shown him. And for a long time after, when that skull appeared in his dreams, he would once again feel that surge of terror and jerk himself awake, just as he did on the night that Shirley accepted his proposal.

"It's okay," she said. "It's okay. Just another nightmare." Her hand rested softly on his chest, a gesture intended to soothe, but the feel of that contact repulsed him. He took her by the wrist and, carefully—as though she was either a very fragile thing or trap from which he had to extricate himself—pulled her hand away.

"I'm sorry. It just never... I'm sorry."

"You don't have to apologize. You can't control what you dream."

"Yeah." He slid from their bed. "I'm going to get a little air."

"Do you want company?"

"No, it's okay, sweetie. I don't want to keep you up. You've got another long day at the secretarial pool tomorrow."

"It's no bother. I'm awake now."

"No, really. Please stay." And he kissed her forehead again.

"Okay," she said unhappily, returning her head to the pillow.

Sitting on the eighth floor of their complex, his apartment balcony offered a view that felt all too familiar to Tommy. At the Crimson Wraith's side, he had gazed down upon Titan City from vantage points this high and higher, scanning for criminal activity through binoculars or following the path of the henchman of some self-proclaimed supervillain. More often-than-not, they wore costumes as ridiculous as what he himself had been convinced to wear.

What a bizarre and brightly colored world they adventured in. It was all so unreal, like one big game, school kids dressing up and chasing each other around a playground in a never-ending period of recess.

In every memory of it, Tommy felt his face smiling and hated himself for it, that joy born of ignorance, trusting that the man he loved had it all figured out—and why shouldn't he? Edward had been fighting crime since he was a boy, after all. Tommy felt safe at his side, safe under his guidance, and safe in his arms. Edward brought him exhilaration and adventure, showing Tommy there was a world where he might achieve even more than the academic and athletic success that brought him to Titan City University on a full-ride scholarship, liberating him from the farm where he grew up. And in return, Tommy filled Edward's dark and quiet house and its echoing halls with love and with laughter.

Out on his apartment balcony at night, overlooking the Titan City streets' interplay of light and shadow, its Kronos-Kola sign burning bright in the distance, Tommy often felt as though the night were looking back at him. Sometimes, he felt compelled to peer into a patch of darkness on the roof opposite and wonder if *he* were hiding there, watching. Would Edward take the same license he felt entitled him to observe the private doings of all Titan citizens to spy upon Tommy after their separation? And almost every time he felt this urge, he was right. Edward spent more nights than he cared to count watching Tommy live a life that seemed as strange and fantastical to him as his own must have appeared to others.

The ache of losing Tommy drove Edward just a little mad. He could not sleep for days because the bed they shared now seemed too cold and too empty after having been so full and so warm for so long. When he did sleep, it could only be on a sofa in the lounge or at the desk of his office, and the sleep he found there did not restore him. Maybe this was why his father never took a serious lover before marrying Sylvia. Perhaps, if he had not been shot in the ribs the night she returned to his life, ending his career as the Crimson Wraith, William might have discovered he was unable to balance romance and crime-fighting. It was more than Edward could bear.

He knew he shouldn't spy on Tommy. He knew that it was disrespectful to his former lover and bad for his own state of mind. If he had a close friend in his life with whom he could confide such things, he would have been ashamed to confess it, and surely such a friend would plead with Edward to stop. But he had no such friend, and Edward did not know how to be that friend to himself. And so, over and over again, he spent some part of his evening patrol watching Tommy's apartment.

And then Edward saw Tommy propose to his girlfriend. He watched the boy who had brought him so much happiness get down on one knee after a humble home-made dinner of spaghetti and meatballs to offer that young woman a small box and the sparkling ring it held inside. Edward saw her face light up and tears shimmer upon her cheeks, and tears began to drip down from his domino mask as well because he had known that exact same happiness she felt. It was hers now, his no longer.

Dr. Oblivion had not been the first villain to capture Tommy, and Edward himself had been held prisoner enough times to have come to expect it as part of the role of the Wily Wisp. It was the role of the Crimson Wraith to come to the rescue, knowing his sidekick was being held as bait for some kind of trap. But when, after five days, Edward at last discovered the location of Dr. Oblivion's secret psychological laboratory, the condition in which he found Tommy was unlike any he had seen before.

"Here he is, your faithful companion!" Dr. Oblivion's voice rang from speakers surrounding the room where he found Tommy blindfolded and bound to a chair. Red light covered everything within with a garish, bloody haze as a disco ball spinning from the ceiling sent disorienting sparkles whirling around them. A cloud of cool fog, smelling both bitter and sweet, floated along the floor around his ankles. "Now, let us observe your heartfelt reunion!" A rhythmic electronic throb replaced Dr. Oblivion's voice as Edward rushed to free his young lover. But as soon as he removed the blindfold and their eyes met, he saw a frenzy overtake Tommy, who leaped from the chair to attack him.

As the two struggled under the red lights, Dr. Oblivion's voice returned to fill the room once more. "Success!" he shrieked. "Here, the patient has achieved perfect metanoia!

And with absolutely no willingness on its part required! No longer will they joke that, for a psychiatrist to change a lightbulb, the lightbulb must *want* to change! Now we can save our victims from themselves whether they want it or not!"

Meanwhile, Edward pleaded with Tommy, as he dodged more attacks than he delivered, "Snap out of it, dearest friend! You know me! You don't want to hurt me! And I will not hurt you!" But Tommy only answered with sputtering screams of rage, until Edward had to throw Tommy to the ground and pin him down. "If you cannot hear my words, then, please, hear this." And he leaned down to kiss his beloved sidekick.

Just as it did for Sleeping Beauty, it took a kiss to break the spell Dr. Oblivion had placed Tommy under. He kissed Edward back, and then, sounding groggy as a waking dreamer, Tommy said, "I'm sorry. I'm so sorry. Please, get me out of here. I want to go home."

But behind them, Dr. Oblivion had entered the room, mouth agape. "Can it be? Is this the Crimson Wraith's secret? That he is afflicted with the mental disease of homosexuality?" And he giggled maniacally. "What a profound perversion! Such a deep-seated sickness of the mind! How delightful!"

Edward had relaxed his grip on Tommy, thinking his sidekick calmed and safe once more, so Tommy easily pushed Edward away to hurl himself at Dr. Oblivion. "You sick son-of-a-bitch!" Tommy shouted. He began beating the sadistic psychiatrist, slamming him face-first into one wall and then another before hurling him into the chair where Tommy had been kept a prisoner. The gas mask still hung at its side, a canister of psychotropic drugs attached. "How about a taste of your own medicine, Doc? Let's see how you like it!" Tommy forced the mask over his captor's face and twisted the canister's knob violently, spinning it all the way open. "Choke on it! Choke on it and die!"

Edward came quietly behind him. "That's enough. He's had enough. You need to let him go." He placed his gloved hands on

Tommy's shoulders. "This isn't you, dearest friend. This isn't justice."

Slowly, Tommy relaxed his grip on Dr. Oblivion. But it was too late. Already, Dr. Oblivion had inhaled far more of the mind-altering chemicals in one sitting than he had forced Tommy to take in all the days before combined. Neither of them would ever be the same.

It was not long after that Tommy left Edward, left Finn Manor, and left the Wily Wisp as well. Having finished his degree at Titan University, he took a job as a stock trader, where his sales number suffered as he struggled just to make it through a day without a debilitating crying fit. But he earned enough for a small apartment of his own and, finally, a ring for Shirley, who worked as a typist at the same office.

The night that Shirley accepted his proposal, having woken screaming from his nightmares once again, Tommy looked out from his balcony and, for the first time since he moved there, he did not sense the night was looking back. It wasn't. It had not been since Shirley accepted Tommy's proposal. Edward had left the rooftop, returned to Finn Manor, and never came to watch Tommy anymore.

2019

Goblins and ghosts in a myriad of masks filled the lobby of the Snyder-Finn building, and with them, princesses, fairies, pirates, spacemen, and superheroes. They screamed, not out of terror, but just because they did not seem to know how to communicate speech at a lower volume, high on candy, thrilled by the prospect of more candy to come.

These were the children of Kevin's employees as well as those assisted by the Finn Foundation's youth charities, invited to celebrate their Halloween safe from Titan City's streets inside a hand-made carnival of cardboard and paper that extended through most of the building's first floor. There were face-painters, balloon artists, and games of chance or minimal skill that offered prizes of some kind for every participant. The cafeteria had been done-up as a haunted house with the mildest of frights, appropriate for ages young as six-years-old. The event ran from 6 to 8 PM, with different groups of children admitted in half-hour blocks and the staff volunteers who ran the event rotating their role each hour.

Gracie spent her first hour on security, greeting visitors at the door and making sure they knew the rules. She had to start at a shout just to be sure she got heard. "All right, you little monsters, listen up! No taking what isn't yours! No touching someone who doesn't want to be touched! No fighting! If you need help, find someone who is wearing one of these badges!" She lifted the lanyard around her neck that held her employee ID. "No sharp objects! And above all, have fun! Any questions?"

A small pirate raised her hand.

Gracie pointed. "Yes, you with the eye-patch!"

The girl had difficulty pronouncing the letter R, which Gracie thought would be problematic for anyone pursuing a career in piracy. "Um, I have a *swowd*. It's *weawwy* sharp. Can I *bwing* it inside, Miss Tutu Teddy Beaw?"

Apparently, Gracie's costume was supposed to be a character from a cartoon that came out in the last few years which Gracie had no reason to have any awareness of. Dressing as Tutu Teddy Bear put her in a full-body suit with fluffy pink tutu attached. Its head totally engulfed Gracie's, a fur-lined plastic globe that rested on her shoulders, with a hole for her face in what was supposed to be the Tutu Teddy Bear's mouth. She wasn't able to put her arms all the way down, due to the costume's wide foam belly, and, of course, the tutu.

Somehow—and she was not quite sure *how* he managed it —but *somehow* Gracie had the sense that Danny had orchestrated things so that was the only costume available in her size. He was there too, up in the Snyder-Finn security booth, where he kept an eye on the monitors while running the electronic elements of the cafeteria haunted house—the lights, the sound effects, and a silly-faced ghost who flew over children's heads, chuckling to itself and telling pre-programmed jokes like, "How does a witch put on her socks? Any *'witch'* way she likes!"

Danny and Gracie had been going over the costumes of previous Crimson Wraiths and Wily Wisps to get a sense of what she might wear when it came time to join Kevin in the field. "Since Michael put on the hood in 1989, the Crimson Wraith costumes have incorporated more and more tech. His was the first to equip the mask with low-light vision, voice modification, and enhanced audio. Each successive version has gotten more advanced, as upgrades allow us to pack more tech with less weight. Kevin's current rig carries GPS, can discretely access wifi signals and nearby phone towers, and can incorporate visual data from any of the Haunts flying into the field with him, effectively putting eyes in the back of his head."

"You get a serious hard-on for this stuff, don't you?" said Gracie.

Danny held up a hand. "Please, let's keep it professional."

But, clearly, his enjoyment of her trying on Esperanza's Wily Wisp outfit blurred that professional line on his end. As she stepped out in the low-rise pants, halter top, and blonde wig, all he said was, "Wow," and that said more than enough.

"Oh, fuck off," said Gracie.

"I mean, it's a good look."

"It's so not me though."

"Yeah, but this is a disguise. It ain't supposed to look like you."

Stephen had brought a full-length mirror down to the Crypt for Gracie, and she looked herself over. Had Captain Villagraña really fought bad guys in this outfit that looked more suited for spinning glow sticks to throbbing techno? But it had been the nineties. She guessed that explained it.

Gracie didn't mind dressing a little sexy for a night at the club, but even then she always put together an outfit that she hoped gave the impression she was still willing and able to kick your ass if she had to. The bright yellow and purple of the Wily Wisp didn't feel right to her, and the long blonde wig was as much an offense as anything else. She stripped that off before turning to go change out of the rest.

"Wait!" said Danny. "You gotta let me take pictures!"

She let her middle finger answer him.

Making it so she had to dress-up as the Tutu Teady Bear definitely seemed like something Danny would do, and he couldn't hide his amusement when he saw her step out into the lobby wearing it during set up.

From across the room, he mouthed at her, "Oh... my... God..."

Gracie just shook her head and mouthed back, "You did this..."

But he shook his head and held up his hands in the most insincere display of innocence.

Anyway, standing out on the sidewalk that cold October night, admitting children into the Snyder-Finn lobby, Gracie did appreciate that the Tutu Teddy Bear costume was warm; she could give it that much.

She looked at the toy cutlass the little pirate girl handed to her. Its foam blade bent easily in her grasp. "Yeah, kid. You're good." Then she turned to the rest of those in front of her. "All right! Everybody inside! Next group!"

After the first hour, Gracie was able to take off the Tutu Teddy Bear in favor of an outfit she'd come to think of as "corporate casual," a pair of khaki pants and navy polo shirt that bore the Snyder-Finn logo. For the second hour, she sat behind a blue curtain that represented a natural freshwater pond—something city kids didn't see too much. The children were guided by assistants on the other side of the curtain to take hold of a fishing rod that had a clothespin on the end of its line and clip to it a little googly-eyed worm made of yarn. They threw their fishing lines over the curtain, then Gracie would unclip the worms and replace them with pieces of candy or little plastic toys before tugging on the lines so the kids would know to pull them back and collect their prizes. It was monotonous, but she didn't have to speak to anyone, so that was preferable.

So far, Gracie wasn't hating working in a corporate office. Yes, its niceness was superficial, but she couldn't deny that she felt safe there, having a doorman check their badges before entry and all. When she would catch sight of the suits assessing her, sure, they gave off a judgmental air. It seemed to Gracie they could still smell on her the last night she slept on a sidewalk and didn't understand what she was trying to prove by not wearing heels and a skirt, but now she slept at Finn Manor, training to fight crime in a mask and hood, so they could all eat shit. Anyway, maybe safe and superficial would be a good way to spend her days if she was going to spend her nights getting very dangerous and very real with the Crimson Wraith.

Her last day at Sprang & Sons had been bittersweet. Brianna brought her a cake with a cowboy hat drawn on it in icing and the words "Happy Trails!" Rich came out to thank her for her time there, which he underquoted by about six months. Whatever. Gracie was in too good a mood to mind.

To every one of their regulars who came in, Brianna announced Gracie was leaving. Each said some version of how they would miss her, and that just felt weird. But, of course, the week would not be complete without Howard showing up for his selections, and he just so happened to do so on that day. It occurred to Gracie that she was actually going to miss his fidgety fretting in pursuit of unattainable reading perfection. Maybe that was how the customers would miss her too, not because of a personal relationship but just the familiarity of being an object in someone else's world, the same way you might get a feeling of loss for an old restaurant you pass on your morning commute that you see is getting torn down, even if you never went inside to eat.

When Brianna told Howard that Gracie was leaving, he said, "Are you sure?"

Gracie smiled, "Yes, I'm sure."

Brianna filled in, "She's going uptown, gonna work for Snyder-Finn."

"Just in the courier pool," said Gracie.

"But that can lead to bigger things," said Brianna, "all sorts of things. You never know where that can go."

Howard nodded in anxious agreement. "You never know. It might be something terrible. It might. I hope you can come back here if there is trouble. You haven't made anyone mad, have you?"

Gracie laughed, "It's not like that, really."

But that didn't calm Howard, who turned to Brianna, "She can come back, right?"

"Well, sure she can," said Brianna. "But this is a good thing, her moving on. You don't have to worry about our Gracie."

Howard's unkempt eyebrows flexed. His mouth twitched as if he were eating an underripe fruit, and each chew brought more bitterness than the last. The notion of not worrying was anathema to him. "I don't know…" he muttered. "I just don't know…"

There was a lot Gracie didn't know; she knew that, particularly starting her training under the Crimson Wraith. No one inside Sprang & Sons knew just how much she didn't know. And one of the things she did not know was that, before the day was out, Kristen would walk through the front door.

She had her hair up in a ponytail. Her dangly earrings brushed the collar of her puffy white coat, and she wore a pair of patterned leggings tucked into Ugg boots.

Seeing her, Gracie felt her heart leap. Zack was gone. Kristen was free. Maybe they could go back to being friends again. But from the look on Kristen's face, Gracie could see that was not the case.

"Can we talk?" Kristen said quietly when she got to the register. She wasn't holding eye contact with Gracie.

"Yeah, sure," said Gracie. She turned to Brianna, "You cool with that?"

"Of course, go on."

They went out to the back alley, and before Gracie could ask how Kristen was, she said, in a quaking voice, "He's gone."

"Okay," said Gracie. To her, that was a damn victory, but Kristen didn't sound victorious.

"I asked him where he was going," Kristen continued. "He wouldn't say. Just took all his things and drove off."

"Okay," Gracie said again. There didn't seem any point Kristen was getting to just yet.

"He's not on social media. Or if he is, he blocked me. Everywhere. It's like..." Kristen gritted her teeth to bite back a sob. "It's like he just died. And it's killing me."

This time, Gracie didn't say "okay." It wasn't okay. What it *was* was making her mad.

Tears came as Kristen continued. "I reached out to Josh—you know, his weed guy? He said Zack just bolted. He isn't even in town anymore. He's just gone. He's just fucking gone." Then she brought her eyes to Gracie's. "Why?"

"Why what?"

"Why did you do it? Was it not enough to nearly cut his leg off? Did you have to get the Crimson Wraith to threaten him too?"

"Whoa..." said Gracie.

But Kristen continued. "He told me. He told me how the Crimson Wraith nearly threw him off a building for you. Why?"

"Why?"

"Yes, why?"

Well, that was just about all that Gracie could take. "Because of you, God damn it!" She didn't want to yell at Kristen. She knew Kristen had been yelled at plenty by lots of people in her life, but Gracie didn't know how to answer without yelling. "Don't you get that? I did all of that for you! Beat the shit out of Zack—for you! Got help from the Crimson Wraith—for you!"

Kristen shook her head with a look on her face as if she pitied Gracie. "This was never going to be a thing between us.

You knew that, right? I mean, a few times making out when we had some drinks was fun and all, but that's all it was, just fun. Zack and I are in love. Don't you know the difference? Don't you know what love is?"

"You think… Wait, you think…" It can be difficult sometimes to understand someone who is just so wrong that you don't know where to start to get to the very wrong conclusion they reached. "You think I was jealous, like romantically?"

"It's not that it wasn't nice, really, but that's not love."

"Why the fuck do you think you were in the hospital? Who do you think put you there? Is that what love is to you?"

Kristen just shrugged, "You can't understand. And you don't have to understand. Just please—*please*—please, tell the Crimson Wraith to back off, okay? I need Zack. I need him. I don't know who I am without him."

"Well, guess what? You're gonna have to fucking figure that out because I promise you that if Zack so much as breathes a whiff of Titan City air, it will be the last breath he ever takes."

The look on Kristen's face hurt her to see. Gracie had never been cruel to her before, and maybe she shouldn't have said what she did. She was just too angry though.

"Don't say that," said Kristen.

"Oh, I'm saying it."

Then Kristen screamed, "Don't say that!" Her voice echoed down the alley.

But Gracie had lost all pity for her former roommate. "I am fucking saying it, and you better believe I fucking mean it! Zack is done, you hear me? Done! And it is time for you to move the fuck on!"

The back door to Sprang & Sons opened, and Brianna peaked her head out, "Hey, guys? Are you okay? We heard some shouting…"

Gracie felt her cheeks burning. "Yeah, everything is fine here. Sorry."

Kristen did not look at all fine though. She shook her head and whispered, "You're a monster." Then she turned and ran.

It made Gracie all the happier to be moving away from Sprang & Sons, on to other things, a job where Kristen wouldn't be able to come find her. And if that meant dressing up as Tutu Teddy Bear or helping kids pretend they were fishing, all of that was just fine by her.

1970

The package arrived at Finn Manor on a Monday without return address. Inside, it bore a little over two hundred pages of a manuscript and a note that read:

Dear Eddie,

Please read this at your earliest convenience. In a week, I will come to talk about it in person. Hope we can come to some sort of agreement.

Sincerely,
Thomas James

As promised, the following Monday, Tommy appeared on the front steps of Finn Manor. He wore a suit and tie, the same as he had worn to his college graduation two years before. Like the rest of Tommy's wardrobe, Edward had bought that outfit for him.

"Hello, Tommy," said Edward.

Tommy nodded, "Eddie. You're answering the door yourself now?"

"I gave the staff the day off. Wanted to make sure we have some privacy."

"Oh," said Tommy. Edward saw a flash of fear. Perhaps he did not want to be alone with the older vigilante.

"Please, come in," said Edward. "We can speak in the study."

On the table beside what he knew was Edward's favorite reading chair, Tommy saw his manuscript. The pages still looked neatly stacked together. "Have you had a chance to read it?" he asked.

"I've read enough," said Edward, opening the antique globe drinks cabinet. "It's still rum and Kola, I presume?"

"Actually," said Tommy, "the wife doesn't like me drinking."

Edward pretended to look around. "Well, I don't see her here."

"Just the Kola," said Tommy, "please."

"Suit yourself," said Edward. Still, he placed ice cubes in a tumbler, popped open the can, and decanted the Kola before handing it over. There was an air of formality in the gesture, as if they had been business partners and not lovers.

As Edward poured his own drink, bourbon on the rocks, he said, "The writing is exceptional. Your professors at Titan University would be proud. That is a very well-constructed narrative you've laid out."

"Thank you," said Tommy. "That's nice to hear."

"And how do you feel about what you've written?" Edward turned to face the young man. Just behind his veil of formality, the hurt and anger burned, revealing itself in the tightness of Edward's lip and a crinkling of the brow, details for which he himself had taught Tommy to look when assessing the attitude of an adversary.

"Good. I think it's good," Tommy sipped at his drink. "You know, I think I will take that rum after all. If you don't mind."

"Not at all," said Edward, taking back the drink and adding the liquor before returning it. "And what sort of title do you have in mind for this story of yours?"

"The agent I've spoken to came up with something he thought would help it sell—*Seduced by the Mask*."

Edward snorted a laugh into his drink.

"You think that's funny?" asked Tommy.

"Well, a little, yes. It sounds like some tawdry paperback romance. But, no, that isn't what I laughed at. You publishing this, taking these words, all this information, having it printed, putting it out in the world—Tommy, you can't."

"You don't think so?" said Tommy.

"No. Goodness, no. A tell-all about your career as the Wily Wisp and as my... No, it is a terrible notion. Tommy, you have a young wife. Probably you want to start a family. Regardless of what you imagine you may have here, the notoriety a book like this would bring you is not a burden you want to bear."

"We need money, Eddie."

"Yes, most people do."

"And selling this book will make us that money."

"But what will the money cost? These are criminal activities to which you are confessing. Criminal. And I don't just mean the sex, which you do a fantastic job of detailing, let me tell you. I'd almost forgotten that night on the rooftop of the Dionysian. You brought it back most beautifully. But there are violent crimes here—vigilantism, breaking-and-entering, invasion of privacy—things to which law enforcement may have turned a blind eye in the past, so long as you and I were promoting civic responsibility with our public appearances. However, if you place this on a bookshelf, I think they would feel compelled to prosecute. Failure to do so on their part would look like negligence.

"That's to say nothing of the criminal element and how they would react. Some of those boys we put away may not be fully reformed once they return to the streets. They may have revenge in mind. Do you want to place a target on yourself and your loved ones? And we haven't cleaned up the streets entirely, you know. That's not how crime-fighting works. There will always be new rogues appearing, angry and ambitious, wanting to give themselves a name among their kind. They would come looking for you, Tommy, putting you in peril to call me out so they might be the one who beat the Crimson Wraith. You've suffered enough already because of that, haven't you? That danger isn't what you want. If it were, you would have stayed."

A tremor in Tommy's tone suggested that the trauma of his captures was returning at Edward's suggestion. "My agent says we can keep it all anonymous. It won't have to be in my name. The author will just be W. W."

"W.W. For Wily Wisp? Really? That's the name you want to use? You'd take the name I gave you? *My* name?" His veneer of civility began to crack. "You would do this... You would do this to me... And not even have the decency to do so in your own name..." Edward broke. He hurled his glass into the empty fireplace where it shattered brilliantly against the stone. "How dare you?"

From his training under Edward, Tommy readied his stance for violence, adjusting his grip around his glass to use it as a weapon if needed. "It's my story, Eddie. I have a right to it. I lived it. I suffered for it. And under that name."

"Of all the selfish, stupid..."

"I'm not stupid, Eddie. I know what this story is. I know people will pay for it. The Crimson Wraith means a lot to Titan City. They will want to know."

"Is that all this means to you? Money? Is this all it ever meant to you? All I ever meant to you?"

"Things change," said Tommy. "I'm not a kid anymore, not like when you met me. I've got a family now. I have someone to look after. You wouldn't understand."

"I used to have a family. You were my family," said Edward. "And together we looked after all of Titan City. What the Crimson Wraith means to Titan City, you were a part of that, Tommy. And someday, maybe, you could have taken that name as well."

"I didn't want that," said Tommy. "I never wanted that."

"Fine. That's fine. You didn't have to. I wouldn't make you. I never made you do anything, did I?"

"No, but..."

"There you go. You say it yourself. You chose all of this. Everything you wrote down here in your book, those were your choices, your responsibility. And now, you are choosing something different. Very well. I hope it makes you happy. I could never bring myself to marry a woman and make a charade of romance, but if you think you can, then I wish you the best."

"My marriage isn't a charade, Eddie. I love my wife. I love being with her. I'm not... I'm not like you."

"So, you're not. My mistake. But don't publish this, Tommy. If you don't see the risk it brings to yourself, think of the harm you might be doing to so many others. What will people think of the Crimson Wraith after they read this? Will criminals still fear him? Will law enforcement still respect him? Will children still listen when he tells them to brush their teeth before bed and do all their homework after school? Will their parents still let them dress as him for Halloween? By focusing on the salacious details of our relationship, you make him sound like some sort of deviant. This book just reeks with page after page of filth. And that's not how I remember it, Tommy. There was nothing dirty about what we felt for each other, not for me."

"So... you did read it..."

"I did," said Edward. "And it broke my heart."

Tommy appeared to consider this. "Maybe I don't have to publish it," he said.

"There you go. Now you're thinking clearly."

"But," said Tommy, "I need you to make up for the money I'd get from it."

"What?"

"Five hundred thousand dollars."

"Five—?"

"Half a million in total. Think of it as back pay, a hundred thousand for each year I was the Wily Wisp. It doesn't have to be all up front. Over time is fine—"

Faster than Tommy could dodge it, Edward slapped him hard across the face. "I took you into my home!" he shouted. "I fed you, clothed you, supported your education, giving you all the love a father ever could..."

"Fathers don't do to their sons the things you did to me."

"The things I did to you? What about the things you did to me? Don't play innocent. I was far from the first man you'd been with. You made that fact clear from the moment we met. Was I even the first well-to-do Titan queen to buy your drinks? To buy your clothes? Or was I just the one who made you the best offer?" He turned away from Tommy, as disgusted with himself as with his ex-lover. "How could I have been so stupid? How could I have placed my trust in you?"

"You trusted me? I trusted you! How many times was I captured by this or that villain? Beaten? Tortured? And Dr. Oblivion..." Tommy clutched the sides of his head. "He's still in there, Eddie, there, in my mind. I can't sleep without seeing him, hearing his voice. Every night he's there. Please. Please, I need this. You can't say no. Not after what we've been through, after what I went through, all for you..." There was a quiver in Tommy's voice, the beginning of tears.

"No," said Edward. "I am saying it. No. Because if you ever had any real feelings for me, you could not come here like this. You could not threaten to expose me like this. And if all of that was just an act, then I can't bring myself to trust anything else you have to say."

"Then trust this," said Tommy. "I will publish this book. It will sell! And then everyone will know. They may not know *who* the Crimson Wraith is, but they will know *what* he is."

With his teeth gritted, Edward spat, "So be it."

"I will," said Tommy. "You don't think I will? I will, really."

"Yes, go on then. Do it." He nodded. "Show me what a man you've become, Tommy. Show me you aren't afraid of what will happen."

"I'm not."

"Good. And neither am I." A laugh burst out of Edward. "Do you know how long... But no, you don't. You can't. Your generation doesn't know what it was like, the hiding, the secrets, the lies, what it meant for someone like us before all this liberation you've come to enjoy, knowing the world hates you and hating yourself just that much and more for something over which you had no control, because your heart was just shaped that way. And you would rip it from your chest with your bare hands if someone told you they could replace it with something 'normal,' a heart that wanted all the things everyone else's heart wants." Edward poured himself another bourbon on the rocks and drank deep. "Go on then, Thomas James. Unmask the Crimson Wraith with your little book. I won't stop you. Let's find out if everyone likes what they see."

CHAPTER FOURTEEN

1971

Seduced by the Mask spent more weeks on The Titan Gazette number one bestsellers list than any book before it, and the fall-out across Titan City was unlike anything ever seen. Its depictions of the Crimson Wraith being a closeted homosexual in his personal life, when not waging his unelected war against crime, captured the general imagination. Citizens did not have to purchase a copy to hear about it. Newspapers, television programs, and radio shows discussed its allegations, bringing awareness to the general populace.

The credibility of its author came into question, of course, but many noted that the references to public appearances throughout the 1960s as well as the thwarting and apprehension of members of the Crimson Wraith's rogue's gallery, lined up with official accounts, with the addition of details that did suggest first-hand experience. Retired police officers and city officials were invited to confirm specific points not part of the public record, and their confirmations made the book's validity seem solid.

Very quickly, other anonymous voices came forward, hoping to make money from their own stories. Publishers shoved onto the shelves titles like *My Night with the Crimson Wraith* and *I was Almost the Wily Wisp*. None of these had a factual basis, but each received substantial sales regardless.

Edward knew the reaction would be bad, but he had not

expected it to take the turn it did. There was one particular point of confusion he could not have anticipated because, to him, it was not confusing at all.

As he promised, Tommy left many details out of *Seduced by the Mask* as a precaution for his and Edward's personal safety. Details of Finn Manor remained a total blank, for instance, and he described the scale of their lifestyle using general terms, saying only that they "lived comfortably." Nowhere did he state that the home of the Crimson Wraith's alter-ego had an indoor swimming pool, century-old bowling alley, or family plot.

But when it came to the subject of their meeting, those broad statements left an unfortunate absence for imagination to fill. Tommy gave it no time nor place, saying only that it happened when he was "young," and then speaking in ominous terms of how it felt in retrospect:

> *I could not imagine what he had in mind for me. All I knew that fateful day was that he seemed kind. He offered me the warmth of his home. I was alone and terrified, so small in a city so large. When he revealed his secret identity, I thought it sounded exciting, like a game of dress-up. I had no way to know the danger lying in wait, danger both to body and soul.*

By not specifying that Tommy was of-age when they met, nor that their meeting occurred in 1963, there existed no point of fact to keep a reader from confusing Tommy James' career as the Wily Wisp with Edward's own.

A narrative arose that the Wily Wisp was not a consenting adult at the time of meeting the Crimson Wraith but was, in fact, groomed for a sexual relationship as a child. Edward never considered the publication of Tommy's book could result in Titan City coming to believe he had sexually abused himself.

The conflation of homosexuality with pedophilia created a fervor that authorities could not ignore. Mayor Kelly

Winchester, associated with the Crimson Wraith since his days as a state senator, felt he needed to repudiate the vigilante to protect his own image. He made up a story that the Crimson Wraith had threatened him with violence, forcing his public support, but his claim was not strong enough to keep him from being voted out of office the next term.

The Titan City Police Department intensified its long-running campaign of harassing businesses that catered to the gay community. For the second time in its history, the Innocents Club was raided and shut down. But this time, it did not go quietly. Riots erupted as those arrested for simply living out their lives did not always allow themselves to be taken peacefully.

Public morality groups called for the arrest of the Crimson Wraith and held mass burnings of the children's merchandise related to him. So much of it went into piles in Keaton Park, consigned to flame. Sometimes Edward attended these displays of moral outrage, but not as the Crimson Wraith. Other times, he did not feel masochistic enough to torture himself with those sights.

Walking around as Edward Finn, CEO of Finn Industries, posed no difficulty except the physical. Decades of crime-fighting acrobatics had taken their toll on the cartilage around Edward's knees, and he sometimes made use of the silver Derby-handled snakewood cane his father employed in his post-Crimson Wraith years. Aside from that, Edward could continue to live the mundane aspects of his existence—attending business meetings, charity events, and social functions. He could go down the street unrecognized by passersby and step into a store for a pack of Chew-Rite gum, just like anyone else. But that was never what he thought of as his real life. In his mind, Edward was not a man masquerading as a crime-fighter but a crime-fighter masquerading as a man. And Tommy had not only destroyed his ability to be the Crimson Wraith in the public eye.

Soon after *Seduced by the Mask* made its impact, Edward

noticed a change in the way his adversaries responded when the Crimson Wraith emerged from his Infernal Mist. They didn't fear him like they used to, either because he seemed less threatening as a gay man or just as a man, a human being, bound by the same appetites and limitations as any other, flawed and susceptible. They could laugh at him, toss epithets his way. And even if the outcome of each combat were the same, with Edward's opponents beaten and bound for collection by the Titan City Police, the fights took longer, their victories won less easily.

Then came the gray and chilly day in the dark of February when a couple of bank robbers grabbed a seven-year-old boy as a piece of insurance when making their escape. Edward heard the announcement on the police radio and hurled himself into action.

Hitting the streets in the Crimson Wraith Roadster once more was out of the question. That attracted too much attention. Detective Goodman had confidentially warned Edward that the TCPD wanted to bring him in for questioning and would no longer provide him with a police escort on his way to the scene of a crime. Besides, the last time Edward drove it, he did not find Titan's citizens waving and cheering at him like before. Instead, they wore expressions of concern and alarm, even revulsion. Seeing those did not help him perform his mission. So, Edward went the old-fashioned way, in a plain white van like the one Chubby drove for him and his father, wearing a false mustache, and glasses to hide his identity as either Edward Finn or the Crimson Wraith.

Having spent twenty-five of his forty-one years alive chasing men like this through Titan City, Edward knew just the sort of shadowy side-streets they would turn down as they fled the flashing police lights, which derelict buildings made ideal hiding places. When, finally, the police lost the vehicle and had to regroup, Edward kept going, and on the third potential hiding spot he searched, he found an abandoned jewelry store whose gravel driveway looked recently disturbed.

The sun had begun setting, and he had the cover of darkness by the time he parked the van in a nearby alleyway and examined the store on foot. Sure enough, he found the getaway vehicle hidden behind the building under a tarp.

After he dealt with them, Edward phoned the TCPD. "You'll find today's bank robbers apprehended for you at Schwartz Jewelers, sealed in the walk-in safe. The stolen cash is here as well. I'm taking their hostage to his parents." Then he turned to the boy. "Are you ready to go home?"

"My mom says I can't play with your toys anymore," said the boy. It may as well have been a bullet in Edward's belly.

"That's fine, but I need to get you back to her. What's your name, son?"

"Ricky."

"Hi, Ricky. I know the children are not supposed to get into cars with strangers, but would you be okay with letting me drive you home?"

Ricky thought about it, and he scrunched up his face to show just how seriously he was thinking as he did. Then he shrugged. "I guess so."

Edward led the boy back to his van, and Ricky told him where he lived. His mom had made him memorize his address in case he ever got lost playing in the neighborhood.

Driving up to Ricky's home, Edward recognized the unmarked police cars out front. Maybe they had been there since earlier that day, awaiting a ransom demand, but he suspected they'd been informed he was coming and wondered if they might try to arrest him. So, he parked around the block to make the rest of the way on foot, creeping through the neighbors' backyards.

"We can't let them see you, right, Crimson Wraith?" said Ricky. "Because people don't like you anymore?"

"That's right, Ricky," said Edward. And just beyond the lights of Ricky's back porch, Edward knelt beside the boy and said, "I'm going to leave you here. Your parents and the police may have some questions for you, and I want you to do everything they ask you, okay?"

"I don't know why they are mad. You seem all right to me."

"Thank you, Ricky. Be safe now. Don't forget to study hard in school."

"I will."

The backdoor of Ricky's home opened, and a woman whose face wore the pain of a day of crying stepped out, pack of cigarettes in hand, lighter at the ready. At the sight of her son, she cried out, "Ricky? Oh, my God, Ricky!" Then, turning to Edward, she said, "The Crimson Wraith... What have you done to him? What have you done to my boy? Get away from him! Phillip, come quick! It's the Crimson Wraith! The Crimson Wraith has our son!"

Before her husband came to the door, before the police waiting in their home followed after, guns out and ready, Edward was running, leaping over backyard fences and ducking into driveways. He heard the officers call out to him, the time-tested warning, "Stop, or I'll shoot!" Then shots fired. But Edward kept on, finally spotting a loose storm drain he could slip inside and let them run past.

As he crouched in the muck, wrapped in his cloak, Edward shook with frustrated rage. To Ricky's parents, the Crimson Wraith seemed just as dangerous as the men who kidnapped their son, maybe more so. He knew he had to accept it and accept that might never change. Edward left his costume there in that storm drain, knowing he could never wear it again, even if he could not imagine his life without the Crimson Wraith in it.

2019

Gracie didn't mind the little specks of rain drizzling down the windows of the Lincoln-Zephyr. Weather like this made people quieter, and, in her experience, that made them a little gentler, easier to deal with.

She would have preferred to be wearing something soft and warm though, not her courier suit. It was too crisp and too new. Even if it fit well, she didn't feel comfortable in it yet. But she understood she had to look a certain way for a prison visit.

The wipers pulsed gently in the background, sweeping away the tiny droplets as Kevin, in the backseat with her, and Stephen, who was driving, told her about the man they were going to see at Titan City Correctional.

Kevin said, "My mentor, Michael, he liked Hank a lot. Michael said that Hank had a really big heart and that he did all his thinking with it. He hated being the one to turn him over to the police, but it was what Hank wanted. And that being the case, Michael wanted to be there for him. While he was training me, Michael asked me to visit Hank in prison and see if he would accept legal aid to try to reduce his sentence. Hank refused. But Michael never gave up."

"Our Michael felt responsible for Mr. Mills," said Stephen. "Had he taken on the role of the Crimson Wraith after Adam's passing, Hank may not have felt the need to do so. And that did not end well for him."

Gracie said, "Because instead of the Crimson Wraith, Michael made himself that all-black costume, right? With the Z-name? The car one?"

"The Zephyr, yes." said Kevin.

Stephen said, "The word means, 'a light breeze,' something subtle, sneaky, hard to catch. It comes from the name of the Greek god of the West Wind."

"A car, a wind, and a god—got it," said Gracie. "And since he wasn't the Crimson Wraith, this Hank guy just decided to jump into the role himself?"

"Exactly," said Kevin. "And he turned out to be pretty effective at it. Maybe he was the kind of Crimson Wraith people needed at the time."

"We did reach out to him," said Stephen. "Edward wished to welcome him formally and offered to support his work. Initially, Hank declined the offer, but his Wily Wisp, Jasmine, prevailed on Mr. Mills to accept some financial support. Edward covered the rent for a two-bedroom apartment to serve as their base of operations and their home."

"Jasmine—she was the awesome-looking one in the sequins?"

Stephen smiled, "Yes, she was quite a remarkable character."

"Okay, but there's still one thing I don't quite get," said Gracie. "You're telling me the Crimson Wraith of the seventies, Adam something..."

"Adam O'Neil," said Kevin.

"Right, so, he died, and there's no Crimson Wraith for a bit, just the Zephyr. If you think Titan City needs some kind of Crimson Wraith, I get that, but why him? Like, you said the Crimson Wraith helped all you guys at some time before you got involved. Did the Crimson Wraith help Hank too?"

"Sort of. Adam arrested him."

Gracie shook her head. "I thought you said Michael arrested him."

"That was Hank's second arrest. His first came from Adam. Hank was responsible for the death of his wife."

"Hold the fucking phone. The guy who decided to become the Crimson Wraith was a wife murderer?"

"Not murder," said Kevin. "Hank was convicted of manslaughter. Apparently, it was an accident, part of a domestic dispute. He pushed her, and she fell down a flight of stairs. When he realized what he had done, he ran, and, as the Crimson Wraith, Adam caught him and convinced him to turn himself over to the police. Hank did. He pled guilty and served five years in prison. After his release, Hank heard the Crimson Wraith was gone, and he experienced a kind of calling. Michael said Hank always seemed consumed by guilt and that he took to the Crimson Wraith's mission as a kind of penance."

"Fucking hell..." Gracie muttered.

There was silence in the car for a moment. Gracie turned to the window. They passed by a billboard announcing, "2-for-1

Everything Bagel Burgers at Burger Bagel!" and another that read, "Catch the BUZZ! Every morning on *Coffee with Cassandra*! You won't believe it!"

Knowing that one of the Crimson Wraiths was in prison for killing a bad guy—"someone who deserved it" as Danny said—was one thing. Killing his wife though, accident or no, that sat like something cold and squirmy in Gracie's stomach. And hearing that it was a fight that got out of hand, she couldn't help but think back to her parents. Sometimes she saw her dad slap her mom. Sometimes she saw her mom slap her dad. Usually, they waited until she was out of the room, and even then, there were mostly things thrown against the walls, not making direct contact. But sometimes it happened.

What if at some point, in some outburst of rage, her dad had killed—actually *killed*—her mom? What if Zack killed Kristen? Maybe neither men would mean to do so and would call it an accident. Would either be able to experience some prison transformation where they left full of remorse and wanting to protect others? Do you have to be a certain type of person beforehand? Could just anyone be a monster one day and a hero the next? She couldn't believe that.

Gracie resigned herself to the fact that the people she'd come to trust trusted Hank, even if it may have been easier for them to overlook violence against a woman since they were all men. She couldn't still the uncomfortable feeling inside, but she decided she could go along with Kevin on this for now.

"Okay, so, the person Hank killed who wasn't his wife, the reason he's locked away right now, who was that?"

"The Troubadour," said Kevin.

"The second Troubadour," Stephen corrected.

Kevin nodded, "The second Troubadour."

"How many Troubadours were there?" asked Gracie.

"So far?" said Kevin, "Just the two."

"Did the first one train someone to follow in his footsteps or something?"

Stephen said, "The second Troubadour had nothing to do

with the first. You see, in the 1960s..."

Gracie interrupted, "Yeah, I read about him."

"You read about him?"

"Sure did, in *Nights of Justice*. Theater student of Cuban ancestry. Thought he was making a point about the *status quo*, and that involved armed robbery, sure, but no one much actually got hurt. Sounded like he even had a fanbase from the —what was that word Goodman used? 'Counterculture.' Yeah, the Troubadour had fans in the counterculture who thought he was sticking it to the Man. The Crimson Wraith caught him in a plot involving the Spirit of Prosperity, and he served a few years. Seemed like he must have gone straight after his release."

Kevin said, "Sounds like your studying is going very well."

Gracie shrugged, "I mean, it's all pretty fucking relevant to me right now, not like memorizing the names and dates of Civil War battlefields in high school."

"Fair," said Kevin. "You haven't read about the second Troubadour yet?"

"No, I guess I haven't gotten that far."

"He came right at the end of Goodman's career. In fact, the second Troubadour was part of what made Goodman ready to retire. His real name was Boland Moore. He wore the same mask as the first Troubadour, and he also saw his criminal activities as art, but with a big difference."

"He was a monster," said Stephen.

"What kind of monster?" asked Gracie.

"A serial killer," said Kevin.

CHAPTER FIFTEEN

1988

Jasmine had a police blanket over her shoulders when Hank arrived. He found her sitting on the front stoop of the apartment she had gone to visit. Emergency lights painted the sides of the tenement buildings and bodegas all down the block. When she saw him walk up, she reached up like a child to be picked up by their father, letting the blanket slip away.

Hank held her. "What the hell?"

Into his shoulder, she said, "It was the worst, absolute worst thing I ever saw."

Detective Jorgé Villagraña approached them, "This is a friend of yours, sir?" It took Hank a moment to realize the detective was calling Jasmine "sir."

"Yes," said Jasmine. "This is Hank."

"I see," said Detective Villagraña. "Were you also acquainted with the victim?"

Hank shook his head. No matter how long it was since his release, police made him uncomfortable. Just the presence of an officer in uniform set him on edge. They carried handcuffs on their belt, handcuffs they might want to put around his wrists again, taking away everything he'd worked for since his release. But he was comforting Jasmine, being strong for her, and that had a way of dissolving his fear. For her, he could be brave. "I didn't know her."

"And where were you this evening?"

"At work."

"Where is work for you, sir?"

"Bobby D's Delicatessen."

"Oh, Bobby D's? Love that place. Can I get your full name just for our report?"

"Henry Mills."

"Thank you, Mr. Mills. And you'll see that Mr. Gates gets home safely?" A little head nod from the detective indicated Jasmine. Again, Hank could not get his head around calling Jasmine "Mister."

"Yeah," he said.

"You take it easy tonight, Mr. Gates," said Detective Villagraña. "We'll call if we have any further questions for you."

Hank could feel both cops and bystanders eyeing them as they walked away, he with his arm around her waist. He knew what they must have thought of their relationship. They could all go to hell.

Back in their apartment, Jasmine went right to the kitchen and took a bottle of Medusa's Head from the cabinet, but she couldn't get it to her mouth. She just started crying. "Who would do that? What kind of monster... I just don't understand... Some Johns, they real sick, Hank. You come to expect that. They want some shit—real crazy shit—they don't think they can get from no wife or no girlfriend. And, hell, it ain't all bad. Some of it's cute even. Like this one guy wanted me to rock him like a baby, and I'm like, 'Aw, honey, let Momma Jasmine take real good care of you...' But this... What the fuck?"

She had gone to visit a friend of hers that night, Mandy. It wasn't anything special, just a social call to gossip about girls Jasmine knew when she was still hooking, paint their nails, watch that TV show *Miss Doug* about a dress shop owner who Jasmine and Mandy both swore reminded them of their mothers, even though Mandy was white.

But when Jasmine got to Mandy's door, there was no answer to her knock, not even when she called out that the bucket of chicken she brought was getting cold. And when the silence got to what her crime-fighting skills told her was way too long, Jasmine tried the handle of the door and found it unlocked. What she saw inside made her scream.

Mandy's body had been decapitated, left naked in a chair that faced the doorway, wrapped in some kind of purple fabric. At her feet, black feathers spelled out the word "NEVER." Then Jasmine felt something wet hit her shoulder and looked up to see Mandy's head hanging over the doorway, dangling from its hair by a hook in the wall.

"We got to get that son of a bitch, Hank. We got to. For her."

They'd never dealt with a criminal like this before, not this kind of killer. Murderers, yes, plenty of those. But they were different. This was strange. Hank didn't understand why someone would do this.

"We will," he told Jasmine. "But I think we are going to need to ask for help."

Later...

Since 1975, they had communicated with each other through messages in the Personals sections of *The Titan Herald*. "Lady in Red seeks a Good Man..." That was how Harlan Goodman, now Commander of the TCPD, knew the Crimson Wraith was reaching out to him. The details of the message would indicate the specifics of time and place. "Remember that day we went riding after the storm? I nearly fell eleven times..." That meant they would meet in Keaton Park at the Stone Horse, memorial to fallen veterans of World War I, at 11 PM.

Commander Goodman wore his civilian clothes, a blue windbreaker jacket, khaki pants, and gray driving cap. He waited on a bench, gazing at the silhouette of the monument rearing up against a patch of night sky framed by the dark limbs of Keaton Park trees around him. Then he felt that sensation on the back of his neck that always told him when his old friend had returned. Funny how regardless of who wore the hood of the Crimson Wraith, Goodman still felt that same sensation. Perhaps it was a secret they passed on to each other.

For the past five years, it had not actually been the Crimson Wraith he met this way but the young man who worked alongside him as the Wily Wisp, now the Zephyr. He too gave Goodman that sensation on the back of his neck. The Commander turned to see the Zephyr. Shadow obscured his domino mask, and he wore a long overcoat to cover his black bodysuit with the "Z" on its chest.

"The Raven," said the Zephyr.

"Is that the name the murderer goes by?"

"No, it's the poem by Edgar Alan Poe. The details of the crime scene are references to lines of it—the head above the door and the body in the chair facing it. The purple fabric over the victim's body came from a curtain; that's from the poem too. And of course, the black feathers..."

"From a raven."

"Bingo."

Two more figures stepped out from the shadows, one was the Wily Wisp, still in her blonde wig and purple domino mask, but wearing a long coat over her usual attire. Beside her loomed the form of the Crimson Wraith, who might have been mistaken for any late-night jogger in his red sweatshirt until one looked into his hood to see the black ski mask with the white skull painted on it.

"Finally, face-to-face," said Goodman, extending his hand to the Crimson Wraith. They shook. "I have a lot of respect for those who wore that hood before you. And you've been doing good work in their name."

The Crimson Wraith said, "Thank you, sir."

Goodman turned to the Wily Wisp. "And you must be his fighting companion."

She grinned, "Fighting companion, personal stylist, surgeon, and spokesmodel, yes."

"Of course. So, the three of you will be working together to catch this killer?"

The Zephyr said, "That we will."

"Well then," said Goodman, "I will put all of my resources at your disposal."

The Crimson Wraith said, "Did you bring the notebook?"

Goodman nodded and reached into his pocket. The personal ad that set up the night's meeting also said, "How I wish to once again hear you read from that little notebook you kept at your bedside, the one with camellias on its cover..." Forensics had found one such notebook at the crime scene, filled with names and dates, all annotated with some kind of code. He figured the white flowers on its cover had to be camellias.

The Wily Wisp took it from him. "This was her client list, from the names they gave her anyway."

"I take it you knew the victim personally?" asked Goodman.

"You can take it that I know what I know."

"My apologies."

Then she found what she was looking for. "Right here, you see these marks? The diamond means something kinky, something the client will pay extra for, but the two Xs means he only seen her twice so far. He's still a newbie, someone she don't know well. Ain't established trust, but guess he offered to pay enough to make her look past that. Looks like he got himself an appointment for 2 PM."

Goodman asked, "So early in the day?"

"Hell, yeah," said the Wily Wisp. "Lots of folks ain't at home, so that's when you schedule something that may get, you know, loud." She shook her head, "Damn it, girl, what did he promise you?"

"Is there a name for him?" asked Goodman. "Any kind of identifying information?"

"Yeah, looks like he told her to call him 'E. Valentino.'"

"As in, Esteban Valentino, the Troubadour?"

The Wily Wisp shrugged. "That's what it says."

"That doesn't make sense," said Goodman. "Esteban Valentino has to be in his forties now. He was let out over a decade ago without a single violation since. And something like this, certainly the Troubadour had a flair for the dramatic but nothing so..."

"Bloody," said the Crimson Wraith.

"Exactly. I helped put him away, and he never had a murder charge—vandalism, public disturbance, multiple counts of armed robbery and resisting arrest, but not one shot fired on any of his capers. The guns he used were prop weapons half the time."

The Zephyr shook his head. "We have eyes on Valentino. This was not him. Trust me."

"Then who?" asked Goodman, "and why the name?"

The Crimson Wraith said, "Maybe he thinks he is like the person who used that name before. Maybe he wants to follow them."

"Like a copycat criminal?" asked Goodman.

The Crimson Wraith nodded.

The Zephyr said, "Those feathers on the floor, in the poem the Raven doesn't say, 'Never.' It says, 'Never-*more*.' Maybe that's a message from the killer. There will be more. He's only just getting started."

2019

Like 6th Avenue, the Robinson Street Bridge had been destroyed on Zero Hour. While the Arch of Mercy provided entry to the newly rebuilt 6th Avenue Bridge, the Arch of Memory stood at the end of Robinson Street, which spanned the Brennert River. And across the Robinson Street Bridge, on the banks of the Brennert, stood the Titan City Correctional Facility.

The TCCF had been home to Hank Mills since 1988, adding thirty-one more years on top of the five he spent after his manslaughter conviction. At the age of sixty-six, Hank had lived over half his life behind bars, and that was working out just fine as far as he was concerned.

The time he spent busting the skulls of Titan City criminals as the Crimson Wraith made it dangerous to keep Hank with the general population. Besides, significant portions of the law enforcement community quietly appreciated Hank's work and wanted to protect him from threats, even if the law required he be incarcerated. So, they placed Hank in a control unit that housed elderly inmates and those living with chronic disease, both of which were more at risk of abuse from other inmates themselves. This offered him some protection. And Hank immediately went about making himself helpful to those around him who could use helping.

This wasn't like his first period in prison. Then, he felt like an awful waste of a human being who needed constant punishment, but this time he came in feeling it was the world itself that was pretty damned awful. And if that was the case, people may as well try to be nice to each other when and where they can. After all, the world sure as hell wasn't getting any nicer on its own. But while some people seemed born with the ability to manage living in the middle of awfulness, Hank didn't figure he was one of them. In his time as the Crimson Wraith, he had gone from thinking he may have been a monster to deciding that, really, he was just too dumb to keep from screwing things up wherever he went, and the smartest thing he could do would be to accept how dumb he was.

That was why, in 2005, when a twenty-five-year-old Kevin Snyder came to him, Hank told him to go away. The kid had money. His father's company, SnyTech, had just bought Finn Industries, and to show their continued commitment to the public good, Snyder-Finn opened up additional funding for the humanitarian work of the Finn Foundation. That included criminal rehabilitation programs.

Kevin said, "Our attorneys had a look at your case and think you'd be an ideal candidate for early release. For over fifteen years now, you've been a model inmate, and there could be post-release opportunities for you—"

"No," said Hank. It wasn't nice to interrupt people, but he had learned there was a point where the tone of someone's voice tells you all that you need to hear, more than any other words will.

But Kevin didn't seem to understand. "Really, there would, both in terms of employment and housing. This could be a chance to—"

"No."

That was the problem, this kid believed there was a chance, a chance for something different, whatever the details, and he wanted Hank to believe as well. But that kind of thinking was only for people who didn't know any better, people who took that something different as a thing to strive for, a thing to break their back in pursuit of. Living in prison, Hank saw men drive themselves crazy dreaming of something different on some magical someday that never came. The ones who did better looked at the here and now as the only reality and adjusted themselves to it.

"Mr. Mills, I—"

"Hank," he said. "My name is Hank."

"Right, Hank…"

The boy seemed confused. Maybe a rich kid like that wasn't used to hearing "no." That made Hank a little sad for him. It meant he had been kept a child for way too long, and it would make things all the more disappointing when life made him grow up.

Kevin tried again, "You know, it was a senior member of our board, Michael Conroy, who personally selected your case. Maybe you're familiar with Mr. Conroy? He used to be the CEO of Finn Industries before the merger. He used to be… well, a lot of things…"

Hank caught the suggestion. Clearly, this kid knew the Crimson Wraith. He nodded. "I know Michael."

"Well, then, you should know that he seems to have really personal interest in giving you another chance out there. You don't have to stay here."

There was that word again, "chance." And Hank had no interest in anything to do with that. "Tell Michael thanks," he said. "But I'm where I'm supposed to be."

Every month since his arrest, Michael had put a little money in Hank's prison account. For the most part, Hank didn't withdraw any, and when he did, it was often to do a favor for another inmate. There came the occasional letter from Michael too and cards on holidays. Soon after Kevin visited, though, he became the one to write the letters. He regretted to inform Hank of Michael's passing away in an industrial accident but assured him that everything that needed to be done in response had been done. "Michael has received his justice," he wrote. Kevin also assured Hank that the Finn Foundation still had his interests in mind and that the monetary contributions to his welfare would continue.

A few more letters followed, but Hank never wrote back. He never wrote to Michael either, but he and Kevin had not known each other beforehand. Within a year, the letters ended, with Kevin saying, "Please, know that you will always have a friend out here if you wish to have a friend. Until you do, I will leave you in peace." Being left in peace sounded good to Hank.

So, when he was told he had visitors, Hank was surprised to hear that but not surprised by who it was. The kid was back, no longer a kid anymore. He had a new kid with him, a girl who looked kind of like a boy, especially in that suit she wore. And Stephen was there. He liked Stephen, Edward's boyfriend, a good cook, and he had helped Hank.

They met in a private room, the kind where attorneys speak with their clients. Hank sat down across from them at a table that bolted down to the floor. And before either Stephen, Kevin, or the boyish girl could speak, Hank went ahead and said it, "No."

1988

It had been two days since Hank last saw Jasmine. She never came back from checking on a friend who said something about a client asking her to buy a white rabbit costume for an *Alice in Wonderland* fantasy. Hank didn't have that friend's address or phone number but had been calling Jasmine's contacts that he knew of. So far, no one who answered knew anything that could help. It was like Jasmine had walked out of their apartment and gotten swallowed up by the city without a trace.

There was no *Alice in Wonderland* murder reported, so that was something hopeful at least. Since the Edgar Allen Poe killing, there had been three others based on *The Scream* by Edvard Munch, Tchaikovsky's Swan *Lake*, and the story of Hansel and Gretel. In all cases, the victims had been women—another prostitute, a waitress, and a student from Titan University.

No doubt as this new Troubadour intended, his bizarre killings grabbed *Gazette* headlines, and Titan City stood on the verge of panic. The TCPD asked citizens, whenever possible, not to walk the streets alone at night. There was talk of instituting a mandatory curfew. Vigilante groups sent to the hospital two innocent men they said had a suspicious look to them.

And so, even though he had not slept for more than a few hours together in days, Hank did not look much more on-edge than anyone else he passed on the way to Bobby D's that morning. The spring air was thick with the bitterness of exhaust and fear. Even through his dulled, sleep-deprived senses, he felt it. And though his vision seemed ringed by darkness, Hank could see in the faces he passed the terror of what might come next. None of them knew where or when or even how the Troubadour would strike again.

It did seem strange to him, however, that he found the front door of Bobby D's unlocked. Usually, he had to tug on the handle for a bit, and then Iris would open it for him, although since Betsy came back from school on her spring break, it had been her. But the door just swung open for him. Very strange.

Then he heard a voice, Betsy's, and it had a strained, shivering quality to it, weak, full of terror. "Hank? Please... Help..."

He saw her sitting at a table, three bowls of oatmeal in front of her. She had been bound to her chair by duct-tape around her body. And where her left arm had been, there was now only a bloody stump, wrapped in bandages and a rubber hose tourniquet.

Hank ran to free her as fresh tears started down her face. Between sobs, she said, "The man, he wore a mask, a weird mask with a long, long nose. He killed them. He killed mom. He killed Uncle Bobby. He said it was because of you, Hank. Why? Why is it because of you? Why us?"

Looking into her wide, horror-stricken eyes, Hank could not say anything but the truth. "Because I'm the Crimson Wraith."

"What? You're... What? No... No, you're not. No..." And then her words disappeared into screams. Hank reached out and held Betsy. She cried into his chest and began beating feebly at him with her remaining arm.

Hank said, "Your mom and Bobby, where are they?"

Betsy pointed to the kitchen of the delicatessen. Hank found Bobby face down in the fryer, hot oil still bubbling around him. A kitchen knife in his back held a piece of paper with one word written on it in block letters: *SHOW*.

Iris hung in the cooler. The blood dripping from her had begun to freeze in dark tracks down her body. In her chest, another knife held another piece of paper with another word: *TIME*.

He left them both as they were for the police, who he called before taking from his pocket the card with the number for Finn Manor. Hank had not called Finn Manor before. He left that to Jasmine. When he heard the click on the other end, it was the first time he spoke the code phrase given to them earlier, the name of the place where they met Michael.

"Golden Sphinx," he said.

"Hello, Mr. Mills," said Stephen. "I am afraid that Michael and Edward are not available at present—"

Hank said, "The Troubadour. He was here."

"Where?" said Stephen.

"He came to the delicatessen. He killed my bosses, the brother and sister. And he left a girl, Bobby's niece, but he... He cut off... He cut off her arm. It's a message. He killed them as a message to me. Jasmine has been missing. He must have her. He must have made her tell him where I was."

Stephen was silent for a moment. Then he said, "All right. How did he kill them? What did he leave for you to find?"

Carefully, Hank laid out the details for Stephen as he found them—Bobby in the fryer, Iris in the freezer, the signs stabbed into them, Betsy left with one arm at a table with three bowls of oatmeal.

"*Dios mio*," Stephen murmured. "It's a children's fairytale. One too hot, one too cold, and Betsy, you say he cut off her left arm?"

"Yes."

"Then all that he left her with is 'just right.'"

"What does it mean?"

"Goldilocks and the Three Bears."

Blood pounded in his skull, and the fury exploded from Hank. He drove his fist into the wall in front of him. Plaster came free from the blow. Hank growled, "He's insane."

"Most certainly. But I think he has also told you where you can find him."

"Where?"

"Mr. Mills, you should know, whatever he is inviting you to come find, it must be some kind of trap."

"Tell me!"

"I will, but please, you should not go after him alone. If you could just wait until Michael can accompany you—"

"He has Jasmine! He has her!"

"I know."

"Then tell me where he is." Hank felt his whole body vibrating, a terrible trembling as if there were gears within him that were jammed, grinding against each other, threatening total collapse.

Stephen said, "The words, 'show' and 'time' add another piece to the puzzle. On Wilson, just off 43rd, there is an old movie theater, closed now for many years. But when it was open, it was called the Regent, and for its insignia, it used the symbol of three golden bears."

Hank nodded. "Wilson. Off 43rd. Got it."

"Mr. Mills, please," said Stephen. "I will reach Michael right away, I promise."

"Tell him to hurry," said Hank, and he slammed down the phone receiver.

Sirens announced the arrival of emergency vehicles. From the kitchen, Hank heard Betsy running outside, screaming to them, "Help! Help us, please!" That would be his last sight of her, seeing her wave her one remaining arm. Then, through the window, he saw Commander Goodman stepping out of a TCPD cruiser, his mouth agape at the sight of her, the only surviving victim of the Troubadour's killing spree.

If he stayed to talk to the police, Hank would have to go downtown. They would take his fingerprints so they could distinguish his from anything the Troubadour left behind. Then they would find his criminal record, and they would ask more questions about that.

But more importantly, he had just disclosed to Betsy that he was the Crimson Wraith. She knew the Troubadour had killed her family to get to him and she might tell the police that. Even if Goodman secretly supported the Crimson Wraith, there would be no way to keep from arresting Hank for his vigilantism. None of that would help Jasmine. Already, that monster must have made her suffer terribly to make her tell him where Hank worked. Hank wouldn't let the Troubadour have her for a single moment more than he had to.

Out the back door Hank fled, ducking down the trash-strewn alley and working his way through the crowd that gathered at the sound of sirens and screams. Some on-lookers would stay to witness every second. Others would only pause a moment to get a sense of the action before going on with their lives. Hank moved among those, not running from the scene of the crime, just drifting away.

In his fist, tightly gripped, he held his usual work bag. It went with him to and from the deli every day, never leaving his side. And tucked within, it held the mask that had become his destiny, the mask he would wear to face the Troubadour, to end his reign of terror once and for all and rescue the Wily Wisp—the mask of the Crimson Wraith.

2019

When they didn't move, Hank repeated himself. "I said, no."

He reminded Gracie of the older male gorilla she'd seen at the Titan City Zoo as a kid. A "silverback," they called him. Now *there* was a name for a superhero, maybe a middle-aged one.

But that was just how Hank looked. His head was shaved in a buzz cut, making a thin crown of gray around his head. His shoulders were rounded, tired from the years of carrying around all his bulk. He still had muscles aplenty, that was for sure, but a heavy belly as well. Gracie remembered the same kind of belly on the silverback. Neither looked any less dangerous for it. As a little girl, when she saw that ape behind the glass, even with its own gray hair and fat belly, she knew it was a monster, strong enough to tear all of them apart if it felt like it. She got just that same feeling from Hank—only there wasn't any glass between them.

Kevin said, "Hank, please—" but he was cut off.

"No. I said, no. And you need to listen."

"This isn't like—"

"I don't care what you have to offer. And I don't care what you think is right. I know where I am supposed to be, and it is right where I am."

"But you don't understand—"

"No, *you* don't understand," said Hank. "I did what I did. Now, I get what I got. That's justice. Justice is what we are supposed to do."

And that was all Gracie could take. "Oh, would you shut the fuck up and listen for one goddamn second?"

Hank turned his eyes to her, and Gracie felt their intensity hit like a fist. "Who are you?" he asked.

Don't be scared of the monster, she said to herself. *It doesn't matter how big he is. You can be a monster too.* "I'm Gracie."

But there was no threat in his words. "Hello, Gracie. I'm Hank."

"Hi, Hank."

"Why are you here?" He directed his attention only at her. It seemed he was done with Kevin.

"Why am I here?"

"Yes. What do you have to do with all this?"

"I'm here because these guys helped me, and now they need help. So, I'm here to try to help them get it."

"You know what these guys do?"

"I do," she said. "And I know it's something you used to do. It's something I want to do too."

Hank shook his head slowly. "Better think about that. You gotta ask yourself if that's going to get you where you want to be."

"You know, I'll be honest with you, I don't have a fucking clue where it's going to get me. But I know this much, I didn't have any idea I'd be here now before I met these guys. And I like being here a whole fuckton more than where I used to be. See, where I used to be, it was *nowhere*, man. I wasn't really living for anything, just out there fighting to survive. With these guys, though, things look just a smidge different. It looks like I could fight for something more. I can have a purpose. I can help make things better. And from what they tell me, that's what you did too, right?"

He looked away from Gracie, answering with a small shrug of his massive frame. "Tried to."

"Okay, cool. You tried. Hell, that right there is about a thousand percent more than most people in the world. You put in the effort, worked to make a difference—that's a rare goddamn thing when you think of it."

"Didn't work out."

"Yeah, sure. I can see that. It's why you're here. I get it. And, hey, if you want to be left here and left alone, I'm sure we can do that, right?"

She looked over to Kevin. Gracie could see his face was torn, eyes sad for Hank but also a little bit of a smile hovering around his lips for her. Seemed like her mentor approved of the job she was doing. He nodded.

"We don't want to take you out of here if you don't want to leave," she said.

"So, then, what *do* you want?"

"Well, Hank," said Gracie, "there's been a murder. Edward—"

"No," he said again, this time not in refusal but disbelief, "Edward? Murdered?"

Then Stephen spoke, "It's true, Hank. Eddie has been murdered. Somebody killed him."

"Who?"

Kevin answered, "We don't know. But we thought maybe you might. It seemed from the evidence of the crime scene that the killer recognized you from the photographs Edward kept on his refrigerator."

"He had a picture of me?"

Stephen said, "He did, Hank. It was from that day the three of us—Edward, Michael, and I—came to eat at your workplace, the sandwich shop, remember? You stayed busy in the kitchen, but we had lunch with Jasmine. She took our photograph. And you can be seen in the background, looking up at her as she took it."

"I remember that day," said Hank. "That was a nice day."

Stephen nodded. "It was a nice day, Hank."

Then Kevin set his briefcase on the table and pulled out a stack of folders. "If the killer recognized you, we think maybe you would recognize them too. These folders contain images of the retirement home staff who seem like they might match the silhouette of the killer we caught on the security cameras from Edward's room. Would you look at these for us, please? Just on the off chance you recognize anything. It might be nothing, but still…"

Hank turned to look at Gracie, questioningly.

She nodded. "Kind of a long-shot, man, but might be the only shot we got."

He nodded back and began looking through images. As he did, Kevin and Stephen exchanged pleased looks, and both turned to smile at Gracie. It seemed like they might have been, well, proud. That felt weird to her, and she liked it.

The sound that came out of Hank sure did seem more like gorilla than man, a guttural, startled cry. In his hand, he held the photograph of a short-haired middle-aged woman.

Tears welled in Hank's eyes as his face contorted in distress. "Betsy…"

They all gathered around him to see the picture as well, a photograph taken by one of the Haunts as she exited her apartment building.

Kevin asked, "Who is Betsy?"

"From Bobby D's, his niece. She worked there." Hank looked up to Stephen. "She was the one. I found her there. You remember? I called you."

Stephen's face fell, horror overcoming him. He held his hand to his mouth and said softly, "That poor girl. How she must have suffered."

Hesitantly, Gracie asked, "Okay, so, what is going on now?"

Stephen said, "She was one of the second Troubadour's victims. He murdered her family in front of her. It was a message."

Hank said, "It was a message for me." Then he looked at the picture confused. "Her arm..."

"It must be a prosthetic," said Stephen. He turned to Gracie. "The killer cut off her arm but let her live."

Gracie muttered, "Jesus fuck..."

"She wanted to know why her family," said Hank. "And I told her. I told her it was to get to me. I told her that I... that I was the Crimson Wraith."

Kevin said. "And she's carried that pain for thirty years."

"So, you're saying she's the one?" said Gracie. "She murdered Edward?"

"No..." said Hank.

"She may hold the Crimson Wraith responsible for all she lost," said Stephen.

Kevin said, "If she knew the Troubadour of the 1980s killed her family to get to Hank, and then saw Edward in the photo with him..."

Gracie nodded, "Might have been all it took to send her over."

Again, Hank moaned her name, "Betsy..."

Afterward...

Hands opened doors for Gracie, Kevin, and Stephen. They pressed buttons to lift gates, allowing the three back out into the world beyond the TCCF. Hands came to fetch Hank, to place his hands in cuffs, and to guide him back to his cell, only releasing his hands there. Immediately, his hands went to his eyes to wipe away the salt of dried tears before he lowered himself onto his cot to lay there, staring at the wall in misery.

And then hands punched into their timecard that they were taking a break. Hands waved for a supervisor's attention and made the gesture of puffing on an imaginary cigarette.

After opening the door outside and walking over to the overhanging corner of the roof that had become the unofficial smoking section, hands pulled first a pack and then lighter from a pocket, selected a cigarette, ignited its tip, and returned the lighter, retrieving next a flip phone.

Fingers opened the cover of the phone, selected "Blue" from the contacts, and began typing. *His visitors just left. Be ready.*

And the response from Blue came right away. *Ready.*

CHAPTER SIXTEEN

2019

When they got back to the Zephyr, Kevin placed a call to Danny on the Crimson Wraith's frequency. He connected his Wrist Comm to the car's audio so Gracie and Stephen could hear as well.

"Line secure, Specter Prime," said Danny. "This is Crypt. What's the word?"

"Subject identified," said Kevin, reading the code scribbled in the corner of Betsy's picture, her initials and birth year. "ED1968."

"Confirmed, Specter Prime. ED1968."

In her head, Gracie did the math. If Hank was arrested in 1988, and that was right when the Troubadour murdered her family, Betsy had to be only twenty-years-old at the time. She looked in the eyes of the image the Haunt had captured of her going about her business at Sunset Gardens. Betsy was smiling as she pushed an elderly woman in a wheelchair, just looked like a regular person, didn't appear to be tangled up inside by thirty-year-old trauma nor capable of murder. Whatever a villain was supposed to look like, Betsy wasn't it.

"Elizabeth DiClemente," said Danny. "Fifty-one years old. Single. No kids. Never married. Employed at Sunset Gardens for the past five years. Got her nursing degree in 1999. Worked the hospitals after Zero Hour. Before that, she attended Titan University for a couple of years before dropping out in... yeah, 1988. Nothing about the murders at Bobby D's though."

"And there might not be," said Kevin. "Since she was under twenty-one years-old, the TCPD wouldn't have released her name among the victims. She may not even have been on payroll at Bobby D's to leave a record on her employment history. A family business like that might just have paid her under the table."

Danny said, "Bobby D's. DiClemente. Damn it, I should have looked into the deli's history. I should have caught that."

Kevin said, "It doesn't matter. We have it now."

Gracie was still looking at Betsy's photograph. "What do you think something like this does to a person? Having your family murdered in front of you? I've lived some pretty fucking fucked-up shit, but this... I just... I just don't understand how you go on from something like this."

"Pain can transform into many things," said Stephen. "Some draw upon it for strength and become a positive force to help others. It depends on the person."

"Yeah, in her case, not so much with the positive force," said Gracie, "More the murdering old men force."

"Indeed," said Stephen.

Gracie said, "So, what do we do with her now? Hank identified her, so that means she is the only Sunset Gardens employee on that list who would recognize the photograph of him on Edward's refrigerator. But that's not hard evidence, is it?"

"It is not," said Kevin. "And we will need hard evidence. Crypt, send us her address. What are her routines like? Is she at Sunset Gardens today?"

"The Haunt posted at her building saw her leaving for work at 2 PM. Based on her patterns, she shouldn't be home until midnight."

"Then we have time to search her apartment," said Kevin.

"We?" said Gracie.

"Yes," said Kevin, "We. I want you coming with me."

"Right, okay. Cool. So, what's the plan?"

"First, disguises. Dressing as building maintenance should

allow us to access her apartment without arousing suspicion. Once inside, we look for hard evidence that may tie her to Edward's murder, specifically any container with traces of aconite, the poison used to kill him."

Danny's voice cut in, "And if you happen across whatever doohickey she used to switch off the cameras, I'd really like to take a look at that thing."

Gracie said, "And this is evidence we use to hand her over to the police?"

"Not quite. Still, no one knows Edward was murdered. The evidence we are looking for isn't for the police. It's so that we can have absolute certainty of her guilt for ourselves. Once we do," said Kevin, "the Crimson Wraith will have a conversation with her."

"You mean like from the top of the Snyder-Finn Building?"

"Let's hope it doesn't require that, but what we need is for her to confess her crime. At this point, her admitting to killing Edward is the only thing that could get her convicted."

"What if she says she murdered him because he was the Crimson Wraith? Doesn't that risk the secrecy of this whole operation?"

"It might."

"Okay, that seems like a really bad idea."

Danny said, "Gotta admit, she has a point."

"We don't really have an alternative," said Kevin. "If we don't pursue her, not only do we not get justice for Edward, we also don't learn just how much she already knows about the Crimson Wraith. Somehow, she created a device that allowed her to manipulate the cameras we placed in Edward's apartment. We need to know how. And Hank's wasn't the only photo on the refrigerator. Edward also had pictures of Stephen, Christopher, and Esperanza. Maybe she wouldn't have connected any of them with the Crimson Wraith, but we don't know that she didn't. For the sake of our safety, we have to find out how much she knows and who, if anyone, she shared that information with."

Gracie said, "So, our options are bad versus super-bad?"

"They are," said Kevin.

Stephen said, "I take it I shall be dropping you off at the Sepulcher on my way back home?"

"If you please, Stephen."

"Of course."

The sun was setting when they arrived at the complex of high-rise condominiums in Downtown Titan. Stephen swiped the platinum membership card that allowed entrance to its parking deck and drove inside.

Kevin explained, "Sometimes Finn Manor is a bit far away for necessary equipment or suiting up. That's why we have a second site, the Sepulcher."

"The Sepulcher, huh?" said Gracie. "That another thing for keeping dead people in?"

"It is."

"You guys really stick to your theme."

"Not much point in having a theme if we don't."

Stephen dropped them off at the condominium's underground parking deck, and a private elevator with shining black walls brought Kevin and Gracie to his penthouse. When the doors opened, the lights within rose to a soft romantic glow. A fire pit ignited. The curtains opened to a view of the city below, and jazzy trip-hop music began to play. "Let me guess," said Gracie. "You also shoot porn videos here."

"Not exactly. There are times when it's good for me to look like I have a love life, so every now and then, I'll bring a date up here and make an anonymous tip to paparazzi so they catch us driving up together. The dates themselves are not that interesting."

"You mean the Crimson Wraith doesn't play sexy mask games in his free time? Too much like your regular workday?"

"What is this 'free time' of which you speak?" Kevin said with a smirk, and then, "*In Pace Requiescat.*" At those words, curtains slid across the balcony windows followed by metal shielding that lowered into place to cover them. A wall panel opened to reveal a computer terminal and worktable, while the fire pit doused itself and rose to show the costume of the Crimson Wraith hung within its plexiglass base.

Gracie said, "Guessing that's not a phrase you'd be likely to accidentally say out loud on a date."

"Not so much, no."

The workbench contained their disguises, and Kevin handed her a generic maintenance technician's jumpsuit. "It's going to be big on you, but no one is going to think it strange if you roll up your sleeves and pant legs. Suits like this tend to fit awkwardly no matter what."

"I know maintenance workers are pretty invisible, but isn't there a chance somebody is going to recognize billionaire CEO Kevin Snyder in a jumpsuit?"

"The disguise needs a couple other features to make it complete." He opened a drawer to select a fake mustache for himself and then a pair of glasses. From another, he pulled a pair of baseball caps and handed one to Gracie. "Glasses, hat, and a change in facial hair make you almost unrecognizable to most people."

"Always wondered how I'd look in a mustache," said Gracie. Kevin smiled and handed her one, but before she had a chance to try it on, a signal light began flashing on the side of the computer terminal.

"That's Crypt," said Kevin. "Danny must have found something." He slid back his sleeve and tapped his Wrist Comm control pad. "This is Specter Prime. What is it, Crypt?"

There was urgency in Danny's voice. "Newsfeed. Coming your way." The monitor in front of them lit up to show an apartment building with smoke billowing from a burning hole in its side.

Then a reporter was speaking to a frantic woman holding a cat. "I just thank the Lord she called to say she was going out of town and ask if I could look after Bobby. I do that sometimes. He's a good kitty and gets along real well with mine. If I hadn't come to get him when I did..."

Gracie said, "Betsy named her cat after her murdered uncle?"

"They are calling it a gas explosion," said Danny. "But it happened right in Subject's apartment."

"Where is Subject now?"

"Just left her place of employment, headed north. Got a Haunt tailing her."

"Then we'll be right behind. Specter Prime out."

"She knew we were coming?" said Gracie. "How?"

"Right now, that doesn't matter." Kevin opened the case that held the costume of the Crimson Wraith. "The only thing that matters is catching up to her."

<u>1988</u>

Over sixty years after an orphan boy named Will Singer had a change of heart about helping a gang of teenagers to mug a man in its alleyway, the man who carried the legacy of that orphan's creation, the Crimson Wraith, approached what was left of the Regent movie theater.

Broken bottles, discarded newspapers, and food wrappers gathered around its papered-over doorway. But in front of one door, the trash extended outward in a neat line, showing it had been opened recently. Hank tried the handle, and it swung out for him too. He slipped on his skull-painted ski mask, pulled up his red hood, and stepped inside.

Officially, the Regent had been closed for seventeen years, since the ill-fated 1971 reunion concert for the Buggies. Their lead guitarist James Starling was shot and murdered on-stage by a man named Niles Aparo, who claimed he found Satanic in their music when he played their records backward. No one ever came back to clean up after. Popcorn bags and ticket stubs sat in piles on the floor, illuminated by work lights attached to a portable generator. These appeared to have been placed just recently. They lit up a series of white arrows spray-painted on the floor, walls, and concessions stand, pointing him toward the auditorium. Above its doorway read the words, "THIS WAY."

The architects of the Regent built the theater in an age when cinema was new, still gilded by an aura of fancy and grandeur. Hank stepped into an ornate auditorium designed to suggest Shakespeare's *A Midsummer Night's Dream*. Its domed ceiling, now chipped and faded, had been painted midnight blue. Once-glittering stars and planets decorated its curves. And at their center stood Diana, goddess of the hunt and the moon, her bow strung and ready to shoot her silver arrows.

Ringing this pseudo-sky, the false fronts of Greek buildings with their carved columns worked their way around the audience. High above the stage, Titania, Queen of the Fairies, cradled her donkey-headed lover in her arms. Flower-crowned pixies peeked out here and there from the façade of the walls, the balcony, the doorways. Years of neglect had cracked their plaster faces, and they stared at Hank with hollow eyes, cheeks half crumbled off, their smiles now more menacing than mirthful.

At the center of the stage, there stood two train boxcars, painted white with rough and scattered brush strokes. Each had a one-word question painted in red over its closed sliding door. Above the left was written, "LADY?" And above the right, "TIGER?"

Then a voice called out to Hank, its source unseen, ringing through the auditorium with dramatic tones that rose and fell for exaggerated emphasis, "Welcome, oh, Scarlet Stranger! Welcome! So glad you managed to interpret my invitation correctly. Truly, in you, I have finally found one with the capacity to appreciate my art. And it pleases me so that you have come dressed for the occasion, wearing your mask and hood even though I now know your true name, Henry Mills. Oh, this will be an excellent extravaganza! You and I, the Crimson Wraith and the Troubadour, dancing this old duet to the tune of Titan City's screams!"

Hank called back, "Where are you? Come on out! Face me!"

"My, my, aren't we eager? But first we must establish terms. You will see me soon, and when you do you must know that I have two things in hand. First, the camera, which you will see quite plainly, and quite plainly is how it will see you, filming your experience of my art, capturing its impression upon you, even though you hide your expressions in a mask."

"I ain't hiding nothing! And I ain't playing no games!"

"Be assured I too play no games, Crimson Wraith, which is why in my other hand I will be holding a revolver, one pointed directly at your heart, just a little encouragement should you contemplate concluding the evening's activities prematurely. We can't have that, now can we?"

Hank said nothing. All the flowery talk just sounded like nonsense to him, but he knew the Troubadour had the upper hand. Until he had Jasmine safe, he would have to play along.

"No words to that, eh? Silent as the grave? Ah, well, since silence implies consent, then let us proceed."

The Troubadour stepped out from behind a curtain, wearing the same long-nosed *Commedia dell'Arte* mask as the one before him, dressed in a white silk shirt, its collar opened wide, tucked into a pair of black denim jeans. On his right shoulder, he held a video camera, aimed at Hank just like the pistol in his left hand. Hank knew he was too far away to try to rush the Troubadour, and he figured the Troubadour knew that too. He seemed to be taking his time to set the scene.

"*The Lady or the Tiger?*" he proclaimed. "Written by Frank R. Stockton and published in a magazine called the *Century* almost exactly a century ago. You are, of course, familiar, being my worthy adversary. It tells of a mercurial king who leaves it up to his prisoners to decide their own fate, presenting them with two doors, each perfectly identical and perfectly soundproofed, one concealing a hungry tiger, who will tear the prisoner apart, and the other a fair maiden to take for wife. It is a metaphor, you see? It is a metaphor for life! A metaphor for our own barbaric justice system that rewards and punishes just as blindly, just as randomly."

Hank could only listen to that yammering for so long. "Just tell me where she is already!"

"Why, she is here!" said the Troubadour, gesturing toward the doorway marked *LADY*. "Or is she here?" he indicated the one marked *TIGER*. "Behind one of these doors, you will find the Wily Wisp, but be careful which you choose because behind the other you will find..." He lost himself in laughter.

"A tiger," said Hank.

"And he is hungry! Oh, yes, a very hungry boy! I know he would just love to 'meat' you." Another laugh. "Get it? 'Meat' you?"

"I get it," said Hank.

"Then get to it!" the Troubadour shouted in a burst of unexpected rage. "Stockton never allowed his reader to know which door held which. The story simply ends without an ending. And since you have decided yours to be the hand to correct the imbalances of our justice system, then yours should be the choice to resolve this unresolved dilemma."

Slowly, Hank approached the doors. The Troubadour circled around him. "One of these has the Wily Wisp," Hank said out loud. "One has the tiger. If I choose the one that has the tiger, what's to stop the tiger from eating you too?"

The Troubadour waved his revolver, "This instrument doth make music to soothe the savage beast."

"And if I open the door that has the Wisp?"

"A tearful reunion! Real Hallmark Moment! Just the sort of *schmaltz* the Oscar committee loves!"

"But you still have the gun."

"Oh, do I? Well, yes, I suppose I do. Now, go on and choose!"

2019

Gracie and Kevin left the penthouse through a different elevator than they entered, a hidden elevator. "How did you get all this secret construction done for the Sepulcher?" Gracie asked.

"Had to get special permission from the owner of the building, which is me, so that wasn't too difficult." Kevin still wore the glasses, hat, and false mustache. His technician's jumpsuit covered the tunic of the Crimson Wraith, and he carried the cloak and mask in his tool bag.

The secret elevator brought them to a private parking deck, where Kevin guided them to a more nondescript car than Gracie could imagine him owning, a gray sedan, about a decade old, that look like it may have been bought used from a rental fleet.

"This isn't exactly the Crimson Wraith Roadster," said Gracie.

"You read about that too?"

"Sure did. Aren't superheroes supposed to have cooler cars than this?"

"If they want to get stopped in traffic, yes." He handed her the keys.

"I, um, I'm not actually that good of a driver."

"Don't worry. It's self-driving."

"*This* car is self-driving?"

"With a little remote help from Crypt, but it shouldn't look like it's driving itself, so you get the driver's seat. I'll be in the back. Easier to suit up there once we arrive at the location."

"Which is?"

"We'll find out."

The interior of the car was a lot more impressive than the exterior. An elaborate computer display greeted Gracie when she sat. At Kevin's voice command, the car came to life and began to make its way out of the parking deck, onto the streets of Titan City, following the Haunt that followed Betsy. After they crossed the Brennert for the third time that day, Danny's voice came from the speaker. "Specter Prime, this is Crypt."

"Go ahead, Crypt."

"Subject has come to a stop and left her vehicle."

"What's the location?"

"Uh, you're not going to believe this but... it's one of the old SnyTech factories, hasn't been operational in at least five years."

"I believe it," said Kevin.

"Yeah, silly me thinking I could surprise you, SP. She's entered the building. Switching to thermal imaging to follow her movements inside."

"Good work, Crypt. We are minutes away."

Gracie said, "SnyTech. That's one of yours?"

"Was, before the Snyder-Finn merger. Some of the old SnyTech factories made the transition. Others phased out over time. This was one of those."

"So, what does that mean?"

"For one," said Kevin, "it means she might know quite a bit more about our operation than she's revealed. Regardless, we should expect her to be prepared for us."

"Prepared for us, how?"

"No way to know. But considering she had her apartment rigged to explode and called ahead to have her neighbor rescue her cat, we should expect that she knew she was followed and that she has something special prepared for us here."

"Fucking hell, like what? Another bomb or maybe some kind of toxic gas? Machine guns? Ninjas?"

"Before I enter the building, Danny will have the Haunts look it over to give a sense of what is waiting inside. The scan will include light, sound, and electronic signals on various frequencies that should reveal living beings, machinery in motion, and most electronic devices. Based on that, I'll have at least a general idea of what is awaiting me and where."

"Awaiting *you*? Not *us*? Am I not going in too?"

"No, I want you to hold back."

"Um, okay, I appreciate your concern for my safety, but..."

"It's not that," said Kevin. "I know you're capable, but if

we have one advantage in this scenario, it's that she may not. Whatever else she knows about the Crimson Wraith, there's a very good chance she doesn't know you have any part of it, since you've only just joined. That's why I need you to stay behind, because you may be the one thing she can't prepare for. Do you understand?"

Gracie nodded. She wasn't sure she liked it, but she did understand it.

When they arrived at the SnyTech factory building, Danny reported on the findings of his scan, as promised. "She's alone, up on the rooftop. Has a few small pieces of electronics with her, but not sure what kind. Also, she's blue."

Through the Crimson Wraith mask, Kevin asked, "What was that, Crypt?"

"Blue. She got up to the rooftop, stripped down to her underwear, and covered herself in blue paint."

"What the fuck?" said Gracie.

"I guess we'll find out," said Kevin. "Specter Second will be staying in the vehicle until needed."

Specter Second? That was her. Gracie had a codename.

Then Kevin reached into his tool bag once more and pulled out a small plastic case that he extended to Gracie. "This is for you," he said, "should you need it."

With his face obscured by the skull mask and his voice modified with a spectral echo, taking the case from his red-gauntleted hand felt somber, meaningful. More than just a gift from the guy who offered her microwave popcorn as he watched a sitcom on his electronic tablet, this came from the Crimson Wraith. Gracie was surprised to feel her hands shaking a little as she opened it to see what was inside.

"Is that... Is that a mask? For me?"

"Sort of," he said. "Tactical goggles. Yes, they will help to hide your identity, but also, they will give your eyes some protection and help you see better in low light. There is also an earwig, so you'll be able to hear and speak on our frequency."

Her voice sounded small to her when she said, "Okay."

"Gracie, you're ready for this. And I won't call you in unless I absolutely need to."

"Okay," she said again.

"I don't want you coming unless I call for you. And if something up there gets too bad, I will use the codeword 'ashes.' That will be your signal to leave. If I say 'ashes,' I want you to get out of here and get to safety. Understood?"

"Ashes. Got it." She inserted the earwig.

"Good," he said. "Specters Prime and Second going quiet, Crypt. Engaging Subject."

"Confirmed, SP. Be careful out there."

"Yeah," said Gracie. "Be careful."

"I will," he said and exited the car.

"Haunts have visual on you, Specter Prime. Specter Second, you should see him on your monitor."

Just like when Kevin hung Zack off the top of the Snyder-Finn Building, Gracie followed his movements in night-vision green, only this time watching from above. She saw him enter the factory building. Then a red diamond appeared on the screen to give his approximate location as he made his way up the stairs inside, finally arriving on the rooftop to face the woman who murdered Edward.

1988

There didn't appear to be any difference between the two doors, nothing to tell them apart except for the words painted overhead. No light came from under either and no sound—not a growl, not a whimper.

Probably it would be too obvious to put Jasmine behind "LADY?" so Hank stepped toward the door under the sign that read, "TIGER?"

"Have you made your choice already?" asked the Troubadour.

Hank stopped. "Yes."

"But are you sure? Think carefully now. This is the most important decision you have ever made, the most important decision you might *ever* make, as it is very, very likely your last."

Turning around, Hank saw the Troubadour's grin under his mask. "You're enjoying this."

"How could I not? This is art! This is drama! The climactic confrontation between fiendish villain and noble hero!"

Noble hero. He knew Hank's name, knew where he worked. But did the Troubadour really know Hank at all? Did he know anything about how it felt to realize he had killed his wife? About his prison fights and then being told he wasn't worth it? About returning to the world and hearing there wasn't a place for him there? About how much it meant being welcomed even just to wash dishes at Bobby D's? About finding Jasmine that fateful night and starting to consider that the two of them together might be something Hank never imagined for himself?

The Troubadour seemed impatient. "Choose! Go on, now! Choose!"

But Hank had already made his most important choice. He chose to wear the hood of the Crimson Wraith. He chose to take up that mission, and that mission was about taking action. He reached for the door.

"But are you sure?" asked the Troubadour, "Can you be sure? Why that door and not the other?"

"It doesn't matter," said Hank.

"Of course, it matters! Everything matters! That is art! Art is making choices, deliberate and conscious choices. It is how we convey meaning!"

"You don't know the meaning of nothing," said Hank, and he pulled the handle of the boxcar door.

Stuck. Hank tried again, harder. No, the door would not budge.

Behind him, the Troubadour circled around, angling to film Hank's masked face. "Yes, let us see. The confusion. The frustration. The plot has a few more twists to it, doesn't it?"

"Why won't this door open?"

"Not every door we try will open. We are presented with a choice, yes, but is it a real choice? Or is it the illusion of choice? Do we ever really choose? Or is free will only a story we tell ourselves?"

Hank glared over his shoulder, right into the camera.

"You had better try the other," said the Troubadour.

If there was any chance of rescuing Jasmine, Hank had to play along just a bit longer. He walked to the other door, carefully gripped the handle, and pulled.

It opened. With the whine of grinding metal wheels, the gap widened, revealing more and more of the space within. But no lady. And no tiger. There was just a roll-top writing desk with a lamp illuminating the crowbar resting on its surface.

"There's nothing here," said Hank.

"Oh, no? Are you sure?" the Troubadour's feigned surprise dripped with barely restrained amusement. "But I could have sworn... Well, you'd better have a closer look, just to be sure..."

Hank entered the room, and the Troubadour followed, narrating for the camera. "And now, though confusion fills him, the hero steps forward, bravely doing his duty, facing his fear, undeterred by uncertainty..."

A string attached a paper tag to the crowbar. On that tag was written, "OOPS."

"What is this?" the Troubadour drew closer. "He puzzles out the last piece of this mystery—oh, the most mysterious piece indeed. Whatever could it mean?"

But from the corner of his eye, Hank saw the gun in the Troubadour's hand lowered slightly, his attention turned away from it and toward the camera capturing the fulfillment of his demented plan. That shift in his opponent's attention was all Hank needed. He spun on the Troubadour and grabbed his gun arm by the wrist. Wrenching the revolver from his hand, Hank shoved the Troubadour against the boxcar wall and pressed the crowbar into his throat.

"Where is she?" Hank roared.

"I can't see," the Troubadour whimpered. "The camera, please, let the camera see..."

"I'm done with your bullshit! Now, tell me!" He pushed harder against the crowbar.

Even struggling to breathe, the Troubadour smiled. "It seems I made a mistake, didn't I? The way it was written, the lady and the tiger were supposed to be placed in two separate rooms. But can't you tell what happened? I must have goofed."

"What do you mean? Where is she?"

When the Troubadour only laughed in response, Hank pulled back the crowbar and drove it into his gut, making him double over, but he never dropped his camera. "They're in the same room!" the Troubadour coughed, "The lady and the tiger, they're in the same room together!"

<u>2019</u>

Betsy stood some fifty feet away from him, and just as Danny said, she had stripped down to her underwear. The color of paint on her body did not register clearly in night vision, which only showed light and dark as shades of green, but it distorted her image with dark splatters, like a kind of camouflage. Beside her stood a large plastic bucket that must have held the paint, based on the dark drips down its side. In her right hand, she held a pistol. In her left, in the plastic fingers of her prosthetic arm, she held a small electronic device. She was clearly cold—naked and wet—and shivering, but how much of that was from the late October chill and how much from being face-to-mask with the Crimson Wraith?

"It's you," she said through slightly chattering teeth.

"It's me," said Kevin. "You know why I'm here."

Her voice came out in a soft, dreamy monotone. "I do. It's because of Mr. Finn. I killed him. I knew you'd find me. I wanted you to find me."

"Why, Betsy?" Slowly, Kevin began to draw closer. "Why did you murder Edward? Why did you want me to find you?"

"You know why I killed him. It's because he's you. He was you, the Crimson Wraith. Just like Hank. Just like Hank was when that thing happened. He's the reason. He's the reason that thing happened to me, to my family."

"What happened to them, to you, was terrible. Something like that shouldn't happen to anyone, not ever."

"It's not fair, you know," said Betsy. "Not fair for you to dress up and make people think you can protect them. Because you can't protect them. People get hurt. They get hurt all the time. You can't stop that. You can't stop bad things from happening."

"No, Betsy, I can't."

"You like to make people think you can, though. You like to make them believe in you. We believe in you, and we get hurt. We live, and we die. But you just keep on going, year after year, decade after decade. Titan City always has to have the Crimson Wraith. We're stuck with you. We didn't ever ask for you, did we? But we're stuck with you."

Watching them on the screen in front of her, Gracie's head was full of alarm bells screaming. This was wrong. This was very wrong. Betsy hadn't even raised her gun. What was she waiting for? Clearly, she was off, broken inside. It showed in the ramble of her words, the nakedness, the paint, the whole set-up, and crazy people don't react the way anyone would expect them too. That's the whole point of crazy. But she had the kind of crazy that still could plan things, and, clearly, she planned this rooftop meeting. It had to be some kind of trap, so why wasn't it springing?

Using his codename, Gracie said out loud, "Specter Prime, you need to end this. Something is seriously not right here."

Danny said, "Agreed Specter Second. He's still not close enough for an effective takedown, though. Just a few more feet, SP. Then toss a flash pellet and end this."

Betsy continued. "But it's not enough that good people believe in you, is it? Good people get fooled all the time. That's the problem with good people. They don't know any better. Bad people though, they believe in you too. The bad people think you are something big and strong for them to fight, something they gotta prove themselves against. So, they do things to get your attention. They do worse things than if you were never around. It's your fault, the things they do. When you put on that mask, you give bad people a reason to hurt good people, and we never asked you to. We never asked you."

"You're right," said Kevin.

No, she fucking is not! But Gracie knew he had to agree with her as much as possible, for as long as possible.

He said, "Maybe I should take off this mask. Would that be better, Betsy? Should I take off my mask?"

"Don't... Don't do that..."

"Don't do what?"

"Don't use my name. Don't say my name like you know me. You don't know me. He knew me, Hank did. But Mr. Finn didn't know me, even though he was the Crimson Wraith and the Crimson Wraith was the reason all those bad things happened. He didn't know what I've been through. He didn't know how he hurt me, how the Crimson Wraith hurt me. Do you know how fucked up that is? To have someone destroy your whole life and never know you?"

"I can't imagine."

"Of course, you can't. You're not the one whose life gets destroyed. What is your life anyway? Your real life? You're standing before me as the Crimson Wraith, but that's not your name."

Danny said, "Almost there, SP. Just another step."

Gracie saw Kevin shift his weight. His left shoulder lowered. His right shoulder raised, readying to pull a flash pellet and throw it from his hip.

Still, Betsy made no sign of movement. "Crimson Wraith is just what you want me to call you. And that's fine, I'll call you that. But there is something I want you to call me in return."

"What's that?" said Kevin.

"I'm the Blue Banshee."

Both moved at once, like Old West duelers launching into action at the sight of the other doing the same, but fast as Kevin was, Betsy had her finger right on the button. That was her play—not the pistol in her right hand but the device in her left.

In Kevin's vision, the blue paint on her body suddenly blazed with blinding intensity. There was no amount of training that could have kept him from averting his gaze, making the flash pellet he threw from his belt fly wide, missing her entirely.

And through the speakers of his mask, affecting everyone listening to the Crimson Wraith's frequency, blared an undulating sonic blast that made Gracie scream and throw her earwig to the floor of the car. It still screamed there, too small and far away to affect her. But Kevin wasn't so lucky. On the screen in front of her, she saw him on his knees wrestling with what looked like a being of pure light as he tried to pull off the mask that she held in place. He was not succeeding.

How much damage would that sound do if he was unable to remove his mask? Gracie knew she had to get up on that roof.

As she crossed the broken asphalt of the SnyTech parking lot, her feet felt as if they flew on their own. Her body knew every action to take before she thought about taking it. Door handles seemed to leap open at her touch. Metal stairs rang under her boots. And, weirdly, her mind circled around the words, "That's how a hero goes, I guess..." Where had she heard that? Was it a movie?

It was Howard. He was reading *Beowulf*. Again. He bought and sold back the same copy about once a year. And he was telling Gracie about the ending, about the death of Beowulf. "As an old man, you see, he has become king. And when the dragon attacks them, well, it's still his job to protect his people, isn't it? Even when all his other knights flee—and why wouldn't they? It *is* a dragon. But Beowulf must stand strong. The only one who stays with him is the youngest warrior. And when the dragon mortally wounds Beowulf, that warrior is the one who finishes the fight. That is why he becomes the next king. But, protecting his people, fighting a dragon, that's how a hero goes, I guess."

Gracie's breath burned in her lungs. *You are not dying on me tonight, Kevin! I am not letting you make me the next Crimson Wraith when I only just met you! That is not my origin story*! The rooftop access door crashed open, and Betsy's eyes shot up at the sound.

<u>1988</u>

Hank threw the Troubadour to the side, scooping up the revolver that he dropped and readying it in one hand while keeping the crowbar in the other. The Crimson Wraith didn't use guns, not usually, but also the Crimson Wraith didn't usually fight tigers. With one hand, he drove the crowbar into the boxcar door and wedged it open, then he swung his other hand forward, revolver ready.

What he wanted to see was his friend, his roommate, his sidekick, facing down the great cat, trying to placate it by saying things like, "Nice kitty... Good kitty..." before looking up to Hank and saying, "Well, it's about damn time! Tony here thinks I'm a box of Frosted Flakes!"

That was not what Hank saw.

Instead of being on its feet, stalking Jasmine, the tiger lay resting, lazily lifting its head at Hank's entrance. Blood smeared its face, from its muzzle to its emerald eyes that wore the sleepiness of having eaten its fill. In the corner lay something dark and wet that Hank knew had once been Jasmine from the sequined shreds of her costume.

Although it was not the tiger's fault to obey its nature, Hank pulled the trigger and kept pulling until every slug buried itself in the tiger's body and it lay as limp as Jasmine. Then Hank ran to her.

"Come on, girl. Come back to me..." He cradled what was left of her. Arms dangled limply. Eyes within that claw-torn face did not move. But still Hank spoke to her as his throat tightened his words into a whisper. "I don't know how to do this without you, Jasmine. Please..."

Behind him, he heard the Troubadour, once again narrating. "And so, it ends, as all things must. Such pathos. What hard heart might remain unmoved by so terrible a tragedy?"

Hank released Jasmine, gently lowering her as if putting her to bed, then rose and turned toward the Troubadour.

"But that is what a hero is for, is it not? To face down tragedy? To overcome? Yes, let us see then. Show us how the drama has moved you." He might have made his escape before then, but no, the Troubadour remained, pointing his camera at Hank even without the pistol to protect himself. "Let us see it! Show our audience your righteous rage!"

The crowbar's first swing spun the Troubadour in a circle. The second sent him in the other direction and took his mask half off his face, revealing the man's pudgy cheeks and scraggly mustache. But still he kept hold of the camera, turning it again toward Hank. Through a torn lip, blood dribbling down his chin, he gurgled, "Thank you... Thank you... Such an ovation..." A third swing shattered ribs. "Too kind... So proud of my cast and crew..."

The fourth and final swing took the Troubadour's legs out from under him. Finally, the camera also fell. Hank dropped the crowbar and leaped on top of him, wrapping his huge hands around his throat.

"Wait!" For the first time, the Troubadour seemed genuinely concerned. "This isn't in the script! Remember you have a part to play! You're the hero! The Crimson Wraith doesn't kill!"

It was true. Hank knew that. He had followed that mission since putting on the mask. Each criminal he defeated, he did not seek to punish himself but brought to public authorities who might administer justice—just as he had received. And so, with one hand still on the Troubadour's throat, he reached up to pull the mask from his face and threw it down onto the floor of the stage.

Below him, the Troubadour's eyes went wide. And as Hank took hold of his throat once more, squeezing the life from him, the Troubadour's face kept an expression of the most elated wonder. Finally, reality proved more profound than art.

Hank still held the Troubadour's throat when he heard Michael's voice from the audience. "What happened? Did you get him? Is she safe?" He approached from the aisle, wearing the costume of the Zephyr.

"It's over," said Hank.

"Well, all right!" said Michael. "That is going to be a huge relief to everyone."

"It's all over."

Then Michael saw the Troubadour, unmoving, unbreathing, underneath Hank. "What... Wait... Is he...?"

"Dead."

"You killed him."

"He killed her!" Hank roared, finally releasing the Troubadour's head. It lolled to one side as he stood to face Michael. "She's back there. He fed her... to an animal... like meat!" It made Hank's brain burn, thinking those words, saying them, hearing them out of his own mouth.

"No..." Michael shook his head, "No, don't say that... She can't..."

"Yes," said Hank. "And now it's over. It's all over. I'm done." He extended his wrists to Michael. "Take me away. I don't want this no more. I ain't the Crimson Wraith. The Crimson Wraith doesn't kill. And I'm a killer."

"You're not..."

"I am. It's all I ever was."

2019

The plastic bucket that had been at Betsy's feet, she now held over Kevin's head, keeping him from reaching his mask. She was much smaller and not as strong as him, nor trained in martial arts, but with her body wrapped around his head, he had a hard time finding leverage. Betsy also did not have the decibels screaming into his brain that he did.

"Let him go!" Gracie shouted, running right at Betsy, never having stopped or slowed her momentum since exploding out of the car door. Betsy still held the pistol in her right hand, which she brought up to aim toward Gracie, but not faster than Gracie could close the distance between them. She leaped, aiming her shoulder into Betsy's midsection, spearing her backward and off of Kevin, who immediately flung the bucket from his head and began tearing at his mask to free himself from its sonic assault.

As soon as Betsy's back slammed against gravel, the pistol flew out of her hand. But Gracie did not release her target. She kept hold of Betsy, rolling with her, controlling their tumble so she could end up on top. Once there, she pinned Betsy down by her shoulders.

This was where Gracie figured she should begin pounding an opponent into unconsciousness with a series of punches to the head, but looking down at Betsy, she couldn't. That wasn't something she could do to an already traumatized middle-aged woman whose left arm had been forcibly amputated by the psychopath who murdered her family. So, instead, she screamed, "Enough!"

It seemed to take Betsy off-guard at least, and she didn't fight back. Instead, she just asked, "Who are you? Are you the Wily Wisp? You're the Wily Wisp, aren't you?"

"I'm... I don't know..." said Gracie. She really didn't.

"Then why are you with him? Are you helping him? Do you

know who he is? Do you know what he does, what happens to the people who help him?"

Behind her, Gracie heard the sound of Kevin retching. She looked back to see he had pulled the mask free and begun vomiting. "Are you all right?"

But she shouldn't have looked away from Betsy, who grabbed a fistful of gravel that she slapped into the side of Gracie's head, stunning her just enough for Betsy to wriggle free and run toward Kevin, grabbing the fallen pistol as she did. Gracie got back to her feet and followed fast behind Betsy but stopped when Betsy wrapped her right arm around Kevin's neck and pressed the gun to his temple.

"Whoa!" said Gracie. "Just hold on! Think about this!"

"No, thank you," said Betsy. "I've been thinking about this plenty. For about thirty years now, I haven't been able to think about anything else. Not a single thing. Only this. Only him. And before you say he isn't the one who did this to me, you ought to know that doesn't matter. If he wants to wear the mask of the Crimson Wraith, then he can get what the Crimson Wraith has coming to him."

"So, are you saying you don't know who he is? You don't even care?" Nausea-stricken and his hair a mess, Kevin might not have been immediately recognizable in the shadows of the factory rooftop.

"Why should I care? No one cared about me. The Crimson Wraith was with my family for years, never once asking us how we felt about it. Maybe we might have concerns about the famous vigilante working right there in our restaurant, making us a target. He didn't ask us. He didn't say a goddamn thing."

"But what happens next? If you kill him, then what happens?"

"Then? Well, that's a beautiful thing, isn't it? A world with one less Crimson Wraith. Two down, two to go. And then we'll be free. We can all breathe easy. We can start to heal."

"Oh, bullshit!" shouted Gracie.

"I don't like the way you are speaking to me."

"And I don't like the way you are holding a gun to my friend's head!"

"Maybe after I end him, then I'll have to end you. Maybe you should think of that before you say anything else."

"If you pull that trigger, I will be on top of you faster than you can aim that gun at me. There is no way you are walking away from this. Think! You already confessed to one murder. Do you really want to add another?"

"It doesn't matter. Healing takes sacrifice. We have to be ready to give our all, whatever it takes."

"Listen, I get your life was fucked up, and I am seriously sorry about that. Under different circumstances, I might want to give you a hug and be there while you cry it out, but you have taken the ticket to Crazy Town and become it's goddamn mayor if you think that justifies triple homicide."

"Don't say that word."

"What word? Homicide?"

"Crazy. I don't like that word. Don't say it. None of this is crazy. It's not crazy to be hurt. It's not crazy to want justice. I'm not crazy. He told me I'm not crazy."

That struck Gracie as odd. "*Who* told you?"

Betsy's face showed that she knew she said too much.

Gracie pushed on that. "Who said this isn't crazy? Did someone tell you to do all this? Did they say you had to kill Edward Finn?"

"I... I can't," said Betsy, "It's... It's confidential."

With her arm around his throat, Kevin croaked, "Someone has taken advantage of you. Please, it does not have to be like this. Let us help you."

"No," said Betsy, "No, you're wrong. I got help. I got good help, the best. I got all the help I need."

"That is not good help," said Gracie, "This is a seriously fucked up thing you did, and if someone told you to do it, then that is seriously fucked up too."

"You don't understand..."

"No, *you* don't understand. I'm not letting you get away tonight, so how about you put the gun down and tell us who talked you into doing all this? Why make things worse?"

Like a cornered animal seeking escape, Betsy's large eyes darted this way and that. She seemed to be fighting in her poor, tortured mind to reconcile what they were saying with whatever had been said to her before. Finally, she looked up, as if the answer to her dilemma would descend from above, and she closed her eyes. "For love…"

"Love?" Gracie asked.

"We give our all for love." Then Betsy opened her eyes and looked into Gracie's. That look told Gracie what was about to happen.

She couldn't get to her faster than Betsy could lift the pistol and place its muzzle under her chin. And since Kevin had not seen that look, he realized too late where the pistol was moving once it left his temple. Neither of them could stop Betsy from pulling the trigger. And Gracie would never be able to forget the way that Betsy went from looking at her to looking at nothing, as everything she was exited out of a hole in the top of her skull.

CHAPTER SEVENTEEN

1972

There is nothing more miserable than misery in summertime. In the movies Edward saw as a boy, a man who lost everything would walk under an overcast sky as cold winds plucked at the collar of his jacket, which he would tug tighter and tighter against his neck to keep out the chill. This was a convenient fiction, telling the audience that when the hero is sad, the whole world is sad with him. Even the sky wears shades of mourning.

But that isn't life. Life keeps happening in its natural way, completely indifferent to human suffering, especially in summertime. Edward walked under a brilliantly blue sky whose sun sent down burning rays to reflect upward from Titan City's searing sidewalks. Cans of uncollected garbage stewed in the heat, and businessmen cooked in their polyester suits. As the afternoon wore on, mostly undressed citizens leaned from tenement windows, struggling to find some balance between indoor shade and outdoor breeze.

And from all over the nation came the tourists, wearing the brightest colors possible to signify they were on holiday. Tourists flooded the sidewalks and clogged the streets, asking any passerby to take their picture as they stood beside no more noteworthy landmark than an "honest-to-goodness" Titan City sausage and pretzel cart. Their naivete might be endearing were it not for their terrible tendency to treat another person's home with the same indifference one might a roadside motel. In response to such entitled attitudes, no wonder Titan citizens had a reputation for being rude, especially in the heat of summer.

Regardless, Edward placed himself right among those tourists lined up at the feet of the Spirit of Prosperity, all gathering to climb up her inner staircase and take in the view of Marshal Bay with the Atlantic beyond. He listened to their little family squabbles and smiled at children who stared at him because he was a stranger and children have a way of seeking out faces they don't know. They did not know him as Edward Finn, millionaire CEO of Finn Industries. They did not know him as the Crimson Wraith, masked vigilante of Titan City. And they did not know he was planning to kill himself by jumping from the arms of the Spirit of Prosperity.

What was it about the view from up there that inspired so many suicidal leaps? Certainly, some of the lives lost there might have resulted from a sudden onset of vertigo, but there were just too many to all be accidental. Over time, the leap seemed to have gained a romantic quality, surrendering to the Spirit of Prosperity's embrace, as if she had ordained their deaths.

It particularly attracted those from the financial industry who found their fortunes turn sour, a sign they had lost Prosperity's favor. Already that year, there had been twenty bodies recovered from Marshal Bay from those making that leap. The economic recession took its toll in more ways than one. And that would likely be the story told when they found Edward, that Finn Industries had suffered a stock decline—which it had—and he just had not been able to bear it. So, the adopted son of William Finn decided to commit suicide only months before his fortieth birthday.

Throughout the climb up the inner staircase, plaques along its inner walls told the story of the Spirit of Prosperity. Erected in 1886 as a gift to the people of Titan City, designed by Finnish sculptor Jonne Hurme, in both World Wars, it served as a military outpost to scout for enemy ships. Various parties attempted to damage the statue in acts of protest, most recently one Esteban Valentino a.k.a. The Troubadour, thwarted by the Crimson Wraith and Wily Wisp.

Edward saw a photograph of that giant nose being lowered by its rigging and then another of him and Tommy in their costumes, smiling for the crowds at the statue's feet. Someone had scrawled "PERVERT" over his face. There had been an unsuccessful attempt to scrub the word away from the plexiglass covering that left the letters blurred but visible.

Edward closed his eyes, feeling dizzy and nauseous. He gripped hard the silver-plated Derby handle of his cane and stood there for a moment. Behind him, a father of three in a straw hat and flamingo-pink shirt barked at him, "Hey, buddy, there are other people here behind you!"

His wife, in her blue paisley *Mumu* with one child on her hip and another holding her hand, said to her husband, "Honey, he's crippled! Go easy on him!"

"Doris, I am going easy! But he ain't going nowhere!"

"My apologies," said Edward. He returned to climbing. No need to engage someone like that, not now. It would all be over soon.

When they reached the shoulders, Edward followed the crowd out Prosperity's right arm, then over the walkway that crossed her chest to her left. He made a show of feigning interest in the view at a few different points. When the family behind him asked him to take their photograph, he did so.

Then, when he came to the downward stair at the statue's left shoulder, he pulled from his pocket a small brass replica of the Spirit of Prosperity he purchased from the gift shop at the base and casually dropped it over the stairwell's inner railing. It banged loudly against one metal support after another, drawing everyone's attention that way. As the crowd leaned over the rail to see what caused the sound, Edward stepped backward, allowing curious onlookers to push him aside, until he had his back against the door to a utility closet with no eyes on him.

From inside his sleeve, he withdrew the Crimson Wraith Utility Pick and slid it into the door handle lock. Carefully squeezing the pick one, two, three times, all the lock's tumblers clicked into place, and Edward turned the handle, slipping inside.

He took an electric lantern from his pocket and set it on a shelf beside the cleaning sprays. Then he pulled out his old copy of Walt Whitman's *Leaves of Grass* from his days at Ellsworth Academy and sat in the suffocating heat to read.

After a while, Edward nodded off. His head rested on a paper towel roll he wedged between his shoulder and the wall. When he woke, the voices and footsteps of tourists had all gone silent. He was alone. There was no one but him and the Spirit of Prosperity herself. It was time.

As he emerged from the utility closet, cool evening breezes caressed him. The sun had set. He stepped out and saw the night sky framed by the doorway on the statue's shoulder. It was a beautiful sight, and not one with which he was familiar. Always on his nightly patrols, he looked inward, into the city lights, into the lives needing rescuing and crime needing justice. But as Edward looked away from Titan City, away from the light, he felt a pull. Searching for the line where the dark of sky met the dark of sea, he seemed drawn toward its infinite emptiness. High above Marshal Bay, he could not smell the scents of the city, just a hint of salt on the wind, reaching out to him from the hungry abyss beyond.

Edward closed his eyes to savor that seductive pull. The promises of that gentle, welcoming nothing overwhelmed him—no more fear, no more shame, no more loneliness, no more regret, no more memory. Edward felt a tear slip down his cheek. Yes, this was right. This was the reason he had never been able to find a place in the world because there was none to be found. This was where he belonged. This was where he had been headed so long without ever knowing.

He opened his eyes and released his cane, letting it clatter to the walkway at his feet. He gripped the rail, readying to jump. Only one last choice, one last action, one last motion. All he needed to do was fight back the voice inside that cried out for him not to, a voice that seemed intent on prolonging his suffering.

2019

Stephen and Danny stood waiting for them at the steps of Finn Manor when the car drove itself up to the door. Kevin was not doing well, having that gunshot happen right above his head following the Blue Banshee's sonic assault. He was still a bit woozy, had a hard time finding his feet. Stephen helped him up to his room.

As they went on ahead, Danny said to Gracie, "That was some bad-ass superhero action out there." Even with Betsy's body paint distorting their cameras, he had been able to get a general image of what happened on the SnyTech rooftop, even if he hadn't been able to hear any of it.

"Thanks," said Gracie. It didn't feel bad ass. She figured being a superhero was supposed to leave someone feeling triumphant. It didn't.

Danny walked with her as she climbed the stairs to her room. "I mean it. You did something special out there. Kevin was right to bring you in, completely. You belong here. You were born for this."

Gracie looked at him like he was a fucking idiot. *Born for this? That shit was so fucked up. You think I was born for fucked up shit? Yeah, thanks, pal...* But she didn't say that. Seeing the look on his face, she could see how much respect he felt for her, how he appreciated her having brought Kevin back alive, and how much he just wanted to help.

And if he wanted to help, there was something he could do. There at the doorway to her bedroom, Gracie threw her arms around Danny, shoved her face into his neck, and squeezed. She wanted to feel something warm and solid right then, and

Danny's torso would do. She squeezed him, and as she held the embrace, she felt his hands hesitantly take hold of her waist. Gently, he patted her side.

Her eyes were wet when she released him. She didn't know when she started crying. Maybe she never stopped. There were waves of tears shed on the ride back home. "Thanks," she said. "Sorry, I should have asked…"

"It's okay," he said, a little too quickly. "All good."

"Thanks," she said again. "Good night."

An anonymous tip directed Titan City Police to the abandoned SnyTech factory where gunshots had been heard. There they found the body of Elizabeth DiClemente, who had been a person of interest in a case of arson at her apartment complex. Her obituary in the *Titan Herald* described her as a loving and selfless caregiver. It spoke glowingly of her service after Zero Hour and her years at Sunset Gardens. There was no mention of suicide, arson, or the murders at Bobby D's, and no connection made to the death of Edward Finn, which to all the world still seemed to have been natural causes.

For two days, Kevin remained sequestered in his bedroom, and Stephen asked that she and Danny keep from playing music or engaging in loud conversation anywhere near that part of the building. He finally left his bedroom, on the night of Halloween. He had his ears bandaged with gauze and carried a dry erase board to communicate with them through writing. His first message was, "I'm so bored. Movie?" They watched some old black and white horror films with the sound off and subtitles on—not at all scary, which suited Gracie just fine. Stephen had been handing out candy to Trick-or-Treaters at the Finn Manor front gate and brought them the remains of the candy bowl to share.

Later in the week, Captain Villagraña came by Finn Manor in an unofficial capacity. She and Kevin spoke privately for some time. His hearing was starting to recover enough for him to have conversations. Gracie didn't know what they spoke about, but she noticed they didn't go down to the Crypt, just stayed in his office. Maybe a Captain of the TCPD wasn't supposed to enter to the secret lair of the Crimson Wraith, even if she used to be the Wily Wisp.

Danny spent long days in the Crypt examining the device Betsy had used, trying to figure out exactly how she managed to control Crimson Wraith technology with it. "It's made from old SnyTech hardware," he eventually explained, "which is what I used for the base of our equipment too. Building off that, there are only a certain number of bands through which we can broadcast and encryption codes available. If she knew that's what we have, then she must have eventually figured out how to hijack the signal our devices use to communicate with each other. It could only have allowed for basic commands, like shutting off the cameras in Edward's apartment and causing that feedback shriek over the audio. I'm going to have to rebuild everything from scratch to make sure someone can't do that again, but the scarier question is, how did she know that's what we were using?"

Gracie asked, "Was that how she made herself look like a miniature sun over the cameras too?"

"No, for that, she used a body paint loaded with an isotope that emitted infrared light when electrified. The device in her hand sent the electrical signal, and her skin carried the charge all over her body. That's why she couldn't just pour it over her clothes. Any device looking at her with night vision would see her lit up like a one million watt bulb, which is pretty smart. If you can't make yourself invisible, might as well make looking at you blinding."

"Wouldn't that, like, hurt?"

"Oh, yeah. She was basically giving herself a really bad sunburn just to fuck with us. Considering everything else she did, I guess she figured it was worth it."

It was well into November before Kevin was at anything close to full capacity, weeks of him banking on his irresponsible mega-rich playboy image to dodge direct involvement with Snyder-Finn financial dealings. But work in the courier pool had been going well for Gracie. She was starting to learn some of the shortcuts to make it across down with a package, and that was surprisingly fun. As for school, she was coming to the end of the semester with a B average in only one class, A's in all the rest. Now and then, she played video games with Danny, but she couldn't get into them the same way Kevin seemed too.

Then came the day Kevin felt well enough to get back into Gracie's training. She was more than happy to. After a half-day in the courier pool, she came back to Finn Manor and joined Kevin for several laps around the manor grounds. It was a beautiful day for it, the sky the dark blue of an autumn afternoon, that cold brightness of the sun angling away from the earth. The cool air felt good on her cheeks as her body temperature rose from the exertion. Somewhere someone must have been burning wood. The acrid bite of mystery smoke smelled delicious.

Once they had finished their run, they sat on one of the stone benches by the rose bushes to rehydrate, and Kevin said to her, "Would you like to say what's on your mind?"

"What?"

Kevin smiled. "You are going to have to get used to not being the best person in the room at reading other people."

He had a point. "Yeah, I guess."

"You don't have to say anything," he continued. "But you can if you would like to."

Saying something never mattered much in Gracie's life, either at home with her parents or after. She learned to do something about what she felt instead of saying something about it. But Kevin had been different from anyone else Gracie met before. He had been from day one and continued to be so.

"Well, I guess, I've been having some questions about, you know, what went down... with Betsy."

"What questions?"

"Was that... I mean... I don't want to put down what we did or anything. It was hard. We tried our best but... What happened with her, was that... justice?" Gracie pushed her fingers through her hair. The thoughts inside her skull weren't sitting well. They felt uncomfortable. She wanted to be able to reach in and poke them around, maybe help them fit in there better.

Kevin asked, "Do you feel bad about our part in what happened?"

"No, I... We couldn't have done anything else, right? I mean, could we?"

"I think probably not. But the fact that you aren't sure about that means you care, and that's a good thing. It's important to care. And it's important to keep caring."

"But we didn't fix it, did we? Edward is still just as dead. Now she is too. And whoever she may have been working with or working for, she took any of that information with her."

"She did."

"And that's it. That's all. She's gone. It's not like she's going to get to go sit in prison and think about what she did, and, I don't know, deal with her shit, maybe try to be better on the other side. I mean, I don't know what prison is supposed to do, if it's supposed to punish someone or make someone not be a criminal anymore, but Betsy isn't having either of that. She's just fucking gone."

"She is."

"So, what was the point?"

1972

Then Edward heard another voice, a man's voice, strangely familiar, calling to him from behind. "Excuse me, sir. I do not wish to be rude, but do you think you will be much longer? You are not the only one intending on making the leap tonight."

Edward turned. And there he was, just as he had been seven years before, right there at the top of the Spirit of Prosperity. He wore no long-nosed mask, carried no fencing foil, but all the same, Edward recognized Esteban Valentino, the Troubadour, smiling ironically with his thin mustache and deeply tanned cheeks.

Esteban continued, "I do not wish to be rude, sir. Of course, this is an important moment for anyone, the very last moment. It is just that, well, I also do not wish to have my courage fail me, and the longer I wait…"

"Of course," said Edward. "I can understand your concern."

"Perhaps it would be possible for me to go out onto our lady's other arm, over there, and commence with my own demise. But I do not wish to disturb yours. I expect that once we hit the water, either one of us will make a particularly loud splash, and that may break the concentration of the other."

"It might indeed."

He didn't seem to recognize Edward, and how could he? While the Troubadour had his mask removed as the TCPD placed him in handcuffs, the Crimson Wraith kept his. Esteban had never seen Edward's face.

"So, I think," Esteban continued, "it is probably best for us to do our jumping one after the other, and since you were here first, I feel as though I need to wait for you to do the deed before attempting it myself."

"How did you get here?" Edward asked.

Esteban grinned, and he reminded Edward of Errol Flynn when he did, so debonair. "Well, I slipped a twenty-dollar bill to the night watchman down below. As it claimed his attention, I ascended the stair. He did not say he had admitted any other leapers tonight. I should have offered half as much if I knew I had to wait, not that I need the money that is, but I do hate to feel I have been overcharged."

"I hid here until after closing," said Edward, "in a supply closet."

"You hid in the closet? Oh, my. It sounds as though you took the advice my *abuelita* gave when she found me trying on my sister's make-up."

"I beg your pardon?" Edward was not prepared to hear the

Troubadour comment on his sexuality so brazenly.

"Does that offend you?" he asked. "Very well then, perhaps you would like to visit some violence upon my person for being a homosexual. That might even resolve our little scheduling issue. You could, say, throw me over the ledge, you know, rid the world of another dirty queer, and then jump off yourself. Or don't. Maybe killing me will make you feel better about whatever it was that brought you to this point."

It was a terrible idea, and Edward's heart ached to hear it, that this man could suggest he be harmed for his sexuality when fear of that very thing kept Edward quietly petrified for so long. "Esteban," he said. "I would never do that to you."

"Esteban? Say now, where do you get off knowing my name? You aren't my guardian angel, are you? Some Clarence from *It's a Wonderful Life* here to show me how much better the world is to have me in it? Do you know my life then, angel? Do you know what I have been doing with it?"

"Actually," said Edward, "I do. A fair amount, at least. For several years, you wore a costume like a Renaissance theater performer, including a mask with a long-pointed nose."

Esteban's eyes narrowed as he stepped forward. "The mask of the character Il Capitano from *Commedia dell'Arte*, a swaggering braggart who hides his true nature. Well done, angel. And then you must know the name I used at that time."

"The Troubadour."

"The Troubadour, yes." Esteban nodded. "I have been trying like hell to put that name behind me. And yet it won't stay put. Wherever I live, whatever job I take, my time as the Troubadour takes it away from me. Sooner or later, someone finds out, and then it is another boarding house, a different floor to mop. So, I come here, looking to make it go away forever by accepting the embrace of Prosperity, and somehow still that name follows."

As his former adversary drew close to him, toe to toe, Edward could not suppress the lifetime of training that told him to brace for a fight. How funny that he could not keep from imagining how to protect his life when just moments ago he felt so ready to end it.

Pronouncing his question like a threat, Esteban asked, "Who are you?"

Being this close to him, Edward experienced a shiver of excitement that he had not felt in so long, and he could not suppress a smile. "Oh, come now, how many of your riddles did I solve in the past, and now you cannot work out even one of mine?"

"My riddles? Solved by you?" Then the comprehension lit up Esteban's eyes. "No," he said. "Oh, no, no, no... It cannot be."

"Cannot be what?" said Edward.

Then Esteban raised his hands to Edward's face, making a little mask between his thumbs and fingers, and looked into eyes that he had only ever seen masked before. "The Scarlet Stranger. *El Fantasmo Rojo*. The Crimson Wraith."

Edward closed his eyes, taking in the other man's touch, the other man's recognition, and the sound of his own name. Those fingers against his skin felt like benediction, and it seemed appropriate in that moment, that moment that still may have been his last, to give confession. Perhaps absolution might follow.

"My name is Edward Burton Finn," he said softly. "I was adopted by William Finn after he rescued me in the guise of his alter-ego, the Crimson Wraith. As a boy, I heard my father's tales of adventure and imagined myself fighting beside him. So, I created a character of my own, the Wily Wisp. When I finished school, I joined his mission to fight crime in Titan City. Years later, he was injured, and he passed to me the role of Crimson Wraith, which I have carried since."

Esteban let his fingers slide down Edward's face, cupping his chin, "You have carried a lot, it seems. And I would say your burdens have increased just recently, with this book that has people saying such terrible things about you."

"It was written by the young man I trained as my sidekick. We had a falling out. I don't think he meant people to draw the conclusions they took from his book. He was younger than me, yes, but he was no child."

"I take it he was the one you had with you when we fought here on this very spot," said Esteban. "Back when I played my little joke of wanting to put a great big silly nose on this face that so many people take so seriously." He stepped back, withdrawing his touch, leaving Edward's cheeks once again cool and vacant and wanting just a little of that warmth once more.

"Yes, that was him."

"And was any of it true, the things that he wrote? It sounded as though the two of you had quite the passionate love affair."

"You've read it?"

"How could I not? After my years in prison, thinking very hard about what I had meant to do with my art and how, time and time again, you showed up to thwart me, someone said they were going to unmask the Crimson Wraith, and I simply could not resist. I've had a lot of time to think on how I felt about the two of us, about the games we played together."

From the look in Esteban's eyes, the way the former Troubadour gazed at him, Edward felt his heart pound with a mighty *thump* against the walls of his chest.

"It was true," said Edward. "He was my lover, some fifteen years younger than me."

"Well, now, how shocking. People will talk. And I do suppose they have. I wonder what they will say next..." Esteban gazed back over his shoulder to the face of the Spirit of Prosperity. "She's a funny one, isn't she, Edward, this goddess who gives and takes at a whim? You think you know what she's about just to have her show another face. Believe that she dispenses mother's milk to all who are worthy, and she may show you just how cruel and spiteful she can be. But when you think there is nothing in her but misery and mockery..." He turned his eyes once more to Edward and smiled, "It turns out the lady has a sense of humor, maybe even mercy."

"Maybe so," said Edward. The wind around the two of them

seemed to pull them closer. "Tell me, Esteban, would you like to leave here with me and go get a drink somewhere. I hope you can agree tonight just got a little too interesting to end in the way either of us intended."

"I do believe I would enjoy that, but you should know I have started going by the Anglo version of my name in order to get a little distance from my past. I ask that you please use that to refer to me."

"And what is your Anglo name then?"

"You can call me," he said with a smile, "Stephen."

2019

Kevin took a sip from his water bottle. "You're asking a really big question, Gracie, and it's an important one. There are lots of ideas about what justice means. The question of whether to punish the guilty, remove them from society, perhaps permanently, or re-educate them in order to make them a better fit for it is something different people are going to answer in different ways at different times and argue with others over forever."

"Dude, that is the most non-answer answer I've fucking ever heard, you know, that right?"

He laughed. "I guess it is."

"Okay, so how about you simple it up for me a little?"

"For you? Gracie Chapel, in the short time I've known you, I figured out there isn't anything simple about you."

"Yeah, I'm super complex, and so is everything else I gotta deal with. So, come on, Kev, can you give me just one simple thing? Go easy on a girl, will ya?"

"All right, here's the simple answer. What happens to someone we try to bring to justice, whether it somehow balances the scales of the harms they've done or helps to reform them, that isn't our job to worry about."

"Say what now?"

"Think about it. The criminal justice system is divided into different parts that do different things. There's apprehension, adjudication, and punishment. You don't have the same person doing all three. The courtroom judge doesn't also catch criminals, formulate arguments for their prosecution and defense, then carry out the sentencing he delivers. He does his one part in the chain and passes whoever comes into his courtroom on to the next."

"Like a factory assembly line?"

"Exactly."

"But that sounds shitty. Shouldn't the whole thing be less mechanical, more human?"

"Honestly? No."

"Why not?"

"Humans being human is where the justice system breaks down. It's where prejudice comes in. It's why different suspects or prisoners get treated differently based on race, social standing, or just reminding an officer or judge or guard of someone else they knew in life and liked or hated."

"You mean... like Betsy," said Gracie. "Edward never did anything to her, but she reminded him of Hank."

"Yes, she discovered Edward's connection to Hank, determined that Edward deserved to be punished for it, and then administered that punishment."

Once again, Gracie thought about her fight with Zack. "She tried to do it all herself."

"She did."

"So, we are just trying to be part of the machine? What part?"

"Effectively, the Crimson Wraith is an unlicensed private investigator. When he catches a criminal, he hands that person over to the police. It's the reason the Crimson Wraith isn't supposed to kill, because that would be judging and sentencing. We leave those to society to decide."

"But society doesn't get to decide on Betsy. She didn't make it to trial. She didn't even make it into handcuffs!"

"Are you saying we failed?"

"I... no..." Gracie could still too easily see the look in Betsy's eyes when she pulled the trigger. "But maybe..." The sound of the pistol firing that was more *pop* than *bang*. "Yes..."

Kevin nodded. "Maybe we did. And we don't have to feel okay about that. But that doesn't mean we never should have tried. And that definitely doesn't mean we should stop trying. At least, I don't feel ready to stop." He looked at her. "Do you? It's okay if you do."

The wobbling wetness rising to her eyes was always so annoying to Gracie. "No," she said. "I'm not ready to stop."

"Good. Because I think you are good at this."

"And you'd miss my sparkling personality, right?"

"I would. Absolutely"

Looking out over the Finn Manor lawn, feeling Autumn chill creep back into her flesh as she cooled from their run, Gracie watched the subtle wave of branches that became more and more bare each day. The season was completing its change. And soon it would change again. Life would just keep going. She could too. Today, Gracie felt sad. Tomorrow, she might not. And in the meantime, Kevin was there, and Danny and Stephen, so she wouldn't have to feel any of it alone.

"Hey, Kevin?"

"Yeah, Gracie?"

"Would you be okay if, like, I put my head on your shoulder or something?"

"I would."

Gracie leaned her head over. As soon as the weight from her neck transferred to him, the wobbliness behind her eyes broke, and she felt its warmth slide down her nose. But sitting with the Crimson Wraith, there on the grounds of his palatial estate, just above his secret headquarters, she could let the tears linger on her face a while before wiping them away.

Elsewhere...

Receiving his message gave Kristen the first night in weeks that she managed to get to bed without sobbing herself to sleep. Many of her posts in groups like *endthewraith* and *crimsonfraud* had received supportive responses. Over and over, in various forms, she said:

How is this fair? How can one man be allowed to do this? Who is he? The love of my life told me that he cannot ever see me again or else the Crimson Wraith will kill him! I made the mistake of inviting this crazy woman to live with us—never again! And after she nearly killed my boyfriend in a fight, we called the cops on her, but the Crimson Wraith held him off the top of a building and said he would kill my boyfriend if he didn't change his story and LIE to the judge to say he started the fight. My life is ruined!

Kristen was far from the only one who suffered a broken heart or worse from the masked vigilante's interference. And it felt good to hear from others who felt as aggrieved as she did:

My man served 3 years for something he didn't do! He didn't never do any of what he got arrested for! And that self-righteous somebody just hand him over to the cops for the third time, not like nobody asked!

And:

What they don't want you to know is having a man run around in a mask like that literally encourages crime! Wake up, sheeple! Check the numbers! He reinforces the status quo to keep you from thinking! THAT's why TCPD doesn't stop him! We need another ZERO HOUR to end these lies with TRUE REVOLUTION!

Normally saying something like there should be another mass bombing would get you on a list for the Bureau of National Safety. But the bulletin board appeared on an encrypted site of the Dark Web. That was the only way to safely air their rage about the Crimson Wraith without fear of retribution.

But none of these comments took away the powerlessness Kristen felt. No one seemed ready to actually do anything. Then she received the message that said:

Your grief is real. Your pain is valid. You have been harmed in a way that should not be ignored. Some of us meet in private to grow and heal together. Nothing but LOVE can make right the things he has done to us. Maybe you can find us some day.

Maybe she could. There was a thought. It was a thought that brought peace.

It took a few more days of messages back and forth before Kristen proved she could be trusted with the location of their meeting place. When finally, he gave her the address, she was surprised to hear they didn't get together in some church basement or community center, but a small shop over in Eastown, just off Pier 38. Her instructions were to go around the side of the building to the door that still had the words *Howard Bros. Fine Cigars* painted above. She would knock three times, pause, then knock four more.

There was no light in the alleyway where Kristen found the door. She could barely make out the words written above it, just the H and the B. That was good enough for her.

There should have been hesitation before she knocked, a little voice asking Kristen if the invitation were real or just some kind of set-up. Maybe the Crimson Wraith or one of his agents had laid a trap to silence critics. But carefully considered caution had never been Kristen's strong suit. A dark alley, late at night, to meet someone whose name or face she didn't know, and with no one else aware of her whereabouts—it was pretty much on par with how Kristen led every other aspect of her life. So, once she had the door found, she knocked in the rhythm she had been told—three, pause, four.

It opened for her, opened by a tall man with kind eyes, a golden beard flecked with white and hair styled upward in a boyish spike. He wore a well-fitting three-piece suit, definitely expensive, showing his toned physique. And with a serene smile, he said to her, "You must be Kristen."

"That's me," she said.

"Come inside."

Kristen followed him into the shop's backroom, which showed no sign of having been active in years, but still the smell of cigars and pipe tobacco remained strong, even over the musty rot of age. A bare bulb hanging from the center of the room flickered dimly, illuminating the dark staircase he led her down.

She asked, "Are you the one I was messaging with?"

"I am. I've been working for a while, putting together our little group in the hopes that, together, we might bring each other the peace of receiving due restitution for how we have been harmed."

"Oh," she said. "Good. So, what do I call you?"

Stopping at the bottom of the stair, he turned and once again gave a smile that told her she was loved, that she was good, and that everything would turn out just fine. "My name is Dr. Oliver James. I'm a psychiatrist. And I too want to find the closure that will only come once the Crimson Wraith is no more. Therefore I have chosen for myself the name of one of his villains—Doctor Oblivion. And I and my compatriots offer you the healing power of love."

Then he gestured into the concrete-walled basement, where Kristen saw a circle of chairs where men and women of different ages and ethnicities, all dressed in everyday streetwear, turned to look at her. In the shadows, she could see their welcoming smiles.

"Love?" she asked.

"Yes, love, L-O-V-E. The League of Vengeance Eternal." Oliver put an arm around Kristen. "And we are just so happy to have you as our newest member."

Those gathered in the circle rose and surrounded Kristen. As their arms collectively embraced her, she wept. Tears spilled down the biggest smile she may have ever smiled, a smile she thought she would never know again. It felt like coming home. This was her new family. And she just knew deep down in her soul that these warm and welcoming people were going to make sure both Gracie and the Crimson Wraith suffered in every way they deserved.

THE END

BE MY HERO!

It doesn't take a mask and cloak to make a difference. For independent artists, the most heroic feat you can perform is to let others know when you like our work. If you've enjoyed reading this adventure of the Crimson Wraith, please leave a review.

You can also sign up for my mailing list and connect with me through social media at jgriffinhughes.com.

It would mean so much. Thank you.

ABOUT THE AUTHOR

J. Griffin Hughes

J. Griffin Hughes was born, raised, and reared in Raleigh, NC. He counts espresso and sushi as much a part of his Southernness as sweet tea and grits. Child of the '80s. Kitchen wizard for fun and profit. Lover of black and white films with detectives and samurai. He received his graduate degree in creative writing from Royal Holloway, University of London.

BOOKS BY THIS AUTHOR

Wouldn't Be Fittin'

"A wandering remembrance that offers astute commentary on the South." — Kirkus Reviews

This book is about Douglas Haas-Bennett, also known as "Miss Doug," owner of Raleigh Creative Costumes, wife of novelist Ben Haas and inventor Willard Bennett, mother, stepmother, and grandmother, humorous, generous, and strong-willed. If you know her, there's a very good chance you love her. If you don't, well, bless your heart.

A descendant of plantation stock, the landed gentry of Eastern North Carolina, Miss Doug witnessed and took part in the twentieth century transformation of Southern culture from "Old South" to "New South," changes in race relations, gender roles, and the very definition of Southernness. The stories here, stories from her and about her, chronicle this transformation with insight, wit, and affection.

Made in the USA
Middletown, DE
30 March 2021